ICONS

ICONS

a novel by
Caroline Winthrop

ST. MARTIN'S PRESS

NEW YORK

Design by Robert Bull Design

Library of Congress Cataloging-in-Publication Data

Winthrop, Caroline.
    Icons / Caroline Winthrop.
        p. cm.
    ISBN 0-312-03729-5
    I. Title.
  PS3573.I559I25   1990
  813'.54—dc20   89-24129

First Edition

10 9 8 7 6 5 4 3 2 1

For Valerie,
маленькой сестре

ICONS

CHAPTER I

New York City: June 1979

The queen-sized mattress sat in the middle of the floor, a raft floating on an endless wooden sea. Piled on the new pink Beautyrest was everything Judith needed to sustain life: telephone, television, a shopping bag half-filled with clothes, and a cardboard box with a carton of cigarettes, assorted candy bars, and a bottle of rum to go with the six-pack of warm Coke.

The telephone began to jangle. Most people gave up after seven or eight rings, but this caller was earning his badge for persistence. Twelve . . . thirteen . . . fourteen . . . Judith turned down the sound on the TV before lifting the receiver.

"Mrs. Klein! Hey, boy, am I glad I finally got hold of you. This is Jim Daley, your insurance agent. Listen, I got the check this morning, and since I'll be passing right by, I thought I'd drop it off."

Judith noticed a tiny speck of white paint on the oak floor, about three feet away from the mattress. No, that was impossible. She had been all over the floor with solvents and polishes, on her hands and knees. How could she have missed it?

Dropping the receiver, she crawled over to the spot and chipped at it with her fingernail. No use. Taking her keys from her pocket, she attacked it viciously with the edge of one, removing not only the spot but a dime-sized patch of varnish as well.

"Damn it!" She sat back on her heels and pounded her fists on her knees. "Damn it, damn it, damn it!" Tears flowed down her cheeks. Nothing was ever perfect. Nothing. Ever.

She heard a noise like a parrot squawking. The telephone. She made her way back to the mattress.

"Mrs. Klein, are you still there? Okay if I bring the check over?"

"I don't understand." Judith raked her free hand through her hair. On the television screen, a gray-haired couple beamed at each other as they spooned their way through bowls of bran cereal in their sun-drenched breakfast nook. The golden years. Children grown. Hand in hand into the sunset. Judith and Charlie. Fifty years from now. Judith and nothing fifty years from now. "Oh, God," Judith whispered, fresh tears filling her eyes. "Oh, God."

"Mrs. Klein, okay about the check?"

She gulped down a sob. "What check?"

"Charlie bought a policy from me after you had the baby. A little extra protection, he called it. He must have told you. Jeez, I never thought we'd have to pay out on that one. Guy was my age, perfect health. Just shows you never know what's coming at you, right?"

Judith dropped the telephone and stared at it. Jim Daley. Another of Charlie's friends. The receiver squawked once more and she held it back up to her ear.

"I called you after the funeral and told you I'd take care of it. Remember? Must have slipped your mind. Wrote up the claim that same day. Don't ask me why they waited six months to pay up; you know how it is with these big companies. Still, a hundred thousand bucks is nothing to sneeze at, right? Hey, okay, Mrs. Klein, I'm on my way. Should be there in twenty minutes."

Judith hung up. She hugged herself and began to rock back and forth, the same motion she had used to comfort little Nellie, but these days the solitary movement brought no comfort, only new tears.

Like that dot of paint. No matter how thoroughly you scraped and scrubbed and painted and scrubbed and polished and scrubbed, some little speck of dirt always escaped your notice. On an otherwise blemish-free world, Daley's extra hundred grand was a *big* piece of dirt.

On the TV screen a kid made a flying leap to catch a ball. In the next shot he handed his soiled baseball uniform to his mom, who wrinkled her brow and shook her head with despair as she dropped the filthy garments into the washer and added a cup of white powder from a box of Brand X detergent.

"Jesus, you pinheaded slut!" Judith shouted at the screen. "You don't know what despair is."

Feet clumped along the corridor outside the apartment. A fist pounded on the door. "Mrs. Klein, it's me, Jim. I think your buzzer's out of order." Judith vaguely remembered hearing the buzzer from the lobby door. Even without her help, Jim Daley had found a way to get into the building. Insurance men were resourceful.

Open up, lady, we know you're in there. Judith switched off the TV and dragged herself off the mattress. Her bare feet slapped the floorboards.

The finish on the hardwood had darkened slightly around the rectangles where Charlie's rugs had been. He had sanded down those floors himself, just as he had built the loft at the end of the high-ceilinged living room and hung the drapes and remodeled the kitchen. The drapes, like the rugs, were gone now, along with everything else, but the loft remained. Judith doubted that Charlie had ever watched an unbroken hour of television in his life. He hadn't had time.

She turned back the dead bolt and dropped the security chain. Jim Daley glided past her, pleasantries dying on his lips as he stood blinking at the vast empty space, nary a smudge, smut, nor smear marring the dazzling whiteness of the ceiling and walls. The glass in the high, wide windows had been cleaned to the vanishing point, and the sun lay broad panels of brightness on the polished floors.

The insurance agent turned to Judith. He was short, barrel-chested, and red-haired, with a wide smile and friendly blue eyes.

"Wow. You really cleaned the place out, huh?"

"That's right." Judith padded back to the mattress. "I really cleaned it out."

Gone were the books, the plants, the paintings, the pieces of sculpture, the handwoven baskets and the primitive carvings and the carpets and the funky art-deco lamps, the odd pieces of furniture they had bought at Salvation Army stores and recovered or restored. Judith could have hired someone, an auctioneer or one of those dealers who bought estates, to take the whole business off her hands. But she had been determined to find a good home for every item. The gallery owner for whom she had been working when she met Charlie had taken the largest pieces of sculpture, after swearing with hand on heart never to sell or trade them away. The rest went to neighbors in the building or to friends. Charlie had had hundreds of friends. Everyone who came to pay a condolence call had left with something, a memento as small as a paperback or as large as a sofa or a bookcase.

All the baby's things had gone to a shelter for battered women in the South Bronx.

Judith had hoped that ridding herself of their possessions would ease her pain. There seemed to be a thousand items, each evoking a hundred or more memories every time she saw them. It hadn't worked. Her own things evoked memories, too: the colorful paisley skirt she had worn to Charlie's birthday party, the cashmere sweater with the stain where little

Nellie had spit up, the shoes she had worn to hike a section of the Appalachian Trail with Charlie. Charlie had hated hiking.

In a frenzy, Judith had piled everything she owned into cartons and carried it down to the sidewalk in front of her building for the winos and the street people to pick through. By morning everything had vanished. Except her pain.

For the next month, Judith had worked feverishly to erase every sign that the Klein family had ever lived in the spacious apartment on Prince Street. Finally, exhausted from scrubbing and cleaning and painting, her hands blistered and raw, she sat and waited for peace.

Then she noticed the chipped porcelain in the tub where Charlie had dropped a monkey wrench, and she heard again the clatter of metal striking metal. His "Shit!" rang out loud and clear, as if he really were in the next room. A series of tiny dents in the baseboard under a window reawakened Nellie's happy laughter as she rammed a toy truck into the obstructive wall again and again before her father stopped her. Voices in the kitchen, laughter in the loft. Two and a half years of noises stored on an endless tape that switched on and off unexpectedly, a nightmare machine that was out of her reach, out of her control.

Jim Daley turned his friendly gaze on her. "So, when you moving?" She knew she looked like hell, but like a good salesman, he didn't bat an eye.

"I'm not moving." Judith took a deep drag on a cigarette. "I just wanted to get rid of it. All of it."

For a moment, Daley looked wary, as if he sensed that something was out of balance here. "You . . . ah, you didn't leave yourself much, did you?"

"I didn't leave anything." Two more puffs finished the cigarette. Judith tore open a fresh pack. "This stuff is new. Mattress. Telephone. Clothes."

She had worn the same jeans and sweatshirt for weeks, taking them off when they were soiled, washing them in the bathtub, putting them on slightly damp. Everything else was in the shopping bag on the Beautyrest, some items still bearing their department store tags.

Daley's smile turned his cheeks into plump red apples. "You ought to get out, get some sun. Use some of that money to buy yourself a trip to Jamaica or someplace. Me, I like the Bahamas better than Bermuda. Don't ask me why. Just personal preference. Here, before I forget." He reached into an inside pocket and produced an envelope. It was unsealed.

Judith glared at him, her eyes brimming. "Charlie had no right to buy that policy. God damn him, why didn't he tell me? Take it and get out of here. I don't want it."

"Now, Mrs. Klein." Daley stood his ground and raised his hands in a placating gesture. "A hundred thousand dollars isn't chicken feed. You got a pretty nice piece of change here. Look, Charlie wanted you to have it. You better take it. I can't give it back to the company. Their computers wouldn't understand."

Judith had just enough ember left on her cigarette to light another. "I don't give a shit about their computers. Burn it. Throw it away. Give it to the poor. Keep it for yourself. I'm telling you, I don't want it!"

Jim Daley laughed. "Hey, don't tempt me. Suppose I kept it and spent it, and then you changed your mind? I'd get arrested and the company would drop me as a salesman. A no-win situation. Look, take the money and have some fun with it. You deserve it, after all you been through." He leaned over and dropped the envelope into her lap. Paper rape.

"Charlie and Nellie didn't deserve to be run over by a hit-and-run driver." Clutching her hair with both hands, Judith began to rock. Forward and back, forward and back. Rocking and keening, her exercise for the past six months. "I don't need any reward for losing my family."

Swiftly, Daley removed himself to a safe distance. He began to pace off the dimensions of the large room.

"Old Charlie sure knew what he was doing when he moved down here. A few years ago, nobody but bums and derelicts lived in SoHo. Now all of a sudden this area is hot. How much rent do you pay, if you don't mind my asking?"

Daley's secretary had typed her name on the envelope: *Mrs. Judith Klein.*

Mrs. Judith Klein. Mrs. Judith Klein. Look at me, Mrs. Klein. Dare you. Go ahead, take a peek.

Judith turned the envelope over and lifted the flap. A one and five zeros. A hundred thousand new burdens.

"Sorry." Daley was standing over her again, rubbing his palms together. "Guess I had no business asking. My wife always says I'm too nosy."

"Three seventy-five," Judith said without looking up, "plus utilities."

"Jeez, that's cheap! My middle daughter's graduating from Parsons in a few weeks, and she and her girlfriends want to find a place in the city. I told them forget it, but hell, you get three, four girls in here, sharing expenses, they could swing it."

"What's your daughter's name?" Judith removed the check from the envelope, folded it in half, and shoved it into the hip pocket of her jeans. The tape in her head started again: Charlie banging pots and pans in the kitchen while he whipped up one of his specials.

"Which one?" Daley gave his big head an exasperated shake. "Middle one's Barb. Got four more. Wife and I kept trying for a boy and finally gave up. Takes a lot of sales to keep these girls in lipstick, let me tell you."

Judith said, "She can have the place if she wants it."

"What?" He looked startled.

"Barb and her friends can have the apartment."

"Gee." Daley hesitated, reluctant to take advantage of her situation, yet unwilling to let the opportunity pass. "You're sure about this?"

"I'm sure. I just needed a little nudge." One hundred thousand nudges. "Do you have a pen? I'll give you the landlord's name and number. Don't let him jack up the rent too high. Charlie turned this building around for him." Daley handed her a ballpoint, clicking it first. She scratched the information on the back of the envelope. "She can have the place right away."

"You mean next month?"

"I mean this afternoon." Judith dug a pair of loafers out of the shopping bag. "I'm getting out of here."

Daley returned the envelope to the same inside pocket he had taken it from. "Best thing," he said heartily, "after something like this. Get away, start over. Lot of people feel the way you do about insurance, that it's blood money. But that's not right. It's supposed to get you over the hump, help you get back on your feet."

Judith dropped the half carton of cigarettes and the candy bars on top of the clothes in the shopping bag. Then she pulled out her keys and tossed them onto the mattress.

"You can have the rum and the Coke, too."

Daley glanced at the keys and then at her. "You just going to leave? Walk out?"

"Is there some law that says I can't?"

"Well, no, I guess not." The insurance man pointed to the mattress, piled with the telephone and television and the rest of Judith's things. "What about . . . what about your stuff?"

"Housewarming present. I don't need it."

"Wow." Daley brushed his soft white hand over his well-barbered head. "You want to tell me where you're going, in case Barb has any questions?"

Judith picked up the shopping bag and carried it to the door. "Barb's a smart girl. She'll figure it out. If she can't, you'll help her." She paused with her hand on the doorknob. "She's lucky to have a father like you. I can't even imagine what that's like, to have a dad you can call on when you have a problem. So long, Mr. Daley."

She left him standing in the middle of the floor beside the mattress, a new castaway on her desert island.

* * *

"Mrs. Klein, we don't usually cash checks of this size."
The officer at Chemical Bank was a black woman in her early forties
wearing a tailored gray suit with a frilly blouse. She spoke in a slow, patient
contralto, even as she was giving Judith one of those wary "How-come-I-
get-all-the-nuts?" looks.

Judith became aware that she had been rocking back and forth. No
wonder the woman looked at her as if she were an escaped mental patient.
She stiffened her spine and crossed her legs. Her foot bumped the shopping bag parked by the side of the desk. "I'll bet there are a hundred banks
within a one-mile radius of this place. Get them each to send over a
thousand apiece and you'll have it."

"That's not the point. We can certainly let you have the money in
cash, if that's what you really want, but we strongly advise against it.
Common sense should tell you—"

"I want the money now," Judith said in a flat voice. "How long will
it take?"

The woman stood up. "I'll have to get the branch manager's okay.
How do you want it? What denominations?"

Judith shrugged. "A few hundreds. Maybe some fifties. The rest in
thousands. Take your time."

After leaving the bank, Judith went into Lord & Taylor and bought
a raincoat and a suitcase and a new handbag. Then, in the ladies' room,
she flushed the contents of her wallet down the toilet and threw the wallet
into the trash receptacle. Everything in it reminded her of Charlie and
little Nellie.

"Who? Judith?" Vanessa's lover answered the phone without turning down the volume on the stereo. Tempestuous Beethoven
raged in the background. "Sorry, Vanessa's not here right now," he bellowed. "I'll tell her you called."

"Where did she go?"

"Actually, I think she's gone to the pub around the corner with a
bunch of her actor cronies. They were making so much noise here I
couldn't concentrate, and so they left."

"Get me the number, Albert. I have to talk to her."

"Well, I don't know if I can even remember—the Elgin, that's it.
Everyone in this area is Keats mad, you know. I think I saw a matchbook
somewhere. Right." He read off a number. Judith made him repeat it three
times because she had nothing with which to write it down. Then she

hung up without saying good-bye and started punching the buttons on the phone, starting with her AT&T credit card number, then the country code for the U.K., then the number for the Elgin. Finally she got through to the pub, which was even noisier than Vanessa's flat. The place must have been packed to the rafters, with the jukebox roaring at full volume. She asked for her sister by name.

"Tell her I want to speak to Jackstraw!" Judith yelled. "Say it's Ben Gunn."

As children, after their father left, Judith and Vanessa had decided to run away from home and become pirates. Judith had taken the name Ben Gunn, the old castaway from *Treasure Island,* and Vanessa was a rollicking freebooter of her own invention named Jackstraw. They had made a solemn pact that any message received from one or the other was to be obeyed at once, without question.

"Judy!" Vanessa came on the line within seconds. "Judy, are you all right?"

"He left me some money I didn't know about!" Judith shouted. Behind her, some New Jersey–bound commuters slowed their hurried pace, pricking their ears at the word *money.* "A hundred thousand bucks in life insurance. I didn't even know he *had* life insurance." She started to sob. "Why did he have to do that? Why?"

"Judy, calm down. I think you ought to hop a plane and come over here this instant."

"Can't." Judith made a pass at her eyes with her sleeve. "I burned my passport. It had entry stamps from the trip we made last fall."

"Judy, for God's sake—"

"I need to get rid of the money, but I don't want to think too hard about doing it. If I give it away to poor people, I'll remember their faces. They'll become Charlie's friends, you see? I can't stand meeting any more of Charlie's friends." Judith began to sob again. "I need . . . I need to find people with no souls. I'll call you when I find them."

"Judy, where are you right now? Tell me, please."

Judith looked over her shoulder. "I'm in the Port Authority, near the Trailways counter. I got panhandled by a junkie and I gave him a hundred bucks of the money and now I can't get his face out of my mind. I can't stand it, Van. I'm getting out of here."

"Judy, you're asking for trouble. Please, honey, you need to talk to someone. Listen, stay right where you are. I'll hang up and call Mother and she'll find someone to take care of you. It won't take long."

"Fuck Mother. I have to do this my way. Bye, Van."

Judith replaced the receiver and hitched up the strap of her new oversized shoulder bag. Its sides were bulging from the quantity of paper money within. As she picked up her suitcase and started toward the ticket counter, a derelict caromed into her and veered off, apologizing. He didn't bother asking her for a quarter. She looked more spaced-out than he was.

CHAPTER 2

Las Vegas: July 1979

*G*imme a six, dice! I need a fat, wet, juicy six." Judith kissed the dice
and rolled them between the palms of her hands.

The stickman, the dealers, and the two boxmen watched her closely.
Not because they suspected her of cheating; she had been shooting craps
at this same table on and off for the past three days, and she had been a
steady and consistent loser. On all three days, she had worn the same pink
silk shift held up by thin spaghetti straps. Every time she leaned forward
to throw the dice, the bodice gaped away from her breasts, which swung
freely, unconfined by cups of wire and lace. One of the dealers on the
graveyard shift had even reported seeing tawny fur on the far horizon. Not
only was the lady a lousy dice player, but she also didn't believe in underwear.

Judith flung the dice. They came up seven. "Little lady's a loser." The
stickman raked the pair in with his hooked bamboo wand. "Next shooter.
We need a new shooter."

Judith straightened up, laughing. "So what else is new?" Her honey-
colored hair was uncombed, flattened on one side and tousled on the
other. Makeup applied and reapplied over several days ringed her eyes in
vivid confusion. Her lipstick was fresh, but the daubs were haphazard and
uneven. "Get me a drink, somebody." Her laughter continued, deep, rich,
and infectious.

A large man wearing a light blue western-style polyester suit and a
cowboy hat stepped over to her and rested his hand on the small of her
back.

"I'll buy you a drink, doll. What'll you have?"

"Hell, I don't care." Teetering on her high-heeled sandals, Judith put her arms around the big man's neck and nuzzled his chin. "Pick two or three things and mix 'em up. Surprise me." She laughed again. "Oh, how I love surprises."

"New shooter coming out." The stickman offered a selection of eight dice to the man on Judith's left, a Chinese. He selected a pair, breathed on them and warmed them in his hands, and rolled a seven on the come-out.

"Seven to win." The dealer doubled the number of chips Judith had left in the Pass Line space. Not satisfied with this sudden spurt of good fortune, she shifted them to the Don't Pass area, betting against the Chinese. Then she tossed a blue chip over to the stickman.

"Give me eight the hard way." She looked over her shoulder and smiled at the crowd. "Don't anybody follow my lead. I'm a wrong bettor from way back." Nobody did. Hard-way bets were one-shot deals, strictly for suckers and novices.

The Chinese rolled a three and a one, and Judith lost her hard-way bet. On the next roll, he matched the four with a pair of twos, a winner. Judith laughed again and waved farewell to the chips the dealer was raking away from the Don't Pass line. The polyester cowboy hailed a waitress and ordered a double Scotch for himself and a Black Russian for the lady, heavy on the vodka.

"Make it two Scotches," Judith said loudly. "A Black Russian is the one drink in the world I won't let past my palate. Hate those rushin' Russians." Judith's words came out garbled and she laughed again.

The polyester cowboy laughed because Judith was laughing. He stepped closer to her and tickled her breast with his crooked forefinger. Judith giggled.

"We sure are having fun tonight, ain't we, baby?"

"We sure are." Judith plucked his cowboy hat from his head and tried it on her own. "You can't spend all this money and still be miserable, can you?" Propping their elbows on the edge of the craps table, leaning against each other like a pair of longtime lovers at a bar, they laughed together.

The cowboy hooked a finger in the middle of her top and helped himself to a private showing. "Listen, honey, when are you and me going to start having some real fun?"

"When the drinks come," Judith promised. "I'll let you sip yours out of my belly button."

"Three easy. The number is three."

Judith tossed another fistful of chips onto the table. "Put 'em on the Come line," she shouted. "It's about time I backed a winner. Whoa!" Her ankle turned, and she lurched into her companion.

"You okay, baby? Maybe we should go upstairs."

"I'm fine. Fine. Gonna stay at my post till the dawn's early light. That which we so proudly hail. Hooray, here come the drinks."

Judith guzzled half her Scotch before spilling the rest down the front of her dress. The sight of the stain spreading over the pink silk sheath amused her mightily, and she laughed loud and long. The cowboy tried to urge her away from the craps table, but she hung back, demanding another Scotch.

"All right, baby. But try and drink this one, okay?"

"Let's try four the hard way." Judith's chips were still riding the three, but she handed the stickman another blue chip. "I don't like anything that comes easy."

"Judith." A young man shouldered his way through the crowd around the table. "Judith!"

Judith didn't hear him until he was right beside her, then she turned and squinted at him in order to focus her wavering gaze. Gradually his features settled into a recognizable pattern: pale skin and pale hair, thinning and white-blond; green eyes behind wire-rimmed glasses; chin solid but cheeks a trifle flabby; mouth thin-lipped and unsmiling. He was well built, thanks to rowing and squash, but no one would ever call him husky. Or handsome. Just typical of thousands of white Anglo-Saxon Protestant males who stepped off the campuses of Ivy League universities into the country's top law firms and brokerage houses.

The first time Judith had met Kenneth Marlowe, he was wearing a little summer suit with short pants and a red bow tie, and oversized glasses that slid down his button nose. Twenty-two years later, his nose had developed the strength and character necessary to support his glasses, and his pants and necktie had lengthened, but the furrows and puckers on his face remained. He had been worried and apprehensive as a kid, and he was worried and apprehensive now.

"Kenny!" Judith flung her arms around his neck. "Kenny, honey, it's so good to see you. Cowboy, I'd like you to meet my baby brother."

"Stepbrother," Kenneth corrected automatically. "Judith, we have to talk."

The cowboy retrieved his hat from Judith's head and placed it on his own before inserting himself between Judith and the new arrival. "Well, stepbrother, why don't you move aside and let the lady have her fun? She can talk later."

Kenneth ignored him. "Judith, we've been frantic. I didn't know where to start looking. Then a friend called and told us he'd seen you here."

Judith chortled. "I bet it was Congressman Hidebound, Democrat from Arkansas. That dirty old tattletale. Wait till I get my hands on him."

"Highland," Kenneth corrected her. "Republican from Illinois."

"Seven, we've got a seven and a loser," the stickman chanted as the Chinese rolled a six and a one. "Who's next? Here we go. New shooter coming out. Let's go, folks. Time to ante up, get into the action."

"Here you go, shooter. Best of luck." Judith tossed a pair of chips down on the Pass Line. "I remember, Hidebound was here last week. We got loaded together. I can't remember if we went to bed or not." She laughed gaily at the gaps in her memory. Then she leaned closer to Kenneth and confided, "You know, Kenny, when that woman he was with wasn't looking, he pushed his hand all the way up my dress."

"It wasn't last week, it was yesterday, and that woman was Mrs. Highland. The congressman telephoned right after they saw you. I took the first plane out."

Judith smiled vaguely and patted his chest with the palm of her hand. "Kenny," she said, "I'm all right. I'm as all right as I want to be."

"Leave her alone, stepbrother." The cowboy threw a possessive arm around Judith's shoulders and drew her away from Kenneth. "She belongs to me tonight. Go and find yourself a girl of your own. You need money? Cash this in." He dropped a blue chip into the breast pocket of Kenneth's wilted seersucker jacket. "This'll buy you the juiciest piece of tenderloin in town, and I don't mean steak."

"This cowboy invests in grain futures." The shooter rolled an eight, double fours. Judith tossed another chip onto the table to back up her Pass Line bet. "He plants the grain and then he bets on whether or not it's going to grow. Somehow, I think that's unethi—unethi—" Her tongue couldn't manage the syllable. She tried out a few variations—"Mythical, mystical, ethanol, ineffable"—before dissolving into laughter. The cowboy held her tightly.

"Later," he said to Kenneth. "Get lost, stepbrother. This is your last warning."

"Please, Judith!" Kenneth's well-modulated baritone rose to a high-pitched tenor. "I can't stand watching this animal paw you like—"

The cowboy hauled back his fist and let loose. The punch caught Kenneth squarely on the chin and he dropped like a sack of feed.

"Wh—where? What? Oh, God, I think I'm going to be sick."

Using a wad of toilet paper, Judith applied the only disinfectant she had on hand: gin, straight from the bottle.

"It's okay, Kenny. You're in my room. Hold still." She dabbed his lip gently. "You shouldn't have insulted him."

"He had no reason to hit me. Ow." Kenneth caught her ministering hand and pulled it away from his swollen face. "That's enough. I'll be okay. I didn't come here to cause trouble. I just wanted to find you, to take you home."

"I'm not going home to Mother, Kenny. I'm too old for that. Besides, I haven't spent all my insurance money yet. A hundred grand, my reward for being married to a dead man. Do you know what kind of service that buys you in this town? I'm a high roller, baby, and a sure loser. That means I own this place."

Kenneth's eyes grew dark behind his glasses. "We've been so worried about you."

"I bet Mother wasn't worried." Judith reached across his body and took a cigarette from the pack on the nightstand. "When Lydia booted her chicks out of the nest, she forgot she ever had us. This was your idea, wasn't it? To come riding out of the west—the east—like a young Lochinvar. But you've got it wrong, baby." She stretched out on the bed beside Kenneth and blew a stream of smoke into the air. "I don't want to be saved. I want to slip quietly down the toilet with the water swirling around my ears and the bright lights fading out overhead when someone slams the lid down. That's it. That's all."

Kenneth sat bolt upright, immediately grabbing his head with both hands. "Oh—oo—ow. . . . You don't mean that, Judith. You can't! It's such a sad waste of a beautiful life."

"So?" Judith shrugged. Her dress strap had fallen down over her shoulder, exposing her left breast. Kenneth stared hard for a moment and then forced himself to look away. "That might not be the way Charlie would have wanted it, I suppose. Other women lose their husbands and their babies. It's sad, it's tragic, but the whole point of life is to go on living, right? Wrong. I don't want to, and no law says I have to. I've packed a hell of a lot of living into my three decades, and I've had enough. Go away and leave me alone, Kenny. This was nice of you, but I don't want to be saved."

"I can't leave you, not like this. Not here. Can't you see how awful it is? How ugly? Look around you, Judith. Look at this place. Look at yourself. What's happened to your pride, your self-respect? At least cover yourself up."

Judith pulled up her shoulder strap, unembarrassed. Her room was identical to every other room in that particular hotel—in the last two weeks she had visited quite a few. The two double beds were covered with striped spreads in western colors, ochre and brown and orange. A huge print of cowboys gathered around a campfire hung on the wall above the television.

The open suitcase on the dresser hemorrhaged lingerie, mostly whites and pastels with a few wisps of black. Nearby, in front of the mirror, stood a clutch of bottles and an ice bucket. The drinks were on the house, as long as Judith kept losing big at the casino downstairs. A bottle of Dom Pérignon had been in the bucket all afternoon unopened; the ice was long melted and the label had fallen off. On top of the television console, a plate of scrambled eggs, bacon, and toast had congealed into an unappetizing mass. A bottle of red pills spilled onto the floor.

A deranged woman blinked back at Judith from the other side of the bottles. The deranged woman was herself.

"Oh, shit." Judith flipped her cigarette into the ice bucket, where the ember expired with a sharp hiss. "It's hard to believe the maid cleaned this place this morning. Jesus, I am so tired of myself. Hold me, Kenny." She turned to Kenneth and opened her arms. "Please. I need someone to hold me, just for a little while."

Kenneth obliged. She wasn't clean. In fact, she smelled of tobacco and alcohol and stale sweat. But he was so captivated by the magic of holding her in his arms that he hardly noticed. Her flesh was unbelievably soft under the pink silk, and when she moved against him, he felt the reverberations clear down to the soles of his feet. His heart began to pound and the banked fire in his gut suddenly sprang to life.

Judith's lips brushed his cheek. "Kenny, I'm glad you came to rescue me. You're so sweet. You've always been sweet."

"Judith, I—" He turned his head, and found her mouth waiting for him: hot, moist, hungry. He hesitated for the merest fraction of a second before kissing her. Their tongues glanced off each other, and the flames in his loins roared higher. When they finally broke off, Judith laughed softly, not her robust fat-girl laugh, which usually made him cringe, but an intimate, throaty chuckle he had never heard before.

"Do it, Kenny." Her fingertips flickered over his face and throat. "For once in your life, give in to temptation. Nobody cares. Big Mama's not watching. I won't tell. Do it."

"Judith, let's get married." The spectacular desert sunset had gone unobserved by most of the inhabitants of the Las Vegas Strip. Now the forest of neon made its own garish, pulsating, rainbow-colored daylight. "Right now. Tonight."

Judith, emerging from the bathroom with one towel wrapped turbanlike around her head and another around her waist, burst out laughing.

"Kenny, don't you know anything? You can't propose to the girl who deflowers you."

Kenneth bristled. "You didn't deflower me. I've had girls—women. Plenty of them. I'm twenty-nine years old, I know my way around. I feel, deep down, that it's right for you, for me, for both of us. Marry me. Please."

"So, you want to make an honest woman of me." Judith flopped across the foot of the bed. She lay on her side, her head propped up on her hand. "You weren't drinking while I was asleep, or snorting something, were you?"

"No. I've been lying here thinking—"

"Dangerous."

"—and I know if we don't do this now, tonight, we'll never do it. It'll be too late."

"Mother"—Judith tickled the bottom of his foot—"will have a bird."

Kenneth retracted his foot and shoved it under the sheet. "She'll have to get used to it. It's not as though we're committing any kind of sin. We're not related by blood, only by marriage. My father won't mind. He's crazy about you. He'll stand up to her."

"Are you kidding?" Judith unleashed a big, mocking laugh. "Preston couldn't stand up to Lydia if somebody shoved a telephone pole up the back of his blue pin-striped suit. Marry you! Jesus." She rolled over on her back and folded her arms behind her head. Her breasts were taut, the nipples hard. Kenneth couldn't take his eyes off them. "You know, the look on Mother's face might almost be worth it. Are you sure you know what you're doing?"

"I do know. Trust me. I know you don't love me, but you're fond of me, I think. Maybe I shouldn't tell you this, but I've hated all the men you've ever been with. I hated them because they had what I wanted most."

"Really? And all this time I thought you were the world's thinnest eunuch." Judith discarded the towels and climbed on top of him. "You're finally ready to do it, aren't you? To tell my mother to kiss off, mind her own business, run somebody else's life for a change. You're going to make the break, move out of her house, get the State Department to assign you to some remote place like Sri Lanka or Bangladesh. By God, Kenny, I believe you're growing up. At long last." She kissed him hard, almost suffocating him.

Fighting for air, Kenneth broke away from her kiss. His defense of Lydia Marlowe was reflexive. "Judith, your mother has been very good to me. I love and respect her."

With a derisive hoot, Judith rolled off of him. "From the moment you walked into our house when you were seven years old, you've let her smother you. She bought your clothes, picked your schools, got you into the diplomatic service, pulled rank with her fancy friends to push you up the ladder, vetted your girlfriends and your co-workers and the guys you play tennis with."

"She has done a lot for me," Kenneth said staunchly. "More than I can ever—"

"She's turned you into a class A wimp, darling. By God, what courage. To spit in her eye! I give myself credit for this, Kenny." Judith ran her fingertips lightly over his chest. He was almost hairless, as smooth as an adolescent boy. "I did this. I've made a man out of you. My only regret is that I didn't do it sooner." Her laughter turned boisterous. "Hell, why not get married? I don't have anything better to do tonight."

"Then—then can we get out of here?"

"Sure." As Judith tossed her head, wet strands of hair slapped his face. "We'll head into the sunset together, just as soon as we tie the knot. But first a little preview of the delights in store for you on our honeymoon."

"Judith, I don't think—"

"That's right, Kenny, don't think. Just lie back and let it happen."

They left Las Vegas at midnight in the car Kenneth had rented at the airport, a bargain-rate Chevrolet Nova with clanking valves and noisy air-conditioning. After an hour the lights of the city were still a dusty glow on the horizon behind them. Judith was wide awake, soaring on amphetamines, ready to drive all night. When Kenneth got sleepy, she persuaded him to let her take the wheel.

"Stay on U.S. Ninety-five north." He folded his suit jacket into a pillow and tucked it between his head and the window. "If you feel sleepy, wake me up."

Ten minutes later, he was snoring gently. Judith turned the air conditioner off and rolled her window down. At night the desert was cool and crisp and dry, as bracing as a good martini.

Married. What a kick. Her mother's blood pressure would go off the charts. Married! "Judy and Kenny" sounded like they should be packaged in cardboard boxes covered with cellophane. Judith had considered telephoning Vanessa in London, but she decided against it. Vanessa would certainly have tried to stop them before they reached the altar. Van didn't have much use for Kenneth. When he was little, she had teased him unmercifully and called him a sissy and a crybaby. Now she simply dismissed him as a wimp, or, mocking his fair coloring and his passion for punctuality, called him the White Rabbit.

Married. Judy and the White Bunny in Wonderland. Right this way, through the looking glass, folks. Please watch your step.

The road was mesmerizing in its straightness. Although traffic from the north was sparse, the headlights of the few oncoming cars dazzled her. Her eyes began to burn like open wounds, and the light abraded them like grit.

Passing through a crossroads town called Scotty's Junction, Judith saw a faded billboard advertising the Swan Motel in Leda. She let out a yip of laughter at the images the name conjured up. The sign outside the motel would have a picture of a naked girl in the clutches of a leering bird, her vital areas discreetly shielded by its spread wings. Judith knew exactly what the room would look like: sun-bleached and seedy, with a strong odor of mildew in the dark bathroom that no amount of disinfectant would ever defeat. The window-unit air conditioner would work only on high, and the television would be mounted on a bracket that was bolted to the wall. What better place to enjoy a honeymoon with one's own brother? Stepbrother. She made a U-turn in the middle of the highway and went back, then jerked the wheel to the right and headed toward Leda. Two miles out of Scotty's Junction she saw another sign for the motel and turned left again.

The road climbed steadily upward, through a nightscape that was as dark as pitch. Judith kept going until the blacktop disintegrated, giving way to unpaved dirt road. The jolting roused Kenneth, who sat up, squinting.

"Where are we? This isn't the main road."

"We're going to the Swan Motel in Leda," Judith told him. "Remember Leda and the swan? Can't you just see the sign out front, and all the swan kitsch in the bathrooms? We have to stop."

"But this can't be the right road. Where's the map? Pull over."

"Not yet, Kenny. Let's keep driving until the road ends or we run out of gas."

"Out here, that's not too smart. Come on, Judith, pull over. I'll get us out of here."

"No, Kenny, just a little farther. Where's your sense of adventure?"

As they rounded a bend on a downhill slope, a rabbit darted out in front of the car. Judith hit the brakes, but it was too late. She felt a slight bump as the tire ran over it.

"Kenny—oh, my God, I've hit something!" As she was slowing, another rabbit dashed into the middle of the road. Blinded and confused, it zigzagged crazily in her headlights and hurled itself under her front tires. She pushed the brake pedal to the floor. The car fishtailed and jerked to a halt, the left rear fender scraping the side of the steep rocky cut through the hillside. Several rabbits frisked in the wash from the lights. Judith was sobbing. "Kenny, make them stop. Kenny!"

They traded places. Kenneth managed to straighten the car on the narrow road, but they were still headed away from the highway. The spinning wheels produced a cloud of choking dust.

"We'll have to keep going until I find someplace to turn around."

Judith begged him to drive slowly, but Kenneth wanted to push on, to get it over with, to reverse direction and head back to civilization. The rabbits, driven out of the parched hills by thirst or hunger or simply by the pressures of overpopulation, jumped out at them, scampered back and forth in front of the car for a moment, their eyes glinting red in the headlights, then threw themselves under their wheels. In less than three miles, they must have crushed a dozen.

"Make them stop!" Judith screamed. "Stop hitting them. Make them stop doing this. It's Charlie and the baby—nobody stopped. Kenneth! We've got to stop, Kenneth! Please!"

"No! God damn it, what do you want me to do, park and wait here until daylight? We'll freeze. I want a warm bed and a hot breakfast. This is our honeymoon, remember?" Kenneth set his jaw. "They're only a bunch of rodents, for Christ's sake."

He finally found a flat spot near a dried-up stream and swung the Nova around. They headed back toward Scotty's Junction and U.S. 95, and the rabbits kept leaping out at them and Kenneth kept running them down. Judith sobbed great, wrenching sobs until she began to retch. Kenneth stopped the car and she vomited out the window. She wanted him to hold her head and wipe her chin, but he didn't move. His hands were frozen to the wheel.

Kenneth found the Swan Motel at four in the morning, only five miles down the road from the place where Judith had mistakenly turned left outside of Scotty's Junction. By that time they were both too dazed and numb to appreciate the blinking strip of pink neon outlining the swan and the toothily smiling Leda, whose arms were outstretched in welcome.

Two months later, Judith told the story at a Washington dinner party. "No marriage ever got off to such a miserable start. Talk about bad omens!" She drained the wine from her glass. Their host promptly refilled it. Kenneth, at the far end of the table, wore a smile as stiff as his black tie. "I thought we ought to find some kind of shaman or tribal medicine man and pay him to take away the curse." Judith laughed. "Poor Kenny. I told him that of all the wrong turns I've made in my life, that one was the worst. Some honeymoon!" Her laughter continued. "The Night of the Kamikaze Rabbits."

CHAPTER 3

Russia, the Countryside Near Moscow: Summer 1979

*A*leksandr Dmitrov gave the soccer ball an expert kick. At the other end of the meadow, his wife, Olga, hugged the folded picnic blanket to her waist and lifted her face to the sky. In seconds, the warm fingers of sunlight massaged away the stresses, the tensions, and the nagging worries she had brought with her from Moscow. These things had no place in her heart today, the first day of summer and the most perfect day of the year.

"Olga, what's the matter with you? You look so strange. You're not pregnant, are you?"

Olga sighed. Her sister-in-law, Marina Seminova, hadn't an ounce of romance or poetry in her grasping Georgian soul. Olga shook out the blanket and handed one end to Marina. The two women spread it over the tall grass, where it lay like a canopy atop the unbending shafts until Marina dropped down and crawled around, pounding the grass flat with her fat knees and the palms of her hands.

Ordinarily the family had their first outdoor picnic in May, just as soon as the corn was up and the ground warm enough to sit upon without catching pneumonia. But a prolonged winter and persistent rainfall had delayed the arrival of spring and forced them to postpone their plans. Now, at summer's start, the grass in the meadow was tall and thick, the birches heavy with leaves, and the pond overflowing its banks. Aleksandr Dmitrov, who had been coming to his mother's villa, or *dacha,* every year since he was a boy, said he couldn't remember ever seeing the water so high.

As Olga bent over the wicker hamper, the scuffed leather soccer ball landed with a *thunk* a few yards away and rolled toward her.

"The ball, Mother. Kick it back!"

The two boys and their fathers were shouting at her, making semaphore signals with their arms. Her Misha hopped up and down like a puppet with springs on the bottoms of his sneakers. He would look like his father when he grew up: tall and strapping, as handsome as an American movie star. His straw-colored hair would darken, as Sasha's had, but he would continue to look at the world with that clear blue-eyed gaze that saw everything. Her menfolk.

"Aunt Olga, hurry up!"

Olga ran over to the ball. Lifting the skirt of her white cotton sundress well above her knees, she took aim with the toe of her sandaled foot and kicked it squarely, just below center. It sailed upward in a high arc and came down just a few feet away from Aleksandr Dmitrov, who called out to her.

"Come out and play! Our team needs you."

"Don't be silly, Sasha! My brother can hardly run at all. You don't need my help." She waved him away, laughing.

The four players raced across the meadow in pursuit of the ball. Daisies and buttercups fell under their feet like stalks of wheat under a reaper's knife. Arkadi Seminov, Olga's nephew, was fighting to keep the ball away from his Uncle Sasha. Aleksandr Dmitrov had the advantage in height and strength, but at seventeen Arkadi was quick and light on his feet. Misha, only seven years old, made swift, darting movements in front of his cousin in an attempt to steal the ball. But Arkadi didn't let these feints distract him. He pressed on toward the goalposts, two birch trees marked with red ribbons.

Olga's brother Yakov was having difficulty keeping up. Since his heart attack three years ago, the bulk in his chest and shoulders seemed to have slipped down to his waist. He had to pause frequently to hitch up his pants and tighten his belt.

"Will you look at Yakov?" Behind her, Marina Seminova fanned herself with a china plate. "He should be more careful. He's not used to this kind of exercise, and in this heat! What if he gets sunstroke?"

"Then we'll throw him into the pond and cool him down." Olga opened the hamper and started lifting things out.

"But what if he has another heart attack?" The flesh on Marina's smooth upper arm swayed gently as she fanned, like the udder of a cow. "I'm so worried about him. I lie awake at night, sick with worry about what will happen to us if Yakov's heart gives out."

Olga removed the bowls and plates from the hamper and arranged them in the center of the blanket. She wondered if she dared hide the vodka until Yakov had slaked his thirst with water. She'd never get away with it. He would recognize her subterfuge and poke fun at her for the rest of the day.

Olga glanced up. Her daughter, Irina, was watching the game from the tall grass at the edge of the birch grove. Although she was only thirteen, she had nursed a crush on her cousin Arkadi for years. Olga had no objection to that; adolescent crushes taught girls how to love. Still, the Seminovs were having serious political difficulties, and Olga didn't want Irina to get hurt as well.

"Yakov's heart," Marina persisted. "Do you think it can stand up to the strain?"

"I gave Yakov a complete physical just two months ago." Olga heard the note of impatience in her voice and struggled to temper it. Yakov's cardiac arrest had been serious, certainly. But must Marina go on and on about it, constantly flapping her hands in despair as if the angel of death were a black bird that she could shoo away from her family? "The heart attack was three years ago," she reminded Marina. "He has recovered splendidly. There is no need to keep upsetting yourself."

As usual, Marina hardly listened. "I can't help it. He's so tense lately. When I touch him, it's like putting my hands on a piece of granite." She dropped her voice. "Olga, something terrible happened yesterday. You know we applied for our exit visas six months ago, and so far we've heard nothing? Well, yesterday two men came to the apartment. They said they were from the Ministry of Defense, Security Division. They told us that Yakov could not be granted a visa without the approval of their department, because his work was related to matters of defense. Defense! Yakov has been at the institute for twenty years, and this was the first time anyone ever told him that his work was related to defense. Yakov—he had been drinking, and I'm afraid he got angry and threw them out. Insisted they leave. He shouldn't have done that, should he? They'll punish us. They'll never give us permission now. Dear God, what will become of us?"

Olga uncovered the smaller basket that held the flatware, the napkins, and the glasses. "I'll bet they weren't from any ministry at all. They were probably KGB."

"But that's even worse!" Marina gasped. "If *they* don't want us to emigrate, we'll never get our visas. I can't take much more, Olga. These six months have been like a nightmare, with the telephone calls and the insults and the rudeness. And if we really have been refused! You know what that means." She clutched at the front of her blouse, a sleeveless yellow nylon shell with orange roses embroidered around the neckline. It was too small for her, and the colors looked ghastly against her sallow skin.

Soviet women didn't have the luxury of choosing clothes for color or style or even fit. "Yakov will never be able to get his job back. How are we supposed to live? How are we going to survive without working?"

"Calm down, Marina," Olga said firmly. "You haven't actually been refused, not officially. As for the nuisance calls and the insults, they want to make it tough on you, that's all. Eventually they'll get tired of it and you'll get your visas."

Out on the playing field, Yakov winkled the ball away from his little nephew Misha and with one mighty kick sent it twenty yards wide of the goal. It landed several feet out in the swollen pond. All the players groaned.

"I'll swim out and get it," Misha offered. "Let me, Papa."

"Why not?" Aleksandr Dmitrov responded. "I've worked up a sweat kicking that soccer ball around. Let's all take a quick swim to cool off before lunch."

Misha squealed with delight and raced toward the pond with Arkadi right behind him. Dmitrov called to his daughter Irina to come and join them, but she shook her head shyly and drifted into the trees as the men stripped off their clothes and waded into the icy water. Dmitrov and Arkadi swam out to the center of the pond and began swatting the ball back and forth, while Misha paddled between them and his Uncle Yakov, who had only ventured in up to his knees.

As Olga stood smiling at the antics of the men, she noticed Marina twisting the folds of her skirt. Olga felt the wriggling worm of anxiety in her own stomach. If her brother and his family really had been refused exit visas, they were in for some rough times. Arkadi's dream of studying engineering at Moscow State University was already finished; just last week, he had been refused entrance. Yakov had been fired from the lab where he had worked for twenty years. Officially, the Seminov family no longer existed. In order to survive, they would have to look for illegal work on the black market side of the economy, and inevitably they would depend on the Dmitrovs for handouts, if not complete financial support.

Why did the system have to be so unfair? What did the KGB gain by persecuting innocents? Deep down, Olga was thankful that her own position in society was secure. Her husband's family was influential and important. Sasha would protect her. He would protect all of them.

Olga knelt down and put her arm around her sister-in-law's shoulders. "Don't worry, Marina. Sasha knows a lot of important people. He'll find a way to help you."

Marina clung to her. Her dark eyes flooded with tears. "I don't know where Yakov got this crazy idea about emigrating. I pleaded with him not to do it, not to apply, but he insisted. And now they're making our lives miserable. My poor Arkadi—all his chances ruined! I don't want to leave. I never wanted to leave. I'll never understand that brother of yours." Her lower lip trembled and tears washed over her round cheeks.

Olga handed her a linen napkin. "Here. It's almost time for lunch. You don't want your husband and son to see you like this." She picked up some Turkish towels and carried them down to the pond, where the men were slogging in toward the bank. She scolded Dmitrov for letting Misha stay in the water so long. "Look at him. His teeth are chattering and his lips are blue." She rubbed her son briskly with a rough towel until he screamed for mercy.

While the brothers-in-law and the two boys dressed, Olga called to Irina, who appeared at the edge of the woods. Slowly, they all made their way back to the blanket, where Marina was keeping watch over the picnic supplies. Only Misha lingered behind at the pond, poking at the muddy banks with a stick.

Yakov grabbed the vodka bottle and filled a tumbler for himself without offering a drink to anyone else. "We gave them a real fight this year," he bellowed. "If Sasha wasn't such a bully, we would have been ahead."

Aleksandr Dmitrov threw himself down in the grass behind Olga, who knelt on the edge of the blanket. "Arkadi's getting too quick for me," he said. "Or maybe I'm just getting old. Next year you two might even beat us."

"God help us." Yakov finished his drink in two swallows. "If we're still here in this blighted country next year, I'll kill Brezhnev with my bare hands. I mean it."

"Yakov," Marina gasped. "Stop! Such bad luck, to talk that way!"

Yakov turned to Olga. "Did she tell you we've been refused?"

Olga waved away a fly. "Don't exaggerate, Yakov. The Office for Visas and Registration hasn't refused you. I suppose you're talking about those two men who came to see you yesterday. They're just trying to throw a scare into you. More KGB harassment."

"They told me they would never let me go. A security risk! What risk? I've been working on polymers for the past fifteen years. Now they tell me my work is defense-related. As if the West didn't know all there was to know about polymers."

Olga smoothed a wisp of dark hair away from her forehead. Her bodice was sticking to her back and her skin was starting to itch under her brassiere. Maybe she would take a swim herself after lunch. "I've already told Marina that we would do what we could to help. Won't we, Sasha?"

"Will you?" Yakov curled his lip in an ugly sneer. "How gracious of you, sister, but aren't you afraid you might get into trouble for helping a Jew? Certainly *being* a Jew has never come between you and your happiness. You had the good fortune—or maybe it was the wisdom—to marry a gentile, and a rich one at that, with good connections. It's different with me. With us. At the institute they've sat on me for twenty years because I'm a Jew. The studies I've done are published, but my name isn't on them. I want my son to have a better life than the one I've had. What's wrong with that? You have a gentile to hide behind. But me, I'm sick of hiding. I'll tell you one thing, if they keep me here, they'll be sorry." He raised the vodka bottle to his lips.

"We'd better eat. This food will spoil out here in the hot sun." Olga twisted around and looked over her shoulder. "Misha, come and have lunch."

"I'm coming!" the boy called back from the pond. "Can we go swimming again after lunch? I'm warm again."

"You're not going in alone, and your father isn't going anywhere until he's had some food. Come along. If you don't hurry, Uncle Yakov will eat all the sausages."

Misha came running barefoot through the grass and threw himself down on the blanket between Yakov and Marina. The boy had rolled the cuffs of his shorts up to the tops of his absurdly skinny thighs. Olga refrained from asking where his socks and sandals had gotten to. He wouldn't be able to tell her.

They filled their bellies. Yakov's mood improved as he ate. Olga felt the familiar hot-weather torpor sneaking up on her: heaviness in the limbs, sluggishness in the brain, and an overwhelming desire to sleep. How pleasant it would be to lie down in the grass next to Sasha, just the two of them. They might doze a bit at first, then Sasha would slide his hand under her dress. Being terribly ticklish, she would giggle and squirm, but eventually she would pull up her skirts and take him into herself. She smiled. The summertime fantasies of a middle-aged matron. By tonight, they would both be too stunned with sunshine and vodka to do anything but collapse in their beds.

Halfway through the meal, Misha grabbed a piece of sausage and a hard-boiled egg and ran down to the pond. Marina fended off flies with one hand while she stuffed food into her face with the other. Yakov took two swallows of vodka for every bite of food. Olga leaned back against her husband. Sasha stroked her arm, and they exchanged smiles that were really wordless conversation. Wasn't this a fine day, with the family together, a good meal, far away from the pressures of the city? Surely, they agreed silently, this was the closest they would ever get to paradise.

After the meal, Irina and Arkadi wandered away from the picnic site.

As they headed through the meadow toward the forest of pine and oak that lay beyond the birch grove, Yakov called out, "Don't get up to anything foolish, you two!" Irina, hearing him, broke away from Arkadi and ran. Casting his father an exasperated look, Arkadi followed her.

"What's the matter with you, Yakov?" Olga handed around slabs of poppyseed cake. "You know how sensitive children are at that age. Irina cries at the slightest provocation these days, and Arkadi has always been so *seriozni*. You shouldn't tease them like that."

"The boy's seventeen. Already he's twitching like a flea in a frying pan. I know how I felt when I was seventeen. And it wasn't sensitive." Yakov reached for an open wine bottle. "Did Marina tell you that I threw those two goons from the ministry out? Told them to get out of my apartment, and pushed them toward the door."

"You're such a hothead." Olga brushed crumbs off her lap. "You'll never learn, Yakov. It doesn't pay to antagonize people. Talk to him, Sasha."

Aleksandr Dmitrov managed a grunt. He was lying on his back, his shirt open, his face turned to the sun, his eyes welded shut.

"One of them grabbed the front of my sweater and pushed his ugly face right up to mine." Yakov pantomimed the scene. " 'Listen to me, Yakov Feodorovich,' he said, 'the only way you'll get out of this country is if you die and they burn you and scatter your ashes to the wind.' "

"Intimidation." Marina knotted her napkin. "Olga says it was just intimidation. Olga says that Sasha can help us. Won't you, Sasha?"

"Sasha? Help us?" Yakov's laughter was ugly and without humor. "My dear wife, that's like asking the fox to patrol the henhouse. Haven't you ever wondered about our Sasha? About the secret life he leads? He disappears on errands for the government for months at a time, and he never says where he's been or what he's been up to. An army officer attached to the diplomatic corps, a 'military attaché.' So he says. But it's a lie, isn't it, Sasha? You're KGB, just like them."

Marina Seminova gasped. "Yakov, no!"

"You're talking nonsense, Yakov," Olga said crisply. "That's what drinking in the hot sun does to fools."

"Am I so foolish?" Yakov waved his glass. "Am I a fool? He's a powerful man, your husband. I'm betting he has important friends sitting in that big yellow building on Dzerzhinsky Square. Any one of them could pick up the telephone, call the head of OVIR, tell him to let the Jew Seminov go, as a favor to a colleague. Why haven't they done it? Because they can't take the risk. I might tell the world what I know: that my brother-in-law is a dirty spy. If I'm a danger to their security, it's not because of their stupid polymers. It's because my brother-in-law is too important. I'm right, aren't I, Sasha? They'll never let us go. Because of you."

"Answer him, Sasha," Olga urged. "Tell him it's a lie."

Dmitrov raised himself up on one elbow. "You don't know what you're talking about, Yakov. If I could have done anything to help with your visa, I would. It's still not too late. I'll have a word with—"

"Lies!" Yakov hauled himself unsteadily to his feet. "He travels to America, to England, to France. A simple soldier? Like hell. He goes, but his wife and children stay here. Hostages. Because the KGB trusts no one, not even their own."

"You exaggerate," Sasha said, his voice calm. "You're imagining things. I travel to military bases, remote outposts, places that aren't suitable for wives and children."

"You bring back gifts: perfumes, silks, cars. From military bases? From places like Cuba and Angola? Don't bother to deny it. We know. Olga knows. But we don't talk about it. We don't even like to think about it, because you're our brother, our friend. But when you're dealing with *them,* you have no friends. You should have said something, Sasha. You should have told me I was wasting my time, wrecking my life for nothing, that an exit visa was out of the question for us. I pity you, Sasha. Yes, you live well, but even I have more freedom than you do. They own you body and soul, Sasha. Body and whatever soul you have left."

"That's enough, Yakov!" Olga snapped. "Sasha is your friend, remember? More than your friend: your brother. Has he ever refused you a favor when you asked? Your car, your apartment—he helped you get those, and you took his help and thanked him. Now the KGB has frightened you and you're taking it out on him. What's the matter with you?"

Yakov sneered. "Without your precious husband, you'd be slaving away in a miserable polyclinic in the worst neighborhood in Moscow, instead of operating on the hernias and hemorrhoids of Politburo members. You can act like a damn Romanov princess if you like, Olga Feodorovna, but we both know that your parents were Jews, and your grandparents and your great-grandparents and all your ancestors back to Abraham. You're a Jew, just like me! But you're too cowardly to admit it. Too cowardly and too comfortable."

Dmitrov filled a glass with vodka and offered it to Yakov. "Drink this, you big idiot. You'll feel better."

Yakov smacked Dmitrov's hand aside. Vodka splashed all over the remains of the picnic. Dmitrov stood, facing his brother-in-law across the blanket, but Yakov was too overwrought to stop himself.

"Ptuh!" Yakov spat in Dmitrov's face. "I spit on your vodka. Ptuh!

I spit on your cars and your apartments, and on your bitch queen of a mother. Ptuh! I spit on your father the general, may his soul rot in hell. He knew where the bodies were buried. Why not? He buried them. Stalin's henchman. He put half a million people into early graves, including my own father. Ptuh! I spit on your dacha in the country, and on all those pictures and icons you're so proud of. You paid for them in blood. Our blood."

Lowering his head, Yakov made a bull-like charge at Dmitrov. Dmitrov sidestepped him neatly and tripped him up. As Yakov fell, he twisted around and grabbed Dmitrov around the knees, and the big man went down in the middle of the picnic buffet. Marina screamed. Yakov jumped on him and started to bludgeon Dmitrov's face with his fists. Dmitrov flipped Yakov off and threw himself on top of his brother-in-law, pinning Yakov's wrists to the ground.

"Listen to me, you lunatic," he hissed. "Loose talk can still send a man to Siberia. You'll dig your grave with your tongue."

But Yakov didn't hear him. All at once the alcohol took effect, dissolving the tension in his arms and body. Yakov's mouth sagged and he started to snore.

"Drunken idiot," Dmitrov growled. "He's passed out."

"Your clothes, Sasha!" Marina wailed. "You have beet juice all over your nice shirt. I'll rinse it right away, in the pond. I'm so sorry. He's been so upset lately, he doesn't know what he's doing."

"Sasha!" The fear in Olga's voice pulled their heads around. "I can't see Misha. He was playing by the pond a moment ago, and now he's gone."

By the time Dmitrov grasped what had happened, Olga was halfway to the pond, running like the wind, her hair and skirts streaming behind her. "Misha! Misha! Misha!"

When Dmitrov reached the pond, Olga had already plunged in up to her waist. Without bothering to remove his clothes, Dmitrov ran splashing into the water.

"Find him, Sasha!" Olga cried. "Oh, God, find him! Misha! Oh, God! Misha!"

After five minutes that seemed like an eternity, Aleksandr Dmitrov found the body of his son a few feet under the surface, near the rushes at the edge of the pond. Dmitrov lifted Misha out of the water and laid him in the grass. Olga Dmitrova, mother and physician, worked grimly to expel the water from her son's lungs. When that failed to revive him, she poured her own breath into the limp, still form while her husband rubbed the boy's arms and a whimpering Marina Seminova stood by wringing her hands and twisting her skirts. But it was too late.

When Irina and Arkadi returned from their walk, they found Olga and Aleksandr still trying vainly to bring their son's inert corpse back to life.

And through it all, Yakov Seminov lay sprawled in the sunshine, snoring like a buzz saw.

CHAPTER 4

Moscow: November 1980

A leksandr Nikolayevich Dmitrov presented his identification to the security officer's secretary. She carried it into the inner office, returning a moment later with an invitation to step inside.

The smiling chief of hospital security stood up and offered his hand across the top of his desk. As they shook hands, Dmitrov caught a whiff of liquor on the man's breath.

"Colonel Dmitrov! What a surprise!" The chief dusted off the front of his green uniform jacket. "They usually tell me when someone's coming. Sit down, please."

"I want to see a patient. Yakov Seminov. The people at the desk told me I had to clear it with you."

"Seminov. Yes, I see. Well, he's in the maximum security ward. I'll have a guard take you up, if you'll wait a moment."

"I can find my way. I've been here before."

"Of course, Colonel." The officer chafed his hands together. "I've heard of you, of course. Your father was a most illustrious man, a Hero of the Soviet Union."

"The Soviet Union has many great heroes."

The security chief beamed at him. "I was there when your father, the general, was rehabilitated posthumously, awarded a Star of Lenin. Surely you attended the ceremony?"

"Oh, yes. It was quite impressive, I recall. I'm sure my father would have approved."

Dmitrov had a vivid recollection of his beautiful mother, wearing black, hamming it up, half buried in bouquets of flowers, and himself, stiff in his cadet's uniform, conscious of the speculative gazes of the older officers present, who were wondering if the sprout would prove anywhere near as tough as the old oak who had fathered him.

After Khrushchev's secret speech to the Politburo revealed the extent of Joseph Stalin's atrocities, many imprisoned heroes were released. Those who had not survived the Gulag had their reputations refurbished, and in some cases, revised. After the country had officially acknowledged General Dmitrov's contributions during the war, young Lieutenant Dmitrov suddenly found himself selected for special duty, given special training, pulled up the ladder by his father's cronies, who had been too afraid to notice him before. His mother had been right when she told him that the award ceremony was more than just a formality. "It will change your life, Sasha," she had said.

The security chief dipped into the top drawer of his desk. "I need to write up a pass. There are a lot of doors between here and Three West. You don't want to keep flashing your badge at all of them."

Dmitrov shook out a cigarette. American, Marlboro. He saw the man eyeing them and offered him one. "Why don't you keep the pack?" Dmitrov said. "I can get more."

"Thanks."

A favor granted, a favor owed. The next time Dmitrov came, the man wouldn't even check his papers.

The chief filled in the blanks: name of visitor; name of patient; room number; security status. He scratched his signature at the bottom of the small square of paper and stamped it with the date and the time, which he read off the rusting wall clock. Dmitrov, the chief noted, was wearing a gold wristwatch, wafer thin, with a band as beautifully and intricately designed as the dead czar's crown.

"Here you are, Colonel." He passed the paper over the top of the desk. "Take the stairs to the third floor. Show this to the guard."

"Who is Seminov's doctor?" Dmitrov asked.

"His doctor?"

"This is a hospital, isn't it? Suppose I want to discuss his condition with someone who knows? Who do I ask for?"

The chief laughed. "Three West isn't the hospital's responsibility, Colonel. It's ours. Why do you think they directed you to me? Seminov is my patient, and he's doing just fine. He won't make trouble for anyone now."

Dmitrov thanked him and went out before his anger forced him to do something stupid.

What is the difference between a hospital and a prison? In this case, none. It had the same stench, the same gritty feeling, the same dank chill. True, more of the physicians here were men—in case their drugs failed to work and extra muscle was needed. Corridors painted green seventy years ago and never touched since; exposed pipes furry with grease and dust, the straps rusted; a pool of water on the floor where a drip just missed the bucket that had been placed to catch it. Stale cigarette smoke, the national love affair with tobacco, almost as intense as the passion for vodka, making common ground between inmates and keepers. In the hall a *babushka* on her knees, swabbing listlessly, pushing the grime from one side to the other, her chapped hands crimson. It looked as though she were wearing rose-colored gloves.

On the third floor, two uniformed men guarded the steel doors to the west wing. One stood at attention, the other was seated at a battered metal desk, writing something in a notebook. Dmitrov handed his pass to the guard at the desk, who took a long time studying it, examining the signature, the seal, the stamps. Dmitrov concealed his impatience. It didn't matter where you went in the country, the world, bureaucrats were all the same: the lowest were the slowest. Their territory was clearly defined and prescribed, but it was their own, and they were cautious of invaders and interlopers.

Finally the nod came, and the head jerked toward the door. "Through there. The hall guard will show you. Visits are limited to twenty minutes."

"This is official business," Dmitrov told him. "I'll stay as long as I like. Clear it with the director if you must."

In reply, he received a shrug.

The standing guard, armed to the teeth, a submachine gun slung from a strap over his shoulder and a pistol holstered on his belt, made a laborious show of unlocking the two sets of locks on the doors and relocking them after Dmitrov passed through.

A young guard who was leaning his chair back against the wall halfway along the corridor righted himself and stood. "Pass?"

"I've already shown—"

"Pass." His hand shot out. He barely glanced at the paper before handing it back. "This way."

They halted in front of a locked door. The guard inserted his key in the lock, and checked his wristwatch. "Knock when you're ready to leave."

Dmitrov stepped into a cubicle about six feet by ten feet. There was a window opposite the door, with a view of the blackened bricks that lined the air shaft. A narrow bed. A sink, with a chamber pot tucked underneath. Not even a stool or a chair for visitors.

Yakov was lying on his side, on top of the covers. His hospital gown gaped open in the back, revealing wasted buttocks and a nasty black and purple bruise over one kidney. Dmitrov went around the bed and leaned over him. Yakov's eyes were open but unfocused. There was a scattering of wounds on his calves, small round scabs about as big as his thumbnail. Cigarette burns.

Dmitrov squatted down on his haunches, putting his hand on Yakov's shoulder. "Hello, Yakov. Do you know me? It's Sasha. Your brother-in-law."

Dmitrov thought he saw a slight flicker in Yakov's eyes. His face was puffy and the skin around his lips was blue. His breathing was labored. Olga had told Dmitrov what to look for. Her brother's heart was failing.

"Would you like to sit up? I'll help you." Would he unbend? Dmitrov wondered. Or was he frozen into this parody of fetal waiting? He leaned closer. "Look at me, Yakov. I'm Sasha. Do you know me? I have some good news. They've given Marina and Arkadi their visas. They'll be leaving next week, for America. At least they'll be out of here. Safe."

"Get away from me." The words came slowly, pushed by a thick tongue, past furry unbrushed teeth, through the slack lips. "Get away from me."

"Yakov—"

"Get out of here. KGB scum. Not my brother. Leave me alone."

Slowly Yakov's eyes came into focus and he tried to roll onto his back, but the effort was too great and he lapsed back into the fetal position.

"I'm still your brother," Dmitrov said softly.

Yakov stared at him and spoke again. "Olga was a good sister. A fighter. Not like Marina. A mouse, Marina. Always terrified. I never thought Olga would let you get away with this. I thought she would stop you. I curse the day she married you."

"I warned you what would happen if you went too far. We had no choice. We had to pull you back."

After Misha's death, Yakov had gone mad with grief and remorse. He blamed his fight with Dmitrov for the accident, and he refused to be comforted. With suicidal recklessness, he began to bait the KGB, daring them to stop him. He published a newspaper, a single sheet written and edited and typed by himself: *Freedom*. He collared a couple of visiting foreigners and gave them messages to the American President, Jimmy Carter, asking him to condemn the Soviet Union for violations of the Helsinki Accords. He gave an interview to a British journalist in which he described his own case and derided the Soviet government for cowardice: "It's safer to keep the Jews locked up here than to let them tell the world what they know." Everyone was surprised that the KGB allowed it to go on as long as it did.

Dmitrov tried everything to persuade his brother-in-law to stop his suicidal course, but eventually Yakov was arrested. He was tried, found insane, and confined to a psychiatric hospital.

"I thought you were different," Yakov mumbled. "But no. You have too much greed. Too much to lose. You march in step with the rest. Right, brother?"

"I have to." Dmitrov sat on the foot of the bed, which dipped alarmingly under his weight. Yakov's body hardly made a dimple in the mattress. Despite the swollen belly, engorged with fluids the kidneys could not dispel, he seemed to have lost half his bulk. "I wanted to speak up, but it would have been a waste, a romantic gesture. I'm not a man who makes romantic gestures. They would have given me the room next to this one. Doctors. Drugs. What would happen to Olga and Irina then? Two families destroyed."

"You threw me to the Wolf."

"I couldn't hide you from him."

"Krelnikov says jump, you jump. You're like all the rest. Just another trained bear. No mind. Brute strength. A KGB thug in an Italian suit. If your father were alive, he would kill you with his bare hands. He hated those people."

"I had no choice," Dmitrov said. His lips were dry and he craved a cigarette. Like a fool, he had given away his pack.

"We all have a choice. Many choices. Even now, I can still choose. I choose not to listen to you anymore. Talk as much as you like. I can't hear you." Yakov closed his eyes.

Dmitrov's jaw tensed. Many times in the past year he had wanted to kill Yakov, to throttle him, to shake some sense into him. Even now, he noticed that he was clenching his hands together to keep from striking out at this poor, sick, stubborn man. It was happening again. A surge of love that hardened into anger, then dissolved into an emotion that felt like hatred. But no. He hated Krelnikov; what he felt toward Yakov was something quite different: loving exasperation.

He said, "I came here today because Olga insisted. She wanted someone to see you before Marina and Arkadi left. I'll soften the details for them. I won't tell them that in my opinion, a psychiatric hospital is the proper place for you. You acted like a crazy man, and in your madness you destroyed yourself."

"I'll be back," Yakov whispered. "To haunt your dreams. I don't dream anymore. What's the point? No mind. The medicines they've given me have taken that away, too."

Yakov's sphincter relaxed, releasing a pool of watery brown stools. A sickening stench filled the air. Dmitrov pounded on the door. When the guard opened it, he said, "Find a nurse or an orderly and clean this man up."

The guard turned sullen. "I don't take orders from you, comrade. Besides, the patients are none of my—"

"Do as I say! At once! Or I'll kick your worthless ass from here to Irkutsk, do you understand me? Move!" He realized that he sounded just like his father dressing down a slovenly subordinate.

The guard blanched up to the peak of his cap. "I'll have to lock the door again."

"Then do it! This man isn't going anyplace."

The door closed. Dmitrov turned back to the bed and looked down at the shrunken figure of his brother-in-law. "You poor bastard. I don't care what you've done. You don't deserve this."

Yakov lay wheezing on his cot. Dmitrov said nothing but waited in silence until the guard returned with an orderly. He watched with folded arms, ignoring the orderly's sotto voce grumbling. His rage was very close to the surface, burning in his throat, trembling on his lips. He shouldn't have stayed to watch, but he couldn't tear himself away. The scene exerted its own horrible fascination. Besides, the sooner he left this place, the sooner he would have to think about what he had seen.

"Give me a hand, will you?" the orderly said to the guard. "I need to turn him over, but I hurt my back last week."

"Are you crazy? He stinks. I'm not paid to diaper lunatics."

Dmitrov grabbed the guard's shoulders and pinned him up against the wall. "What are you paid for, then? Can you tell me that? Are you paid to prod him with the butt of your rifle, and burn him with cigarettes? Both of you, get out of here."

The two men shuffled out, rolling their eyes and muttering to each other. Dmitrov took the sponge from the basin and cleaned Yakov the best he could, then he finished changing the soiled linens. There was a heavy rubber pad under the bottom sheet. No wonder Yakov was sweating. Dmitrov considered removing it, but when he lifted the corner, he found that the mattress itself was stained and filthy.

When he had completed his chores, he tapped on the door. The guard, who didn't care how long the visitor was locked in with the patient, was long in coming. Dmitrov leaned over the cot.

"Good-bye, Yakov. If these people know anything about mercy, they'll let you die quickly." He leaned over and kissed the fevered forehead.

When the guard opened the door, Dmitrov shoved the soiled bed linens into his arms.

"My report will be on the security chief's desk in the morning. I'm citing you for insubordination, cruelty, inattention to duty, and slovenly appearance, and that's just the beginning. Do you have anything to say to that?"

The man snapped to attention in the corridor outside Yakov's cell. "No, comrade."

Two minutes later, Dmitrov found himself standing on the sidewalk in front of the hospital. He couldn't recall how he got there. The air was bitter, tangy with coal fumes, thick with the promise of more snow. He shoved his hands into the pockets of his raincoat and started to walk. A black Chaika limousine pulled up abreast of him and the rear door opened.

"Colonel Dmitrov. Which way are you going? I'll take you."

Dmitrov stared down at the Wolf. Bald-headed and bullnecked, Ivan Krelnikov smiled habitually in order to show off the two gold canine teeth in his upper jaw. With each passing year, Krelnikov's resemblance to the animal he had been nicknamed for became more marked, even as his reputation for ruthlessness and viciousness grew. When the Politburo created the KGB's Fifth Chief Directorate in 1969, Krelnikov had been appointed head of the special Jewish Department. Although he had since been promoted, he maintained a keen interest in the people he cynically called his "Hebrew children." At Dzerzhinsky Square he was credited with being the first to suggest that anyone who disagreed with established policy was clearly insane. To him the Soviet Union owed the perversion and politicization of psychiatry. Now, eleven years later, thousands of dissidents like Yakov had been confined to "hospitals," where they were drugged and starved and deprived of their dignity. Eventually, many of these "psychiatric patients" actually did lose their minds.

"No, thank you." Dmitrov turned away from the Chaika. "I prefer to walk."

"Of course. You want an opportunity to brood in solitude about the fate of that poor bastard you've just seen. Don't be a fool. Ride with me. I'll drop you anywhere you like."

Dmitrov climbed in and pulled the door closed. The car glided smoothly away from the curb. The Wolf chuckled. "Here." A silver flask appeared under Dmitrov's nose. "You need this."

Dmitrov sipped. Not vodka but French brandy, Rémy Martin. The Wolf liked to show off. The brandy washed away the sour taste in Dmitrov's gut. He took another long swallow and returned the flask to Krelnikov.

"I suppose your *stukach* in the security office called you the moment I left him?"

"If he hadn't, he would have been dining on his own balls tomorrow. He's not the only man I have inside that hell hole. Really, it would have been better if you had stayed away. Seminov's heart is failing. He won't last the month. Is that how you want to remember him?"

Dmitrov stared straight ahead. Yes, that's how I want to remember him, how I must remember him. "I want him moved to a real hospital," he said. "He's dying, isn't he? Put him somewhere where he'll be comfortable."

Krelnikov shook his head. "I'm not authorized to do that. He is a psychiatric patient."

"He's no crazier than you are."

"That may be, but I don't go around denouncing my government at the top of my lungs. Sane men know the importance of discretion. Like you. You never say what you think, do you, Aleksandr Nikolayevich? Right now, you'd like to break me over your knee, wouldn't you? But you'll keep your hands to yourself and bite your tongue. You have too much to lose by telling the truth."

"Not at all. If you really wanted to destroy me, you'd manufacture the evidence. You don't need me to tell you anything." Dmitrov leaned forward. "Will you let me off here, please?"

The driver waited for Krelnikov's consent. "Pull over to the curb," Krelnikov said. "Ah, we're very near the Bolshoi, I see. When you see your mother, please give her my regards. She's getting on in years, isn't she? When she dies, you'll find yourself with fewer friends, I fear. The ranks of the old lady's admirers are thinning. The men who begged to be allowed to perform favors for her are dying off. I hear that Stalin himself once sipped champagne from her ballet slipper. Is that so?"

"I wouldn't know. I wasn't there."

"But you've heard the story, surely. Thousands of times. She likes to tell it. Did you know that I worked for her once? It was a long time ago. I was a new recruit, fresh out of the army. I worked hard, did my job, waited for someone to notice me. The ballerina needed a driver. Since her admirers were likely to include foreigners, and since I understood English and German, they assigned me to the task. I lasted one day. She took one look at me and said, 'How am I supposed to dance after looking at your ugly face? Get away from me and don't come back.' I've never forgotten that."

"That's her way." Dmitrov stepped out onto the sidewalk. "She likes to insult people."

"I sense a restlessness in you, Colonel." The Wolf's gold teeth, wet with saliva, gleamed like nuggets at the entrance of a treasure cave. "You have a reckless nature. No one else has seen it, of course, because you are skilled at concealing it. But it will emerge. Given time and the proper circumstances, it will show itself. And when that happens, fifty famous ballerinas won't be able to save you. Good-bye."

Dmitrov watched the car pull away. The policeman at the intersection stopped the flow of cross traffic to permit the Chaika to pass without slowing. A few pedestrians glanced at the limousine curiously, but the curtains over the side and rear windows concealed the occupant. A good thing, too. Those people didn't want to know that man, the one they called the Wolf.

Dmitrov pulled the collar of his coat up around his ears.

"They own you body and soul, Sasha," Yakov had taunted him on the day Misha died. "Body and whatever soul you have left."

CHAPTER 5

Warsaw: November 1981

J udith Marlowe gave a shout of laughter. "Have you lost your mind,
Kenny? That necklace is the most disgusting piece of crap I've ever
seen. I wouldn't wear it to a street brawl. If Byron wants to show off his
genius as a jewelry designer, he can wear the damn thing himself. And you
can damn well tell him I said so."

As Judith swung around on the stool in front of her dressing table,
clear liquid sloshed out of her glass and splashed her husband's shoes.
Immediately Kenneth whipped out his handkerchief and wiped them off.
Judith was drinking Polish vodka, one of the stronger brands, one hundred twenty proof and powerful enough to melt the wax off his dress
pumps.

He said in an urgent whisper, "Will you please watch your language?
For God's sake, the neighbors!"

"Fuck the neighbors," Judith said cheerfully. "It's time they were
learning basic American. I'm more interested in the bugs our Soviet brothers have planted in our boudoir walls. Hey, comrades," she sang, "wake
up!" Dropping her voice to a gravelly contralto, she crooned, "We've got
a good scene going here."

Wearing only a brassiere and black silk panties, Judith planted herself
in the middle of the blue and cream carpet, propped her hands on her hips,
and unleashed a torrent of rapid-fire Polish. Kenneth cringed. Whenever
Judith studied a new language, she always mastered the obscenities first,
what she called the herbs and spices of social intercourse.

"And when you've finished all that," Judith concluded grandly in

English, "you can stick your collective noses up Comrade Brezhnev's ass."

Kenneth struggled to keep his voice steady. "If you recall, Judith, you put on quite an act when Byron gave you that necklace. Anyone would think you adored it. Byron did. And now he's starting to wonder why he never sees you wearing it."

Judith flopped backward onto the bed. "Tell him I wear it when we screw," she laughed. "It turns you on. It's become a sacred object, a fertility fetish, too precious to show to strangers." She waggled her tongue at him.

"Please, Judith." Kenneth fixed his gaze on a spot on the wall above the carved headboard. "Byron is our country's ambassador. I am an embassy employee. That makes him my boss. I agree, the necklace is a trifle overdone—"

"It's a grotesque piece of shit." Judith rolled onto her haunch. "I wouldn't be caught dead in it. I wouldn't even wear it to my mother's funeral. Only the gladdest rags will do for that happy occasion."

In May, the American ambassador to Poland, Byron Harcourt, had hosted a small gathering at his official residence in honor of Judith's birthday. When he presented his gift, Judith, who had put away a lot of champagne at dinner, barely managed to restrain a burst of derisive laughter. Byron Harcourt boasted of how he had designed the piece himself, how he had taken the design to a jeweler in Vienna, how the man had made the necklace to his exact specifications. At first the guests thought it was a joke, an appalling piece of kitsch: two clawlike hands, elongated and deformed, one wearing an emerald ring, the other a clanking bracelet encrusted with diamonds, reaching around from the back of her neck to clasp an enormous pearl at the base of her throat. Those jewels couldn't possibly be real. But they were.

After the party, Judith pitched the thing into the bottom of her closet and never looked at it.

Kenneth lowered himself gingerly onto the foot of the bed. "Look, I know you hate it, but—"

Judith shuddered. "It's macabre. It reminds me of dead babies. Where did he buy it? Oven Art Limited, in Auschwitz?"

"I agree that it was completely inappropriate for him to give the wife of one of his undersecretaries such a costly gift," Kenneth said carefully. "But he did, and as I recall, you accepted in a voice dripping with graciousness."

"Course I did. Mother taught me manners. But she put a high shine on yours. My surfaces don't take a shine too well."

"That's fine, but by doing so, you put me on the spot. The stupid bastard keeps asking me about it. He won't let it rest. And he's perfectly capable of screwing up my career because of it. I ran out of believable excuses in June. I've tried telling him that I've never had any say about your wardrobe or your accessories or anything you do, but he won't let it drop."

"Why doesn't he ask me about it? I'll tell him the truth."

Kenneth mustered a weak smile. "I would prefer that you temper your honesty around Byron. I realize you've probably got some principle at stake about being your own woman and all that, but I'm asking you to compromise. If you think about it, I interfere in your life very little, but as your husband, I have a right to ask you this as a personal favor to me. Can't you wear it tonight, just this once?" His tone became slightly wheedling. "The Chopin Ball is a big event in this town. Everyone will be there. The necklace will get plenty of attention, and Byron can bask in reflected glory. Maybe this will shut him up so that we can concentrate on more important business, like how we're going to respond when the Russians invade."

Judith snorted. "Respond! What a joke. By the time you diplomats have finished your outraged twitterings, this town is going to reek of borscht and Russian cigarettes and the sweet smell of Soviet socks hung out to dry on gun barrels. Solidarity will be a happy memory and Lech Walesa will be rotting in jail. Respond, indeed."

The independent labor union known as Solidarity had begun with a workers' strike in the Gdansk shipyards in August 1980. An unemployed electrician named Lech Walesa had climbed the fence surrounding the shipyard in order to join the strike. Six months later, he won the Nobel Peace Prize. For the past five hundred days, Walesa and the movement he helped found had made headlines around the world. Encouraged by the government's capitulation to the shipyard workers' demands, Poles from all walks of life flocked to the union: miners, farmers, machinists, intellectuals, students. For the first time since World War II, all levels of Polish society were united against a single enemy, only this time it was their own Communist government. One prime minister had resigned amidst charges of incompetence and corruption. The country's new leader, an austere army general named Wojciech Jaruzelski, was struggling to contain the discontent before it erupted into full-blown revolution and brought Russian tanks streaming across Poland's borders. Yet at this very moment, with the economy in chaos and the Soviet Army hovering nearby, Solidarity's leaders were meeting in Gdansk to formulate a new list of impossible demands. Walesa, although highly respected, was losing control.

Kenneth leaned forward and grasped Judith's hand. "Will you do it? Please, Judith. As a favor to me?"

Judith gazed at him steadily, saying nothing. He was the first to look away. She chuckled softly. "All those courses in diplomacy and tact have really paid off, haven't they, Kenny? You'd like to box my ears or wring my neck, but you won't. Properly brought-up gentlemen never abuse their wives, no matter how trying we may be. And I've really given your patience a workout, haven't I?"

Kenneth kept his tone neutral. "It hasn't been so bad."

"Not for me. I can have a good time wherever I go. But what about you? Your first overseas posting, a choice plum like Warsaw. Mother must have called in a whole bunch of markers to get this for you. You're starting to climb the ladder of success, and what happens? You look around and discover you've got a weight strapped to your ankles, a hundred and twenty-five pounds of untamed female. Your wife. I tried to warn you what it would be like."

Kenneth went into the bathroom and tossed his soiled handkerchief into the wicker hamper. He continued through the connecting door to his own bedroom, where he selected a clean handkerchief from the stack in his bureau drawer.

"I was under no illusions when I married you," he said on his return. "My eyes were wide open."

"The hell they were! You were so drunk on sex and the thrill of rebellion that you couldn't think straight. It was fun at the beginning, after that disastrous first night. Remember? Playing hooky. Driving up the coast to San Francisco, stopping wherever and whenever we felt like it. You kept wanting to call Mother, to tell her what we'd done, but I wouldn't let you. Then we flew home, and when she finished chewing your balls off, you could hardly bring yourself to look at me, much less to touch me. And that's where we stand two years later. The fact that we're still married means that we're both getting something we need. But what? If you ask me, we're both sick."

"You will wear the necklace, won't you?" Kenneth's left eyelid twitched. "Just this once? I promise, I won't ask again."

Judith expelled a long sigh. "Quit whining, Kenny. I'll wear it. But I'm telling you right now, I'm going to drop that sucker into the collection plate at Saint Kasimir's on Christmas Eve."

"Fine. Wonderful. After tonight, I don't care what you do with it."

Judith sat up and swung her long legs over the side of the bed. "Now run along and let me finish creating the illusion of perfection. The way I'm feeling, it's going to be an uphill job."

"I'll bring the car around." Kenneth moved toward the door. "Ah, don't take too long, please." He glanced at his wristwatch. "We're running late as it is. You know what a stickler for punctuality Byron is."

"Sticklers," said Judith, "deserve to get stuck where they'll feel it most. I have an idea; why don't you go without me? Tell him I'm having early menopause. Flashes so hot I incinerate men on contact."

"No, no," Kenneth said hastily, "that's all right. I'll wait."

After he had gone, Judith lit a cigarette and took a long time smoking it while she finished her drink. The door buzzer sounded: Kenneth reminding her that the BMW was idling in front of the entrance and that they had an appointment to keep. She stubbed out the cigarette, dragged herself off the bed, and opened the door to her closet. As she stood there, contemplating her wardrobe, the corners of her mouth began to twitch, and even without an audience to hear her, she began to laugh out loud.

They arrived at the Hotel Forum forty-five minutes later. Kenneth pulled the BMW up to the curb, leapt out, and hurried around to open Judith's door. As they walked into the hotel, a familiar figure scurried toward them.

"It's about time!" Byron Harcourt had been pacing off the dimensions of the Forum's lobby for nearly an hour. "I thought I was going to have to go through that damn receiving line by myself."

Judith kissed him on both cheeks. "It's all my fault, Byron," she said. "It took me simply ages to dress. I had to find just the right costume to set off this marvelous necklace." She touched the weighty piece of gold that gleamed at her throat.

Byron Harcourt beamed at her. "I'll forgive you anything, honey, if you'll let me have another kiss." This one was full on the lips, wet and rather prolonged. Judith held her breath until it was over. Harcourt let his arm linger at her waist. "You're here now, pretty lady, that's all that matters."

With his long, hefty torso and stubby legs, America's ambassador to Poland cut a less than striking figure in his evening clothes, and even suspenders could not pull the waistband of his trousers up over his protruding gut. A lifetime of self-indulgence had blunted his features and coarsened his skin. Tonight, primed with too much Scotch, Harcourt had dressed carelessly; the impressive gray crest of his toupee rode his shining forehead at a slight angle. Judith wondered if there was a diplomatic way of telling him about it. She could see the question on the Foreign Service exam: *Your ambassador makes an appearance at a public function looking less than tidy—*

Kenneth came up behind her. "May I take your coat, Judith?"

"Certainly."

The coat was Italian, yards of white wool with padded shoulders and kimono sleeves, and elongated lapels that reached the floor. When tossed mufflerlike over the shoulders, it had a togalike appearance. Judith unwrapped herself slowly, almost teasingly, looking back and forth between the two men. When she finally opened the front and let the garment slide off her shoulders, Kenneth blanched. Byron Harcourt cleared his throat. Judith started to laugh.

"What's the matter, darlings? Has that nasty wind ruined my hair? Do I look a complete and total wreck?"

Kenneth's jaw tensed. "What in hell do you think you're doing? Take that thing off at once."

Judith's eyes widened. "But darling, you said you wanted me to wear Byron's necklace." She appealed to the ambassador. "It is lovely, isn't it? I just adore it. The reason I haven't worn it before is that I'm a hoarder. I hate sharing my most beautiful possessions with strangers."

"Sure, honey." Harcourt's smile looked a little strained, as if he suspected her of making fun of him but couldn't quite believe it. "You look . . . great."

Kenneth grabbed her arm. "We're not talking about the necklace. That damn button. Take it off right now!"

The two men gazed horror-stricken at the six-inch badge pinned above her left breast, red letters on a white background reading SOLI-DARNÖSC. Judith had cinched the waist of her flowing white Grecian gown with a broad red sash. She looked like the spirit of Polish liberty.

"Oh, Kenny." She shook off his hand. "Don't be so stuffy. Out of the fourteen million workers in Poland, ten million belong to Solidarity. That means that for every three Poles you brush up against at an affair like this, two out of three are likely to be Solidarity members."

"Not here. Not this bunch. The whole idea—"

"If the button goes, so do I," Judith said sweetly, switching on her brightest, falsest smile. "And you and Byron can escort each other through the receiving line."

Byron Harcourt shrugged. "She's your wife, Ken, but I do admire her courage."

Kenneth Marlowe swallowed, and at the same time he narrowed his lips so tightly that they disappeared. Judith wondered if he were trying to turn himself inside out.

"Why are you doing this to me?" he demanded in a low hiss. "Why? I ask for so little. I've given you as much freedom as you need, with the understanding that you are not, repeat *not,* to make a fool of me in front of Byron and the people who are our hosts. I insist that you do as I ask."

"You can't insist and ask at the same time," Judith told him. "And you don't give orders around here. Not to me."

"Hell, I can take the heat if you can, Ken," the ambassador said. "Shall we go in now, Judy honey?"

"Sure, Byron." With a merry laugh, Judith turned away from Kenneth and slipped her hand through the crook of Byron Harcourt's elbow. "I just love making scenes. Stick with me and we'll have lots of fun."

"Sounds good to me. You heard from your mother lately?"

"No." Deep, infectious laughter bubbled up under her words. "But I can almost guarantee that I will be hearing from her very soon. At the highest possible decibel level."

The Solidarity button created a gratifying sensation in the receiving line. Eyebrows lifted, expressions tightened, but nothing was said until Judith and Byron had moved past, leaving a ripple of outraged hisses and murmurs in their wake. Judith smiled at the women, flirted and laughed with the men, and ignored the pointed stares and the gossip. These highly placed Polish bureaucrats and their elaborately coiffed wives were no different from the sponsors of the charity affairs she had attended as a debutante.

Byron seemed tense, but no more so than usual at a big affair like this. He was a newcomer to international politics, an outsider, a wealthy, conservative businessman and who had obtained his posting by contributing generously to Republican coffers. Divorced and lonely, he had come to rely on Judith as his hostess, dinner companion, and escort. Kenneth, his indispensable assistant during the day, was becoming an unnecessary nuisance at night.

After a prolonged ceremony during which the Minister of Art and Culture awarded Chopin Medals to Poland's most promising young musicians, a three-piece band assembled on the dais and the floor was cleared for dancing. Declaring that he had been waiting for this all night, Byron pulled Judith into his arms and began to push her along in front of him as he bulldozed his way across the floor. His after-shave was particularly obnoxious that evening, and combined with the aura of nervous perspiration, Scotch whiskey, and cigar smoke, it made her want to vomit. He held her uncomfortably close, his mouth pressed against her cheek. Occasionally, his right hand strayed down her back and groped through the folds of soft wool crepe, searching for something to squeeze.

The dance ended. Judith wriggled away from Harcourt. "Byron, darling, I have to pee in the worst way. While I'm gone, why don't you dance with Frau Schultz? She speaks excellent English."

Byron balked at the suggestion. "I can't dance with her. She's bigger than me."

"But very light on her feet." Judith laughed and gave him a push. "Remember your ambassadorial responsibilities. I don't want to monopolize you for the whole evening."

As she watched him walk away, Judith felt a tap on her arm. Looking around, she saw Ivan Pushkin, the local TASS correspondent, bowing to her and grinning under his pointed foxlike nose.

"Madame, you look delightful tonight." His eyes slid past the button on her shoulder and went straight to her cleavage. "Quite the most beautiful creature in the room. Would you be so kind as to dance with me?"

"Why not?" The dance was a foxtrot, which almost everyone in Poland danced as a side-to-side two-step shuffle. Pushkin was no exception, but Judith noticed that he kept twisting his neck around as though he were looking for someone. Finally he made a small clicking sound with his mouth and stopped dancing.

"Here is someone who would like to meet you," he said. "A new arrival to our *corpse diplomatic.*" Pushkin's execrable French accent was a joke among the Western diplomats and their wives. It was even funnier than his English accent, which sounded like a Peter Sellers parody of a Russian.

Following Pushkin's gaze, Judith saw a man moving toward them through the crowd. He was half a head taller than everyone else in the room, and even from a distance, Judith could see that his eyes were blue, with a slightly Eastern cast. His eyebrows were a shade darker than his hair, which was light brown. Under high Tartar cheekbones, his face was lean and strong. A deep dimple at the left corner of his mouth softened his sternness, and the crinkles at the corners of his eyes suggested either nearsightedness or a powerful sense of humor. Judith suspected the latter. Why not? Everything else about him was perfect.

He stopped two paces from Pushkin and waited while the journalist made the introductions.

"Mrs. Marlowe, I am pleased to present our new cultural attaché, Aleksandr Dmitrov. He has recently arrived from Moscow."

Judith offered her hand. Instead of shaking it, Dmitrov cradled it gently and kissed it, Polish fashion. Judith was willing to bet that he hadn't bought his blue pin-striped suit off the rack at GUM. The jacket was beautifully cut, showing just the right amount of shirt cuff, as well as gold links and a gold Rolex on the left wrist. His broad shoulders needed no padding.

"So you're the newest addition to our diplomatic ghetto," Judith said. "Warsaw is a very exciting place to be right now, don't you agree?"

"I have always enjoyed visiting this city." His English accent was more British than American, and he had a slight tendency to overarticulate his consonants.

"Yes, the Poles are generally very hospitable to guests, if not to conquerors." Judith laughed and flashed him a wicked smile. "You didn't arrive in a tank, did you?"

Pushkin coughed and excused himself hurriedly. Dmitrov's smile did not dim. "Perhaps you will honor me with the rest of this dance?"

"I was just waiting for you to ask."

He swept her onto the floor. The movement was so easy and graceful that it caught her by surprise. After a moment, she realized to her astonishment that he was actually dancing an honest-to-God foxtrot, and dancing it to perfection. She had never had such a skilled partner. Once she realized she could follow him effortlessly, she gave herself up to the enjoyment of the experience.

"That was wonderful!" Judith exclaimed when the music stopped. "And much too brief." She noticed that he had steered her over to the edge of the crowded dance floor, to a quiet spot behind a battered aspidistra in a hammered copper washtub.

"I quite agree." Dmitrov's left hand still caressed hers.

Judith smiled up at him. "I had no idea that Russian diplomatic training included dancing classes."

"Ordinarily, it doesn't."

"What about the KGB? Does it like its spies to master the social graces?"

Dmitrov grinned back at her. "I have no idea, madame. I am a diplomat, not a spy."

Judith laughed and tossed her hair. "You don't expect me to believe you, do you? Spies and diplomats are the most skilled liars in the world. It's my policy never to believe a word any of them says."

"A wise move in any social interaction." Dmitrov looked solemn, but his eyes were sparkling. "Particularly one between a man and a woman."

"Then I can trust you never to tell me the truth?"

"Only when I cannot avoid it, like now. If I say you are quite the most enchanting woman I have met in many years, you must believe me."

Judith laughed delightedly. "Oh, I'll accept that. But don't think for a second that I've swallowed that lie about your being a minor functionary at the Soviet embassy. Your clothes give you away. If you didn't have that jacket tailored for you in London, I'll eat it."

"You may have to dine on wool from Ukrainian sheep. My tailor lives in Kiev."

"Then you've never been to London?"

"My job is to inform people all over the world about the glories of Soviet culture. Naturally I have traveled widely."

"That means you're either a trusted party member or your rank is very high. I'd say both."

"You are grilling me very thoroughly, Mrs. Marlowe. You must be either a very good cook or a skilled CIA operative."

Judith laughed again. "I ought to know better than to try to extract information from a Russian. Why don't you dance with me again?"

"Your husband won't mind?"

"Oh, you don't want to dance with him. He'll step all over your feet"—she glanced down—"and scuff those lovely Italian pumps you're wearing. But perhaps I'm in error again. Those shoes didn't come from Milan, did they? They're part of the last shipment from the number-three shoe factory in Tbilisi."

The orchestra struck up a waltz. Dmitrov took her in his arms and whirled her away. They spun so rapidly that it seemed her feet hardly touched the floor. In his arms, she felt that she could do anything, even fly, if that's what he wanted of her. The music, cranked out less than brilliantly by the usual trio of piano, violin, and drums, was strangely intoxicating. Giddy from the sheer joy of moving so fluidly through space, Judith laughed out loud. Dmitrov's eyes never left her face. His smile grew broader, until he was laughing, too. Kenneth's face flashed past, a study in suppressed anger.

The dance ended too soon. Dmitrov was breathing easily, as though the exertion had been effortless, but Judith was puffing and her cheeks were burning. Once again he piloted her into a shadowy corner.

Judith laced her arms around his neck and leaned against his chest. "Take me, you tiger. I'm all yours."

Dmitrov looked startled. "I beg your pardon, Mrs. Marlowe?"

"I'll tell you anything you want to know, only promise you'll dance with me again before I die. State secrets? I've got plenty. Kenny is a fiend for chocolate. Belgian chocolate. But he can't eat too many because he gets pimples on his back. You want more? The ambassador buys shirts with a size sixteen collar, but he really should be wearing sixteen and a half. His shoes are too small, too. He's vain about everything except the size of his brain. He hasn't one. I don't know about his penis. He'd love to show it to me, but I have a weak stomach for deformities." The band had struck up a slow dance. Judith slid her hands down to Dmitrov's shoulders. "Will that do for now? This torture is exquisite."

He slipped his arm around her waist and cradled her right hand against his chest. They began to rock slowly back and forth, hardly moving from the spot. "I assure you, Mrs. Marlow, dancing with you is a delight sufficient unto itself. You may keep your state secrets."

"Playing it cagey, Mr. B? Excuse the pun. The urge comes over me sometimes. I can't help myself."

"I don't understand."

"Cagey; B: KGB. You, *Sovietski*. Me, *Americanska*. You prey upon the weak and the stupid. Following orders. Unless you just wanted to get close enough to read my button."

"A pleasure I couldn't resist. Although beauty like yours requires no ornamentation."

"That's what I told my husband earlier. But he wouldn't listen. In any case, I've fallen hopelessly in love with you. When can we consummate our passion? Is right now too soon?"

His dimple deepened. "Where do you suggest we make love? In the pantry behind the kitchen?"

"In the back seat of the ambassador's limousine?"

"The wine cellar?"

"The party cadre's office?" They laughed together. "You, Mr. Dmitrov, have been very well schooled in the care and handling of diplomates." Judith touched his bottom lip. "Either that, or you have a sneakily un-Soviet sense of humor."

"We bears are occasionally docile, and frequently playful."

"My dear dancing bear, I wish I could believe you loved me for myself alone. Perhaps I'm rushing things a bit, wishing you would kiss me before my mouth dries up from all this idle chitchat."

"A kiss? Here? With the eyes of Warsaw upon us?"

"Why not? Let's make 'em pop." Judith lifted her face, and with a slight pressure on the back of his neck, drew his head down. He hesitated, but her lips were insistent. He crushed his mouth against hers. They stopped dancing.

"Wow," Judith said breathlessly when they came up for air. "You must have gotten your Ph.D. in seduction. Wish I'd been there when you defended your dissertation."

Dmitrov cleared his throat. "Forgive me, but it hardly seems proper to seduce you before I've told you why I was so anxious to meet you."

"I thought we'd already gotten the preliminaries out of the way. Who needs 'em?"

"I have a message from your father."

"So soon?" Judith chuckled. "Jesus, Kenny didn't waste any time playing tattletale. I suppose Preston wants me to be a good little girl. So what else is new?"

"Not your stepfather, Mrs. Marlowe. Your real father, Phillip Abbott. As you probably know, he lives in Moscow now. We are acquainted."

Suddenly Judith felt hot and so heavy that she pictured herself sinking right through the floor, a sort of mini nuclear meltdown. Dmitrov looked at her with concern.

"Mrs. Marlowe, are you all right?" He placed a steadying hand under her elbow. "I didn't mean to distress you. But he is old. And ill. He wants to see you."

Without taking her gaze from his face, Judith shook her head. Just then Kenneth approached them and, throwing his arm around her shoulders, drew her away from Dmitrov.

"Time to go, Judith. I have an early day tomorrow."

"Mr. Marlowe?" Dmitrov offered his hand. "I am Aleksandr Dmitrov, the new Soviet cultural attaché. Your wife has been welcoming me to Warsaw."

"I saw." Kenneth ignored the proffered hand. "The whole room saw. Try not to take my wife too seriously, Mr. Dmitrov. She has a quirky sense of humor."

"He means I often drink too much," Judith said unsteadily. "As an excuse for not conforming, it's somewhat overdone, but it still works."

"You see what I mean?" Kenneth's smile was beginning to crack. "Come along, Judith."

As they walked away, Judith called over her shoulder to Dmitrov, "Next time wear your hand-tailored flak jacket, comrade. Socially, I'm a loose cannon."

As the Marlowes made their way across the dance floor, the other diplomats and their wives avoided looking at Judith. When they reached the door, she turned and pulled off the Solidarity button.

"Lucky winner gets a free trip to Moscow. Bye, everybody." She tossed it discuslike over the heads of the crowd, but Kenneth jerked her away before she could see where it landed.

CHAPTER 6

*Y*our mother is right about you. You're a lunatic, a dangerous lunatic. I should have you locked up, committed, put away someplace where you can't hurt yourself or anyone else."

Judith took a long drag on a cigarette. "My mother is not right and you know it. I'm saner than you are. And I have a lot more fun."

The five-room apartment on Aleje Ujazdowskie was their first real home together. Judith had purchased all the furnishings locally, from antique and secondhand dealers. She liked cluttered, cozy rooms filled with flowers and fabrics and bric-a-brac and family pictures. Kenneth, who suffered from allergies to dust and molds, would have preferred a sterile cube with a couple of abstract paintings on the walls.

He stopped pacing the floor in front of the overstuffed sofa. "Do you have any idea who that man is?"

Judith shrugged from the depths of the cushions. *"Sovietski.* This town is crawling with them. So what?"

"So he's probably KGB and GRU and God knows what else. What did he say to you?" Kenneth bent over, pushing his face close to hers. "More to the point, what did you tell him? What? I've got to know."

"Jesus, Kenny, I was flirting with him." Judith stubbed out her cigarette in the ashtray. "I was so glad to get away from Byron, to see a genuinely tall man with real hair and his own teeth that I lost my head for a minute. Back off, will you?"

"I will not back off. You must have talked about something? What?"

"I can't remember." Judith reached over the arm of the sofa and took another cigarette from the jade box on the end table. "Dancing. We talked about dancing. He's a good dancer. And chocolates. I told him you preferred Belgian but they give you zits. Is that such a crime? Oh, and I gave him Byron's shirt size."

"Zits! Byron's shirt size!"

"I was making a joke, all right? Having fun."

"Not all right." The muscles in Kenneth's neck grew taut. "It's not all right at all. What do I do now? We are supposed to report any suspicious approaches by Soviet agents. Half of Warsaw saw you with him, and chances are if I don't tell the security people at the embassy, someone else will. But I don't want to blow this all out of proportion. It might well have been an innocent encounter. I've got to know. Did this man actively seek you out? Did this meeting seem prearranged?"

"I don't remember." Judith pursed her lips and expelled cigarette smoke in a narrow stream. "I saw him across the crowded room and he saw me and we sort of drifted together like in the movies and then we danced. It was very pleasant."

"He kissed you," Kenneth charged.

"I kissed him," she corrected. "It was my idea. Can you blame me for taking advantage? A gorgeous hunk like that? If I hadn't kissed him, I'd be kicking myself from here to Gdansk. I sure won't get another chance. I tried to get him into bed, but he turned me down. Clumsy me."

"Do you know what you are, Judith?" Kenneth ground his teeth. "You're a whore. Worse than that, you're a stupid whore."

Judith peered up at him from under the tumble of curls on her forehead. "No, Kenny," she said softly, "I am not stupid. And I am not a whore. I've never taken money for it."

"You're irresponsible," Kenneth raged, "thoughtless, and totally selfish. You see a man you like and you spread your legs. No questions, no hesitation."

"The operative word is 'like.' " Judith chuckled. "I have to like them. I liked you well enough to spread my legs, didn't I? I even paid you the enormous compliment of marrying you. As I recall, it was your idea."

Kenneth tucked his hands under his armpits. "I must have been insane. Temporarily out of my mind."

Judith kicked off her shoes and drew her feet up under her buttocks. "The night you ran down all those poor rabbits. I knew then that you didn't have any feelings."

"You're disgusting. Do you know that?"

"I'm disgusting?" She rested her head on her arms. "You let my mother turn you into the palace eunuch."

"We should never have married." Kenneth resumed his pacing, stopping in front of a primitive oil painting Judith had found at a flea market in Lublin. It showed a girl in peasant costume standing under an apple tree loaded with purple fruit. The subject's skin was yellow. The leaves on the tree were black.

"Thus spake Lydia from on high," Judith said with a soft sigh. "If I cared enough to think about it, I might feel sorry for you, Kenny. You let her write the lyrics, score the music. Can't you trust yourself to hum your own songs? We weren't committing any crime. So, we were step-brother and stepsister. Who gives a hoot? It's not incest, it's not even interesting. Sure, we raised a few eyebrows in Washington, but in that town you can raise eyebrows by wearing brown wingtips with a blue suit. We would have been all right. Without Lydia."

Kenneth drew himself up and moistened his lips with his tongue. "I think you should leave Warsaw. You're not cut out to be a diplomat's wife. You don't fit in."

Judith laughed. "Actually, I think I fit in very well. Most of your fellow diplomats adore me. I add interest and humor to their dull little lives. So I'm not going to leave, Kenny. Not yet. I'm still your wife. And besides, I've got no place to go. Vanessa has her own life, her own friends. She doesn't need me butting in, hanging on her. I won't go back home to Mother. Jesus, I'd rather live in the Y than do that. Remember where you found me? One step up from the gutter. If I left you, I'd just go back there. Nothing has changed for me, not really. Inside, I still feel cold and dead. Funny, I had some idea that if we got married, you'd take care of me. After all, I'm still your big sister."

Kenneth turned on his heel. "Good night, Judith."

Judith glanced at the clock on the mantelpiece. "Two in the morning. That means it's midafternoon in D.C. Still time to run over to the embassy and put through a quick call to Mom before you go to bed, tell her about my latest outrage. You know what you'll get? A big, fat raspberry that means 'I told you so.'"

Kenneth gnawed the inside of his lower lip. "I am not going to call Mother. I see no reason to upset her needlessly. But I'm warning you: stay away from that Russian. This isn't funny. As it is, I'll probably have some explaining to do to the security people tomorrow."

"Tell 'em I was sloshed." Judith shrugged. "That's the usual excuse for disorderly diplomats, isn't it? Listen, I've kissed a few of those security guys under the mistletoe. They know what I'm like." She got up off the sofa and moved toward him, hips swaying. "You know what they're wondering, your fellow embassy drones? Everybody from Byron Harcourt on down to the marine guards? They would dearly like to know why you don't shape up and act like a man. Knock me up. Give me a baby. Keep me so doped and happy with sex that I won't have the energy even to look at someone else. The big Why. I'd like to know, too. Is it my breath? Should I change deodorants? Lydia doesn't have her periscope aimed at my bed. If you gave in to your carnal appetites more than twice a month, she'd never know."

"Good night, Judith." Kenneth stomped into his room and closed the door. The key turned in the lock.

"You bastard," Judith said aloud. Then she threw herself at the door, pounding on it with her fists. "I'm your wife, damn you! I'm not going to rape you. Just don't lock me out! Kenny, please! Please."

She could hear him moving around, emptying the change from his pockets, placing his keys in the tray on the dresser, hanging up his clothes and stuffing the wooden trees into his shoes. Turning back the bedspread, putting on his pajamas and slippers before he went to the bathroom. He never strolled around his own house naked, not even when he was alone. He always locked the bathroom door, even when he just went in to wash his hands or brush his teeth. He had learned, at an early age, the proper way to do things, and he had never seen any reason to deviate from those standards in adulthood, not even when his wife was scratching at the paint on the bedroom door with her fingernails.

Judith stumbled to the credenza and filled a tumbler with Scotch. Her tears flowed, salting the Scotch slightly, chapping her cheeks, depleting the fluids in her body quicker than she could replenish them. When the glass was half empty, she dragged a couple of large cushions into the kitchen and lugged over the telephone on its long cord. Between sobs, she dialed her sister's number.

CHAPTER 7

London: November 1981

*V*anessa left the North Circular Road at Neasdon, crossed Finchley Road a few minutes later, and headed toward Hampstead Heath. Halfway up the hill, she turned onto the little street called Keats's Grove, where the poet had lived for a time. The house was closed to tourists now, but in the morning the literary pilgrims would start to arrive. After viewing the house, a few of them would tour the neighborhood. Their walk would take them past her own neat brick house, purchased with her share of the money that had been left in trust for the two girls by their grandfather, Senator Lymond. Her mother had made a few stinging remarks about would-be expatriates who couldn't appreciate American values, but even as executrix of her father's estate she could not withhold Vanessa's money. Vanessa had thrown a housewarming party for herself at which she had proclaimed her exile official and irrevocable. She had not, however, given up her American passport.

The house was divided into four flats. Vanessa lived at the front, on top, where, if she'd been nosy and a homebody, she could keep an eye on the street. Perhaps one day someone would tack up a plaque beside the door: IN THIS HOUSE LIVED AMERICAN ACTRESS VANESSA MARLOWE.

Some bastard had parked in her spot, right in front of the door. She drove past and found a space in the next block. Her living room light was on, which meant that Albert was home. Probably working late. She unloaded her luggage from the back, and locked her Triumph.

The car that occupied her accustomed space was a dusty Ford Cortina. Its hatch was open, and Vanessa could see that the rear was loaded with cartons and clothes. The front door to the house had been propped open with a brick. So far as Vanessa knew, none of her tenants had given notice. Perhaps the heavy-metal rocker downstairs had found himself a new roommate to share expenses. She would call on them in the morning. Right now, all she wanted to do was sleep.

She shifted the strap of her bag higher on her shoulder and dragged herself up the stairs. The door to her own flat was standing open. Deaf Kitty lay across the sill. When he saw her, he meowed plaintively and rubbed against her legs. Vanessa stooped to pet him.

"What's going on, lovey?" He arched his back, telling her that he was glad to see her.

Just then Albert came out of her bedroom, a load of clothes slung over his arm. When he saw her, he reached behind him and pulled the bedroom door closed.

"Vanessa! What—why . . . ? I thought you were in Wales."

Vanessa unkinked her back and let her bag slide to the floor. "They wrapped up the shooting a day early. What's going on? Are you house-cleaning?"

Albert swallowed. "I'm leaving."

"Leaving." She uttered the word with no expression, in the flattest of her many voices.

He continued in a rush. "I suppose I should have told you, but . . . There's this other girl, you see. I met her about a month ago, and things happened so quickly. I wanted to be sure. We—we've decided to get married."

"Married." No change in intonation. Totally flat.

"Please, darling, try and understand. You and I—we've been friends for two years, but I could see we were going nowhere. You do agree, don't you?"

"No." Vanessa crossed her arms. "I don't."

Albert cast a quick glance over his shoulder at the bedroom door, then he draped the load of clothes over the back of the sofa. "You're so dead set against marriage, anything that smacks of domesticity. I can understand that. I went through my rebellious phase too. But now I'm ready for something deeper, something more. Real commitment. I want to have a family. You'd be the first to agree that you're—ah, difficult. Brilliant, but difficult. Your moods. Oh, God, I'm making a muck-up of this." He raked a freckled hand through his thinning red-blond hair and laughed nervously. "Look, couldn't you go out and come back again in twenty minutes? I really hadn't planned on telling you like this."

"How were you planning to tell me?" Vanessa asked evenly. "Were you going to leave a note propped against the clock on the mantelpiece?"

At that moment, a girl burst out of the bedroom balancing two cartons in her arms, one on top of the other. "Here's the rest of your stuff. If I've left anything—" She stopped short, seeing Vanessa. "Oh."

Vanessa stared at her coldly. "And this, I presume, is the lucky young slut."

Albert blanched and started to stammer, but the girl, who liked to think of herself as plucky, spoke up. "That's right. I'm Christina Ballard. And you're Vanessa Marlowe."

"I don't need you to tell me who I am. Get out of this flat before I call the police and have you both arrested for trespassing."

"Now, Vanessa, there's no need," Albert began.

Christina tossed her blond curls. "I've heard all about your bullying and your tantrums. You don't frighten me. You actors are only comfortable when you're pretending to be someone else. It's pathetic really, that you can't have any kind of real life offstage. Maybe if you thought a little less about yourselves and a little bit more about the people who cared about you, you'd be happier."

Vanessa set her jaw. Her eyes flashed. "Don't you dare lecture me, you brainless piece of fluff. This is my bloody house and you are bloody well not welcome. Out! Out!" She lunged toward Christina, who dropped her load and took refuge behind the sofa. Vanessa snatched up one of the cartons, took it out into the hall, and threw it over the banister. It hit the stairs, sprang open, and spilled its contents: hair dryer, books, shaving kit, running shoes, and a pair of five-pound dumbbells.

"You evil bitch!" Christina shrieked. "Someday you're going to wake up old and sick and alone, but you won't need to ask why. All you'll have to do is remember what a wicked, ugly person you are!"

"Out!" Vanessa screamed. "You, too, you craven bastard. Out of my house! You've clung to me like a damn leech for two years, eating my food, living here rent-free, writing your so-called novel, and you've never done a thing to help out."

"That's a lie," Christina asserted. "He put hundreds of scripts on tape for you, because you're too stupid to read them yourself. You—"

She didn't finish. Vanessa grabbed her hair and dragged her toward the door. "Get out, get out, get out! Out!" In the hall, she booted Christina's bottom. The girl plunged shrieking down the stairs. Vanessa started to follow, then she saw Albert's typewriter standing near the door. She grabbed it, ran with it to the window, raised the sash, and threw the typewriter out, right onto the roof of the Cortina, where it left a deep dent. It bounced against the windshield, cracking it with a report like a gunshot, and crashed to the pavement. The case sprang open and the machine tumbled out, shedding cast metal letters and keys like confetti.

"You're mad," Albert gasped. "I'll—I'll have the law on you. That was an expensive—"

"Which I bought and paid for because you said you needed a new one." Vanessa threw herself on his pile of clothing and started removing items. "I gave you this, and this, and this. And this and this. I'd rather send the stuff to Oxfam than let you take it with you. Set the law on me, go ahead. I'll charge you with stealing, and if you think I won't, you don't know me. Nobody walks out on me. Nobody." She scooped up the rest of the clothes and sent them after the typewriter. From down in the street came an anguished howl from Christina. "Now take your bloody tart and get out. I suppose she's all impressed with herself for springing you from the trap. A novelist! She's in for a surprise. Not only have you not written anything in two years, you're a lousy lover, too."

"I'll pay you back for this," Albert promised as he stumbled to the door.

"I can't wait." Vanessa sneered. "If you're thinking of writing this up and selling the story to the tabloids, just remember that there are laws about libel. And don't forget to spell my name right."

"You really are mad. I always suspected—but this! I'm not surprised. Your father's a traitor and your sister's a whore. Why should you be any different?"

Vanessa grabbed a potted plant from the windowsill and hurled it toward his head. He dodged out the door. The pot hit the jamb and shattered. Vanessa hung out the window, breathing hard. When she saw him emerge from the front entrance, she grabbed another pot and let it drop. It missed him by inches. Christina pulled another shriek out of her repertory of outraged cries.

"Get out!" Vanessa screamed. "Get out, both of you! Get out, get out!"

Albert jumped behind the wheel and drove away before Christina had pulled her door closed. A farewell scream accompanied their getaway. Vanessa stood at the window, panting, until she felt the spray of rain in her face. She closed the sash and pulled the shade.

She helped herself to a large brandy and drank it while pacing the floor of the apartment: into the kitchen, out again; the bedroom, in chaos, the bathroom, equally disgusting. Her ex-lover and his slut had showered together after making love and had left their sodden towels on the floor. She scrubbed the tiles, changed the sheets on the bed, and dragged the dirty laundry into the pantry behind the kitchen. Finally, taking a dustpan, brush, and wastebasket, she went downstairs and swept up the potshards and broken plant stems from the sidewalk outside the house. She would change all the locks tomorrow, a nuisance for the other tenants, but that couldn't be helped. Albert had taken her keys.

When she reached the top of the stairs, her neighbor's door opened and an elderly man poked his head out.

"Ah, Miss Marlowe, are you all right? I heard a terrible disturbance. I hesitated to call the police. Artists are so temperamental."

Vanessa swallowed the bile that burned her throat. "Everything's fine, Mr. Tidyman. Just fine. I'm sorry if we awakened you."

"Oh, dear me, no, you didn't awaken me. At my age, one doesn't need much sleep. I was reading. My favorite pastime. I'm going through Gibbon's *Decline and Fall* for the fifth time. Do you know it?"

"Only if it's been on the BBC," Vanessa said rudely.

"Ah." Mr. Tidyman cocked his head. "Is that your telephone I hear?"

"Yes, it is." Vanessa continued to stand in the hall outside his door until with muttered good-nights and apologies he retreated back inside and closed it. "Nosy old fart," she said loud enough for him to hear. She walked into her own flat, slammed the door, and slipped the security chain into its slot. The ringing of the telephone persisted. She lifted the receiver. "Hello?" She listened to herself critically. Not even a tremble or a throb. Wonderful how all those years of training and practice paid off. She was in total and complete control of her body. Total and complete. "Hello!"

The caller was silent, but the line was still open. Vanessa could hear the hiss along the wires.

"Hello? Who is this, please?"

"It's—it's me," came a small voice.

Vanessa's heart sank. "It's all right, Judy, I'm here. You can tell me. What's wrong?"

The story came over the wires in lurching gasps, between choking sobs: the Chopin Ball, Byron Harcourt's dreadful necklace, Judith's prank with the Solidarity button, the handsome Russian, the dancing, the drinking, then Kenneth's rage.

"He said horrible things to me. Horrible. He—he called me a whore."

Vanessa flinched. For the second time that night, someone had defamed her sister. They dared to judge because they didn't know how deeply she had been wounded, how desperately she needed to be loved. But Vanessa knew.

"Screw Kenny," she said staunchly. "He's an idiot. I've always said so."

Judith was still sobbing. "He said—he said that I needed professional psychiatric care, maybe even hospitalization. Vanessa, don't let him put me in a hospital. I couldn't stand that again. I'd probably jump out a window or something. Or eat a pack of cigarettes. Nicotine is supposed to be poisonous if you ingest it, isn't it? He—he sounded just like Mother. It was horrible."

"I know, baby. I know. Screw 'em both."

"I mean, my God, I wasn't fucking the Russian, I was only flirting with him. I made him kiss me, but it was just a social kiss. For fun. Kenny wanted to know everything the Russian said. It was all nonsense. Except for the one thing, the big thing, and I couldn't tell Kenny about that. I couldn't. It's none of his business."

"What big thing, Judy? Slow down, take a deep breath. What happened?"

"He said—the Russian, that is—he said he knew Daddy. In Moscow."

With the portion of her brain that studied human behavior and stored it for future use, Vanessa observed her own reaction: the frozen, dead feeling in her core, somewhere above her stomach and below her heart; her fingers on the telephone receiver not really white-knuckled, but gripping hard enough to ache; dry mouth, leaden feet, light-headedness. Standard panic symptoms. She already knew about them.

But why? Why be frightened of a man she hadn't seen in twenty-five years, a man who was as good as dead?

"Is that all?"

"He said Daddy wanted to see me. There might have been more, but I don't remember. I was standing there trying to take it all in when Kenny came over and said we had to leave."

"It must be a joke," Vanessa said after a long pause. "I thought he was dead."

"So did I." Static disrupted the connection. Was someone listening? No, only Judith blowing her nose. "After chewing me out, Kenny went to bed and locked the door. I hate it when he does that." Vanessa heard another burst of sobs.

Vanessa raked her fingertips through her hair. "Maybe you should have told Kenny, babe. This Russian is undoubtedly some kind of spook, and the whole thing is just a trap."

"What if he's not?" Judith sniffed. "What if Daddy really does want to see me? Oh, Van, I don't know what to do."

"Forget it," Vanessa advised. "Pretend the whole thing never happened. If you see the Russian again, tell him to get lost. That's a part of the past that we don't need to dig up."

"Aren't you curious about him, Van? Wouldn't you like to see him again?"

"No." Vanessa's tone was bitter. "I don't even think about him, and when I do, I take a drink and he goes away, like a bad conscience. He never cared about us. If he did, he wouldn't have gone. He would have stayed and faced the music. He knew when he defected that he'd never see us again."

"Defected," Judith repeated, and Vanessa heard her voice start to go out of control again. "I've always hated that word. It sounds like 'defecate.' "

"Don't you remember what it was like, what he did to us? People swarming all over the house, asking Mother questions, searching through our things. And the newspapers—reporters and photographers everywhere we went, pictures in the papers: 'Spy's Wife in Seclusion.' If she hadn't married Preston and changed our name to Marlowe, they'd still be calling us 'spy's daughters.' Phillip Abbott betrayed his country. He deserted his family. I don't care if the Russians zap his balls with cattle prods or hold burning cigarettes up to the soles of his feet. I wish they'd hang him up at the crossroads and let the crows pick out his eyes. It's no more than he deserves."

Judith was silent for a long time. Then she said, "You really hate him, don't you? You're not just angry; you hate him. I guess I didn't know. We hardly ever talked about him. Mother wouldn't allow it, and then we just forgot."

"I didn't forget. I still remember how I used to sit on his lap while he read stories to me. He played games with us before he put us to bed. He made funny little toys for us, and took us to the park, and bought us a puppy even after Mother said we couldn't have one, remember? And then one day, he just disappeared. Vanished. Didn't even say good-bye. And he never wrote and he never called, not even on birthdays. They have telephones in the Soviet Union, for God's sake. He could have done something to let us know that he still cared. But he didn't. And now it's twenty-five years later, and he's an old man, and we've messed up our lives without any help from him. If he'd been around, things might have been different. Who knows? I hate him. I hate him so much." Tears sprang to Vanessa's eyes. She bit her lip to keep from sobbing aloud.

Judith leapt to her sister's defense. "You're not a mess, Van. I'm the one who did time in a mental ward. You've got a wonderful career and so many talents, and you've got Albert—"

"Not anymore I don't. He just left. Tonight. Packed up his rubbish and carted it away. He's going to marry some bint named Christina. I came home and found them, and I went crazy. A wild woman. He was going to leave a note! For me, a note! Funny, isn't it, that the one thing that sets me off is a man walking out? I don't need a psychiatrist to tell me where that comes from."

Judith hiccupped. "Separation psychosis, one of mine called it. Jesus, men are bastards. I'm sorry, Van."

"I hated him," Vanessa said. "I went from liking him, maybe even loving him, to hating him in a split second. I wanted to murder him."

Another long silence, then Judith said, "Do you think there's something wrong with us, Van?"

Vanessa snorted. "Of course there's something wrong with us. But we're big girls now. We can't keep blaming our parents for screwing up our lives. We have a right to live even though we're not perfect. Listen, Judy, why don't you leave Kenny and come here for a while? I've finished that television thing and I'm not going to commit to anything else until I've made up my mind about that Irish play I told you about. Will you come?"

"No, I'm all right." Judith sighed deeply. "I don't want to leave right now. The Russians might invade or the Poles could rebel, and I don't want to miss the excitement. But if you really need me—"

"No, I'll manage. Resilient as hell, we Marlowe girls. Thank God for work. What are you going to do about this Soviet and his message from Moscow?"

"Nothing right now. Don't tell Mother. She'd shit bricks."

"If she did, they'd be neat and tidy and wrapped in gold foil."

After another minute, Judith said she was starting to feel sleepy. She told Vanessa she loved her, and Vanessa did the same, and they hung up.

Vanessa went into the kitchen and poured herself a shot of Irish whiskey. It would make her feel like hell in the morning, but that didn't matter. She wasn't filming. A conference with the director and the play-wright at ten, a pub lunch, more blather, enthusiastic noises. The play had some problems, but she had an idea or two that would help.

Vanessa had no doubt that she could persuade them to see things her way. After all, she was a diplomat's daughter.

CHAPTER 8

Warsaw: December 2, 1981

A cold December rain pelted the rooftops and boosted the misery level
of the weary shoppers, who had been waiting in line all morning
hoping to find some extra meat or a few treats for the holidays. The force
of the downpour dragged the last frost-blasted chestnut leaves from the
trees. A rushing brown tide sluiced along the gutters to the sewer open-
ings, carrying the detritus of city living: cigarette butts, useless tram and
bus passes, scraps of newspaper.

Judith ducked into the main PEWEX store on Aleye Jerozolimskie.
She paused for a moment inside the door to let the water drip from her
hat and the folds of her coat. Unlike most of the other stores in Warsaw,
here the shelves were loaded with merchandise. Money was worth something, provided it was hard currency: dollars or pounds or francs—anything but Polish zlotys. Foreign residents and tourists shopped here, as did
those Poles who had either connections with the black market or relatives
abroad. Even when the other shops in the city were stripped bare of
essential goods, one could still find canned ham and bars of soap and
American cigarettes at the PEWEX, as well as imported liquors of every
description.

She selected her purchases: a carton of cigarettes and a bottle of
vodka for Jan and Ewa, chocolate for the children, a can of peaches, a few
rolls of toilet paper, flashlight batteries, lavender-scented soap. Nothing
very expensive, but all useful items that were otherwise difficult to obtain.
She had developed a keen sense of how much a friend could give without
looking like a charitable donor. It was all right to flaunt your connections

and your privileges—like the right to shop at the PEWEX—but not your wealth. Byron's necklace was proof of that.

She waited while the salesgirl wrote up her purchases on a slip of paper, which Judith carried to the cashier. She waited another fifteen minutes in the cashier's line, paid for her purchases, and took her receipt back to the original salesgirl, who handed them over. The process of buying anything in an Eastern bloc country was tedious and time-consuming, but the notion of self-service was far too radical for them. Judith stuffed the items into the string bag she carried everywhere with her and slid the bag into a plastic sack to protect it from the weather.

Outside, the rain had the sting of ice. The woman behind the cashier's desk had predicted snow before nightfall. Judith was grateful for her broad-brimmed felt hat, which kept her dry as effectively as an umbrella.

As she hurried down the street, she collided with another pedestrian. They disentangled themselves and stepped back, apologizing in Polish. Then their eyes met. Judith recognized the Russian, Dmitrov. He smiled charmingly. "It's Mrs. Marlowe, isn't it?"

Judith let out a delighted cry. "Darling, I'm so glad!" Then she lowered her voice and cast a furtive look around. "But we must be careful. They will stop at nothing to keep us apart."

Dmitrov frowned slightly. "I beg your pardon. Perhaps you don't remember me. I am the man who—"

"Remember you! Of course I remember you! How could I forget? We danced the night away in each other's arms. It was like a dream. And then we kissed, and time stood still. Until my ape of a husband intervened. He subjected me to a brutal interrogation, but I kept the faith. I didn't breathe a word of our secret."

He stepped closer, sheltering her with his umbrella. "Our—secret?"

"Our continuing affair. From Istanbul to Idaho, Asbury Park to Rangoon. Nights of passion in the world's finest hotels. Promises of eternal fidelity, which I have kept. Endless plotting, the lies we're forced to tell, the people we must deceive if we are to remain true to each other."

"I see." Dmitrov listened for a moment to the drum of raindrops on nylon. "You are making fun of me."

Judith sighed. "Don't be so wooden, darling, so . . . *Sovietski*. Don't Russian women flirt and play games? Don't they get crazy and frisky and silly? Apparently not, if you find this so astonishing. But why underestimate my charms? I am the most fascinating woman you've ever known." She peeked at her wristwatch. "Alas, we cannot slip away to your hotel for an afternoon of mad, passionate love. I'm supposed to be giving an English lesson. Don't just stand there, my dear dancing bear. Point me toward the nearest tram and offer to carry my bag. It's brutally heavy."

Dmitrov took the sack. "I beg your pardon. My car is right over here, if you would like a lift."

"A lift! Just the thing on this wretched morning. The trams are always so crowded, and these days everyone looks like they're on their way home to put their heads in the oven. It's the tension, the waiting. Will they or won't they? Can you tell me, darling? Are we peaceniks going to be sticking carnations down Soviet gun barrels anytime soon?"

"Really, I have no idea. I am concerned only with promoting art and culture." With a firm hand on her elbow, Dmitrov guided her across the street and down the block to a red Mercedes two-seater.

When Judith saw it, she halted and let out a shriek of laughter. "This is yours? Your people don't mind spending money on the tools of seduction, do they?"

The interior of the car smelled of new leather, wet wool, and American tobacco, and now the delicate floral scent of Judith's perfume. She settled into the leather bucket seat as Dmitrov turned the key in the ignition.

"Please don't tell me what you did to deserve this. I don't want to know how many Afghan rebels you nuked, or how many dissident Jews you tortured. But it's a little flashy for someone of your age, don't you think? Do you really think you can catch up with your lost youth in a fast car?"

Dmitrov maneuvered out of the tight parking space and pulled into the line of traffic. "I thought this model would appeal to my daughter. She will be sixteen in a few months. I hoped she would be impressed."

"I suppose she put on an elaborate show of boredom. I remember sixteen. All too well." Judith removed her hat and shook out her hair. "Married with children. My heart is broken. Why didn't you tell me?"

"Divorced, actually. With one child. By the way, where are we going?"

"A block of flats near the Central Station. But you can take the long route. I've trained my student to expect tardiness from her teacher." Judith shifted sideways so that she could study his profile. "Divorced, eh? Let me guess. You were suffering from falling hair and rising anxiety about the onrush of middle age, so you found yourself a nice piece of ass not much older than your daughter, and your wife threw you out. Am I right?"

Dmitrov resisted the impulse to check his hairline in the rearview mirror. "My wife and I agreed to separate. 'Mutual consent' is the term they use in your country, I believe."

"Sometimes I think about mutually consenting Kenneth out of my life." Judith sighed. "But what would I do then? He's my stepbrother, so he'd never be completely out of my life, and I'd probably attach myself to another loser. Except for my first husband, my track record is abysmally poor."

"Mr. Marlowe seemed rather irritated at finding us together. I didn't mean to cause trouble for you."

Judith's jolly, rolling laughter filled the car. "You have no idea how irritated! He even threatened to slap me into a psychiatric hospital. And that's an experience I am not particularly eager to repeat."

"Oh?" Dmitrov swung around a slow-moving tram and nearly ran down an elderly pedestrian who was jaywalking. He braked hard, skidded a little, nearly hit a lamppost, pulled out of the skid, and ducked in front of the tram. A glance at Judith showed her to be completely unperturbed by these maneuvers. "You seem a trifle eccentric, if I may say so, but not really mad."

"I have suffered from shattered nerves, with the mind still intact. My first breakdown was in college, at Bryn Mawr. I was screwing my French professor, or he was screwing me—I can't quite remember, it was such a long time ago. Anyway, we set up housekeeping, he the daddy figure, me the nineteen-year-old piece of ass who was supposed to persuade him that he was as virile and vigorous as jocks half his age. Eventually he thought better of what he was doing and went back to his wife. I slit my wrists on their doorstep. I was probably high on something, but the drama was higher. I can still remember all those people screaming, and the sirens blaring. Quite a night. Mother had me locked up in a private nuthouse for a month. The worst month of my life."

They were driving past Old Town, the medieval heart of the city. Like the rest of Warsaw, this section had been razed by the Germans during their retreat from the Soviet Army in 1944. When the war ended, instead of scraping away the rubble and planting a forest of concrete cubes in its place, the city planners decided not only to rebuild, but to restore the area to its original state. With the aid of the original architectural plans, they did just that. Every detail was authentic, down to the last door handle and hinge. The streets were narrow, lined with quaint, half-timbered buildings with cafés in the basements, shops that offered handicrafts and antiques, and restaurants designed to please not only tourists but the locals as well.

Traffic in the area was heavier than usual that day because of the rain. Dmitrov tried detouring around Krakow Street, but even the side streets were clogged with cars. They crept along at a pace that the slowest pedestrian could better.

"You do like to create an effect, don't you?" he said.

"The world is my stage, Mr. Dmitrov." Judith sighed contentedly and stretched. "May I say that I'm thrilled that you've decided to make your entrance at last? I've been waiting for you, you know."

He slowed for a traffic light. "Waiting for someone like me, you mean? An occasion for scandal, or another spectacular scene to upset your husband and your ambassador?"

"No, you, personally. The minute I laid eyes on you, I had the feeling that I knew you. I recognized you."

"Really? I don't think we've met before." Dmitrov drew his eyebrows together in a thoughtful frown. "I would remember."

"How does one French poodle recognize another? Noses touch, and after some not so discreet sniffing, tails wag. Dogs know when they've met another of the same breed. Why should people be any different? And if it wasn't recognition, perhaps it was reincarnation, spiritual recycling. We were lovers in the past. Or friends? Father and daughter, mother and son? Something. Our souls responded to each other. They knew. Of course, it's rather inconvenient for the man of one's dreams to wear the uniform of the enemy. But what's a love affair without risk? We'll take our cues from Romeo and Juliet. Love will find a way."

"You have a vivid imagination, Mrs. Marlowe."

"Why not? It's my own way of filling in the gap between cradle and grave. Some people pray. Others watch television or read pornographic magazines. Sex is nice, too, to pass the time. And when all else fails, you can always spin daydreams. Why not? Ask our Polish friends. It's harmless and cheap and you can do it anytime, even while you're standing on line waiting to buy a pair of cardboard shoes from Riga."

Judith watched a couple of old women in their dark woolens, driven along by gusts of rain. Since the rise of Solidarity, the streets of Warsaw were busier than ever. Even as the economy continued its treacherous downward spiral and the Cassandras warned that a Russian invasion was imminent, the Poles maintained a breathtaking pace, as if they were trying to extract maximum benefit from this heady atmosphere of liberation before it all turned to smoke.

"I feel sorry for you, Mr. Dmitrov," she said. "Another rainy day in Warsaw with a boring job to do. When it's finished, you can go home to your bachelor digs in Moscow and your ex-wife and your sullen teenager and your well-stocked liquor cabinet and wonder what the hell it's all been for. Pushing fifty and all you feel is . . . emptiness."

"Fantastic," Dmitrov said. "You should be a writer."

"I know what I see. My eyes may be glazed with vodka from time to time, but they don't miss much. I looked up that night and I saw myself in your skin, teetering on the brink. That makes two of us." Judith turned and smiled at him. "So tell me, what are we going to do about it, Sasha?"

His foot jerked on the accelerator. "You're very familiar, Mrs. Marlowe. Only my family and closest friends call me Sasha."

The now-familiar peal of Judith's laughter filled the interior of the little red Mercedes. "You're the one who offered me a lift, remember? If I'm making you uncomfortable, just stop the car and put me out. I won't mind. I love rejection. I swallow it like a bitter pill and drink it down with one-hundred-proof or better."

Her laughter hung in the air and made the car feel very warm and close. Dmitrov concentrated on the blurred scene that appeared between swipes of his windshield wipers.

"Your father would like to see you before he dies," he said. "I tried to tell you the other night, but you weren't listening."

"I heard you. To tell you the honest truth, darling, I'm not interested. My father opted out of my life a quarter of a century ago. I may have needed him at one time, but I don't now. Whether he's alive or dead makes no difference to me. I'm not about to start thinking of him now."

"Can you help it, knowing that he still cares about you?"

"I don't know any such thing, and you'd better believe I can keep myself from thinking about anything I choose. I just bathe my sores in alcohol, and they fade gently away. I'd advise you to try it, if I didn't think you already have. How much does it take to stop your hurt? I'll bet you have an awesome capacity for self-punishment. A fifth a day? More? I must be getting old. Forgetfulness is costing me less. Three or four drinks and I'm beyond pain." Judith's laughter came again, automatically, but it had a hollow ring and broke off quickly.

Dmitrov made no reply. He was remembering the empty vodka bottle he had left on his bedside table. An empty bottle and a brimming ashtray, and a lacy brassiere hanging on the bedpost.

"And tonight you'll find yourself another girl," Judith said, reading his mind. "The whores who hang around the Hotel Forum are pretty and clean, country girls. They're cheap and they give good value for the money, so don't be niggardly with your tip. They like Swiss francs the best, although dollars and pounds will do. Never, but never, offer them Russian rubles. They'll spit in your eye."

"Thank you for the advice. I'll keep it in mind."

Judith tucked her hair up under her hat. "Turn here, if you don't mind. It's those cinder-block palaces on your right, the seventh one in. Seventh heaven in the workers' paradise." She reached back between the bucket seats and hauled her shopping bag into her lap. "I suppose your people will be invading pretty soon if this country doesn't shape up. We may not see each other again. If that happens, I have a message for my father, in standard colloquial English. Here it is: 'Fuck off, you son of a bitch.' And don't you dare sanitize it, either."

Dmitrov pulled over to the curb, put the car in neutral, and set the hand brake. "You don't want to see him."

Judith laughed. "That's it in a nutshell, baby." She leaned over and kissed Dmitrov on the cheek. "So long, you big, beautiful bear. Thanks for the ride."

She walked up the crumbling concrete path to the entrance, then turned and waved. A gust of wind threatened to steal her hat. She clapped her hand on top of her head and hurried inside.

The elevator had been broken ever since Judith started visiting the apartment on Chmielna Street. By the time she reached the fifth floor, she was overheated and thirsty. She pounded on the door. After a moment, Ewa Nowicki cracked it open.

"Oh, it's you, Judith." Her English was hesitant. "I—I forgot you were coming today."

"Forgot? Tuesdays and Thursdays. I haven't missed one yet. I stopped at the PEWEX—just a couple of things for you and the kids." Judith handed over the shopping bag. "What's going on?"

"Jan is home today, and his friends." Ewa always reminded Judith of a frightened laboratory mouse, with her white-blond hair, her short, pointed nose, and her protruding eyes under heavy lids.

Judith stepped into the living room to find ten pairs of eyes staring at her. Jan Nowicki was seated at the head of the dining table. He was five feet eleven inches tall, slender, and hollow-chested, with a mass of untidy black hair, a scholar's stoop, and wire-rimmed glasses. The others were scattered around, sitting on the sofa, standing against the walls. Poles had not adopted the American habit of sprawling on the floor when all the chairs were taken. Judith couldn't blame them. The average floor in a Warsaw home was concrete, as hard and as cold as a crypt.

"What's this?" Judith said in her halting Polish. "Are you plotting revolution or assassination? For heaven's sake, don't look so guilty."

They laughed a little and the tension eased. Jan said, "This is Mrs. Marlowe, a friend of Ewa's. An American. She understands Polish. Come in, Judith. Sit down." He switched to English. "Police were outside Solidarity headquarters this morning, checking the papers of anyone who went in or came out. We decided to meet here instead."

A burly steelworker vacated the chair on Jan's right and bowed to Judith. Judith smiled at him and seated herself. "What's the difference?" she asked in Polish. "They all know who you are anyway. Their files are stuffed with photographs, dossiers."

"It's a game we play," a young man said. Judith had met him once before. He was one of Jan's students from Warsaw University. "We know who they are, they know who we are, but why make it easy for them?"

Ewa placed Judith's bottle of vodka in the middle of the table, next to an empty one. She gave Judith a clean glass. Jan poured drinks all around. "To Poland, mother of us all," he toasted. They drank.

In the corner, three men started to argue about what would happen if the Soviets invaded. "Our army will resist," a chubby man in a red sweater insisted. "They won't stand by and let the Russians shoot their fathers and their brothers and their girlfriends. They will fight for us, for themselves."

"The officers won't let that happen," said a gray-haired man in a duffle coat. "They're loyal to the government. If they turn traitor, they'll lose everything they have, after they've lost their lives."

"The younger officers and the enlisted men will rise up and overthrow the leadership," declared a youth in blue denim jeans and jacket. "They'll take command of the tanks and the guns and turn them against the Russians. My cousin is a gunnery sergeant. He says all the men think as he does. They won't let the Russians take over without a fight."

The steelworker spoke up. "Another battle for Warsaw, for the soul of our country. Lives will be lost, but when the world witnesses Soviet atrocities against Polish people on Polish soil, they will come to our aid."

The student gave Judith a resentful look. "The West didn't help Hungary in 1956 or Czechoslovakia in 1968. All their fine democratic rhetoric was so much hot air."

"The West could not respond with force," Jan said quietly. "The risk of nuclear war was too great, both times. The same thing will happen here. NATO thinks in terms of defensive strategies. They don't have the manpower to invade, even if they could. And by the time the Americans get through bickering about their War Powers Act in Congress, two million Poles will be dead. No, once again we Poles are going to have to fight our own battle, without help from anyone else."

"Nothing changes." The student glowered into his empty glass. "During the uprising, we fought the Germans while Russian divisions sat on the other side of the river and did nothing. This time the West Germans will sit on their hands and watch the Russians destroy us. The patterns of history are always the same. Only the nationalities change."

"And the Poles always get screwed," said Red Sweater.

During the discussion, Ewa flitted in and out of the kitchen. Judith thought she had lost some weight in the past week. Her skin was pastier than usual, and her hair needed washing. Judith had the impression that Ewa had something on her mind and that she was trying to work up the courage to speak. Finally she stopped behind Jan's chair and blurted out,

"I have had a letter from my brother in Cleveland. He wants us to get out before it's too late. He's offered to send us the money. But Jan won't go."

Ewa was trained as a biologist. After her graduation from college she could find no work at home, and so she had gone to France as an au pair girl. She lived frugally and returned to Poland with a tidy sum of money, which enabled her to marry Jan, who taught history at Warsaw University. Lately, Jan had become active in Solidarity, and the newly formed trade union had elected him secretary of the Warsaw branch, located on Mazo-wiecka Street.

"Hush, Ewa," Jan hissed. "We don't need to talk about that here."

"Why not?" Judith looked around. The faces of the men had turned impassive. Those who were smoking studied the ends of their cigarettes. The rest stared into the depths of their glasses. "Jan, you can't honestly believe that things are going to get any better here."

"I have a duty to my friends," Jan said passionately. "To my country and to the other members of Solidarity. We must stick together."

"That damn Solidarity!" Ewa cried. "Are our lives any better since it started? Has the government made any important concessions to the workers? Is there meat on the shelves, and fresh fruit, and shoes for the children? It's all talk. Dreams."

"Be quiet, woman," Jan hissed. "You're embarrassing me."

Judith lit a cigarette. "Ewa is right, Jan. The inevitable won't be pleasant, whatever happens. I should have my Russian boyfriend talk to you. He'd tell you to leave."

"What Russian boyfriend?" Ewa asked.

"The one who drove me here. He's wonderfully handsome. I met him at the Chopin Ball. He calls himself a cultural attaché, but everyone knows that's a euphemism for KGB."

Ewa clutched the front of her blouse. "Oh, my God. My God! The KGB, and you brought him here?"

"He didn't follow me upstairs. At least I don't think he did."

"You brought him here!" Ewa shrieked. "He'll ask questions of the other people in the building and they'll tell him who you come to visit every week. You're crazy! You must be crazy to do such a stupid thing! Isn't it bad enough we have our own secret police breathing down our necks? Do we have to have Russian thugs as well? And Jan says they can't arrest everybody! Well, I'll tell you, they'll arrest him and me, too, and then who will look after the children? You? You can't even have one of your own."

Judith finished her drink and looked around the table. "Maybe I just haven't found the right man." She winked at Jan before turning back to Ewa. "What if you're right about him? It won't help to get hysterical."

"I'm not hysterical!" Ewa clenched her fists. "I just want enough milk for my babies. I want to buy food without standing in line for three hours. I want to be able to get a decent wage for my work. You Americans don't know what it's like to live here. If you had to live like we do, you would go mad. You couldn't take it. You're selfish and spoiled by your easy lives, and you don't know what it is to pull yourself out of the ashes after the war, to fight for survival."

Judith grinned at the men. "If she hates America so much, why is she so desperate to go there?"

"You are a wicked woman," Ewa cried. "A whore. I know what you're like with men. Look at them." She swung her arm violently, as if she wanted to decapitate all the occupants of the room. "Like sheep. They can't take their eyes off you. They don't know that you have no soul. You come here to feed off us, because there is no love in your life, no children. You're the worst kind of parasite. You do no work. You think it is chic to have a Polish friend, so you can amuse your rich friends with stories of our poverty and our backwardness. But we don't want you here. We don't want your friendship, and we don't want your vodka or your toilet paper or your chocolate." She waved her arm over the table, knocking the vodka bottle on its side. Jan's student righted it at once. "Go away and leave us alone!"

Ewa stumbled into the kitchen, a curtained alcove just off the living room. They could hear her sobbing.

After a long silence, Judith stood up. "I'd better go."

Jan said, "I am sorry. She has been very upset lately. I will walk you down."

"You don't have to. I know the way." Judith put on her coat and cast a smile around the room. "Good-bye, everybody. I wish you luck."

Jan followed her down the stairs. On the first landing he spoke her name and she halted. "You mustn't think too harshly of Ewa," Jan said. "She didn't mean all those things."

Judith leaned against the cement wall. The rough concrete snagged her raincoat. "Of course she meant them. Why else would she say them?"

"She is jealous of you. But at the same time, she loves you and wants to be your friend. She talks about you all the time, you know. Your hair and your clothes. The countries you have visited. The important people you have met. Statesmen and movie stars. I am grateful to you for spending so much time with her. I am away too much. She hasn't many friends of her own."

"I enjoyed the lessons. Ewa was making progress. It's a shame we have to stop."

"No, you mustn't stop!" Jan cried. "That would be terrible. Please,

I will talk to her. Come again on Thursday, as you always do. I know that's what she wants. It would break her heart to think she drove you away. She really wanted to shout at me, but she couldn't do it in front of the others. It's me she's furious with. Because I refuse to emigrate."

Judith cocked her head to one side. "Why are you being so stubborn?" she asked. "Recent history should tell you how this thing is going to end. Why not get out while you still can?"

Jan shrugged. "I still have hope. I believe in my heart that this new generation of workers and intellectuals will save the country. If enough of us band together to voice our discontent, the leaders will have to listen. I know it will happen. We have won so many concessions already. They can't take them away."

"You can't eat concessions," Judith said wryly. "You'd better get back to your guests. Good-bye, Jan."

As she turned away, Jan put his hand on her arm. "Will you come again? Please? It would mean so much to Ewa. And to the children, of course."

Judith glanced at his restraining hand, and then at his face. "And what about you, Jan?"

He flushed. "Of course I would like to see you again. You have been a good friend to our family. Please?"

"You're very persuasive." Judith laughed. "Oh, what the hell, I've got nothing better to do with my time. Tell Ewa that all is forgiven. I'll see her Thursday."

"I will tell her." Jan let his hand linger. "Thank you."

As Judith left the building, a passing truck sent a tidal wave of filthy water surging over the tops of her shoes. She shook her fist at the driver and cursed him in Polish, but he sped away without turning his head.

She should have invited Aleksandr Dmitrov to visit the Nowickis with her. Talk about setting the cat among the pigeons! Even Jan wouldn't have forgiven her that lapse in judgment. But at least Dmitrov would have been around to give her a ride home. Now she would have to walk to the Central Station in her sodden shoes and take a tram.

She would treat herself to a hot bath—if the water heater cooperated—and a hot drink to ward off the chill that was already numbing her feet and climbing up her legs. Irish coffee, maybe. Or a hot toddy with lemon.

The only thing missing was someone to love her.

CHAPTER 9

*J*udith emerged from the bedroom wearing a simple black wool jersey dress and a string of pearls around her neck. Kenneth was holding her coat, the mink he had given her on their first wedding anniversary. "Byron just called," he said. "He's swinging by to pick us up. I couldn't say no."

"It's not that hard." Judith poked her arms into the sleeves of the coat. "You say no to me all the time. Place the tip of the tongue against the roof of the mouth, form the lips into an O and hum, then release the tongue. 'No.' Or, 'No, thank you, Mr. Ambassador.' Or, 'My wife says you give her the creeps, Your Excellency.' See how easy it is?" Judith laughed.

"He won't want to stay long. It's not a diplomatic gathering, after all. We'll just pop in, have a drink, and go out for dinner somewhere."

"Yuck." Judith made a face. "I don't think I can stand another meal with Byron. All the while he's acting the gracious host, he's groping me under the table. You go out with him. Let him squeeze your knee."

"Look," Kenneth said testily, "he's about to send in my evaluation, in case you've forgotten. Would it be too much to ask you to go along with him? Please, Judith, we have only eight more months in Poland. Let's not screw up now." The buzzer sounded. "There he is. Do you want me to make up some excuse?"

"And miss the best party of the season? Certainly not. Markowsky serves the best booze in town."

They rode the open cage elevator down to the lobby. The curving marble staircase twisted around them like a dragon holding them in thrall. When the Nazis destroyed the city in 1944, this building, like every other substantial structure in Warsaw, had been flattened. Only the staircase had remained, rising miraculously from the rubble, reaching for nothing and supported by nothing. Some romantic-minded Polish architect had decided to construct a block of flats around this monument to Polish invincibility. The resulting apartments were the usual Stalin-era concrete boxes, poorly designed and shoddily constructed. But at least, Judith thought, the building had an old soul.

Like the rings of Hell in Dante's *Inferno,* each floor of the building had its characteristic odor: boiled cabbage and boiling diapers for the East Germans; garlic and rosemary for the French from Provence; freshly brewed coffee for the Americans, an RCA electronics engineer and his wife.

Ambassador Harcourt was waiting for them at the foot of the stairs. "Hey, how's my Judy-girl?" he boomed. Judith felt the edges of her charm-school smile harden. The only person she permitted to call her Judy was Vanessa. No one ever called her Judy-girl.

"Hey yourself, Byron-boy." She offered her cheek, but the ambassador pulled her around and kissed her long and hard on the lips. Judith struggled, half-laughing and half-squealing, and finally managed to push him away. "You want to watch that sort of thing, Byron-boy," she gasped.

Judith looked around desperately for Kenneth, but he had stepped outside; she could see him through the glass doors, chatting with the driver of the ambassador's car. She looked back at Byron. "You have lipstick all over your face. Kenny-boy might beat you up if he sees it."

Harcourt chuckled and scrubbed his mouth with his handkerchief. "It was worth it. I haven't seen you in a long time. I've missed you, honey. I bet you've missed me, too." As Judith moved toward the doors, Byron caught her arm and drew her back. "Just a second, Judy. We never seem to have any time to talk alone together."

Judith had the urge to slap him, but she restrained herself and switched her smile back on. "What do you want to talk about, Byron?"

"It seems to me that you and Kenneth are having some problems." Byron moved closer and cooed into her ear. "Maybe I can help."

Judith looked amazed. "Why, Byron, I can't imagine where you got an idea like that. Kenny and I are doing just fine."

"Sometimes I wonder if he's man enough for you, that's all."

Judith laughed. "Byron, don't let Kenny's cool exterior fool you. He's a stallion. With a little encouragement from me, he can go all night. If he seems a little tired and listless some mornings, you can blame me."

"You're a hell of a woman, Judy-girl."

"You'd better believe it, Byron-boy." Judith escaped through the glass doors to the waiting car.

Their host that evening was Adam Markowsky, Poland's Minister of Trade. In the flush of optimism that followed the rise of Solidarity, he had brokered numerous rich deals between foreign investors and the Polish government, which was already deeply in debt to Western banks. Markowsky lived like a millionaire, in a mansion in the eastern suburbs of Warsaw. He was known for his bonhomie, his loud talk and laughter, and his stinging anti-Soviet banter. His unrelenting hostility toward the Soviets had convinced many people that Markowsky was actually an agent for the KGB, but such suspicions did nothing to tarnish his popularity with Poland's party-loving elite.

Though there were shortages and endless lines at the meat counters, the Minister of Trade had secured a variety of tempting items to entice his guests. The hors d'oeuvres buffet was loaded with chunks of kielbasa, herring in sour cream, assorted cheeses and fruits out of season, smoked salmon, and pâtés served with grainy French mustard and cornichons. As Judith helped herself, she thought about Ewa, who spent most mornings standing in line with a hundred other Polish housewives to buy meat, only to be told when she reached the counter that the supply had run out. Rumor said that the government was hoarding foodstuffs, hoping to enrage working-class Poles in this busy pre-Christmas season and to turn them against Solidarity.

As Judith pondered the offerings on the buffet table, a passing waiter offered champagne. It was French, ice cold and delicious. Judith downed a glass quickly, and felt her annoyance at Polish bureaucrats and certain American diplomats begin to ease.

As always, the guests drifted into sexually segregated groups, the men talking diplomacy and politics, the women discussing child care and shopping. Stories about other people's cute and clever children depressed Judith. She joined the group around Madame Cartier, wife of the French second secretary. Madame Cartier was describing her adventures with Gustave, the long-haired dachshund puppy she and her husband had recently brought from Munich. Madame disliked dogs, but Monsieur Cartier had insisted that she needed protection in these dangerous times, and now the floor of her apartment was thickly padded with the Polish Communist Party daily.

"I can't think of a better use for it," Judith remarked. Her hearty laughter prompted an outburst of giggles from Madame Cartier, who accidentally sloshed champagne on the front of Judith's dress. The little

Frenchwoman was horrified, and offered to accompany Judith upstairs to help her sponge it off.

"No, no, it's quite all right," Judith reassured her. "I'll just run up. You'll see, it won't even leave a mark."

As Judith hurried out of the main salon, Byron Harcourt gazed after her. He was standing by himself, near the bar. He asked the waiter for a Scotch, neat, drank it down, and scanned the crowd to see if anyone was watching. Then he set down his glass and left the room.

He prepared himself to produce a grin and an excuse in his lame Polish, but they weren't needed. The lavish upstairs bedroom assigned to the ladies as a lounge was empty. Byron heard the sound of running water in the adjoining bathroom. Very quietly, he closed the door and turned the key in the lock. A minute later, Judith came out of the bathroom and headed toward the dressing table and the mirror. When she saw him, she stopped abruptly.

"Byron, you silly man, you're in the wrong room!" Judith laughed. "The gents' is downstairs, near the billiard room."

"Any room you're in is the right room for me, Judy." Harcourt cleared his throat. "I have to talk to you, but we never seem to get the chance to be alone together, have you noticed that? You never come to the embassy during the day, and at night there are always too many people around."

"You'd better talk fast." Judith stepped over to the mirror and opened her purse. "Of the eighty women downstairs, half need to use this room right now, and the rest are fighting the urge to pee until it becomes irresistible. Believe me, you don't want to stand between the bathroom door and a woman with a bursting bladder." She laughed.

"They can go someplace else," Byron said. "I guess you know it's time for me to write up my yearly reviews of my staff's performance. Ken's been a little distracted lately, I've noticed. I'd hate to give him a bad report. It might help if I knew more about you."

Judith touched some blush to her cheeks with a sable brush. "If you have some criticisms of Kenneth's work, you'd better tell him."

"Now, Judy, you don't want to put a crimp in Kenneth's career at this point. Warsaw's an important post. From here he could go to London or Rome, or maybe Moscow. Or even an embassy of his own, a little one. You don't want him to end up a junior functionary in a place like Upper Volta, do you?" Byron chuckled. To State Department insiders, the small West African state was the metaphorical equivalent of Siberia, a hardship post, the bottom of the barrel.

"I don't know." Judith smiled as she dabbed perfume in the hollow of her throat and on the insides of her wrists. "I've never been to Upper Volta. It might be very pleasant."

Byron Harcourt moved closer. "You're laughing at me. Hey, I don't mind. In my experience, a pretty woman can get away with anything. Even wearing that crazy Solidarity button. Remember? That would really hurt Kenneth if I put it down on paper. Embassy wives aren't allowed to get involved with local politics. It would look bad on his record."

Judith put her mascara away and took out her lipstick. "But if I sleep with you, you'll forget all about it, is that right?"

"That sounds like a fine idea, just what I had in mind." He stepped behind her and wrapped his arms around her waist.

Judith kept her voice even. "Oh, for God's sake, Byron, there are laws about sexual harassment—"

"Don't quote laws to me, Judy. Men and women make their own laws. What's the harm?" He slid his hands upward and cradled her breasts. "Upper Volta is pretty hot in the summertime. I'd give it some thought if I were you."

"Byron, if you don't take your hands off me right now, I'm going to scream the place down!"

"You've got no reason to scream. I'm not going to hurt you, Judy. I just need to let you know how I feel."

His shallow breathing left her in no doubt of what he was feeling. The mirror reflected back the glazed look in his eyes. Panic swept over her, and she opened her mouth to scream, but her throat had turned to chalk. In one movement, Byron dragged her over to the bed, tipped her over, and threw himself on top of her. He proceeded to cover her face with wet kisses while he forced his knee between her legs. Judith twisted her face to one side, but that only exposed her neck, which was like offering a bone to a hungry dog. She kept trying to yell, but she couldn't even breathe. She felt as if she had been crushed by a Soviet tank.

Byron clawed at her panties. She squirmed and wriggled, but in a moment he was inside her, boring away like a blind mole. She continued to struggle, with no effect. Why didn't anyone rescue her? Of course, Byron had locked the door. Where was Kenneth? Ordinarily, he stuck close to Byron. Unless he knew, had hinted, had lent encouragement.

No, God, not that.

Judith heard scratching, then the sound of the door opening and closing again. The weight on her body lifted. Aleksandr Dmitrov stood over the bed holding Byron Harcourt by the collar, like a puppy he had found messing on the rug. Byron's face was bright red. Dmitrov's was pale, and veins stood out prominently on his forehead.

"You are a stupid man, Mr. Ambassador," he said in a low, angry voice. "Adam Markowsky likes stupid men. From time to time he provides girls for his friends and invites them to use this room. There is a video camera behind that mirror."

"No," Harcourt whimpered in a strangled gasp. "Let—go."

"For Mrs. Marlowe's sake, I will confiscate the videotape. But if you bother this woman again, I will see that the *Washington Post* gets a copy, and I will urge Mrs. Marlowe to take you to court. The evidence is undeniable. With any luck, the judge will sentence you to prison. In my opinion, jail is too good for an animal like you. You belong in a pigsty."

Judith rolled over on her side in time to see Dmitrov hustling Harcourt away. He thrust the ambassador into the corridor, then closed and relocked the door.

"He—he—" She swallowed, gagging.

Dmitrov approached the bed slowly. "He's gone. It's over."

"He—he raped me." She sat up and pulled her skirt down over her thighs. "Raped me. Oh, my God, he really did. Oh, my God."

She started to shake. Dmitrov sat beside her and put his arm around her. She was shuddering violently, as if she had caught a severe chill.

"They're going to say it's my fault. But I never thought . . . He's been working up to it for a long time. Heavy hints. Heavy breathing. Oh, God, I—I think I'm going to be sick." Tears streamed down her cheeks. She bent her head over her knees.

Dmitrov said, "Come into the bathroom. You'll feel better if you clean yourself up."

Judith clutched his sleeve and leaned against him, sobbing, as he guided her around the bed. "I don't want anyone to know, to see me."

"I won't say a word to anyone but your husband. He will take you home."

"Don't leave me!"

"I'll lock the door from the outside and take the key. You'll be quite safe until we get back."

Judith leaned against the sink and stared at herself in the mirror. "How did you get in? I thought he'd locked the door."

"I saw him follow you out of the room. You were both gone a long time, and I became worried. So I picked the lock."

"What about the film?"

"There is no film. I merely wanted to frighten him. I'm sorry I didn't come sooner." Dmitrov pressed her hand. "It's over. You're safe now. I'll be back soon with Mr. Marlowe."

Dmitrov found Kenneth Marlowe debating the relative merits of Volvos and BMWs and Mercedes Benzes with the British Third Secretary.

"Mr. Marlowe, a word with you, if you please." Deftly, Dmitrov separated Kenneth from his companion and urged him toward the entrance hall. "Your wife is upstairs, in one of the bedrooms. Your ambassador forced himself upon her. She is in a very bad way."

Kenneth pulled away and scowled at the Russian. "What are you talking about? You leave my wife alone."

"Mr. Harcourt raped her. So far no one else knows. But Mrs. Marlowe is deeply distressed, to say the least. She needs you. Will you come, please?"

The irritation in Kenneth's expression turned to dismay, and then to anger. He set his jaw. "Damn her," he said under his breath. "I knew something like this would happen. Where is she?"

Dmitrov led the way up the stairs and unlocked the bedroom door. Judith was sitting in front of the dressing table. Her face was still streaked and smeared and her clothes were in disarray. Kenneth turned to Dmitrov and dismissed him as if he were a servant.

"That will do. You may go now."

"No." Judith turned away from the mirror. "Let him stay. He knows what happened."

"Why, was he next in line?" Kenneth snarled. "What did you expect? I could have told you this was coming, the way you hung on Byron's arm, flirting with him."

"Of course I flirted with Byron! You—you encouraged it! 'Make him feel at home,' you said. You used me to make yourself look better, and when you should have been sticking close to me, protecting me, you walked away and left us alone together, again and again."

"Why shouldn't I leave you alone with him? You're always telling me that you can take care of yourself."

"Then you're not going to do anything?"

"What do you want me to do, punch him in the nose? Challenge him to a duel? He's my boss, for Christ's sake. I don't care how influential Mother is, this man has power where it really counts. He used to own the land where the man in the White House built his ranch. And the President is known for his loyalty to his friends. You've really done it this time, haven't you? I don't know how I'm going to fix this."

"You're my husband!" Judith cried. "Tell him to stay away from me! Act like a man!"

"I am not going to be made a laughingstock, Judith. I've given you a long leash until now, but—"

Judith's lips trembled. "What are you going to do, Kenny, chain me to my kennel?" She pointed to Dmitrov, standing with his back to the door. "What kind of marriage is it when a stranger, the enemy, is kinder to me than my own husband?" She stood up and stumbled toward the door. Dmitrov stepped aside and opened it, then after a moment he followed her out.

Kenneth thought frantically about how he could control the damage. Ambassador Harcourt must have been drunk, of course. And Judith as well. A slight misunderstanding. Byron wouldn't blab about it, and neither would Judith. But what about Dmitrov? A KGB man, conveniently on the spot. He was certainly in a position to try a spot of blackmail. Dear Christ, what a mess. What a miserable, infuriating mess.

By the time Dmitrov reached the foot of the grand staircase, Judith had vanished. Markowsky's majordomo informed him that Mrs. Marlowe had stepped outside. No, she had not taken her coat.

"Let me have it, then."

Dmitrov found her standing in the middle of the drive, shivering. He draped the mink over her shoulders. "My car is over here."

Judith nodded dumbly. She desperately needed a place where she could sit quietly and pull herself together, a place with no diplomats, no diplomats' wives. Dmitrov guided her gently to his Mercedes and seated her inside. He drove toward the outskirts of the city, past concrete apartment complexes and sports palaces, until the man-made elements of the landscape dwindled to only a few farmhouses and the odd church or fencerow. He had plugged a cassette into the tape deck, Rudolf Serkin playing a Mozart piano concerto. The music soothed and settled his passenger, and after a few minutes, she closed her eyes and put her head back.

"Are you feeling better?" Dmitrov asked. He had been watching Judith out of the corner of his eye and gauged when he could speak safely.

"I could use a drink. You don't have a pocket flask, do you?"

"I'm afraid not, but we're not far from a place I know."

"Smarmy bastard. Strutting little creep. I hate him. I hate both of them. Kenny's worse, a simpering, ass-licking little toad."

"He is trying to protect his job," Dmitrov said.

"Don't I know it? That son of a bitch raped me, and all I got from my husband was a serves-you-right. Are you sure you don't have a bottle stashed in here someplace?"

"Quite sure. It won't be long now."

"Jesus, where do we have to go for this drink? Siberia? Oh, oh." She bent forward, resting her head on her knees. "I'm going to be sick again. You'd better pull over."

Dmitrov did as she asked, then he reached across and opened her door. "Take deep breaths," he ordered. "Deep."

"Damn stomach. I always—"

"Don't talk. Breathe deeply. That's good." He waited while she did as he told her. "Are you better now?"

She sat up. Her eyes were bright with new tears. "I—I'm so ashamed. He—he was right—right about me. Whore."

"Hush." Dmitrov gathered her into his arms and held her. "It wasn't your fault. Never listen to what anyone says about you. They don't know anything. Only you know yourself."

Judith sobbed. As Dmitrov rocked her gently and smoothed her hair and patted her, he murmured endearments in Russian: "Little girl, pretty little girl, kitten, sweet child. Don't cry. Don't pay any attention to what they say. Hush now. Hush."

When she was empty of tears, he mopped her face with his handkerchief and planted a fatherly kiss on her forehead.

"Thanks," she murmured.

"Not at all," he said. "How do the Americans put it: what are friends for? Close your door and we'll be on our way. The bear is hungry and it's past his dinnertime."

They drove into a quaint little town with a domed church and a half-timbered city hall. Judith recognized it: Otwak, about fifty miles from Warsaw. Dmitrov helped her out of the deep bucket seat and put his arm around her waist as he guided her along the icy sidewalk. Judith was grateful for his strong physical support. She felt like an invalid or a person of advanced years, too feeble to be proud. They rounded the corner from the main street, went down a flight of stairs, and opened a large plank door.

Under a low vaulted ceiling, between sturdy plastered pillars, stood several small round tables set with sparkling white linen and shining crystal. Each one held a vase of fresh flowers, almost impossible to obtain in Poland in the wintertime, and a candle in a brass holder. As they entered, a few diners looked up. With their slowly moving fat cheeks, they looked to Judith like a herd of placidly ruminating cows.

The headwaiter greeted Dmitrov politely and showed them to a table in a quiet corner. Judith went to the bathroom, where she washed away the dried semen from her thighs, combed her hair, and fixed her makeup. Ten minutes later, she returned, looking considerably brighter. The waiter had brought two glasses of lemon vodka. Judith swallowed hers in one gulp, and expelled a long breath.

"Ask him to come back, and this time leave the bottle."

"Food first. The habit of drinking without eating is very unhealthy."

"Absolutely," Judith said wearily. "It can lead to flirtation and fibbing and unsolicited sexual intercourse—by which I mean rape, of course. Jesus, thirty-three years old, half a lifetime of stupid behavior, and it's taken me this long to get raped. I can hardly believe it. Raped! By a sawed-off runt with elevator shoes and a hairpiece. This is one for the books. And you wonder why I drink? Come on, let me have one more vodka, will you? I'm still feeling the effects of the shock."

"Which is precisely why you should temper your consumption of alcohol." Dmitrov produced a pack of Marlboros. "Have a cigarette instead."

Judith studied the occupants of the room. They were well-dressed, well-fleshed, and largely untalkative. "What is this place, some sort of secret hangout for the people who don't want the peasants to see them eating caviar and quail eggs en croûte?"

"Something like that. Those who have profited by their positions of power in the people's state. Markowsky comes here often, I believe. Ambassador Harcourt brings his mistress here from time to time."

"His what? You're joking. If he's getting it off with somebody else, what the hell was he doing dipping his wick into me? Are you making this up?"

He shook his head. "My sources are impeccable."

"I'll bet. KGB snoops. The best in the world. Their file on me probably fills three volumes, and you've read every line, haven't you?"

Dmitrov let the question pass. "Right now, I am interested in what I would like to eat. They serve a good saddle of venison here, with wild mushrooms and potatoes so tender and small they look like marbles. May I order for you?"

The waiter appeared at his elbow. He and Dmitrov discussed the menu in Polish.

"Not bad," Judith said when they were alone. "They've really primed you well for this expedition, haven't they?"

"Languages come easily to me."

"Me, too, but I don't know fifty varieties of mushrooms."

"I had a Polish nursemaid when I was a child. By the time my mother replaced her with someone who spoke what she felt was a more useful language, English, I had absorbed quite a few mushrooms."

"Our nursemaid was French," Judith said. "Until my stepfather became ambassador to Costa Rica; then we got Spanish-speaking ones. Listen, if I eat all my peas, can I have some wine with dinner?"

"Anything you like. But only if you eat your peas."

The soup arrived, liver dumplings and smoky mushroom caps floating in a rich broth. Another waiter brought out an unlabeled bottle of wine. Dmitrov tasted and nodded his approval. The waiter poured and Judith sipped. The wine evoked the spicy air of a pine forest in the autumn, sun-warmed grass, icy streams.

Judith blew out her breath in a long sigh. "This was worth waiting for, if not being sexually assaulted for."

"After your ordeal, you deserve a bit of pampering." Dmitrov ripped a chunk off a loaf of hot bread and offered it to her.

"Maybe Kenny's right." Judith dipped the crust in her bowl of broth. "I should surrender myself to the psychiatric establishment. I don't deserve to live in the real world. I can't cope worth a damn. I'm just going through the motions."

"Don't do that," Dmitrov said sharply. "Forgive me. What I meant was, please don't start feeling sorry for yourself. That sort of thing is very tiresome in beautiful women. It never rings true."

"I have valid reasons," Judith protested. "My father deserted us, my mother was too busy being Mrs. Republican to pay any attention to us. I have rotten luck with men. And I have no abilities at all, apart from drinking and screwing. And to top it all off, I am now a rapee. I don't dare set foot in the Soviet Union. They'd ship me to the Gulag for being an unproductive consumer of good air and strong spirits. A parasite."

"I think I could guarantee your safety." Dmitrov lay down his soup spoon and smiled at her across the table.

"Ah, yes, your errand of mercy again—or whatever it's an errand of. Reuniting father and daughter. You might have better luck if you fixed up a meeting on neutral ground. Paris, for instance. I don't even need a bad excuse to go there."

"That won't be possible, I'm afraid. Your father is not able to travel."

"You mean they won't let him out? Good for them." Judith twirled the stem of her wineglass. "You've been very nice to me tonight. Because it suits your purposes, whatever they are?"

"Not at all. I'm rather taken with you. I admit, I found you somewhat perplexing at first. So different from other women, certainly Soviet women, just as you implied. But I have decided that the best way to enjoy your company is to treat you as a rare work of art: simply to settle back and enjoy the experience."

Judith wrinkled her nose at him. "That's pure bullshit, but I love it."

"My compliments are somewhat labored and heavy-handed, which means they are typically Russian." Dmitrov sighed. "Forgive me. But I assure you that I am in earnest. I wish I could think of some way to make you laugh again. Your laughter is delightful, charming—no, it's much more. Since laughter is the trait that sets us apart from the animals, that makes us human, you, with your delicious laughter, are the most exuberantly, contagiously, extravagantly human being I have ever known. You are also female, which makes you irresistible."

"Kenny tells me I laugh too much, at all the wrong things." Judith smiled at Dmitrov over the rim of her wineglass. "There's definitely a lot of charm in this corner tonight, but all of it's emanating from you. You're good, comrade. The most unlikely Soviet I've ever met. Leonid Brezhnev as played by Cary Grant. Farfetched, I grant you, but I'm willing to suspend my disbelief for an evening."

The waiter arrived to remove the soup plates. The owner of the restaurant presented the fish course himself, trout sauced with a puree of fresh vegetables. Judith asked, in Polish, about the wine they were drinking. It was from his private cellar, the man said. Made for him by a farmer near Lodz, whose family had been making wines and fruit liqueurs for two centuries.

"I am delighted that Madame is pleased with it. Most of our customers have not the palate to appreciate such a superb creation. To them, I give French wines."

After he had gone, Judith said, "I really love being treated like royalty. But I feel like a hypocritical skunk for eating like this when most of the local Poles are half starving."

"Don't feel guilty. They wouldn't envy you my company."

Judith laughed out loud. The outburst was so unexpected, so genuine and infectious, that the other diners turned to stare at them. Dmitrov grinned back at her.

Judith stubbed out her cigarette and lifted her fork. "You're right, darling. They certainly wouldn't. Let's eat."

CHAPTER IO

*S*o." They had finished the meat course and moved on to coffee and after-dinner cigarettes. "How does a nice proletarian lad like yourself end up with an English-speaking nursemaid?"

Dmitrov's eyes crinkled at the corners. "My mother was rather well known in her day. I believe that millions of people in the United States saw her dance on 'The Ed Sullivan Show' when the Bolshoi Ballet made its first tour. Galina Valenskaya. Perhaps you have heard of her?"

Judith gaped at him. "You're making this up. Valenskaya's not your mother."

"I swear"—laughing, Dmitrov raised his right hand—"as Lydia Lymond Marlowe is your mother, Valenskaya is mine. I suspect, if they met each other, that they would find a lot to talk about, a lot in common. Power, for example, and how to wield it."

"My ma can lick your ma." Judith's eyes were shining.

"I rather doubt that. I've seen my mother take on generals, premiers, ballet masters."

"Presidents, ambassadors, geniuses from think tanks," Judith countered. "Lydia eats nails for breakfast."

Dmitrov waved the boast aside. "My mother dines on wrecks of cars, Zils and Chaikas." They laughed together.

"Valenskaya," Judith marveled in a faraway voice. "We actually saw her. My sister and I. In New York. I've never forgotten it. A lot of little girls are ballet-mad. I know I was. She did *Sleeping Beauty.* Vanessa and I danced up and down the halls for months afterward. And all the while she had kids of her own."

"One kid. Myself."

"That must have been tough."

Dmitrov shrugged. "I learned diplomacy at an early age. The art of well-timed withdrawals, placating language, the charming words needed to change a foul mood into a cheerful one." He noticed Judith frowning at him. "What's the matter?"

"You really are making this up, aren't you?"

"No, I'm not. Why?"

"Because that's how we grew up. You're lucky you're a man. They're not as warped by their mothers' disapproval. When the time came to make the break, you probably told her to take a flying leap. Didn't you?"

He chuckled. "As a connoisseur of scenes, you would have enjoyed that one, I think."

"How old were you?" Judith asked eagerly.

"Eight."

She laughed. "My, you were precocious! I still haven't been able to tell my mother in words. She's supposed to get the message from the way I behave."

"Wouldn't it be simpler to speak the truth?"

Judith's smiled faded, and her eyes darkened. "I'm not after simplicity, comrade. Never-ending torment is what I crave, for both of us." She looked around the dining room. They were the last patrons. Their waiter was polishing glasses at the bar, glancing their way. "Speaking of torment, I think you'd better take me home. It's already tomorrow."

"Of course." Dmitrov paid for the meal in American dollars. He did not ask for a receipt. They went outside, into the blast and sting of a sleet storm. "From the northeast," Dmitrov said. "Another gift from Mother Russia."

He drove cautiously on the slick roads. It was nearly two in the morning when he turned a corner onto Aleye Ujazdowskie and pulled up in front of Judith's apartment building. She looked up at the windows on the corner of the top floor, where the glow of a lamp still burned.

"Give me one good reason why I shouldn't go in there," she begged softly. "Please."

Dmitrov cradled her face between the palms of his hands and kissed her. The kiss answered what they had been wondering since the beginning of the evening: Would she? Would they? He made a U-turn in the middle of the street and headed east, toward the river. At that hour the city was nearly empty of cars. A number 36 tram rumbled along Marszalkowska Boulevard, on its way to the Citadel and the northern suburbs. The passengers, many of them power plant and hospital workers, dozed inside their dimly lit capsule.

Snowflakes danced in front of the Mercedes's headlights. They crossed a bridge over the Vistula and parked in front of an apartment building that faced Skaryszewski Park. The bulb inside the elevator couldn't have been stronger than fifteen watts. The cage jogged to a halt on the sixth floor. Dmitrov selected a key from his ring and fitted it into the lock of a door.

"My friend said I could use this apartment. He's in Paris, making a film. It has been a lifelong dream of his, to work in the West. Solidarity made it possible. Knowing Tadeusz, I'm sure he'll take full advantage."

Dmitrov switched on the harsh overhead light. The walls of the living-dining area were plastered with posters for French, American, and Polish films. Judith stopped in front of one that had been mounted and framed. "I saw this one. Is he your friend? Tadeusz Olsewski?"

"Yes. I saw *Circuses* in Moscow a few years ago and liked it very much. On my next visit to Warsaw, I called on him. We shared a bottle of vodka, and by the time we'd finished it, we were good friends."

The apartment was impossibly small and crammed full of mismatched pieces of furniture, the kinds of odds and ends a young couple might beg from their parents when they set up housekeeping on their own—assuming they were lucky enough to get an apartment.

"Do you want a drink?" Dmitrov asked. "I imagine that Tadeusz has a bottle somewhere."

Judith shook her head. "I'm already regretting all the drinks I've had today. For once in my life, I wish I were completely sober."

"Why is that?"

"Because I don't want to miss anything." They gazed at each other a moment, then she said, "Hold me, Sasha."

He stepped close to her, rested his hands on her shoulders, and planted a light kiss on her forehead.

"Like a blessing," she sighed. "Byron, Markowsky's house. It was years ago, wasn't it?"

"A lifetime." His arms tightened around her. Her head fell naturally into the hollow of his shoulder and she nestled there, content. He reached over and switched off the light. When he lowered his head to kiss her, her lips were waiting for him.

"Why did you do that? The lights, I mean?"

"The three most basic elements in human history." He fingered her hair lightly. "A man. A woman. And the darkness that drew them close together night after night, century after century. Everything else is . . . optional."

Even as a boy, Aleksandr Dmitrov had delighted in the feel of things: texture, density, coldness and wetness and liquids and solids. He loved to experience his world tactilely, and now, with the room in darkness, he explored this new treasure he had been given. Her fragrance distracted him at first, until he gave up trying to identify it. He had never smelled it before, not on her body. He marveled at her hair, so fine and silky, and her skin, as soft as a child's. The fur of her coat, the hard smoothness of her pearls. A ring on her finger. The wool of her dress.

Judith slipped out of her coat. Slowly, Dmitrov unzipped her dress and drew the bodice down over her shoulders and breasts. She wore lace underthings, a brassiere with a pair of hard curved wires under her breasts, a garter belt that rode high over her hipbones. No panties. Byron Harcourt had ruined them, and she had discarded them. The skin between her legs was even softer than the skin of her belly. He stroked the thatch of curly hair, felt the promise of wetness.

In the darkness, freed of the necessity of using her eyes, it seemed to Judith that her other senses grew more acute. She was able to gauge Dmitrov's excitement by the quickening of his breathing and the surging pulse beneath her fingertips. She relished every detail, every discovery: the appendicitis scar, the striation of the muscles on his arms and calves, the smooth hardness of his back.

Dmitrov had seldom made a leisurely business of his lovemaking, not since he and Olga were newlyweds with large chunks of eternity to spend in bed together, before the children were born, before the pressures of their professional lives started to pull them apart. He had never kept a mistress, and he used and discarded whores with little thought for the pleasure he might give them. After all, that wasn't what he was paying them for.

But this time he found himself trying to match Judith's patience, wanting to reciprocate her generosity. Even as he felt himself succumbing to his desire for her, he wanted to exert the same powerful spell over her. He wanted to learn her secrets, to imbed them in his flesh, which would never forget.

By the time she let him know that she was ready for him, they were both sweating. Judith stretched out on the mink and drew him down, onto and into her. They found their proper rhythm at once, without missing a beat, as though they were longtime lovers. When Dmitrov dug his fingers into her buttocks and lifted her up to him, she raked her fingernails down his back. They both drew blood, but neither felt any pain. He held himself back until she was choking on suppressed screams, then he emptied himself into her, prolonging his thrusts until her moans had faded to murmurs. Welded together, they drew the mink coat over themselves and slept.

Judith awakened to see a light in the kitchen. She asked Dmitrov what he was doing.

"Making tea," he rumbled. "All I can find are those silly little bags with strings. What's the matter with these people?"

Wrapping herself in the mink, Judith went looking for the bathroom. She found the bedroom first, a chamber so small that an ordinary double bed took up most of the floor space. Cartons and bundles were stacked against the footboard, leaving only a narrow path to another door in the opposite wall. When Judith opened it and switched on the light, she found herself in one of those tiny cubicles that results when builders proceed haphazardly without following any precise architectural plans.

The walls and ceiling had been painted a bright blue and decorated with fluffy white clouds and colorful floating balloons. A crib in the corner took up half the room. It stood under a canopy of white lace, which hung from a hook on the ceiling and cascaded down to the floor.

On the white-painted bureau stood a framed montage of photographs. The subject of all the pictures and snapshots was a round-faced, smiling cherub with masses of dark curling hair: laughing up from a blanket on the grass, splashing in the sink where she was being given a bath, tugging at the earflaps on her knitted winter bonnet, sitting on her mother's lap, being hoisted into the air by her father, whose delighted grin told it all. Daddy's girl.

Inside the crib lay a few soft toys. Judith lifted out a soft, white plush rabbit with shining glass eyes and an idiotic embroidered grin and held it to her cheek. It smelled like a baby, flowery sweet yet slightly sour.

"I thought we deserved some vodka. I hope you don't mind the pepper. I couldn't find anything else."

Dmitrov stood in the doorway, a bottle in one hand and a couple of small glasses in the other. He had fashioned a blanket into a sort of toga.

"You bastard." Judith spoke without turning away from the crib. "You slimy, stinking bastard. You don't care you how low you stoop, do you? I could kill you for this. I could stick a knife into your chest and dig out your heart and leave it in a gutter for the rats to chew."

"Judith, I don't understand." He sounded mystified. "What's the matter?"

She whirled. "Did you have a hard time finding one that looked like my Helen? Same curly hair, same round face." Still holding the toy, she thrust out her arm at the photographs. "The only difference is, this one's alive somewhere. I'm amazed you didn't try to spring her on me in person."

Dmitrov set down the bottle and glasses on the small white-painted bureau. "You're not making any sense, Judith. If you'll go slowly and—"

"You're such a damn liar. Did my dossier go into detail? Or did they stick to the bare facts? Helen Vanessa Klein, born November fourth, 1976. Struck by a drunken driver while her father was wheeling her stroller across a Manhattan street. Both killed instantly. End of marriage. End of motherhood. End of sanity. End of fucking everything. Down the toilet in Las Vegas and leave it to Kenneth Marlowe to fish her out."

Dmitrov was too stunned to speak for half a minute, then he said, "Judith, this was not intentional. I didn't know, I swear it. Please, believe me."

"I wore white to the funeral." Tears coursed down Judith's cheeks. "Charlie never liked me in black. Papa Bear's coffin and Baby Bear's. It was obvious to everybody that there should have been one more, medium-size, for Mama Bear."

"Judith, forgive—"

"The bastard who killed them spent thirty days in jail, was released on bail because it was a first offense, and skipped to Florida. That's American justice. I've murdered him a thousand times in my imagination. I've crucified him and run him down with his own car. Bastard. You're all such bastards. They sure picked the right bastard for S and T: seduction and treachery. I've never had better. That shows you how stupid I am. Even while I was being raped for the second time tonight, I didn't know what was happening. I enjoyed myself. Enjoyed? Hell, another session like that one and I would have followed you to Irkutsk on my knees."

She hugged the wall, the stuffed rabbit clutched to her breast. Dmitrov held back. He had read her file. He knew that this was the scar she bathed with liquor, the wound that wouldn't heal. But the bald phrases in the dossier had never hinted . . .

"Judith, please, listen to me." He spoke softly, urgently. "I know what you must feel. Two years ago, we lost our son in an accident. He was eight years old when it happened. He drowned. It was a hot day, we should have been watching, but instead we—" He shook his head helplessly. "He took our lives down to the bottom of that pond with him. After that, nothing was the same. My wife couldn't talk about it. She still can't. The hurt is terrible, and I don't expect it will ever go away. I would not have brought you here if I had known. My God, it's the last thing I would have done."

Judith narrowed her eyes. "If that's a lie, it's a despicable one. Sick and twisted and disgusting. And if it's the truth, you ought to be ashamed of yourself, using your kid's death as another weapon in your arsenal. I may be stupid, but I'd rather be violated by ten Byron Harcourts than let a sleaze like you fuck me over again. Get out of my way."

She ran past him into the living room. Dmitrov watched silently as she pushed her feet into her high-heeled pumps, gathered up her clothes in a bundle, and left, still naked under her mink coat. He stepped to the window and looked out. After a minute, she emerged from the building and trotted toward the bridge. In another minute, she was gone.

He supposed that her rage would protect her. Perhaps he should have followed her. But no. He would spare her further twaddle, lame excuses, lurching denials.

He blamed himself. He had given the apartment only a cursory glance when he arrived in Warsaw, and he had even admired the nursery as just the right touch of verisimilitude: the home of real people, with a real foundation in their marriage. He didn't recall seeing the photographs of the child. He was sure that they were a recent addition, the decorator's finishing touch. But he hadn't cared enough to check the place out again before bringing Judith here tonight. He was slipping, getting careless, growing old.

He yelled, "Did you hear that, Pushkin? Did you hear that, you piss-brained moron? You've ruined everything, you and your helpers. What are you going to do now, you drooling idiot?"

A minute passed. The telephone rang. He ripped the cord from the wall. He wasn't going to waste words on a telephone receiver. Eventually Pushkin would turn up in person, and Dmitrov would flay him alive for the meddling fool that he was.

The tantrum failed to console him. He should have paid closer attention. He should have made the connection. He had no doubt that the moppet in the photographs was the spitting image of the late Helen Klein.

He retrieved the bottle of vodka from the nursery. Pepper vodka, the favorite Polish nostrum for bellyaches. If you can't cure it, burn it out; or numb the area so you don't feel it. He poured himself a drink and knocked it back. The pepper made his eyes water, and the vodka burned his gut.

Ivan Pushkin clucked and waggled his head. "You're ashamed of your own clumsiness, so you try to blame me. Just because you failed to handle the situation adroitly—"

"I failed? I didn't get a chance to fail. She saw those blasted photographs you planted and she went crazy. What did you expect her to do, fall into my arms and agree to come to Moscow with me? If that's so, then you're even more of an idiot than I thought."

Pushkin shoved his spectacles up the humped bridge of his nose. "There is no need for you to talk to me like that. I will report to Comrade Krelnikov that you have been stubborn and uncooperative."

Dmitrov told him what he and Krelnikov could do with their reports, and their opinions of him. "I was told I could handle the matter in my own way, without interference from morons like you. Very well, I have finished with this particular assignment. Perhaps you'll have better luck working your own charms on Mrs. Marlowe."

Dmitrov started toward the door. Pushkin hurled himself at his retreating back.

"Wait, comrade, where are you going?"

"I'm driving back to Moscow. Today."

"But the job's not finished."

"Maybe not, but I am. Thanks to your clumsiness, we've lost more ground than we've gained. I have no credibility left. None. She won't let me near her, not after tonight. You'll have to try again with someone else."

"But that could take weeks. Months. Meanwhile, Abbott might die."

"That's not my problem. Why don't you bring him here?"

"I can't do that. It's too risky. These Poles aren't to be trusted. One of them would spot him and tell the world. We'd have every Western journalist in Warsaw beating at Abbott's door."

Dmitrov shrugged. "Send him to the country. Put him in a hospital."

"You don't understand, we want him at home, enjoying free give-and-take with his circle of friends. We want to observe him. We want to see him together with his daughter, in his natural setting."

"Why?" Dmitrov had asked the question before, back in Moscow. Krelnikov hadn't even bothered to evade it. He had simply said bluntly, "That is none of your concern."

Pushkin waved his hands. "I can't tell you that. It's confidential."

Dmitrov snorted. "You mean you don't know, either. You're all idiots," he said to the listening walls as he pulled open the door. Pushkin followed him out.

"All right, what do you want?"

"I told you, I want out. I'm leaving. Get someone else to do your dirty work." S and T: seduction and treachery; the sort of assignment he hated most. No, the sort of assignment he hated himself for doing, because he was good at it.

"You can handle the affair any way you wish," Pushkin said. "Free rein. If you need anything, ask us, but otherwise, go your own way. I won't even ask you to report until you've got her consent. That's all we care about. You'll think of something. Do you know how many men would love to have this assignment? Don't be a proud idiot, Dmitrov. All right, we made a mistake. But from here on, it's your show."

"We're both wasting our time, comrade. She won't speak to me."

"What's the matter, are you losing your taste for American girls?" Pushkin's eyes glittered behind his thick lenses. "Those long, slim legs, those fine breasts, that honey-colored hair, those green eyes, that lovely, wide mouth just made for kissing? Can you really walk away from her after you've tasted those? Apologize to her. You'll find a way to convince her that you mean well. Look, you told her about your son's accident, didn't you? She'll remember that, she'll think about it. Pretty soon she'll decide that she was mistaken about the photographs, that she overreacted. Brush up against her socially. Let her know you're staying here, in the apartment. She'll come around. You'll see."

Dmitrov looked down his nose at him. He found Pushkin despicable, and he didn't care if Pushkin knew it. But if he walked away now, someone else would pay the price. Krelnikov would see to it. His mother might start experiencing difficulties with grocers, telephone and maid service, her teaching job at the Bolshoi school. His ex-wife would be assigned the worst shift at the hospital. His daughter—

He didn't want to think about what they could do to his daughter.

He said, "Get your damn bugs out of the apartment. I don't want somebody listening to me every time I take a crap. If something happens worth reporting, I'll let you know."

Pushkin nodded eagerly. "A reasonable request. I will take care of it this afternoon."

"Make sure you do. And no tricks. I'll check the place over myself."

"Of course. Of course, Colonel." Pushkin grinned. "I'm glad we've resolved this little dispute. Nothing is so terrible that it can't be settled by talking, eh?"

They rode the elevator down together and stepped outside into the predawn chill. The sleet of the night before had softened into snow, big, sparkling flakes that fell slowly, like the glitter the stagehands sprinkled from the flies during the first act of *The Nutcracker*. Pushkin asked Dmitrov for a lift back to the Soviet compound.

As they drove, Pushkin praised himself and the TASS organization for their adroitness in spreading disinformation. Even the Western press was beginning to blame Solidarity for the shortages in vital commodities like meat and coal. When the movement was finally crushed, outsiders would agree that trade unionism in Poland had promised much but delivered nothing.

* * *

Two days after the nightmare evening at Markowsky's house, Judith received a letter from Dmitrov, hastily scrawled in black ink on heavy cream-colored stock:

My Judith,

We conceal our hurts so well, but a word, a picture, a reminder can make us bleed again. Seeing the anguish in your eyes, I felt my own once more. I am not sorry for dancing with you, for talking to you, for making love to you. Only for hurting you. That was never my intention. I remain your lover and your friend—

He had signed it with a flourish, his full name, Aleksandr Nikolaye-vich Dmitrov, and given the address of the apartment.

Judith crumpled up the letter and discarded it. But before Kenneth returned that evening, she fished it out of the wastebasket and pressed it flat in a volume of Shakespeare's plays, a book she was certain Kenneth would never open.

CHAPTER II

Warsaw: Sunday, December 13, 1981

γou're still up, I see."

Kenneth emerged from his room, his eyes puffy behind his glasses. He wrapped his plaid woolen robe around his torso and looped the sash over itself.

Judith lay stretched out on the sofa. "I'm having trouble sleeping." Her words came slowly. "Apparently it's common among victims of trauma. Particularly women who have been raped."

Kenneth let that pass. "I'm not very sleepy myself. That curry you made tonight was pretty hot. Do we have anything for an upset stomach?"

"I am not familiar with the contents of our medicine cabinet. I wasn't trying to poison you."

"I'm not blaming you," Kenneth said too quickly. "But I do have a rather delicate stomach, you know."

"Have you? I would never have guessed." Judith chuckled. "It seems to me that you would need a pretty strong stomach to accuse your wife of provoking the man who raped her. Talk about ferocious loyalty! You never did say anything to Byron about it, did you?"

"I didn't see any point." Kenneth approached the sofa. "He got drunk that night and he passed out in the car on the way home. The next day, he could hardly remember his own name."

"Now that's what I call a convenient loss of memory." Judith sat up partway and draped her right arm over the back of the sofa. "I'll bet he hasn't mentioned my name all week, has he? He's forgotten that I exist. You probably wish you could do the same. 'Whatever happened to what's-her-name, your wife, the loony?' 'Wife? Wife? Sorry, but I don't know what you're talking about.' " She rubbed her eyes. "Don't mind me. I'm just jealous of anybody who can drink enough to blank out unpleasantness. I never could."

Kenneth parked his hip on the arm of the sofa. "Look, Judith, I know this business has done serious harm to our marriage, and I'm sorry, but—"

"We don't have a marriage, Kenny." Her voice was sad. "We never did. We formed a dubious alliance. I had my reasons, you had yours. But I have learned, to my sorrow, that you are an untrustworthy ally. The one time I needed you to stand up for me, you couldn't do it. Not only wouldn't, but couldn't. I can't make up my mind whether you're gutless, or if your job really means more to you than I do. I guess I don't want it to be either of those things."

He sighed. "Do we really need to rake all this up again, at two in the morning?"

"No, we don't need to do anything." She rubbed her hand through her touseled hair. "Need. I've taken a lover, you know. He's been here every day this week. He comes at one and leaves at three. And between us, we make those old bedsprings sing."

Kenneth's face turned ashen. "Who is it? Not—not that . . ."

"My pet Soviet? No, I'll spare you that jolt to your heart, and your gut. A Pole. He teaches at the university, or did. I give his wife English lessons and I take presents to their kids. I've decided to get pregnant, you see. When I finally blow this town, I'm going to take something of Poland with me, even something as small, or as great, as a single Polish sperm."

"I see." Kenneth moistened his lips with his tongue. "I suppose I deserved this."

"Hey." Judith flipped her hand in a half-cocked salute. "I'm doing my part for international diplomacy. Giving him something to remember me by."

Kenneth stood. His hands went to the pockets of his robe. "And just when are you leaving?"

Judith waved her empty glass. "I haven't decided yet. When I get pregnant or when my lover lands in jail. Whichever comes first."

"So he's one of those." Kenneth sounded grim.

"You bet. A rebel with a worthy cause. Shall we have a drink to Solidarity?"

Kenneth stalked out to the kitchen. He dumped a spoonful of bicarbonate of soda into a glass of water. He swallowed it in two gulps, burped loudly a couple of times, and returned to his room without wishing Judith good night.

Eventually, exhaustion pushed Judith into a sleep so deep that she didn't hear the murderous rumble of iron treads until the tanks were right in front of their building. She awakened to see Kenneth standing at the window in his pajamas, peering through the curtains.

"The Russians," he whispered when she asked what was happening. "The invasion."

From their darkened living room, they watched the heavy vehicles moving into the city from the south, like a parade of lumbering dinosaurs. Kenneth was relieved when he identified them as Polish rather than Soviet, not tanks but armored personnel carriers, each with a single cannon thrusting up from its turret.

"I'd better call in, see what's going on." But the line was dead. The television stations weren't broadcasting, either. The only radio they could pick up was some late-night jazz on Armed Forces Radio from Frankfurt.

Kenneth began pulling on his clothes.

"Where are you going?"

"The embassy. Whatever's going on out there, come morning all hell's going to break loose, and I want to be on top of the situation."

"I'm coming, too." Judith pulled on a pair of woolen slacks and a heavy sweater, then she dived into the bottom of her closet for her fur-lined boots.

Kenneth tried to persuade her to stay home, but she insisted on accompanying him. They bypassed the elevator and ran down five flights to the street. As they were walking toward the car, a young soldier intercepted them.

"Excuse me, sir and madame, but no one is allowed out in the streets at this time." Kenneth tried some diplomatic bullying, but the sight of his credentials left the soldier unmoved. "A curfew is in effect until oh six hundred. Please return to your home until then. Everything is under control here. Return to your home." He rested his hand on the stock of his rifle.

They went back to the apartment and retired to their separate rooms. Kenneth set his alarm for five-thirty and promptly fell asleep. Judith lay in the darkness, listening to the pounding of her heart, feeling the rage building inside her. Dmitrov knew about this, she was sure. He must be congratulating himself now on the smooth execution of the operation, perhaps writing a report to the men in Moscow: *"Poles accepting control readily, with no show of resistance."*

At the embassy the following morning, staff members crowded around their television sets to hear General Jaruzelski's proclamation. Judith thought he looked like an invading alien, with his light-bulb–like head, his bald pate, his thick, dark-tinted glasses. The stirring strains of the Polish national anthem introduced him, and when he finished telling the Poles that the army had assumed control of their lives and their destinies, he quoted a line from the anthem, whose chords then accompanied the fade-out.

The embassy workers were no better informed than the citizens in the street. Telephone and telex lines were down all over the country. In its zeal, the army had completely destroyed a major switching post, rendering all internal and external communication impossible. Even emergency calls for police or medical assistance could not go through.

Kenneth told Judith he would probably spend the night at his desk. Managing a crisis of this proportion would take every waking minute. The coup would have big repercussions at home, in the White House and State Department, where sympathy for Solidarity was strong, and Washington would be relying on their men in Warsaw for news and intelligence.

Byron came striding in at eleven-thirty. He called for reports, demanded that his staff bring him up to date on everything that was happening. His glance slid over Judith, sitting in an armchair in the anteroom outside his office. He didn't smile but hurried into his office, Kenneth trotting at his heels. The door closed behind them.

Judith left the embassy. Out in the street, walls and lampposts were plastered with posters that listed the main points of life under this new rule: censorship, arrest, curfew. Although the police state had reasserted its power of terrorism and repression, the roads were crowded with cars, the sidewalks were jammed, and the tramcars overflowed. Denied the use of their telephones, people were rushing off to visit friends and relatives, eager to get news, or to pass on what they knew. In the squares, at intersections, and on the bridges, policemen or soldiers stood guard, ready to ask for personal documents or to shoot down resisters. No one resisted. The citizens of Warsaw had been expecting something like this for a long time, and now that it had finally happened, Judith saw expressions of despair and resignation, and even relief. Solidarity was all very well, and although it had made life interesting, even exciting for a while, it hadn't put bread on the table. With Christmas only twelve days away, the stores were emptier than ever.

She hurried to the Nowickis' apartment, a few blocks from the Central Station. To her relief, Jan was there, holding court in the living room. He kissed her hand, compressing it between both of his and holding it far too long.

The cramped space was jammed with friends and supporters. Some of Jan's friends in Solidarity had already been arrested, and the question was whether those who were still free should go underground.

"I have tried to persuade Jan to go to Vienna at once," Ewa told Judith in English. "Or to go to his brother in the country. He could hide there until this is all over. But he won't listen to me. Can you . . . can you talk to him?"

Judith shook her head. "If he won't listen to you, he won't pay any attention to me. If the police haven't come by now—"

"It's early days yet. There are so many, too many. You will see, the arrests will go on for weeks. I am so frightened."

Judith tried to comfort her, but she couldn't make it sound convincing. The danger to Jan and his friends was real, and imminent.

At nine o'clock in the evening the visitors began to leave. They talked passionately of rebellion and resistance, but they didn't want to risk being caught away from their homes after the ten o'clock curfew. Judith was about to join the exodus when she caught Ewa's eye. She hung back.

"Sofia won't go to bed unless you kiss her good night. Do you mind?"

Judith followed Ewa to a corner of the living room that had been partitioned off with blankets. Jerzy, the two-year-old, was already fast asleep; he had dropped off in his father's arms at the height of the frenzy and argument. But four-year-old Sofia was sitting up on her cot, hugging her knees. Judith sat beside her and lifted her onto her lap.

"Shall I tell you a story, Sofia?" The little girl nodded. "Once a little girl named Sofia put on her prettiest dress and went out into the forest looking for a friend. On the road she met a cat, and the cat said, 'I will be your friend, Sofia.' And Sofia said—"

Someone pounded on the door. Judith stopped in mid-sentence, tightening her hold on Sofia. On the other side of the curtain, Jan said, "It's probably that windbag Frederic wanting to get the last word in."

Judith heard a cry. Sofia bounded off her lap and pulled the curtain back. Two men in olive drab uniforms were standing in the center of the room. One was holding Jan's coat. The other was holding Ewa.

"You can't take him!" Ewa screamed. "No, leave him alone! Jan, tell them, make them stop!"

Judith threw herself at the man who was restraining Ewa. "Let her go, you're hurting her!"

The policeman planted his hand in the middle of Judith's chest and shoved. She stumbled and fell against the back of the shabby plastic-covered sofa.

"Bastard! Leave her alone!" Jan cried, rushing to her side.

Righting herself, Judith pushed past Jan and charged again, fists whirling. This time the policeman clipped her under the chin with his gun and she dropped to her knees, stunned.

"No! Judith, my darling, my own one. Judith, I love you! Judith!"

Crazed and furious, Jan hurled himself at the man who had attacked Judith. The other cop drew his truncheon and struck him over the head. Jan grunted and went limp. The men grabbed Jan's arms and dragged him through the open door. Out in the hall, a group of neighbors had gathered.

"Do something!" Judith cried dazedly. "Stop them!"

No one moved. Ewa stumbled to the door. "Jan! Jan! Oh, my God, where are they taking him? Jan!"

Judith dragged herself to her feet. "They won't tell you anything. Don't worry, Ewa. He'll be back. A few days—"

"Are you crazy? He struck a policeman. That's a crime. They'll lock him up for twenty years. What am I going to do? Oh, God, what will become of us?"

Little Jerzy had awakened and was screaming. Sofia stood clutching the edge of the hanging blanket while tears rolled down her cheeks.

"I want my papa!" she wailed. "Why did they take him away? I want my papa!"

Ewa fell to her knees beside the child and engulfed her in a hug. As she gazed at Judith over Sofia's head, her eyes narrowed. "You did this. He got himself hurt trying to defend you. He loves you. I heard him say it. I saw it in his eyes. You're lovers, aren't you? Don't lie to me! You've seduced my husband!"

Judith rubbed her jaw. It was plenty sore, but the bone wasn't broken and her teeth were still intact. "That's not true, Ewa."

"You're lying. I know you're lying. I've never had any other man but Jan. We were children together. I can't remember a time when we didn't love each other. Even lately, with all the worry and the arguing, I thought he still cared about me."

"He does," Judith insisted. "Of course he cares about you. Everything will be all right, Ewa. You'll see."

"How am I supposed to live without him?" Ewa wailed. "Can you tell me that? You can have any man in the world, just for the asking. Why couldn't you leave my husband alone? You took him away from me. Can you give him back? Can you? Get out. Get out of my house. I hate you." She collapsed sobbing on the floor at her daughter's feet. Baby Jerzy toddled out from behind the curtain, bawling. Sofia started to scream shrilly.

Judith escaped. Halfway down the stairs, she lurched to a halt and hung gasping over the banister. "Hell," she moaned aloud. "Oh, bloody bloody hell."

Ewa was right. Judith had no business interfering in their marriage. Somehow, she had to give Jan back to his wife.

She reflected that she knew a hundred people of influence in Warsaw. Of the Poles, half would be in jail by now, and the other half would be preoccupied with staying out of jail. The diplomats would be struggling to remain neutral. Kenneth—and everyone else at the American embassy— would want nothing to do with a known troublemaker like Jan Nowicki.

And then there was Aleksandr Nikolayevich Dmitrov.

On Monday morning, as the reality of the situation sank in, the city seemed to be in the grip of a hangover. All the schools except the nursery schools were closed, as were many of the factories and offices. The police continued their sweeps through the city, scooping up Solidarity members and whisking them off in vans to unknown destinations. Although telephone service to the rest of the country was still cut off, the radio and television stations were broadcasting regular pronouncements and orders to the population.

Glancing out of her bedroom window, Judith saw a gray police van parked across the street. As she watched, two men in plain clothes came out of the opposite building, leading three people between them, two men and a woman. Neighbors whom she had never met, on their way to some detention center or internment camp. She would never get to know them now. The thought of all those missing spouses and parents and friends filled her with rage.

For sixteen months, the Polish secret police had bided their time. They had listened to conversations in cafés and classrooms. They had infiltrated Solidarity meetings, taken notes, logged information into their files, constructed lists of names, addresses, and charges. When the time came, they knew just where to pick up the radicals and the liberals and the social misfits, all the people who dared not only to dream of freedom but to do something about it.

Judith noticed that her hands were shaking. She clasped them in front of her but it failed to quiet the tremor. The telephone was still dead. The only TV station left on the air featured an announcer in military uniform, reviewing the terms of the martial-law proclamation for the thousandth time. The coup must have been in the works for quite a while, to get posters up so quickly, soldiers in place, and the television announcers togged out in uniforms tailored to fit. Judith felt a little sick. Dmitrov and his cohorts could be proud of themselves.

When she left the apartment at six, a light snow was falling, and the slush underfoot was turning to ice. She crossed the Poniatowskiego Bridge on foot. The guards posted at either end did not challenge her.

Another soldier stood at the entrance of Dmitrov's building. For a moment, Judith thought he would ask for her papers. They eyed each other warily, then he turned away.

She shared the elevator with a dumpy old woman who was laden down with bulging plastic shopping bags from which peeked rolls of toilet paper, a pair of boots, even a coat. The items represented a triumph of cunning, or else magnificent luck. Judith was curious.

"Where did you find all that stuff, Pani?"

"I have friends," the old woman said vaguely. "These days, everyone needs friends." Having survived the German occupation, the Warsaw uprising, the Communist takeover, and a host of minor troubles, the woman was not about to reveal her source of supply to a stranger, and a foreigner at that.

Judith rapped sharply on Dmitrov's door. She told herself that he wouldn't be home. He would be busy observing, interrogating, reporting. But she heard movement, and a moment later the door swung open. Dmitrov was wearing jeans and a blue cashmere pullover that matched his eyes. His feet were bare. She thought of the hard, battle-scarred body under those casual clothes, and she swallowed.

"Well, you've had a busy week, haven't you, Mr. Secret Agent?" Judith lounged against the doorjamb. "You can be proud of yourself. Nice, tidy job. Clever, too, getting the Poles to take care of the problem themselves. Swift and clean and deadly. The Soviet trademark. But this looks so much better in the international press. Congratulations."

Dmitrov kept his expression neutral. "Will you come in?"

He stepped to one side. Judith sashayed past him and strolled over to the wall where the movie posters were displayed. "Poor Tadeusz Olsewski is missing all the excitement. Oh, well, he can read about it in today's *Figaro* or *Herald Tribune*. He'll cry a little, and he'll gather with his fellow exiles to commiserate. But he won't come back. Why should he? His country's under martial law, the days of liberation are past, and he's got a Russian spy occupying his apartment. But of course, this isn't really his apartment, is it? It's a fake. Like you, darling." Her smile was slow and shallow, with no warmth in it. "I'm glad we made love in the dark. When I tried to remember what you looked like, I couldn't. All I got was . . . shadows."

Dmitrov shook a cigarette from a pack and snapped his lighter. "I remember it very well. Or rather, my hands remember." He moved his fingers in the air. "They have never experienced such an orgy of delight."

Judith felt herself growing warm inside her sheepskin. "I want to issue a complaint to the management. The military's nasty little coup has put a crimp in my love life. The pigs have arrested the man I've been sleeping with. I promised his wife that I'd see what I could do to get him out. Somehow betrayed wives arouse more compassion in me than cuckholded husbands. Most women don't deserve that kind of betrayal. Most men do."

Dmitrov gave her a lopsided smile. "Do they?"

"You bet." She tossed her head. "It doesn't take much to make a woman happy. A few kisses, a compliment or two, a nice screw now and then. But men seem to require endless attention and constant reassurance. Forgive me, I'm straying from the point. You're an influential man. Would you mind springing Jan Nowicki from the calaboose so that we can get back to making a baby?"

"Ah." Dmitrov crossed his arms. "Is that what you're doing?"

"That's what I'm doing." Judith sauntered over to him and stood with feet apart and hands in her pockets. "This will surprise you, but I was good at mothering. I was good at it and I liked it. After our little scene the other night, I decided that that's what I was missing in life. A sense of purpose." She stared at him. "Well, what about it?"

Dmitrov shrugged. "I will see what I can do for you. And Mrs. Nowicki, of course. He's a lucky man, this Jan." He tapped his cigarette above an overflowing ashtray. "Would you like something to drink?"

"No, thanks. This isn't a social call. Just wanted to hit you up for a favor. I figured you owed me." Their gazes locked. "How do you figure it?"

"I've already said I would see what I could do. That must mean I agree with you."

Judith conceded the staring contest and turned toward the door. She hesitated. "You people couldn't stay out of it, could you? You couldn't let this country resolve its own difficulties."

"On Saturday," Dmitrov said, grinding out his cigarette, "the leaders of Solidarity in Gdansk issued a pronouncement. They demanded a national referendum on Prime Minister Jaruzelski's government, the establishment of a non-Communist opposition party, and free elections. To ask for just one of those things was tantamount to suicide, but all three! Their actions forced the government's hand." He shrugged. "If you ask me, the whole business was typical of the Poles. They're romantic, headstrong, impetuous, and self-destructive."

Judith whirled on him. "Oh, does that have a familiar ring to it! Like the Jews—'They brought it on themselves.'"

"You shouldn't have bought shares in their bankrupt dreams," Dmitrov said in a hard voice. "It was a bad investment. The so-called free-trade movement known as Solidarity was deformed in utero. It should have been aborted before it ever saw the light."

The ugliness of his metaphors made Judith flinch. "But it was born. And it grew. The best way to discipline an errant child, I suppose, is to bring the nailed boot crashing down, grind him into dust, shovel him into a jail cell or an internment camp, leave his family wondering and afraid. A lot of fathers in this city are wondering where their sons are right now. You wouldn't sound so smug if your boy was among them." Judith's eyes flashed. "Your kid did you a favor by dying, Sasha. At least you don't have to lie to him anymore."

She had the door partway open when Dmitrov grabbed her shoulders and pulled her around. The muscles around his mouth and eyes were taut, and he spoke in a harsh, throbbing whisper.

"My son didn't ask to be born, he didn't ask to die. They start out the same, the children, unmarked, no scars, no nothing, and we do this to them. Life does it, turns them into us. I'm lucky he never found out what kind of man his father was, never knew. I don't pray—God means nothing to me—but I have prayed to my son. 'Forgive me, Misha. I'm sorry, Misha. I couldn't stop myself, Misha.' What Christians call sin we Russians call living. Surviving. And he was spared all that. He went swimming one hot summer day and God took pity on both of us and let him drown."

His sorrow filled the room. It sucked the oxygen and warmth out of the air, leaving Judith feeling cramped and dizzy and cold. She cowered against the door.

"You think I didn't secretly hope that maybe this time a bunch of slaphappy zealots might actually pull it off? It made me sick to watch them making a mess of it, playing into the government's hands. I could have told them what to do, shown them how to plan their moves. But no. I have to live, too. Typical Russian. Every day I do my job, and every night I soak my tired spirits in vodka." Dmitrov released her. He stood unmoving for a moment, then he gave his head a violent shake, as if to clear it.

"Be careful what you say," Judith begged in a whisper. "They can hear you."

"No, they can't. I told them to take their nasty little devices out of the walls. And I went over every square inch. I can speak more openly here than I can in my own apartment in Moscow." He turned away and sat on the sofa. "You Americans don't know what it's like, day after day, the lies you hear, the lies you tell, the lies that are your life. You don't know."

Judith removed her coat and threw it over the back of a chair. "You're right, I don't know. Tell me about it."

"I'm no different from the Poles," Dmitrov said with a bitter laugh. "Born to self-destruct. Forget it. You'd better get out of here. They're going to be strict about the curfew." Judith didn't move. Dmitrov leaned forward, bracing his elbows on his knees. "Does this Nowicki have a son?" he asked without looking up.

"One."

"He'll be proud of his father, until he's older; then he'll ask why the old man didn't do more in December 1981, risk more. Why he didn't fight if he believed he was right. And Jan Nowicki won't be able to tell him."

Judith allowed the silence to lengthen. Then she said, "Who drafted that letter for you? Some hack in the S and T department?"

"No one." Dmitrov gripped his hands together. "It was my own, and sincerely meant. Not that I expect you to believe me."

"Do you have a picture? Of Misha?"

He hesitated a moment, then he pulled out his wallet. "My wife took this the spring before he died. The last photograph we have of him." He extracted a color snapshot encased in plastic. He kept it in the deep pouch in the back, with bills of large denomination.

Judith sat on the arm of the sofa and studied the snapshot. It showed Dmitrov and a towheaded boy with long legs and big ears. They were standing in the sunshine, in front of some wooden steps that needed painting. The boy was holding a soccer ball on his hip and grinning at the camera, exposing the gap where his two front teeth should have been. The likeness to Dmitrov was unmistakable. Judith handed it back. Dmitrov restored the picture to its place in his wallet and slid the wallet back into his hip pocket.

Judith said, "I'll bet you looked just like that when you were his age."

He shrugged. "So my mother says."

"Cute."

"We had a hard time getting him to smile. His teeth. He was terribly embarrassed." Dmitrov glanced at his Rolex. "I'd better drive you back. It's nearly ten."

"Maybe I don't want to go back," Judith said.

Dmitrov turned to her. "Why not?"

"Because I want to stay."

"Why?"

Judith shrugged. "When you start thinking about the . . . thing in your life, the thing that shouldn't have happened, it can eat you up. Like Charlie and Nellie and me. He was a cop. Do you believe it? The rich-bitch phony hippie radical and the fuzz. I was working at a friend's gallery in New York and he came in one day and flashed his shield. He said, 'I'm Charlie Klein of the Art Squad.' Thefts, forgeries, you know. When I stopped laughing, he asked me if I would come to dinner. Not *go* to dinner, mind you, but *come* to dinner, at his place. He lived in a big apartment in SoHo, and it was better than any gallery I'd ever seen. He didn't know anything about art when he joined the force, but he hated feeling ignorant, and by the time I met him, he was an expert. He already had a master's degree in art history and he was getting his doctorate at NYU. One wall of books, one wall of paintings, and pieces of sculpture instead of furniture—he slept on a mattress on the floor. He spent all his money on art. He was a mean cook, too, but he refused to divulge his recipe for fettuccini Alfredo. The only way I could get it out of him was to marry him. It was a hard chase, but I wore him down. Nellie was born, and I thought things just didn't get any better than that. You probably felt that way, too, didn't you? With Misha?"

"Yes."

"Sure you did. Children have that effect. Little miracles. This sounds awful, but when they told me about the accident, I felt relieved in a way. I realized that all that time, all that wonderful time, I'd been waiting for the boom to fall. I didn't deserve him, or the baby, and somebody finally rectified the mistake. I'll never forget Charlie's mother at the funeral. She's a survivor of the camps, but she's not a victim. Gold jewelry, red wigs, short skirts, a string of boyfriends in Miami—she reinvents her life every minute. But that day, as we watched them putting Charlie and Nellie into the ground, she turned to me and said, 'This is worse than Belsen.' " Judith stopped and took a deep breath. "I sold his collection, got rid of everything that had anything to do with us as a family. I thought I could localize the pain by eliminating the associations. Stupid, but I wasn't thinking. Six months later, an insurance check turned up. It was the prod I needed to leave New York. I cashed it and got on a bus and got the hell out of there. No matter what happened to me, I didn't care, because I'd been someplace that was worse than Belsen. Are you listening, Sasha?"

He nodded.

She slid down onto the cushion beside him. "Sometimes you start thinking about it, the whys and the wherefores, and you can't stop. You can drink, or you can ram your head into a brick wall, but you can't stop. On nights like that, being alone is a bitch." Judith stroked his cheek. "Something I wouldn't wish on my worst enemy."

Dmitrov drew her into his arms. She came willingly, and they held each other tightly for a very long time.

CHAPTER 12

udith set the breakfast tray down on the corner of the bed and pulled
the curtains open. Outside the sky was hard and textured like granite,
and tinted with a pinkish wash. Snow was falling. Dmitrov lifted his head
and squinted at the light.

"What time is it?" He groped for his Rolex.

"Just after eleven. Top of the morning, tiger." Judith ruffled his hair,
kissed him, and placed the tray over his knees. "I just hope I'm as vigorous
as you when I get to be your age."

"If you try to maintain this pace, you'll never make it." Dmitrov
sniffed. "Coffee? Where did you find coffee?"

Judith poured two cups. "Second floor, apartment at the rear.
There's a one-crone black market down there. Anything you want, at the
most exhorbitant prices imaginable. It seems that her grandson, who lives
in Houston, wants to go to Harvard. I just financed his freshman year.
Brought home potatoes, ham, vodka, all sorts of lovely things, without
setting foot out of doors."

"You're incredible." Dmitrov peeked under the large cooking pot
Judith had inverted over the plate on the tray. "Don't tell me you had time
to cook as well?"

"The way you were sleeping, I would have had time to translate Julia
Child into Polish. French toast with some melted brie on top, and some
honey-butter glop I threw together." She shucked her boots, peeled off
her jeans, and crawled into bed beside him. "Only one plate. I hate
washing up. Do you mind sharing?"

"Do I have a choice? I see you've annexed my sweater." He plucked at her blue cashmere sleeve.

Judith unfurled the two handkerchiefs she was using as napkins and handed him one. "I notice you've cleaned out the kiddie junk from the back room. You must have thought I'd come back."

"I hoped you would. I'm glad you did. I don't like unfinished business." He took a bite of eggy bread fried in butter. "My God, you really can cook."

"Only when I'm in the proper frame of mind. I do my best work when I'm in love."

"Oh, have you decided to fall in love with me?"

"Of course." Judith nestled close to him and stabbed at the plate with her fork. "Why not complicate matters a little? Get crazy. Have some fun. Break my heart. Maybe get a Russian baby instead of a Polish one. Do you mind? You don't need to reciprocate. That's the sort of complication we don't need. A couple of star-crossed geezers, lovers from the wrong side of the ideological tracks, meeting at the Metropole in Moscow every May Day, mooning at each other's wrinkles over the blinis. It's too pathetic for words."

"Let me understand." Dmitrov swallowed. "You are perfectly free to fall in love with me, but I am not permitted to fall in love with you?"

"Certainly not. Didn't you learn anything in spy school? Rule number one: Don't get involved. Stay detached. Do the job and get out, and if you're a good little agent, you'll get a medal when they pension you off."

Dmitrov dipped a bite of bread and cheese into the pool of sweetened butter. "You're in this for kicks, then?"

"Now, there's a dated bit of English slang." Judith laughed. "What if I am? In it for kicks, that is. Is that any worse than what you're in it for?"

"Which is?"

"A score, a top grade on your report card, a pat on the head from whoever is running you and Pushkin and the rest? I don't mind your trying, I really don't. It's simply not . . . important. I would like to think that we touched at some point, the real you and the real me. Last night, or maybe it was when you were consoling me and saying nice things to me in Russian after Byron did what he did. Your son is as real to you as my daughter is to me. They force us to be real to each other. Every now and then. When we can't help ourselves."

Dmitrov sipped his coffee in silence. Judith hummed to herself, an atypically melancholy Cole Porter song: "It's All Right With Me."

"What are you thinking?" Dmitrov asked.

"How about a nice soufflé for lunch? Pani's larder doesn't run to salad greens, I'm afraid. Only cabbage. And me without my cookbooks—

Creative Cabbage Cookery, translated from the Crimean."

"I don't like cabbage," Dmitrov told her. "In fact, I hate it."

Judith reared back, mouth open in mock astonishment. "What kind of son of the steppes are you, Sasha? A bad seed? You should be ashamed of yourself."

"Potatoes are another matter. I am very fond of potatoes."

"Settled. We'll have potato pancakes. Just what my waistline doesn't need. But what the hell? Why not live a little while the revolution rages around us?" She drew circles in the air with her fork. "A few stolen moments of happiness, a fevered embrace in the shadow of an oncoming tank, a wrenching farewell at the station. By God, life is more like the movies than the movies."

Dmitrov took the fork from her hand, placed it and her coffee mug on the tray, and put the tray on the floor. "Take off my sweater, please."

"Why?"

"Because I don't want to stretch it out of shape."

On their third evening in the apartment, they bathed together in the small tub, a riotous business that probably flooded the apartment below them. Judith offered to shave Dmitrov. He declined.

"Then I'll watch."

She leaned against the wall behind him as he bent over the basin, the razor in his hand. His features emerged as the fog on the mirror cleared.

"Whom do you look like? Your father or your mother?"

"Father." Dmitrov pulled his mouth to the left and scraped his right cheek.

"I should have guessed. I can almost tell you what he was like. Stern and forbidding, eyes glaring under dark brows, cheekbones thrusting up like breastworks, nose protruding like the barrel of a cannon. A fortress face to guard the fortress man. Am I close?"

"Not bad." Dmitrov worked around his dimple. "He was not a man given to emotion."

"I'll bet he was plenty frisky with his mistresses. I have a confession to make, Sasha. I sneaked past the guards when they weren't looking. I'm inside. I've peeked at the throne room and the guardroom and the dungeon, and the chamber where they pile the cannonballs. I don't know everything yet, but I've got a good idea of the general layout. A spy within. You're vulnerable, baby. But then, most warriors are. Remember the lesson of Achilles and his heel?"

He swished his blade in the basin. "It's the first lesson they teach at spy school. The instructors are especially strict in warning against involvements with strange women, particularly attractive Americans who might be working for the CIA."

Judith laughed. "I'm flattered. The CIA would never recruit a burnt-out flower child like me. I'm not reliable. Too likely to get involved with Russian nationals who might be working for the KGB." Pushing herself away from the wall, she slid her arms around Dmitrov's waist and rubbed her cheek against his back. "I love being with you, Sasha. Holding you, being held. I love the talk and I love the silences. And all the phases of lovemaking. The glance, the touch—we don't need much to get started, do we? Being animals together. Sleeping it off afterwards. You don't mind if I warm my cold feet on your fanny. I don't mind it when your eyes go blank and all of a sudden you're a thousand miles away. I don't mind because I know you'll come back to me. No distance is too far. It's been perfect."

"Even perfection can become boring." Dmitrov rinsed his face and toweled it dry.

"Russian fatalism." Judith sighed. "Why bother to be happy? It won't last."

"I need a drink." He flung his towel over the bar on the back of the door. "You?"

"No, thanks." She trailed him out to the living room. "You're drinking a lot. Funny, I haven't felt the need since I've been here. But we've already put Pani Prybowitz's grandson through medical school on what we've spent on vodka."

"Is this the point where the honeymoon starts to sour?" Dmitrov wondered as he tipped the bottle over his glass. "When we start bickering over unimportant things like my drinking? I was wondering when it would happen."

"Sorry, I didn't mean to nag. I was just curious about why I need it less and you need it more."

"In my case, you have no comparison to make. I have always drunk a lot. I'm used to it. It doesn't bother me."

"Right. Let's hope Pani Prybowitz's kid becomes a liver surgeon. I'll take a drink. Why not? Just to prove we're still friends."

They finished the bottle at midnight. Dmitrov wanted to go down to their black marketeer for more, but Judith dragged him back to bed. Their lovemaking was unsatisfactory, a lot of huffing and puffing with manufactured excitement and no tenderness. Dmitrov nearly set fire to the bed by falling asleep with a lighted cigarette in his hand.

When they finally turned out the lights, Judith grunted, "That's more like it. A couple of old married farts."

In the morning, Dmitrov stumbled out to the living room to find

Judith sitting fully dressed on the sofa, her coat in her lap. He went into the kitchen, helped himself to coffee from the pot on the stove, and came back.

"So you're leaving. I don't blame you."

"I'm an old hand at love affairs, remember?" Her smile looked strained. "At this point, we're getting on each other's nerves a bit. We need a brief separation to regroup and remind ourselves that we're still us. Good God, will you listen to that tortured syntax?" She plucked a loose thread on her coat. "Tell me something. Is my father dying?"

Dmitrov sat beside her and buried his nose in his coffee mug. "We're all dying. But he's being very aggressive about it."

"You mean he's trying to kill himself?"

He shrugged. "His heart is enlarged and his lungs are weak. He insists on smoking three packs of cigarettes a day. His liver is beyond hope, thanks to a steady diet of cheap vodka, the kind that would eat the varnish off that table if you spilled it. He has had extended periods of treatment in a rehabilitation center, but they did him no good at all."

"Were you responsible for him? Officially, I mean?"

"No. I met him only once, at the ballet. He is quite a fanatic, apparently. My mother introduced us. I suspect he reminds her of the charming but unprincipled rogues she knew as a young girl, in the dear old days before the revolution."

Judith hugged herself. "My mother got rid of everything after he left. She was so angry, so bitter. She couldn't talk about him. It was too painful. Maybe that was a mistake. If she had let us talk about him, Vanessa and me, we might have gotten him out of our systems."

"And you wouldn't have to sleep with aging Russians who drink too much." Dmitrov finished his coffee and extracted a cigarette from a nearly empty pack. "I'm sorry about last night. I behaved badly. I think."

"We both behaved badly, to stop ourselves from being too happy, I suppose. I've been awake for hours, thinking about him. Daddy." Judith whispered the word. "We never called Preston Marlowe 'Daddy.' Vanessa refused, even after he adopted us, so I wouldn't either. He was always Preston. Mother didn't like it, but Vanessa can be as stubborn as hell when she feels like it, and I followed right along. I remember Vanessa looking at Preston and announcing, 'You're not my daddy. My daddy went to Russia.' And that was that. He was good-natured about it, of course. Preston always is. Good-natured. Easily led." She sighed deeply. "When I was twenty, I tried to find out what happened. I read some books and looked at the old newspapers in the library. Do you know about it?"

"Some. It was fairly widely reported."

"In 1956," Judith said, "my father was working at one of the Eastern

European desks at the State Department, handling the Hungarian crisis. The Hungarians were desperate for freedom. They kept looking to the West for support. But the Russian tanks rolled right over them. Do you know why?"

"Tell me."

"Because my father passed confidential information to the Soviets, assuring them that no matter how far they went in crushing the rebellion, they wouldn't meet any opposition from the freedom-loving people of the United States or NATO. He unbolted the door and let them in."

"They would have come anyway," Dmitrov told her. "Soviet leaders are terrified that their satellites will turn against them. It's their biggest nightmare. The only reason they're not here now is that Jaruzelski's coup preempted an invasion. He was able to put his own house in order. Otherwise—" He made an eloquently hopeless gesture.

"The fact that my father defected proved his guilt. It was a terrific propaganda coup for your people. A terrific embarrassment for our side. We couldn't even pretend that we were sympathetic to the Hungarians. Our refusal to act showed the world that we didn't care. And that we weren't serious about stopping Communism."

Dmitrov said, "Eisenhower and Dulles weren't about to start World War Three with Budapest as the principle battleground. It would have been a disaster. They made the correct decision."

"Which my father revealed to the Soviets. I remember 1968, the year your boys overran Czechoslovakia and stamped out those nasty bonfires of freedom. I felt guilty about that, too. Stupid, isn't it? Is it my fault my father was a shit? I'll bet when Solidarity started here, there was plenty of head-shaking in Budapest and Prague. They knew how it would end. But I keep wondering why. Why did he do it? He was a loyal product of the establishment, the best schools, family dedicated to public service, Medal of Honor winner in the Pacific, superpatriot, all-around good sport. I've heard he had a mean pitching arm in college. He even considered turning pro, but the call of diplomacy was too strong. His family had money, and God knows, my mother had plenty. Why would he throw it all away like he did?"

"Why don't you ask him," Dmitrov said quietly, "before it's too late?"

"Don't you understand?" Judith appealed to him. "I can't! He's a stranger who's not a stranger. The thought of seeing him terrifies me. It makes me sick, right here." She ground her fist into her middle. "I don't really want to know what went on twenty-five years ago, and yet I do, because it was such a big fucking deal and because it twisted all our lives so badly that we'll never get straight. I want my daddy, but it's too late for a daddy to do me any good. Mostly I want to hear him say that he didn't do it just to get away from Mother, and from us. That's what we thought, Vanessa and me. Kids are so damn self-centered. But even if he did say it, I wouldn't believe him, because he's a traitor and a liar. I want to make peace with him, and I want to kick his teeth in. I'd better just stay away." She stood and put on her coat. Dmitrov rose with her.

"Will you come back?" he asked.

"Are you kidding?" She smiled at him. "I'll probably start missing you before I've reached the other side of the bridge. I'll run home, grab a toothbrush and some clean underwear, leave a note for Kenny, and be back before you've finished your second cup of coffee. Hold me, Sasha." She put her arms around his waist. "I don't mind the wild parties. It's the mornings after I can't take. I feel like hell."

"Me, too. You're right, I must be drinking too much. I've never set the bedclothes on fire before."

"As a hiding place, a bottle has its drawbacks. I know. Sasha." Her fingertips brushed his lips. "If this is making you unhappy, we'll stop. Right now."

"It's not you, Judith. Other things, perhaps. I don't know. I shouldn't let myself think. Come back, please."

"We have no future."

"I'll give you a baby. That's future enough. A son whom you will name Aleksandr, and you will call him Sanya, not Alec or Alex or Al. Sanya is a nice Russian diminutive. I will always be with you, in him."

"What if it's a girl?"

"Then she'll have to come to Russia to live with her papa, so that he can see you in her eyes." He smoothed Judith's hair away from her forehead and kissed her. "Do you want me to drive you?"

"No, thanks, I need the walk."

When she had gone, Dmitrov pulled the cord to open the living room curtains so he could watch her. He saw Judith emerge from the building and turn left, toward the Vistula. She moved gracefully, swinging along the icy sidewalk, oblivious to possible pitfalls and slick spots. Suddenly she turned, scooped up a double fistful of snow, and sent a white missile hurtling toward his window. It fell short, but he had to give her points for style. He waved, and she waved back, and ran laughing toward the bridge.

As Dmitrov stepped away from the window, a movement down in the street caught his eye. A man had been lounging against the fence that surrounded the park across the street. He pitched a cigarette into the gutter and hurried after Judith. Dmitrov frowned. If the fellow was in such a hurry to go someplace, why had he been loitering under their window?

The wind off the river was cold and biting. Not the sort of weather to stand idly smoking a cigarette. Only spies, criminals, and cops did that.

With a curse, Dmitrov pulled on his clothes and grabbed his coat.

Judith halted in the middle of the bridge to pull down the rolled brim of her knitted hat and to button the top button of her sheepskin coat. To her left, through the vapor of her own breath, she could see the statue of the Mermaid, Warsaw's symbol, draped in snowy vestments. A few flakes sifted down from the leaden sky. The other pedestrians looked sullen and cheerless. In two days it would be Christmas, the grimmest of seasons when your larder was bare and your friends were all in jail.

Hearing a cry, she turned. Two men were struggling a few yards away. The shorter of the two was pressed up against the bridge railing. To Judith's horror, his attacker grabbed the shorter man's legs and tipped him over into the water. Then the attacker turned and ran toward Judith. Dmitrov.

He grabbed her arm. "Let's go."

"Sasha—what—why—"

"Come on! He isn't going to tread water forever."

They ran, slowing only when they came to the end of the bridge, where a couple of soldiers stood guard. The incident had happened so quickly that no one had noticed, although a small knot of people had started to gather at the far end of the bridge, drawn by the shouts of the man in the water. The guards glanced at Dmitrov and Judith and let them pass.

When they were out of earshot, Judith ducked into a doorway and shook off Dmitrov's hand. "Will you please explain to me why you attacked a perfectly innocent stranger? What's going on?"

"He was following you."

"Following me! That's crazy. Why should anyone follow me?"

"That's what I'd like to know. He didn't see my face. I kept my head down so he wouldn't recognize me."

"You mean he was a Russian?"

"No, I don't think so."

"What, then? A Pole?"

"No. American."

Judith stared. "You mean a CIA man? Now I know you're crazy. Americans don't spy on each other."

"They do if they think one of their countrymen is being suborned by a Soviet agent."

"Oh." He watched the understanding dawn in her eyes. "Well, for God's sake. How did they find out?"

"I would like to know that, too. Did you tell anyone about the apartment? The Nowicki man? Your sister?"

"No one. I never mentioned it." She chewed the finger of her glove, then she raised her eyes. "Your letter. I kept it. Kenneth must have found it."

"Perhaps." Dmitrov stood very still, his hands at his sides, his gaze fixed on a spot over her head. Finally he expelled his breath in a frosty cloud. "I need to see your apartment."

"But Kenneth—"

"I'll wait on the corner. If he's not at home, lower the shade twice and then raise it again."

He guided her through back streets and narrow alleys, glancing behind him every now and then to make sure they weren't being followed. Up in her apartment, Judith found a note from Kenneth on the kitchen table, dated that morning:

Taking the train to Vienna this PM to meet with our people there.
Hope you're all right. Back in a few days.

She checked the kitchen, the bathroom, the bedrooms. Kenneth's overnight case was gone. His dresser drawers were empty of shirts and underwear.

Back in the living room, she signaled with the window shade. Half a minute later there was a tap on the door and Dmitrov slipped in. He pressed his forefinger to his lips, warning her to be silent. *Letter,* he mouthed.

She took the Shakespeare off the shelf and flipped through it. The letter was gone. Dmitrov shrugged.

While Judith watched from the sofa, he methodically searched the apartment. He felt under the furniture, checked the phone, the lamps, the seams on the upholstery. One by one, he removed the pictures from the walls, the colorful prints and paintings Judith had collected. He noticed a wrinkle on the paper backing of a framed old French playbill advertising a performance by Papillon, a famous clown. He peeled back the paper and removed a small metal disc no bigger than his thumbnail. He carried it into the bathroom and flushed it down the toilet. Then he vanished into Judith's bedroom. He came out bearing a tape recorder and a microphone.

"The first bug was Soviet, old model, probably dead. This thing is voice activated, and the batteries are brand new. It was attached to your bed, a special strap screwed onto the back of the headboard. From the amount of dust that has gathered on the top, it hasn't been there for more than a few days."

"My bed!"

"You said you told your husband about Nowicki. Perhaps he wants to find out if your trysts are really as free of political content as you would have him think."

"Kenny?" Judith was outraged. "Kenny did this?"

"It was certainly done with his knowledge. Someone needs to check the machine on a regular basis, rewind the tapes, change them, replace the batteries. You say the letter is gone. That means he knows we are more than just casual acquaintances. He knows the address of the apartment, and that we made love. He wants, or someone wants to know just how serious this affair has become. I'm surprised they haven't dragged you in for questioning yet."

"Why should they?" Judith demanded. "I don't have anything to tell them."

"Don't you? They'll want to know what we said to each other, every word, every intonation. What did you reveal about the personalities at the embassy? The petty feuds? The people you suspect of working for the CIA? They will interrogate you ruthlessly, as if you were the enemy and not I. What did you learn from me? Did I reveal anything of the slightest importance when we were in bed together? Did I say anything about any of the Soviets and their function here? After a few days, they will release you, caution you to be more careful in the future, and put you on a plane to America, out of harm's way. But the mark on your husband's record will be enough to keep him from ever being assigned overseas again." He shook his head. "It's not a casual love affair anymore, Judith. It's a diplomatic incident. I don't blame them. If the situations were reversed and one of our women were involved with one of your men, I'd do the same."

Judith was staring at him. "Is that all I am to you, Sasha? Diplomatic business? Nothing more?"

"You could be a great deal more, if I let you. But I can't." Dmitrov placed the tape recorder on the end table. "It would be foolish, suicidal."

"And you'd rather drink yourself to death, is that it? Slow but sure. The Twenty-Year Plan." Judith went to the bottles displayed on the credenza, filled two glasses with vodka, and carried them back to the sofa. "Might as well get it off to a good start. Good luck, comrade. And while we're at it, Merry Christmas and Happy New Year."

"And good-bye," Dmitrov said softly.

Judith shrugged and swallowed. "If that's the way you want it."

"There's no point in continuing, Judith. No point. They know about us."

"We're a matched set, baby, remember? A couple of randy poodles. Have you looked in the mirror lately? The dead look that was in your eyes when we met is almost gone. You're starting to feel something, and you don't like it. Hence the big rush to the bottle and out the door."

"There is no point," Dmitrov repeated, stressing the words.

"No point in stopping, either. Why should we? So far, nobody's arrested me for espionage or anything else. Kenny's in Vienna, beavering away for Uncle Sam. If the CIA breaks down the door, they won't throw you into jail. This is your turf, after all. I'll be the one they dip into hot water, and I don't care. So why not stay the night?" Judith toyed with the button on his jeans. "Stay two while you're at it. Let's play the game as long as it pays, and when we start to lose, we'll cash in."

Dmitrov stayed her hand. "If we can."

"We're grown-ups. We know the rules. We pay as we go. Hearts don't break, they bleed for a while, but so what? There's another man waiting for me just as surely as there's another woman waiting for you. But for the time being, we have each other. Let's enjoy it." Grinning, Judith fell back among the chintz cushions. "That's my tough-girl act. How do you like it?"

Dmitrov smiled. "It's good, but I don't believe a word of it. You've already announced your intention of falling in love with me. When I leave you, you'll probably have one of your famous suicidal nervous break-downs."

"And when I recover, I'll find myself another lover as quickly as you can say"—Judith snapped her fingers under his nose—"Wojciech Jaruzel-ski. I wonder if he's available?"

"I'd better go." Dmitrov pushed himself off the sofa. "I'm sorry, Judith."

She shrugged. "You'll never get a better offer. But I won't argue. Good-bye, darling. I'm off to shampoo my hair. You know the way out." She kissed him softly, not trying too hard to provoke a response. Then she went into her bedroom and closed the door.

Two minutes after she stepped under the shower, he joined her. "I forgot to ask if you wanted your back scrubbed."

She slid her soapy hands over his body. "A woman would have to be crazy to turn down an offer like that."

CHAPTER 13

Warsaw: December 29, 1981

S o, the neighbors are interested in Mrs. Marlowe's lover." Pushkin pressed his folded hands against his receding chin. His fleshy lower lip drooped over his forefinger. "Someone, her husband perhaps, told them about your interest in her. Otherwise, why would they bug her bedroom? But I do not understand why they haven't acted to remove her from danger. If she were Soviet, we would have sent her out of the country at the first sign of trouble. I suppose we should simply count ourselves lucky that you still have an opportunity to work on her. Are you making any progress?"

Dmitrov shrugged. "It's hard to tell. She's obsessed with her father's crime. She's curious about him. At the same time, she's terrified of a meeting."

"You don't have much time. Sooner or later, someone is going to put an end to Mrs. Marlowe's latest escapade. Her husband returned from Vienna last week. That could be a problem."

"We're safe enough for now. As far as they know, she hasn't seen me since I threw that fellow into the Vistula. American, was he?"

Pushkin shrugged. "Not known to us, if he is. He and another man are taking turns watching her apartment, following her when she goes out."

"She hasn't left the apartment for a week," Dmitrov said. "They must be rather tired of standing in the snow, waiting for something to happen."

* * *

Dmitrov stepped into a workers' café and ordered vodka. The other men in the place glanced at him, then looked away. He was a foreigner; he could not help them in their troubles. At least the vodka was good, biting but smooth. He tipped it down his throat and closed his eyes for a moment as he visualized it melting the core of coldness inside him, like boiling water poured over ice. Somehow he had to humanize himself again, become pliant and responsive. But lately the thermostat in his brain was increasingly harder to regulate.

When he reached Aleye Ujazdowskie, he entered a restaurant, flapped his special identification at the headwaiter, and made his way through the dining room to the kitchen. Without saying a word to anyone, he opened the door to the cellar and went down into the main storage area. With his skeleton key, he unlocked a door that led to an adjoining basement. During the war, members of the resistance had chipped out tunnels all over the city to facilitate movement against the Germans. When Warsaw was resurrected from the ash heap, many of those old passageways remained. Dmitrov moved through three basements, past heating plants and furnaces, under dripping water pipes and sagging lines of laundry hung up to dry. Eventually he mounted another flight of stairs, which led to an enclosed fire escape. He climbed up five flights and pulled open the door into the main corridor. Ahead of him he could see the openwork cage of the elevator awaiting the summons of its next passenger. He tapped on the third door to his left and waited. After a moment, a lock turned and the door swung open noiselessly on oiled hinges. He stepped inside and Judith threw herself into his arms.

"You've been drinking again," she said after they kissed. Her hands played over his face, searching for new lines, new troubles. "If you hate this so much, why don't you just stay away?"

"Because I can't." He clasped her to his chest and buried his face in her hair. "God help me, I can't. And I don't want to."

The top of Judith's baby grand piano held a small gallery of photographs, including a photograph of Judith and Kenneth taken at the chapel in Las Vegas where they were married. Kenneth looked stunned; Judith, stoned. Her body seemed limp, almost in a state of collapse. She and Kenneth leaned against each other, supporting each other for the first and probably the last time in their married lives.

There were several photographs of Judith's sister, Vanessa, an actress who lived in London. Dmitrov's favorite was a snapshot of the two girls taken at the ages of four and six respectively, Judith with her jaunty smile, Vanessa with a wary frown and a worried pucker on her forehead.

Lounging on the deep sofa with its flowered chintz slipcovers, Judith lay across Dmitrov's lap, her head resting against his shoulder.

"After our son is born," she said, "I'll take him home to America. When he's grown up, eighteen, say, I'll tell him about his father. He might even make a pilgrimage to Moscow to see you. You'll be hoary with age by then, but still erect and distinguished, your manly chest hung with medals and ribbons, with a mob of half-grown sons by your second wife. You and he will find that you don't have much to say to each other. Eighteen years. The year 2000. Can you imagine what relics we'll be by then? Who knows, by that time, maybe he won't even need a visa to travel to Russia. A world without borders."

"We Soviets will have asserted our mastery of the globe by then," Dmitrov said grandly. "The West will be overrun by starving refugees from the Third World, taxing their resources to the limit. They will have nothing left for weaponry, while the Soviet people, accustomed to deprivation and hardship, will still be standing in line for bread and meat, but safe under the canopy of a dazzling array of nuclear and conventional arms." He made a face. "Not a very pleasant vision."

"Our son will ask you what it means to fall in love. You will go to your Lenin computer, punch in the word, and get the definition: 'an obsolete term defining the archaic practice of conceding complete trust and friendship to a stranger, which may or may not lead to physical consummation resulting in genetically unreliable offspring.'"

Dmitrov laughed. "I like our old-fashioned world better."

A knock on the door brought them to their feet. Dmitrov said in a whisper, "Don't answer."

"But Kenneth—".

"He has a key. He wouldn't knock."

The hammering continued, and then a man began to shout, "Judith, Judith, please be at home, I beg you! Please, I must talk to you. Judith!"

"It's Jan Nowicki." Judith chewed her lip. "If I don't talk to him, he'll stay out there all day making a fool of himself and attracting all sorts of attention. Go hide in the bedroom while I get rid of him."

"That might not be so easy," Dmitrov said. "Men in love aren't rational."

She looked at him sideways. "You're as rational as ever. That's a bad sign, I guess."

"Maybe I'm just a good actor." He kissed her, then ducked into her bedroom and closed the door.

Judith knotted the sash of her robe more tightly around her waist. She caught Jan by surprise. About to hammer with both fists, he found himself without a target and fell head first into her arms.

"My darling one! They let me out of the detention center this morning. I haven't been home yet. I had to see you."

"Shhh." Judith stepped into the hall and pulled the door closed behind her. "Kenneth's home with the flu. You've got to get out of here."

"No, that can't be. He is never at home during the day. What—"

"He's in bed right now, sleeping. Things have changed, Jan. We can't go back to the way it was before the—before. Try and understand."

"I only understand one thing, my sweet Judith." Jan captured her hand and brought it to his lips. "I have to talk with you, make love to you, sleep with you. I have so much to tell you, my darling. Can't we go someplace else? I have friends."

Judith pressed her back against the door. "Jan, no, I'm not going anywhere. I can't see you anymore. Or Ewa. You gave the whole show away the night you were arrested, and she hates me now. I don't want to hurt her anymore. Just go away."

"I won't! I don't care about Ewa. I care about you, my sweet love, my precious darling. I want to go away with you. We'll run away together, elope. I can stay in Vienna until your divorce is final, and then we'll go to America. You can get me a job teaching in a university there. I'll give you a dozen babies, one for every month of the year."

"Jan! Listen to me, please. I don't love you. I never loved you. I want you to go away right now, and don't come back."

At last, he seemed to grasp what she was saying. "Go?" His eyebrows converged over the bridge of his nose. Behind his wire-rimmed glasses, his eyes grew cloudy. "I can't go. All those nights in that stinking detention center, listening to the farts and the groans and the weeping and the praying. It was horrible. I thought I'd go mad, but I closed my eyes and thought of you. Of us. You saved me."

"That's nice"—Judith tried to make her voice sound soothing—"but you should have been thinking of Ewa."

"No, you!" Tears welled up in his eyes. "You got me out of that place, didn't you? You used your influence to help me. Everyone else who was arrested with me is still in jail, waiting. But they freed me. Me! Why? Because I had a friend on the outside, a champion. You did that great thing for me, I know you did. That is why I don't understand why you want to send me away. Why?" He gripped her upper arms. "Why are you being so cold to me now?"

"Jan, let go of me. Please, calm down. It's too dangerous for us to be friends now. Kenneth—Kenneth knows. I told him. He was furious with me. You've got to go."

"I won't go!" Jan shouted. "I have no home. I can't live with Ewa anymore. I hate that miserable apartment. I hate the darkness and the drabness and the ugliness, and I hate living with a woman who is drab and ugly. I want to be free, I want to be with you. A beautiful woman in a beautiful place, where we can eat beautiful foods and talk about beautiful ideas. Judith, Judith, I beg you, Judith, don't send me away. I won't let you. I won't let you!" With a jerk, he pulled her close and started kissing her.

"Stop it, Jan!" Judith pressed the heels of her hands against his chest. She felt no muscle under the shabby clothes, only the hard ridges of his ribs. "Stop!"

Dmitrov stepped into the hall. He was fully dressed. "Maybe you'd better hear it from me." Taking Jan by the lapels of his coat, he pushed him up against the wall and said in Polish, "This is no place for you, young man. Go home to your wife. She'll take you back. Your children need you. Go home and forget you ever saw this woman. She doesn't want you anymore."

Jan began to blubber. "This—this man isn't your husband. Who are you?"

"A friend," Dmitrov said.

"He's my new lover," Judith added bluntly. "You were away too long. I'm sorry, Jan."

Jan's mouth opened. He tried to speak, but couldn't. He stayed frozen for a minute, saying nothing, then he burst into tears. When Dmitrov released him, he whirled and stumbled down the stairs. Dmitrov drew Judith back into the apartment.

"You didn't need to do that," she said. "I could have handled it."

"Oh, yes, I heard how well you were handling it. Were you trying to get raped again?"

"He loves me." She crossed the room to the piano and sat on the bench. "He really loves me. Funny, isn't it? Jan loves me, but I love you, and you love—who? Somebody? Anybody? Christ, I feel awful."

"He wants you to rescue him, to take him away to America, find him a job, give him a house, a car, a new wardrobe. He's using you."

"Partly." With one finger, Judith picked out the opening melody of a Chopin nocturne. "But the rest was real enough. I can tell. . . . I would do it with you. Run away. To Switzerland, or Italy, or South America. Somewhere where no one would find us."

"No place is that remote anymore." Dmitrov moved around behind her and rested his hands on her shoulders. "People are so disgustingly mobile these days. Let's bring back the days of the troika and the stage-coach, when it took a month to travel five hundred miles. Love affairs were easier then. When one's husband went away, he was guaranteed not to return for at least half a year."

"You're a spy." Judith rubbed her cheek against the back of his hand. "You know how to hide. We'll get wigs, false noses, plastic surgery. I want more of you, all of you. This isn't enough. What if—what if you defected?"

His hands stiffened. "I have a mother and a daughter back home. I know what happens to the families of defectors, the repercussions. I won't do that to them, Judith."

"Then I will." She turned and hugged him around the waist. "Your people in Moscow can have a father-and-daughter defector team. Quite a propaganda coup."

"Don't make jokes." Dmitrov stroked her head. "You know what life there is like. Once you got there, you couldn't leave. You'd be a prisoner. Our leaders aren't as fond of defectors from the West as people think. Your gesture would have very little propaganda value."

"Don't be so bloody rational! People in love are supposed to damn the consequences."

"In Russia, no one damns the consequences. Don't think about this anymore, my darling. Come to bed."

"I'm frightened, Sasha." Judith hid her face in the fullness of his shirtfront. "I don't want to lose you."

"You won't lose me." He combed his fingers through her hair. It was fine and silky and abundant, and it smelled of roses. "Come, let's make a citizen of the twenty-first century."

Jan stood on the sidewalk looking up at the apartment. They were in there together. Making love in that lovely bedroom, with candles burning and fresh flowers releasing their fragrance into the over-heated air, the scent mixing with the animal odors of saliva and semen and sweat. The street tipped, and he thought he was going to faint. Was it overwhelming desire, or simply hunger and weariness? He didn't know. He leaned against the wall to the right of the entrance and closed his eyes.

He wanted to love her and he wanted to kill her. He wanted to kill himself, but he hadn't the courage or the strength. Prison had shown him his limitations. He was powerless to affect history. He could only stand to one side while it swept past, and years after the fact he would read about it and interpret it. History always happened to someone else, to the dead.

A pair of young women jostled him as they passed. He snarled at them to watch where they were going. They cast him a brief pitying glance before moving on. They knew what he was. He looked like a prisoner, smelled like one.

Pulling up his collar, he began to walk, and he kept on walking until his legs began to ache. He had no idea where he was going, in what direction. Finally, exhaustion forced him to stop. He looked up and read the street sign. He was only a few blocks from the American embassy. His feet must have brought him there for a reason. He had only to look into his heart to find it.

Jan approached the American marine who stood guard outside the gates. "I want to see someone inside," he said in English, "an American official."

"The consular section is closed, sir. Come back tomorrow."

"But I'm not applying for anything. I just want to speak to him, a quick word. Mr. Marlowe. Mr. Kenneth Marlowe."

"Look, I'm not supposed to let anybody in now. Move along or one of your own cops will arrest you for loitering."

"But I need to tell him that his wife is being unfaithful to him right this minute. There is a stranger in his bed. A man has a right to know these things. If your wife were screwing another man, wouldn't you want to know? Wouldn't you want someone to tell you?"

The marine shifted his rifle from one shoulder to the other. "I don't know."

"Please, let me give him a message. I won't make trouble. You can search me. I don't have a weapon. No knife, no gun, not even a pencil. They only let me out of jail this morning. I haven't even been home yet. I just want a word with Mr. Marlowe, and then I'll go. Do you know the man I'm talking about? I've seen his photograph. He has fair hair, and glasses like mine."

The soldier wished the crazies wouldn't come around on his watch. "Look, I'll give him the message. Maybe he'll come out. That black BMW parked across the street is his. Wait over there."

"Yes, thank you, friend, thank you. Thank you." Bowing, saluting, smiling like a servile waiter, Jan backed away. The marine disappeared inside for less than a minute before returning to his post. Across the street, Jan waited for some acknowledgment, but none came. Finally, after twenty minutes, a man stepped out of the embassy and spoke to the marine. The marine nodded at Jan, waiting half frozen beside the black BMW. The man from the embassy hesitated, then he crossed the street and approached the car.

"Mr. Marlowe?" Jan said in precise English. He had used his time to compose his denunciation, to memorize it, to practice his delivery. "I must tell you something. It is about your wife. Will you listen, please?"

"Moscow is beautiful in the spring." Dmitrov rubbed the palm of his hand over the small of Judith's back. She had no patience with light-fingered stroking. Like an old dog, she liked hard, deep massage. "At dusk, people go into the Lenin Hills above town, and they sit there until dawn, hoping to hear the nightingales sing. Of course, the lucky ones who live in the country can just open their windows. The kiss of spring comes in on the song of the nightingale."

Judith rolled away from his hand. "Is this a travelogue or an invitation?"

"Both. I'm being recalled to Moscow. I just found out this morning."

She sat up. "When?"

"Two weeks. I don't know when I'll get another assignment out of the country. They're plums, you know, and I am not very popular with the men currently in charge."

"But it's not fair! I don't want you to go. I'm—I'm not ready to—to—"

"To give me up and find a new lover? To say good-bye?"

"I don't want a new lover. Haven't I made it clear that this is different? You're still holding out. You won't admit that I matter to you. But I know I do. I know the signs. You want me every bit as much as I want you. We can't just let it end, Sasha."

"It might be the best way," he said gently. "We have no future. We both knew this was inevitable."

"But not yet! So soon! No. No!" She hurled herself against his chest. He clasped her in his arms.

"We'll see each other again," he promised. "In a few more months, when the snow melts and the wildflowers bloom. I'll be waiting by the door of the dacha my father built fifty years ago with his own hands. We'll make love in the soft grass under the birches, while the nightingales sing over our heads. But who knows? Maybe by that time you'll have forgotten all about me. You'll be lying on the Riviera with some handsome French boy—"

"Stop it!" Judith drew away from him. "Stop patronizing me. Stop acting like I'm a cheap whore just looking for my next trick. If you don't know better than that by now—"

"I'm sorry, my darling. I didn't mean it."

"You're as cold as ice, aren't you? You let your guard slip only once, when you talked about Misha, but it's been up ever since. You won't let yourself feel. Well, what did I expect? After all, you're a spy, aren't you? You've had your heart surgically removed and your guts wired directly to your brain. You don't let yourself feel. It's too dangerous. This is the payoff, isn't it? Decision time. You've been trying to rig a meeting between me and my father, and now you're putting on the squeeze. Well, I won't go. Not to hear your fucking nightingales. Not to see some superannuated old fart who doesn't even remember the times I sat on his lap and called him 'Daddy.' It was a nice cast, Mr. Dmitrov, but I'm not in the biting mood today."

She pulled on a black negligee and flounced out to the living room. In a moment, Dmitrov heard the crashing chords of Chopin's Ballade in G Minor. She played badly, although in the time he had been with her he had noticed improvement. An ungifted amateur, she called herself. He glanced at his watch. He would have to time this carefully.

Five minutes later, he sat beside her on the bench and rested his head on her shoulder. He was naked. "I'm sorry. I know that I seem cold. My wife has accused me of it often enough. But the old habits are hard to break. If I don't say I love you, it's because love frightens me. Loss is so much harder to bear when one loves."

"Oh, Sasha." She lifted her hands from the keys. Tears filled her eyes. "I love you so."

"And I love you." He kissed her again and again until the anger in her body was gone, until she was limp and pliant in his arms.

Judith murmured, "I'll go to Moscow, but I don't want to see him. My father."

"If you refuse to see him, they might withhold your visa."

"But why? What difference does it make?"

"I don't know. Perhaps they want him to be happy in his last months."

"Will you come with me?"

"It might not be possible. It all depends on them, what they want."

"I'll refuse to see him unless you come with me."

"You will find that the Soviet government does not take kindly to ultimatums. You'll find yourself locked out. And they'll punish you by keeping you away from me forever."

"Spring. I can't wait. It's too long."

Dmitrov smiled. "Now you sound like a child in a hurry for her birthday to arrive."

"I'll leave Kenneth. I can't live with him anymore."

"It might be better to wait until after the visit," Dmitrov advised. "If your people become suspicious, they won't let you go. They'll confiscate your passport. It is in their national interest to keep us apart."

"What happens if, after May, we decide we can't live apart?" Judith wondered.

"Then we'll make another plan. Don't cry anymore, my darling. We have a future after all." He pulled the silky garment away from Judith's shoulders and kissed her throat and her breasts. When she was ready, he slid to the floor and drew her down on top of him. Then he gave her the ride of her life. Her eyes closed, her head fell back, and she dug her fingernails into his thighs.

She collapsed on top of him just as the key turned in the lock and Kenneth Marlowe stepped into the room.

"My God," Kenneth said, "you really are disgusting. Get up and get dressed, both of you," he barked. "Now, damn it!"

He stood to one side while they disentangled themselves and stood up, then he followed them into Judith's bedroom.

"I always thought you were crazy," Kenneth said to Judith, "but now I know. This is the stupidest stunt you've ever pulled."

Judith sighed. "He was a damn good fuck, I'll say that much for him. The best I've ever had."

Dmitrov quickly pulled on his jeans and boots and an Aran sweater, and picked up his overcoat. He bowed to Judith, who had pulled on a robe. "Thank you for a most enjoyable afternoon, Mrs. Marlowe."

"Get out of here," Kenneth snapped. "Judith, pack your bags. You're leaving Warsaw tonight."

Judith gave Dmitrov a slow smile. "You're more than welcome, I'm sure, comrade." Their gazes locked for a moment in silent communication. Then Dmitrov went out. Kenneth followed him through the living room and locked the apartment door after him.

"Where am I going?" Judith called from the bedroom. "Not that it really matters."

"As far as I'm concerned," Kenneth said in a choked voice, "you can go straight to hell. There must be plenty of women there just like you."

Judith laughed, the particular juicy laugh that always made Kenneth grind his teeth. "And plenty of hard-hearted bastards just like you."

CHAPTER 14

London: January 1982

*V*anessa Marlowe had been asleep for only three hours when the buzzer screamed, slicing into her dreams like a saw. She burrowed under her pillows to escape it, but the din persisted. A bleary-eyed glance at the clock told her it was only eight-thirty. She cursed and wished her caller in hell. At the foot of the bed, Deaf Kitty slept on, oblivious to the disturbance. His whiskers twitched once when she threw back the covers and stumbled from the room, but he did not open his eyes.

She went to the window, threw open the sash, and picked up a flowerpot. Judith waved up at her from the sidewalk. A black taxi idled at the curb while the driver unloaded three enormous Vuitton suitcases and a bundle of shopping bags.

"Van, it's me! Open up! Happy New Year!"

"Judy?" Vanessa croaked. "Judy, what are you doing here? My show doesn't open for two weeks."

"I got thrown out of Poland." Judith let out a peal of laughter. "It's a long story. Open the door."

Vanessa put down the flowerpot and pressed the button that released the latch on the street door, then she pulled on a pair of jeans and a sweater and went down to greet her sister. Judith met her in the small entryway and engulfed her in a fur-lined hug.

"Oh, Judy, I'm so glad."

"I woke you up. I'm sorry, I should have waited, but I couldn't. I have so much to tell you."

Vanessa stifled a yawn. "I stayed late at the theater, working with one of the actors. I didn't get home until three. Where did you come from?"

"Boat train. Made a stop in Paris to do some shopping. Oh, Van, you should see all the wonderful stuff I bought. Wait until Kenny gets the credit card bills. He'll bust an artery."

The taxi driver carried the heaviest suitcases up to the second floor. Judith added an extravagant tip to the fare, which was sixty-eight pounds, and wished him a safe trip back to Dover.

"Dover?" Vanessa ground her fists into her eye sockets. "You took a taxi from Dover?"

"Of course. I couldn't picture humping all this mess on and off trains. The crossing was lousy, of course."

They carried the last few items up the stairs. Vanessa's neighbor opened his door and peeped out. The elderly white-haired man looked somewhat desiccated but was smartly dressed in a blue pin-striped suit and immaculate white shirt.

"Ah, Miss Marlowe, I was expecting a visitor myself. Forgive me."

"Good morning, Mr. Tidyman. This is my sister, Mrs. Marlowe. She's here for the opening."

"So happy to meet you, Mrs. Marlowe." His dentures whistled a little on the sibilants. "Always so lovely when a member of the family comes to visit. I'll wish you both a good morning." He retreated.

"Insufferable old busybody," Vanessa growled.

Vanessa's living room was high-ceilinged and spacious. She had covered the walls with cream-colored moiré fabric and painted the woodwork the same creamy white. The draperies were made of cocoa brown velvet, backed with panels of ivory lace from Belgium. Her carpet was a red silk Senna from the last century, but her furniture was modern, a tan leather chesterfield and two comfortable armchairs covered with a nubby cream and brown striped material. A vase of pink hothouse tulips sat on the coffee table.

An enormous glass-fronted bookcase stood against the wall to the right of the door. A complicated sound system occupied the center, and the remaining shelves were crammed with thousands of records and cassette tapes.

"Honestly," Vanessa grumbled, "this is the last time I rent to an old-age pensioner."

"He seems nice enough." Judith hung her mink in the closet near the door. She was wearing black: black velvet trousers tucked into the tops of floppy black suede boots, and an oversize black sweater with a drooping cowl neck. Her silver earrings were half moons with leering comic book faces.

"He's a bloody nuisance, always spying. And his lease runs for three years, can you believe it? Talk about dumb. I should have signed him up for six months. Now I'll probably have to shovel him out when he dies."

Judith laughed. "What about the guy downstairs who was supposed to drive him out?"

"Mad Mylton of the Hypo Dermicks? Quiet as a nun, the bastard. He comes here for a dose of peace and quiet, he says. Complains when *my* stereo's turned up too loud. Can you stomach instant coffee?"

"Let me." Judith rummaged in one of the shopping bags. "I brought you some special beans, and a new coffee maker, one of those French jobs with a plunger."

"I don't know why you bother. The junk you bring always ends up in the back of a cupboard." Yawning, Vanessa followed Judith out to the kitchen. The open shelves were bare except for wine and cat food and crackers. Vanessa ate in restaurants, or from cardboard take-out containers.

Judith set to work clearing the plants off the top of the stove. She removed some ivy from the tea kettle, which she rinsed, filled, and set over the gas flame.

"How's the play going?"

Vanessa sat at the table. "It stinks, of course. I stink worse than anybody. I don't know why I got involved. To think I turned down Beatrice in Leeds for this. I should have my head examined."

"You're always so negative at this point in the rehearsal," Judith said, "and on opening night, you're always brilliant."

"No, this time I'm really worried. I rewrote all my dialogue myself. O'Breen's was so bad I couldn't say it without gagging."

Judith sliced some bread and cheese and made sandwiches. They took a tray into the living room. As they were sitting down, Deaf Kitty wandered out of the bedroom and hopped up into Vanessa's lap. She hugged him.

"He's lucky he can't hear my Irish ranting. Handicaps are blessings in disguise, aren't they, boyo?"

Deaf Kitty endured the mauling good-humoredly for about half a minute, then he began to squirm. When Vanessa set him down, he began feverishly to lick his ruffled fur. He was a dandy, never a hair out of place.

Vanessa alternated sips of coffee with drags on a cigarette. "All right, your turn. What's going on? What do you mean you got thrown out of Poland? What about Kenny?"

"He did the throwing. Caught me in flagrante, I'm afraid. Before I knew what was happening, I found myself on the evening train to Vienna."

"What about the man?"

Judith lifted one shoulder, half a shrug. "He's just a man. No different from the rest."

"I don't believe you. You've been smirking ever since you got here. You've gone and fallen in love, haven't you?"

Judith nodded happily. "It's real, and it's wonderful, and he's wonderful. I'm happy and sad and angry and delirious all at the same time. I've never felt like this before, Vanessa."

"Since the last time you felt like this, you mean." Vanessa glowered at her. "You're not on anything, are you?"

Judith laughed. "I'm all natural, one hundred percent pure, high on love. He's beautiful, Van. When we're together, it's magic time."

"Well, I hope he's not coming here. I am not giving up my bed to you and one of your weird boyfriends."

"No, he's not. I won't be seeing him for a while, until spring. I thought I'd die when he told me. That's when I knew I loved him, really loved him. But we'll work it out so that we can be together. We have to."

"What's this paragon's name?" Vanessa asked. "J. Christ?"

"I can't tell you. You'll be angry with me."

"Why, do I know him? Why all the reticence, Judy? What's going on?"

Judith took a long breath. "His name is Aleksandr Nikolayevich Dmitrov."

Vanessa sat stunned. "A Russian? A Russian! No! Oh, no, Judy. Oh, God, it's worse than I thought. Why? Why did you have to go and fall in love with a fucking Russian?"

"The operative word is the adjective. We couldn't help it."

"Yes, you could." Vanessa slammed her cup and saucer down on the tray. "But you didn't. You're hurling yourself headlong into heartbreak and nervous breakdowns and all the rest. Nothing changes. How many more times are you going to put yourself through one of these impossible romances? God knows, I thought you were nuts when you married *Kenny,* of all people. But this is worse. Dear God, I don't know what's the matter with you. Yes, I do, and if I could fix it, I would, but I'm not licensed to do lobotomies. Christ, I can't do a blessed thing but stand on the sidelines wringing my hands until you fall flat on your face, and then run and pick you up and wash off the blood and wipe away the tears. Why? Why are you doing this to me?"

Judith looked sorrowful. "You sound like Mother when you say things like that. I'm not doing this to hurt you. I need him, and he needs me."

"Relationships based on need—"

"We're good for each other. Don't scold, Van. I can't stand it. We saw each other and the miracle happened. It's good and right. For the first time in years, I feel like I'm living."

"Is he going to defect?"

"Oh, no, of course not. Neither am I." Judith sighed. "I don't know how it's going to work out, only that it will. It has to."

"He's the man you danced with, the one with the message from Daddy. Isn't he?"

"Yes."

Vanessa wanted to say more, but she held herself back. She lit another cigarette and gazed into the muddy depths of her coffee cup.

"Don't be angry," Judith begged. "I don't think up these things deliberately to upset you, Van. I'm not smart enough. They just— happen."

"You're plenty smart. Don't run yourself down."

"Would you be happier if I, uh . . . if I stayed someplace else? A hotel?"

"Oh, for God's sake," Vanessa snapped. "What a stupid suggestion. I'm not angry. I just wish I knew why you keep doing this to yourself. Reckless endangerment, I call it. And so many of them are losers. You deserve better, Judy."

Judith hugged her. "I'm learning to recognize quality when I see it. He's different, Van. I wish you could meet him."

"Remember the time when you were seven years old and you made a parachute out of a tablecloth and jumped off the garage roof? You haven't changed. Still taking risks, just for the hell of it. I'll tell you, Judy, you make theater look tame. A decent writer could get ten plays out of your love life alone."

"I wouldn't watch them. I'm too busy living them."

Vanessa punched a cushion. "Here's some news you won't like. Mother and Preston are coming to the opening. I thought it was strange. She's never gone out of her way to see me in anything before. She said they were coming to London on business anyway."

Judith sat very still. "She must know about Sasha. Either Kenny told her, or someone else. It's me she's coming to see. I'm going to catch hell for this. Help me, Van. She doesn't know it's serious. We made it look like a casual fling. If they knew I was planning to see him again, they'd try and stop me."

"Oh, Judy. What a mess."

"I'm not afraid of being hurt, Van. You have to take a few risks in life, or you'll turn into a vegetable. Besides, there isn't anything that can happen to me that's worse than some of the things that have already happened. Don't worry. I know what I'm doing, honest."

The old refrain. Vanessa had heard it over and over again, through the succession of Judith's boyfriends, lovers, husbands, tragedies, triumphs. She manufactured a brave smile.

"All right, I believe you. Show me what you bought in Paris. I'm depending on you to shop for me while I'm here. My wardrobe is in rags and I haven't had time to do anything about it."

"Hang on to your soul, Denny O'Halloran," Megan Riley crooned. "Your body is gettin' weaker, but your spirit is growin' stronger. Remember our Lord? His own spirit was powerful enough to gather up the scattered atoms of his corpse and to make it live again, forever."

The stage was pitch black except for the cone of blue light that enveloped the actors.

"The pain," Denny groaned. "I've never known such pain."

"It's only the body livin' hard at the end, livin' so hard it hurts, fillin' itself with fifty or more years of livin'. It'll be over soon. You're gettin' older by the minute, Denny. Every second of pain is a whole year of your life. Your old wife is here, holdin' your hand. And the children you fathered those many years ago are standin' round your bed. Can you see them? They're old themselves, with lines in their faces. The little ones are playin' outside. For all you're in here dyin', it's still a lovely day, the last day of your life. The sun is doin' a roarin' trade out there, tradin' its light for flowers. The priest has paid his last call. Your sins are forgiven. To be sure, you didn't have that many, no more than the average man."

"But I'm dying—I died when I was still a lad, only twenty," Denny said.

Megan shook her head. "You dreamt it. The cell, the filth, H Block. All a dream."

"What about Ireland?"

"What about Ireland?" Megan asked kindly. "Nothin' changes in Ireland. Nothin' ever changes. Only the faces, the hands that hold the guns, the feet slitherin' through the darkness on some errand of peace or death. Which is it? Did anyone ever know? Part of the past, Denny. Leave it lay. How's the pain now?"

"Not so bad anymore. I'm just tired, like."

"You've a right. All that livin', all that history you're makin', compressin' it into a few minutes. It's hard work, livin'. Who decides the measure of a man's life? Someone, the Lord perhaps. Perhaps He holds His hands close together, or else He spreads them apart, as far as his arms can reach. The difference between twenty years or ninety, the sweep of those hands in the air, and empty space between them. A life span."

"Not so empty," Denny breathed. "I had a wife. . . ."

"Yes?" Megan said encouragingly. "What was her name?"

Denny crinkled his forehead, trying to remember. "Maura. Or Nora. Yes, Nora. And sons. Five of them. I was a good father to them, for all the times I cuffed their ears and they spoke back to me. But they found work, all of them. Honest work. And none of them, not one, ever put his hands on the cold steel of a gun. That was my doin', too."

"You've done well, Denny." Megan rocked him. "You can be proud of yourself. But it's time, my love. Time to say good-bye. Nora's weepin', and the boys, too. They don't know the sweetness in the body when the pain ends, finally. You try to tell them, but you can't. No matter. They'll learn it soon enough for themselves. It's time to leave them now. Your old man's body is too heavy for you, Denny. You're as light as thistledown, me darlin'. The chains can't hold you. The walls are like paper. You're through them, beyond them. Look over there. Do you see that meadow, Denny? Aw, Denny, you young rascal, I can hear you laughin' behind me. You can run faster than that, Denny. Faster! Look, now, we're nearly there. Take my hand and we'll run there together. Come on, now. We're nearly home."

The lights went out, then came up again on a tableau that mirrored Michelangelo's *Pietà*. Vanessa and the actor who was draped across her lap stayed frozen in position until the lights went down a second time, then they cleared the stage. A wardrobe assistant waited for Vanessa in the wings. Vanessa ripped off her garish blond wig and thin wrapper, fluffed her own short brown hair, and slipped on the black shift the girl held over her head. The actors were taking their places for the curtain call. Out in the house, the noise had started to build, not just thunderous applause but stamping feet, earsplitting whistles, raucous shouts, and cries of "Author!"

The actors filed on first, eight men made up to look like IRA Provisionals in Belfast's Maze Prison, the "Blanket Men" who refused to wear prison garb and daubed the walls of their cells with their own excrement.

They arranged themselves across the breadth of the stage of the Olivier Theatre in London's National Theatre complex on the south bank of the Thames. Then the two men in the center parted and Vanessa stepped between them. The applause and the shouting grew louder. She had given the audience a gallery of angry and weeping and pious Irish women. In the first act, wearing only the simple black dress and using a handful of props, Vanessa had played a grieving mother, a new bride, a teaching nun, a stern grandmother, a featherbrained mistress, a twelve-year-old schoolgirl, and a pregnant wife.

The entire second act took place in the hospital room of dying hunger striker Denny O'Halloran. In his ravings, he conjured up the prostitute Megan Riley. Megan twitted, mocked, seduced, and drove him mad. Vanessa had made up heavily for the part. She wore a frowsy blond wig and high-heeled black pumps, and a garish silk wrapper that occasionally fell open to reveal naked breasts and thighs. In the final scene, the seductress became the Virgin Mary. She led the weak and dying man in prayer and urged him to confess his sins, and then she held him in her arms as he expired.

The playwright, Les O'Breen, faked a reluctant entrance, allowing two actors who were his personal friends to drag him on from the wings. He joined the players who had brought his words to life.

He gave Vanessa a sloppy kiss on the cheek. "Lovely, darling. You had 'em in tears."

Vanessa gritted her teeth as the crowd gave O'Breen a thundering ovation, but her strong theatrical discipline kept her from announcing that she had rewritten the whole play. Les O'Breen had never seen the inside of any prison, certainly not the Maze. He had not spoken to any of the prisoners on H Block. In fact, he had never even been to Belfast. He was twenty-eight, a Cambridge drop-out who had persuaded his wealthy father to finance his first venture in the theater. Now people were calling him a genius.

Les urged Vanessa to take another solo bow. He escorted her down to the footlights, turned to her, and applauded her himself. She gave him a terse nod of acknowledgment and bowed deeply to the cheering audience once again.

"Christ," O'Breen chortled, "a fucking standing ovation."

Then Vanessa saw Judith in the third row, jumping up and down and applauding madly. Vanessa grinned broadly and threw her a big kiss.

In the box nearest the apron at stage right, Lydia and Preston Marlowe clapped enthusiastically as they beamed down at the stage.

"Good heavens, I'd forgotten how exhausting modern theater is," Lydia clucked. "Wouldn't the Senator turn over in his grave if he knew his granddaughter was making her living as a stripper?"

Preston chuckled. He was tall and gaunt, with a shock of wavy white hair, square black-framed glasses, and a disarmingly boyish grin that was the envy of many politicians. A man who normally favored bow ties, he looked perfectly at home in a tuxedo. "I imagine the Senator would have enjoyed the play immensely. Gosh, Vanessa was terrific, wasn't she? I didn't know she could look so beautiful."

"Vanessa was truly magnificent," Lydia agreed. "Of course, a little makeup, some pink lights, and the advantage of distance would make anyone look good, even Vanessa. Now, darling, when I'm ready to have my little talk with Judith, stay out of the way, will you? And if you can, try and keep Vanessa occupied. As you well know, she can't be trusted to leave her histrionics in the theater."

"Of course, my dear." The cast had vacated the stage. Members of the audience were starting to leave their seats. "Interesting." Preston stepped behind his wife's gilded chair. "Puts a whole new light on the Irish problem, don't you think?"

Lydia left her program under her seat. "Oh, I don't know. The sex lives of terrorists don't interest me very much, I'm afraid." Lydia joined the stream of playgoers heading toward the exits, and Preston trailed after her.

"I was so proud of you." Judith hugged her sister for the hundredth time. "Every time I see you, I'm impressed all over again with how good you are, but tonight— Oh, God, you were wonderful!"

In the ballroom of the Savoy Hotel, the opening-night party hosted by Lydia and Preston Marlowe was in full swing. Critics and friends mobbed Vanessa, showering her with compliments like handfuls of rice at a wedding. Vanessa was beaming, deliriously happy. Almost twenty years in the theater had not satisfied her hunger for praise and approval.

Judith scanned the crowd. "Wow! Mother isn't wasting her largess on just ordinary folk." The guests included some of the most distinguished actors and actresses in England, as well as a staggering number of titled personages, including Princess Margaret. Judith spotted John Mills talking to Sean Connery, and Derek Jacobi laughing with a woman she thought she ought to know. "Jesus, Van, this party is going to keep the society columnists busy for weeks."

"Check out Les," Vanessa said out of the corner of her mouth. "He looks like a well-fed snake basking on a hot rock." Les O'Breen certainly seemed to be enjoying the adulation and the champagne. Every time a waiter passed bearing a tray of brimming glasses, O'Breen helped himself to two.

"The power of my poetry doesn't really need all that overacting," the sisters heard him bawl. "Vanessa's Megan was marvelous, certainly, but not quite what I had in mind."

"What mind?" Vanessa grunted. "God, he's such an idiot. He's so stupid he doesn't even know we rewrote the whole play."

Judith laughed. "The perfect playwright for you, Van. No lines to learn. But tell me, what did Mother say? Did she like you? Was she shocked? I've avoided her so far."

Vanessa shrugged. "The usual faint praise. She said I had some nice moments—nice!—and that I seemed to have lost some weight. End of topic. Preston was more generous. He told me I looked marvelous, and then he asked me how I remembered all those lines. If I had a nickel for every person who's asked me that question—oh, look, there's Sir Ralph! Was he really there tonight?"

"Yes, of course. I saw him at intermission. Had to stop myself from asking for an autograph."

Vanessa slurped down her drink. "These people didn't come to see me. The only reason we had a full house tonight was because Mother sent out invitations to everybody and his orangutan. A command performance, with a bash at the Savoy to make it worth your while." She grabbed another drink from a passing tray.

"Don't be dumb, Van. The audience loved the play. I eavesdropped all over the place at intermission. Everyone was talking about you. Somebody called you the next Glenda Jackson. They loved you!"

Vanessa was still writhing on the crucifix of her own insecurity. "No wonder we sold out. O'Breen doesn't have enough friends to fill even one row. Oh, God, here comes Preston. What does he want?"

Preston smiled at them. "This is some party, isn't it? Vanessa." He grasped her shoulders firmly and rotated her one hundred and eighty degrees. "Do you see those folks over there?"

"The Oliviers! Them, too!" Vanessa exclaimed. "I can't believe they're here."

Preston chuckled. "Your mother and I have known them for years. Come on over and say hello. Excuse us, Judith."

Judith watched smiling as Vanessa and Preston made their way across the room. Then she felt a touch on her arm.

"Hello, darling. I think it's time we had a little talk, don't you?"

Judith steeled herself. "Can't it wait, Mother? This is Van's party, after all."

"I'm afraid not. Preston and I are leaving tomorrow night, and we have a thousand things to do before then. Our suite is right upstairs. I won't keep you long."

Judith permitted herself to be led. She knew she couldn't avoid this moment forever, but she had hoped to postpone it until she was a little drunker.

"You're looking well, dear," Lydia said as they stepped into the elevator. "You've put on a bit of weight. It's very becoming. You look less like a waif."

"Or a hungry hooker." Judith gave vent to an elaborate sigh. "Why this sudden obsession with weight, Mother? Vanessa's lost, I've gained. Who cares? You're maintaining, I see." She cast a quick glance over her mother's petite, slender figure. "You ought to tell the world how to do it. Gentle starvation on club soda and celery. Too bad we don't all have your strength of character."

Lydia led the way down the red-carpeted corridor and unlocked the door to her suite. "As bristly as porcupines, my two girls. At the ages of thirty-three and thirty-five, they are still stuck in that stage of adolescence where Mother can do nothing right. I wonder when they'll get over it?"

As Judith and Lydia entered the room, a man rose from the sofa and turned to them. "Good evening, Judith."

Judith stopped in her tracks. "Hi, Kenny," she said, recovering quickly. "How's Warsaw?"

"No change politically. Lonelier." Kenneth shrugged. He wore a dark gray suit and red tie. "Would you like a drink?"

"Need you ask?" Judith collapsed on the sofa. "But I'm not sure my duenna will allow it. Mother, may I?" She turned to look at her mother.

Lydia Lymond Marlowe gave a brief nod of assent as she lowered herself gracefully onto a straight-backed chair. She was wearing a floor-length gold sheath with a scoop neckline and long sleeves, and a stunning emerald necklace. God, Judith thought, she could be my sister. Lydia looked at least twenty years younger than her sixty-two years. An occasional face lift, stringent dieting, daily tennis, and semiannual visits to Elizabeth Arden kept her trim and lovely. Her hair was probably white under the honey-gold dye, but Judith was certain that only her mother's undertaker would know the truth.

As a child, Lydia Lymond had played amid the statues in the Capitol Rotunda. While she was waiting for her father to finish work in his office, she had raced alone down the long corridors outside the Senate chamber. Her father, Horace, was the son of a plumber who was also a Republican precinct captain in Philadelphia. The Republican machine in that city sent Horace to Congress when he was only twenty-five. He was elected to the Senate ten years later, and he served there for thirty years. Guests at the Lymond table had included Vice President Richard Nixon, John Foster Dulles, President Eisenhower's Secretary of State, and John's brother Allen, the nation's chief spy. General Douglas MacArthur was also a frequent visitor. From them, Lydia had learned about politics, war, and the art of compromise. She had also learned about the rampant evil that was Communism.

Horace Lymond had entered Congress a virtual pauper, a green young lawyer who had never pleaded a case. When he died forty years later, he had amassed a fortune, much of it in real estate. He confined his purchases to the area that was later enclosed by the Washington Beltway—a coincidence that did not pass unnoticed in the Washington press. The swamps and farmlands he owned were now covered with subdivisions, condominiums, millionaires' estates, federal office buildings, and even a secret military communications center. Apart from the trust he established for his granddaughters, Lydia was his only heir.

"If you think you need to fortify yourself with more alcohol in order to have a conversation with your own mother, go right ahead," Lydia said. "Ginger ale for me, please, Kenneth."

Judith took out her cigarettes. "Splurging a bit on the calories, aren't you, Ma? Bourbon, Kenny, and go easy on the ice. Let me guess why you're here." Her lighter flamed. She knew perfectly well that her mother detested cigarette smoke. "It's about the guy Kenny caught me screwing, the Russian. All right, I boobed. Bad girl, very naughty, won't happen again, so sorry. Anything else?"

"There are a few more items on the agenda." Lydia steeled herself against the cloud of smoke that drifted her way. "The gentleman in question." She reached for a manila folder that lay on the coffee table and opened it in her lap. "Aleksandr Nikolayevich Dmitrov, age forty-five, Moscow State University, Soviet Army, colonel. He has served with various diplomatic missions, often in politically sensitive areas: Kabul, Havana. There is no doubt that he works for the KGB, but in what capacity is not known. Certainly he is highly placed and well trusted. He might even be following in his father's footsteps. At Stalin's behest, General Dmitrov purged the military of spies and traitors in the late 1930s. He himself was executed in 1947. He was rehabilitated posthumously after Leonid Brezhnev came to power, and that's when young Aleksandr started his own rise within the KGB. Your lover, my dear, is the son of a murderer. And very likely a murderer himself."

Kenneth handed Judith a tumbler. The drink was strong, just what she needed, but she put her glass down after the first swallow. Suddenly she felt the need to stay alert and sober.

"That's all very interesting, Mother, but no longer a worry, since I am not likely to see the colonel again. He told me he was being called home, and I doubt I'll be returning to Warsaw before he leaves." She lifted her glass in Kenneth's direction. "The affair, alas, has ended."

They heard a knock at the door. Kenneth went to answer.

"Step aside, brother." Vanessa barged past him into the room. "I'm not letting Mother stick pins into Judy's hide tonight. This is my party, damn it!"

"Let her in, Kenneth." Lydia suppressed her annoyance at Preston. Really, he was not at all dependable.

"We were discussing my deplorable affair with Sasha." Judith patted the cushion beside her. Vanessa flopped down and glared at her mother and stepbrother. Kenneth had taken up a position behind Lydia's chair. "Kenny's playing bartender, and doing it very nicely. Mother's been reading horror stories about my lover boy from some file she conned away from the CIA. Ain't she terrific?"

Lydia sighed. "That's enough, Judith. I realize that you could go on in this vein all night, but I do not choose to waste time listening to your prattle. Colonel Dmitrov is a powerful and dangerous man, not some low-level operative who makes a practice of seducing the bored and foolish wives of certain highly placed diplomats."

Judith was outraged. "Are you saying that he's too good for me?"

"In a sense, yes, that is exactly what I'm saying. They could have dispatched any reasonably handsome and virile young stud to find out Byron Harcourt's shirt size. Or"—she shot a baleful glance at Kenneth—"my son-in-law's preferences in sweets. The point is, why? Why did they roll out a big gun like Dmitrov and point him at you? Didn't you wonder about that?"

"Not at all." Judith tossed her head. "I was too busy enjoying myself. I have to say, of all the men I've known, he was—"

"No doubt," Lydia cut her off. "But while you were having fun, you were also putting a good many careers at risk. Kenneth and I have taken great pains to keep this story from getting back to Washington. If it does, Kenneth will be finished in the State Department. His wife consorting with a colonel in the KGB, in his own apartment!"

"But not his bed," Judith murmured.

Lydia pressed on. "And Preston. Judith, it won't hurt you to know that there are changes ahead in the administration. If our present Secretary of State resigns, and many expect him to do so shortly, Preston will undoubtedly be chosen to succeed him. We cannot afford to jeopardize that appointment. Your 'deplorable affair' may have ended, but the repercussions will still be felt. And so I am asking you this question, and I am begging you to answer me honestly and straightforwardly. What did he want? What did Dmitrov really want from you?"

Laughing, Judith threw up her hands. "What do all men want? Despite Kenny's opinion to the contrary, Mother, some men find me attractive and desirable. Circumstances threw us together. He comforted me after I'd been assaulted. We had dinner. We talked. We went to bed. Why does it have to be anything more than that?"

"Because of who this man is, and what he does. Did he say anything about me? Anything at all? Please, Judith, I must know."

Judith looked amazed. "No, he didn't talk about you. He has his own mother to talk about."

Vanessa, who had been listening in silence, suddenly blurted, "I think you ought to tell her, Judy. She has a right to know."

Judith turned on her. "Van, I thought you were on my side!"

"I am, but this is serious. It concerns the whole family. Not just you, but me and Mother, too."

"Thank you, Vanessa." Lydia's gaze was steady. "Judith?"

Judith took a long swallow of bourbon. "He said—oh, hell, this is so boring. I mean who cares about a dead man? He said that Daddy—that Phil was dying and wanted to see me before he went. That's all. I told him to forget it. We dropped the subject and went on to other things."

Lydia's hands tensed, becoming claws. For a half a minute she looked every year of her age. "What else, Judith? What else did he say about Phillip?"

"Not much." Judith swirled the ice cubes in her glass. "He's old. He's got a bad heart. He doesn't take care of himself. He's going to die soon. That's about it."

"And he wants to see you."

"Is that so strange?" Judith lifted her head. "I am his daughter."

"So is Vanessa his daughter. Why didn't they approach Vanessa? Why you?"

"Because I was handy, I guess." Judith shrugged. "Right there in Warsaw. Why not?"

"So." Lydia sat back. Her hands relaxed. "After twenty-five years, Phillip has finally remembered that he fathered two daughters. How touching. How pathetic. And you, Judith, I suppose you're planning to visit Moscow? To see both your father and Colonel Dmitrov? Why not? You're probably curious about Phillip. But I would advise you to remember what he did, how he betrayed his country and his family, deserted us, abandoned us."

"Poor us," Vanessa said under her breath. "Where would we have been without Granddaddy's millions?"

Lydia's head came around slowly. "No, Vanessa, I am not talking about money. I am talking about the devastating experience of losing the man I loved." Her lower lip trembled, and she swallowed hard. "I loved Phillip. I thought he loved me. He was—oh, God, he loved you girls so.

I . . . we . . . our life was as perfect as life can be. Your father—Phillip—he wrecked a marriage and a wonderful career and the lives of four people, including himself, not for idealism, not for money, but because—" Her hands flew to her mouth and she closed her eyes while silent sobs shook her petite frame. Tears ravaged her makeup, but she did not wipe them away.

Judith and Vanessa watched in silent horror as their mother's self-control crumbled. In an instant, she looked decades older. Kenneth stood paralyzed behind her chair. None of them had ever seen Lydia Lymond cry.

"Mother . . ." Kenneth leaned over her, but Lydia rebuffed him with a gesture.

"No," she croaked, "you have to know, all of you. Phillip—oh, God, how can I say this?" Lydia took a deep breath and straightened her spine. Her eyes were dark with sorrow. "Your father was a homosexual. Phillip had love affairs with men, even while he was pretending to be my husband and fathering two innocent little girls. I never dreamed, never even suspected. I don't know when the Russians recruited him. After we were married, I suppose. They threatened to expose him. He used me as a front, even as he used the Senator to further his career. And when the FBI became suspicious, Phillip defected. He left us without a word, without even a good-bye."

The heavy brocade curtains muffled the roar of traffic down in the street. A single horn blared, and was silent.

"I couldn't believe it when they told me. An agent came to see me with the news of his defection, and the next day it was all over the papers. I searched your father's desk before the FBI could impound his papers. And that's when I found the photographs." Lydia squeezed her eyes closed. Tears seeped out from under her eyelids. "You'll never know what that was like. The horror I felt, looking at that—that pornography. The sickness. Those pictures meant that everything we had shared was a lie. Our love. Our marriage. His love for you. Lies! I destroyed the photographs. I suppose it was a crime, but I couldn't let anyone see them. I didn't want my children to know what their father was really like. The only thing that stopped me from killing myself was you girls. You needed me, and that need kept me alive. Yes, I forbade you to speak of him, to ask questions. Is it any wonder? The truth was so ugly, and I felt so . . . besmirched by it."

Judith groped for Vanessa's hand. They didn't look at each other. Their mother's agony commanded their complete attention.

Lydia stood up. "Judith, I beg you not to go to Moscow, to stay away from him. No creature on earth is so despicable, so morally repellent as

Phillip Abbott. He deserves to die horribly, slowly, without the comfort of family and friends. Please, let him die without tainting us again." Walking slowly, like an old woman, she crossed the floor and entered her bedroom. The door closed behind her.

Judith and Vanessa and Kenneth stayed still for a long time, shocked into immobility.

Kenneth broke the silence. "I guess I'll go up to my room. It's late." The women gave no indication that they had heard him. "Judith, would you mind stopping in to see me before you leave? I'm in room two forty."

After he had gone, Judith broke down and began to weep. Vanessa, dry-eyed, held her sister in her arms for a long time. Finally Judith straightened up and dried her tears.

"God, we're such a mess, aren't we, Van?" she sighed. "What a way to open a show. I think Mother has just upstaged you. I'd better talk to Kenny. I owe him that much. Wait for me downstairs?"

The two sisters hugged each other again. Then, after a farewell glance at their mother's door, they left the room.

Kenneth's door was slightly ajar. Judith tapped twice and pushed it open. Kenneth was sitting on the bed, fully dressed. He stood as she entered.

"What's this, a new open-door policy?" she said with manufactured brightness.

Kenneth gave her a steady look. "I'm on my way back to Washington, Judith. I've been pulled out of Warsaw, reassigned to Africa. Zambia. It's crazy, isn't it? I mean, here I am, a specialist in Eastern European affairs, and . . ." He lifted his hands and let them fall. "But you have to expect that sort of thing when you work for the government, I guess."

Judith shook her head. "Byron must have given you a big fat F on your report card. I'm sorry, Kenny."

"Things could be worse." Kenneth managed a weak smile. "This assignment isn't really a demotion. More like a sideways move, a slap on the wrist. If I do a good job, I'll probably get a better posting next time. What I'd like to know is, will you come with me?"

Judith blinked. "I can't believe you're serious. After what happened—"

"I'll take my share of the blame for that. I'm sorry. I know what you're like, and I know I'm the wrong man for you, but I still love you. Will you?"

Judith wandered over to the window and pushed the curtains aside. The Strand was clearing out as the after-theater crowd and the party-goers from the Savoy made their way back to their homes.

"That's downright nice of you, Ken doll. I don't know what to say. I'm tempted to make a joke about your feeling right at home in Africa with the superb horns I put on you, but I know it's not funny. I wish you hadn't walked in on us like that. Things aren't really ugly until they rear up and smack you in the face. Adultery is ugly, isn't it, especially if the victim is you and the perp is me? I'm sorry it happened the way it did. That's the best apology I can muster and still stay honest."

"It's a fine apology. Will you come? Please say yes."

Judith considered the invitation for a long moment, then she laughed. "Hell, why not? I've got nothing better to do in the near future. Besides, I've never been to Upper Volta."

"Zambia," Kenneth corrected gently.

"Are you sure you know what you're doing, Kenny?" Judith sounded skeptical. "This is your chance to consign me to the junk heap of history. God knows, you have good reason."

Kenneth's gaze was direct and earnest. "Strange as it seems, I am not ready to give up on this marriage."

Judith smiled at him. "Well, bully for you, old boy. Maybe there's hope for you yet. All right, my love, in exchange for this stirring vote of confidence, I will promise to do my best to keep my nose from dripping into the soup at diplomatic banquets and to choose my lovers from among the ranks of the socially acceptable, which is to say, Western and white. It's the best I can do, considering the strained state of our love life."

Kenneth flinched. "I was hoping we could make some changes in that department. I've been under a good bit of stress lately. We both have. The pace in Zambia should be a lot slower. We can start over." He gave a nervous laugh. "Maybe the lover you choose will be your own husband."

"That would be different," Judith said with a smile. "Almost unheard of these days."

Kenneth approached her and took her hand. "May I—may I telephone you at Vanessa's tomorrow?"

"If you like. Not too early, though. Actresses need their beauty sleep. Good night, Kenny." Judith gave him a warm kiss on the mouth, and made her way to the door. "God damn Vanessa. If only she hadn't made me tell Mother about Phillip. I have no intention of going to Moscow."

"She did the right thing." Kenneth followed her. "It's better that we know the whole story."

"Good old American need-to-know." Suddenly angry, Judith turned to him. "What's so awful about ignorance?" she demanded. "Can't we let anything just happen without analyzing it and interpreting it? A love affair? A dying queer?" She gave her head a frustrated shake. "It's all part of life, Kenny. Ordinary, everyday events. Does everything have to be more than what it really is?" She waited a moment for Kenneth to reply, but he remained silent, watching her with an expression of desperate longing in his eyes. Wishing to escape it, Judith ran out of the room without saying anything else.

       The next morning Kenneth found his mother-in-law seated at the writing desk in her suite, responding to an invitation that had arrived in an envelope bearing an embossed crest and a red wax seal.

"Judith has agreed to accompany me to Lusaka," he announced. "She's not planning to go to Russia."

"Thank God." Lydia signed her name with a flourish and capped her fountain pen. "That would be a disaster." She fanned the note in the air for a moment, then folded it in half and stuffed it into an envelope. "It's like one of those awful horror films, where a withered hand reaches up out of the grave and grabs you. Why couldn't Phillip just stay dead?" She tossed the note aside and slammed the palms of her hands down on the desk. "Why is he bothering Judith? I hate him. I hate him for doing this to me."

Kenneth sat down on the sofa. "And you're not too fond of me right now, I'll wager."

"I'm furious with you." Spinning around, her head lowered, Lydia fixed him with her iciest stare. "You should have told me about Dmitrov at once, before things got out of hand. You are fairly intelligent, Kenneth, even bright, but you're no match for Judith. Which is why your marriage was such a terrible mistake. You have no control over her, because you don't have her respect. She looks at you and she sees a kid with thick horn-rims and buck teeth."

Kenneth looked affronted. "I have never worn horn-rims. And my teeth have been straight for years."

"Believe me, she hasn't noticed." Lydia began to pace. "I will never understand, never comprehend what made you do it. Marry Judith! It was a breach of trust, a betrayal, an act of supreme stupidity that I will never, never forgive."

"So you've told me," Kenneth said softly. "Many times."

Lydia expelled a long breath. "But the damage is done, and we must live with it. As we must live with that bastard Phillip Abbott, until he dies or his keepers decide to quarantine him." Her pacing brought her back to the desk. She picked up her gold fountain pen, a gift from her father on her thirteenth birthday. She studied it for a moment without really seeing it and threw it down again. "That wretched, horrible scandal. The timing on this couldn't be worse. If the press picks this up, Preston will never be confirmed."

"Surely this won't touch Dad." Kenneth twisted around and looked at the door to Preston's room. "Is he there?"

"No," Lydia said. "He had a breakfast meeting with Mrs. Thatcher."

"Well, nobody could question his loyalty. Or yours." Kenneth followed Lydia with his gaze as she started to move again. "If they were giving Patriot of the Year awards, you'd win, hands down."

"Yes," Lydia said bitterly. "And why? Because I have worked like a demon to lift my name and my reputation out of the gutter, to clean off the mud that son of a bitch splashed on me, to rehabilitate myself in the eyes of my father's friends and colleagues, to gain the respect of my party and my president. And as hard as I have worked on my own behalf, I have worked harder for Preston. I built him up brick by brick, but every time somebody mentions Phillip Abbott's name, the structure teeters. Can you imagine, the Secretary of State's stepdaughter ferrying back and forth to Moscow to visit her real father, a defector! And like it or not, I *was* the defector's wife. That is too close to Preston not to damage him. What an intolerable situation!"

Lydia Marlowe drew her tiny hands into fists and beat helplessly at empty air.

"Why, why, why didn't that wretched pervert die then!"

CHAPTER 15

Huntingdon County, Pennsylvania: May 1982

*T*he gray Oldsmobile passed the end of the driveway three times, but Owen Adair kept the spray attachment of his hose trained on his roses. He wondered if he should run inside, bar the doors, and get out his gun. Finally the car turned in and parked behind Owen's Ford. The driver stepped out. He stood for a moment rubbing the small of his back and squinting at the tidy backyard, the trim lawn, the masses of peony and iris blooming in the English-style borders.

Owen's heartbeat decelerated. His greeting was gruff, concealing his fright. Moments like this made him realize how much he valued his little, self-contained existence. "Were you really lost or just casing the joint?"

Owen's visitor laughed. "To be honest, I couldn't believe my eyes. This place looks like a honeymoon retreat. You haven't gone and gotten married again, have you, Owen?" The man advanced, his hand extended. They shook hands, and the warmth they had shared in the distant past returned. "You're looking well. How have the nuns been treating you?"

Owen turned his sprayer back on the roses. "Not too bad. We have our disagreements, of course. When I taught John Donne last year, we spent two classes discussing the various aspects of carnal and spiritual love. The girls had a grand time, but the chairman of my department gave me the Man of the World speech—'You're a man of the world, Mr. Adair, and I am sure that you look upon deviant behavior with an indulgent eye, but our young ladies are unspoiled and unsophisticated.' You can fill in the rest. Some of her unspoiled darlings would hump the belfry on top of the administration building if they could climb that high. And she knows it."

Owen released his finger from the sprayer's trigger. "Just passing, are you, Billy?"

Billy Whistle smiled. "I might be."

"You're the only man I know who would take a long drive on a warm Saturday wearing a three-piece suit and a necktie and keep his shirt collar buttoned. Don't tell me you were in the neighborhood. Saint Theresa's isn't in the neighborhood of anything. Ask my unspoiled young ladies."

Whistle sighed deeply. "I never expected you to end up in a place like this. A Catholic women's college in the middle of nowhere. I didn't know they still made them."

"A rare find," Owen admitted. He turned off the water, detached the sprayer, rinsed it, and propped it upside down on the back step to drain. "But it has its advantages. I'm not so overwhelmed by work that I don't have time to pursue my own private interests."

"Which are?" Whistle followed him into the kitchen. In contrast to the neatness of the outdoors, the interior was a shambles. Books were everywhere, heaped on the kitchen table and the counters, stacked on the windowsills, spilling off the chairs.

"John Milton. There hasn't been a good biography for a while. I've taken it upon myself to write one. Decent old boy, Milton. He had a few words to say about those who stalk the corridors of power in Washington: 'I did but prompt the age to quit their clogs/By the known rules of ancient liberty/When straight a barbarous noise environs me/Of owls and cuckoos, asses, apes, and dogs.' Coffee or whiskey, or a combination of the two?"

Whistle laughed. "Just water. Doctor's orders. I'm supposed to stay away from alcohol, caffeine, and nicotine."

"What's left?" Ignoring him, Owen took a bottle down from the cupboard over the sink, tipped it over a pair of pony glasses, added ice, and handed one to his guest. "Sex?"

"With caution." Whistle sipped, and smiled. "Why is it that your Scotch always tastes better than anyone else's?"

"Out here it's the ice. My water comes from five hundred feet below the ground. Let's go into the living room. I'll clear off a chair for you."

The living room was small and dark, its windows shaded by the thick screen of hemlocks that grew at the front of the house, concealing it from the eyes of passersby. Every horizontal surface was cluttered with books, file cards, newspapers, scholarly journals, and phonograph records. Owen swept a pile of blue examination booklets off an armchair and motioned his guest to be seated. He perched himself on the bench in front of an old pump organ. A book of Bach preludes sat on the music rack.

"How are things back at the shop?" he asked.

"The same as when you left, only different. There aren't too many people left from our generation. The young ones are faster and meaner, but no smarter. If you mentioned John Milton to most of them, they'd ask you what department he worked in and what his GS rating was. I hold my breath waiting for something to go wrong, and when it does, I put on my overalls and repair it as quickly as I can before the leak turns into a torrent. I'm tired, but I don't have your extracurricular interests, and so I'll probably stick with it until they push me out. And then one bright, sunny morning, I'll eat a bullet for breakfast, and everyone will shake their heads wisely and say, 'See, Whistle wasn't as tough as he pretended to be.' In fact, I'm only as tough as I need to be. I envy you, Owen."

"Sure you do." Owen grinned. "But you'd rather die than live like this. Okay, Billy, let's have it. You didn't drive way up here from Washington just to cry on my shoulder. A phone call would have brought us up to date quicker."

Whistle raised his empty glass. "I might as well have another, so long as you're twisting my arm."

"I'll bring the bottle."

"No, two's my limit."

Owen refreshed their drinks and resumed his seat. "I imagine you're driving back today, so let's not waste any more time."

Whistle nodded, pleased that they had gotten through the preliminaries so quickly. "This is no more than a whisper, and it might be false, but the story is that Phillip Abbott's dying."

"Is he? It's about time." Owen pulled a pack of cigarettes out of his shirt pocket. Somewhat absently, he offered it to Whistle, who waved it away.

"Long past time for some, I imagine. His wife, for instance. Yes, the man is dying, and he's asked to see his daughters before he goes. For reasons we don't understand, the Russians are cooperating. They've approached the younger one, Judith. She married her stepbrother, remember? Just so happens she's learning Russian in her spare time."

Owen sucked on his cigarette. "What else do you have?"

"That's it. I can't pursue the matter. Preston Marlowe is on the White House's short list for Secretary of State, and I don't want to stir up any dirt that would hurt his chances. I certainly don't want to upset Lydia Lymond. I don't look too good with deep scratches all over my face and torso. But I don't have to tell you about Lydia. You've already been blooded."

"I see." The long ash from Owen's cigarette fell between his knees and vanished into the grubby patterned carpet. "You've come here because an official probe is out, and an unofficial one is risky, so you're hoping to persuade me to get my banner out of mothballs and limp back into the fray. No, thanks, Billy. As far as I'm concerned, Phillip Abbott is deader than John Milton. I'm not eager to exhume that particular stinking corpse."

Billy Whistle leaned forward, elbows on his knees. "That case put a big black smudge on your record right at the start of your career. If you hadn't been so all-fired brilliant and indispensable, it would have ruined you. You learned your lesson and you never made another slipup, but I gather you've never forgotten, either. I'll bet you still have nights when you sit in this chair drinking your Scotch and wonder how he could have operated so well, and for such a long time, and with such damaging effect, without anyone spotting him. The big question was, and still is, who? Who ran him? Who protected him and helped him, and who pulled his nuts out of the fire in the nick of time?"

Owen set his glass down on the organ, on a small round shelf designed to hold a candle. "To tell you the truth, Billy, I don't ask myself any of those questions. Because I'm not interested in the answers. And that's that. Did I tell you I'm learning Greek? I'm hoping to start translating the *Iliad* next summer. That ought to keep me busy until they paint my face with makeup and dress me in one of those blue suits that split up the back."

"Lydia won't tolerate the Agency nosing in, pestering her precious daughters." Billy went right on as though Owen hadn't spoken. "But I would dearly like to know why the Russians are suddenly getting sentimental in Abbott's old age. Why, after twenty-five years of denying him access to Westerners, are they not only permitting but encouraging a visit from one of the girls? It must mean that the person or network that worked with Abbott is no longer in place. Maybe they're all dead. But who were they? Either Abbott is no longer a danger to them, or there's another, more pressing reason, and something they need more than secrecy. The Agency wants to know what that could be."

Owen shrugged. "If the Russians won't let Abbott out of Moscow, they must want any communication between him and his daughter to be under their control. The girl could be in considerable danger. But I don't see how they can touch her without creating an international incident of phenomenal proportions. It's crazy. She's the stepdaughter of the almost–Secretary of State. It doesn't make any sense."

"Maybe not. But it still might be worth pursuing. For someone who has the time and the inclination, that is. And the anonymity."

"Damn you." Owen's face flushed. "Damn you for playing me like a kitten with a ball of yarn. Tweak the string and I pounce, is that it? I'm not your errand boy anymore, Billy. I'm nobody's lackey. I don't take orders from anybody these days but Sister Mary Evangelist. That woman could get the pope himself to turn somersaults."

"Owen," Billy said gently, "I'm not ordering, or even asking for a favor. I merely thought I'd pass along the information. Do with it what you will. You're under no obligation to me or the Agency. It's probably nothing. An old man's dying wish, and he's so far gone, they didn't see any reason to turn him down. It's nice to know the Soviet bureaucrats are sprouting wings and halos these days. Makes a change. Well, I'll push off." He stood. "Chew it over, see how you like it, and if you decide to spit it out and forget it, I won't blame you. You were a green kid when it happened. You did your best."

"Maybe that's why they picked me for the job," Owen charged, "because I was so green. They thought they could rely on me to screw it up."

"Maybe." Billy kept his tone neutral.

"My inexperience didn't mess me up and you know it. I was tied hand and foot. I couldn't move. With all the obstructing of justice going on, J. Edgar himself couldn't have cracked that case."

"Hoover knew his limitations," Billy Whistle said with a reminiscent smile. "He wasn't averse to sweeping unpleasant matters under the rug, and national security be damned. Well, so long, Owen. You're pretty comfortable here. I don't blame you for not wanting to budge. Cultivate your garden, keep the mind agile, don't let the rot set in. I won't give anyone your regards. You haven't seen me."

Owen walked his visitor to his car and saw him off. When he returned to his living room, he noticed a sheet of paper lying on the cushion of the chair Billy had occupied. It was an update on the Abbott girls. Judith was a Marlowe again, by marriage this time. Her husband had been assigned to the American embassy in Warsaw before moving to Lusaka, Zambia. No children. Some reports from Poland of Judith's erratic behavior: drinking, infidelity. Vanessa lived in London, worked in the theater, highly respected as an actress. Owen studied the paper for two minutes, committing it to memory, then he tossed it into the empty fireplace and touched it with a lighted match. Not that anyone would have found it in this mess, but old habits died hard.

Lydia's girls . . .

Owen Adair had first seen Lydia Lymond Abbott twenty-five years ago, in 1956, a week after Phillip Abbott's defection. Lydia had an intellect that would have made a Jesuit's head spin, if he could manage the double trick of taking his eyes off her lovely face and ignoring the graceful arrangement of curves and angles below. And when it came to her daughters, Lydia was a lioness defending her cubs.

"Just what is it that you want to know, Mr. Adair? I have two terribly upset children who have lost their father. They need me. I'll give you exactly two minutes."

"Don't hold out on me, Mrs. Abbott. We believe your husband may have had some—ah, strange friendships. You're obliged to tell me everything you know about anybody he was seeing."

The second interview took place after the initial shock of both Phillip Abbott's defection and the discovery of his homosexual proclivities had worn off. They sat in the drawing room of her father's mansion on M Street. Lydia wore a high-necked white blouse and a straight black skirt slit to the knee. Modest, less daring than today's liberated nuns. But Lydia was no nun. She leaned forward in her chair, intercepting a beam of sunlight. She sparkled like gold. But she was iron.

"Let me tell you something, Mr. Adair. My first obligation is to protect my children from further taint of scandal. They will have to live with the knowledge that their father was a traitor, but I will not have them thinking of him as a pervert as well. If the merest whisper of his unsavory affairs reaches my children or the press, I will hold you directly responsible. I will destroy you. Is that clear? Don't underestimate me because I'm a woman."

He remembered his reply: "That's a mistake no Irishman would make, Mrs. Abbott. We know better."

And Lydia's: "You patronize me at your own risk, Mr. Adair."

The blue books were waiting, fifty-two final exams from the three sections of English he had taught that semester: freshman composition, Milton and the Seventeenth Century, and The English Novel From Defoe to Dickens. Except for two or three, their essays would be unintelligible, barely literate, superficial, and completely devoid of sense.

If he started on them now, he could be on a plane to London by tomorrow night.

The man who stepped into Vanessa's dressing room was in his mid-fifties, not tall but well-built, with a full head of graying hair and startling black eyebrows.

"Miss Marlowe? From the way the young lady announced me on the telephone, you're probably expecting Fred Astaire, but my name is Adair and I'm a terrible dancer."

Vanessa swung around on the stool in front of the makeup mirror. "She never gets the names right. She also said you were a friend of Billy Whimple. She meant Whistle, right? Good old Uncle Billy. I haven't seen him in years. Do you work for him?"

"We share a common interest. He writes poetry in his spare time. I teach it."

"Take a seat." Vanessa gestured toward a tubular chrome chair with orange plastic cushions. "You're staring. What's the matter? I guess you weren't sure which of the ladies in *Troubles* to expect."

"You're right." Owen threw his trench coat over the back of the chair and sat. He dropped his tweed hat onto the floor at his feet. "You're lovelier than any of them."

Vanessa's smile was wary. "I'm not Irish, but I know blarney when I hear it."

She was thirty-five, but in her baggy sweater and tight faded jeans, she looked like a teenager. Her short brown hair curled damply around her scrubbed face. She smelled of soap. Her feet, propped on the rung of the stool on which she sat, were bare, slender, and powerful-looking. She had an ideal actor's face, mobile and highly expressive, with a broad forehead, strong chin, and large eyes. Not a beauty like her mother, but pleasing to behold.

"If you know Uncle Billy, then you've probably met my mother." Vanessa picked up a brush and began to comb out the wig she had worn as Megan. The short, irritated strokes were a warning, but Owen wasn't sure what she was warning him away from.

"I have," he admitted.

"I thought so. I can always tell. I don't like comparisons, not when I suffer by them. My sister got the looks. Some say she got the talent, too. I just struggle along with what's left."

Owen sat back, amazed by her bitterness. "I assure you, Miss Marlowe, I meant no unkindness by staring. If I was rude, forgive me. In truth, I was thinking how lovely you are up close, far more beautiful than you are onstage."

"Don't patronize me," she snapped. "Don't you dare patronize me! I don't stand for that from my mother, her fancy friends, or anybody else."

He sat quietly for a moment while he wondered how to salvage the situation. Vanessa continued to brush the wig with unnecessary vigor. Owen cursed Billy's report as too cursory and brief. He might have warned Owen that he would be walking into a briar patch.

Owen looked around. The room was small, garishly lit with fluorescent tubes overhead and incandescent bulbs around the makeup mirror. A glimpse of white tile through the door to the left of the dressing table indicated a bathroom. On hooks along one wall hung Vanessa's costumes, the black dress and the gaudy silk dressing gown. A few dog-eared greeting cards and congratulatory telegrams were stuck to the mirror with cellophane tape. Behind the wig form on the dressing table stood a bouquet of fading roses.

"I'm remiss," Owen said in a conciliatory tone. "I should have brought you flowers. I'm afraid I'm not up on protocol. I've never visited an actress in her dressing room before."

Vanessa arranged the wig on the Styrofoam form and secured it with a couple of lethal-looking pins. Owen felt his own scalp tingle. "I'd take you to the green-room bar for a drink," she said, "but the din gets on my nerves. What did you think of the play? And don't you dare lie to me."

"You were wonderful," Owen said simply. "You reminded me of so many women I've known, Irish women, strong and beautiful no matter what their age. My mother, for one. You brought her back to me. Thank you for that. I can't recall when I've been so moved in a theater."

Vanessa ducked her head and scratched her foot. "Thanks." Owen permitted himself a quick smile. She was ready to come to the treaty table.

He said, "I'm afraid the play itself didn't come up to—"

"Don't fart around." Her head came up. "You thought it was terrible, a self-indulgent piece of confessional excess that would earn Mr. O'Breen a failing grade from you and every other English teacher you know. Isn't that what you want to say?"

Owen laughed. "Something along those lines, and I couldn't have phrased it better. Your speeches . . . I don't suppose you wrote them yourself, did you?"

Vanessa flushed. "How did you know?"

"They didn't fit. In fact, they were too good. And the cadences sounded like you, the way you talk offstage."

"I didn't write them, not really. I reported. Before we started rehearsing, I spent a couple of weeks in Northern Ireland, talking to women, listening to them. Megan was a whore in Derry. She wouldn't sleep with Protestants, no matter what they paid her."

"How could she tell?"

"Beats me." Vanessa pulled on some white athletic socks and a pair of worn running shoes. "But she knew. She could spot them by their accents, tell exactly what neighborhood they came from. She fell down on the wealthy types, though. Not that she had too many of those. A lah-di-dah university accent sounds the same whether it's Catholic or Protestant.

She had an altar in her room, a picture of the Sacred Heart on top of the television with a row of votive candles in red holders burning in front of it. When I'm doing Megan, I picture that altar."

She tidied up the table, wiping off the jars, shaking the brushes free of powder, capping the tubes and the pencils and the little pots of color. When that was done, she stowed everything in its special niche in a large black case that looked like a tool chest. The leather was scuffed, the handles worn.

"You've been at this a long time, haven't you?" Owen said. "That bag has seen a lot of wear."

"Oh, it's been to all sorts of interesting places. I filmed a thing for Granada in the Outer Hebrides last fall. Christ, it was cold. I never wanted to leave the dressing room."

Owen took a breath. Now or never. "I saw you for the first time when you were about ten. But you won't remember me. It was too long ago."

Vanessa gazed harder at him. In her mind, she peeled away the layers of age from his face as she might peel away layers of makeup from her own. She erased the tired lines around his mouth and the pouches under his eyes. His brows were black, which meant that his graying hair would have been black also, blue-black and shiny and full. Twenty-five years ago he would have been in his late twenties, slender and darkly handsome. She continued to stare, and finally recognition came.

"You came to our house," she said slowly. "I remember you. First you came with another man, then you came alone to talk to Mother. I listened from the other side of the door, in the dining room. Then Granddaddy came in and he started shouting. It was right after my father—after Phillip—went away." The corners of her mouth dipped down, and she shook her head. "Don't you people ever give up? Thanks for stopping by, Mr. Adair, but I don't want to talk to you anymore."

"Miss Marlowe—"

"If you're not out of here in thirty seconds, I'll call the guard and have you thrown out. You can't let it drop, can you? You're ridiculous. Pathetic. Look at yourself. You've grown old persecuting us, and you still haven't sense enough to quit."

Owen stayed seated. "We never persecuted you. We had to know who your father was seeing, what sort of activities he engaged in."

"We didn't know anything about his 'activities.' The part of him that was a traitor had nothing to do with us. We were his children, his wife. We were the victims, not you. Whatever secrets he gave away are old hat now. The world has changed. Half the people in it weren't even alive twenty-five years ago. So why don't you go away and leave us alone?"

"Because there is a truth somewhere that has never come out. Twenty-five years ago, I was assigned to find that truth, bring it to light. But it's still hidden. Who helped him? Are those persons still in place? I need to know. For my own self-satisfaction, I want to know how he worked it, how he got away with it for so many years without anyone suspecting. I believe we would have found the answer if your grandfather hadn't stepped in with his charges of harassment and villainy. I certainly did not enjoy questioning your mother. She's a hell of a woman, but back then she was shocked and distraught and angry, because the man she loved had betrayed her. I felt sorry for her, and for you and your sister, but I had a job to do."

Vanessa pulled herself up, eyes glittering. "Are you saying now that Granddaddy had something to do with Phil's defection? Because if you are—"

"No, no." Owen shook his head. "Senator Lymond loathed the Communists as much as any of us did back then. I'd stake my life that he wasn't a traitor. But he enjoyed a lot of power in Washington, and I use 'enjoy' in both senses of the word. He had it, and he delighted in using it. The scandal barely touched him, because he did his damnedest to deflect it. By protecting his daughter, he also protected himself. He was elected to another term in the Senate that fall, and he won it by a ridiculously wide margin. But that doesn't change the fact that he sidelined our investigation." Owen patted the side pocket of his jacket and brought out a bruised pack of cigarettes. "You've heard from your father, haven't you? You or your sister."

"So you know about that." Vanessa took the cigarette he offered, a sign that she was willing to grant him a momentary if grudging truce. "He's old, he's sick, he's dying. Maybe he just wants to say he's sorry. Well, I don't want to hear it. I've hated him for too many years, and I don't forgive easily."

Owen's lighter flared twice. "What about your sister?"

Vanessa lifted her chin and sent a stream of smoke toward the ceiling. "You're on the right track, but a little slow off the mark, Mr. Adair. She's on her way to Moscow right now."

"What?! Is she going to see him?"

"That's the idea. He sent a message, an oral one. Maybe he's ready for a deathbed confession." She shrugged. "I don't know."

"When is she coming back?"

"I have no idea. Knowing Judy, she might never come back. My little sister is unpredictable. Not like me. All it takes to make me lose my temper is for someone to mention my old man. I don't care if you're a reporter or a teacher or a down-and-out retired spook who's still dreaming about the one that got away. You've committed the unpardonable sin. Now, if you'll excuse me, I'm getting out of this place. My working day ended an hour ago." Vanessa stubbed out the cigarette. She slipped into her raincoat and pulled an oversized beret down over her ears. "Leave it alone, Mr. Adair. Take up fishing. Learn to golf. My father isn't going to live forever. Let someone else worry about him."

"I'm not as old as I look, Miss Marlowe."

"Don't make me laugh. You have the eyes of a man who's a hundred and ten. Let me guess. The outfit you worked for sucked you dry, then they nudged you out of the way, didn't they?"

Owen Adair took a deep breath. "Something like that."

"And now you're back in harness. One last fling. For what? Old times' sake? You don't owe them anything."

"For myself, Miss Marlowe. Because I care about the truth."

"Is it going to set you free? Or any of us? I doubt it. The truth is a bloody great two-edged sword. It liberates some and decapitates others. In the wrong hands it can be lethal. As you bloody well know."

She strode out, leaving the door open. Owen finished his cigarette and turned out the lights. A taxi was parked in the cab stand in front, and as it carried him across Waterloo Bridge, he glanced out and saw Vanessa Marlowe striding along, her head down, her hands jammed into her pockets. Apart from her looks, he reflected, she and her mother were a lot alike: set apart from the ordinary run of women by their strength and their intelligence, unable to hide their impatience with fools, yet quick to take advantage of them when necessary. Twenty-five years ago, he had scrapped with Lydia Lymond Abbott and had emerged somewhat the worse for wear. Vanessa Marlowe had made those old scars smart anew.

He instructed the cabbie to pull over at the end of the bridge. He paid his fare and walked back to meet Vanessa.

"As you guessed, I have no official standing in this matter at all," he said. "But middle age does have its advantages, Miss Marlowe. One is less likely to judge quickly, or to condemn. I'm not out to crucify your father or to upset the women in his family. And one also learns patience. If the truth continues to elude me forever, then so be it."

Vanessa stood with her feet wide apart, hands still stuffed in her pockets, her head thrust forward. "What do you want, Mr. Adair? I don't know anything that can help you."

"Perhaps not. But I know a great deal that can help you get to know your father. With a few vital exceptions, I can tell you everything he was involved in until his defection. We never met, but I know him inside out. His taste in food and liquor, the books he liked to read, his favorite games. Everything. If you ever want to talk about him—"

"No, thanks, Mr. Adair. I've come to terms with the man who wasn't there. I've learned to know myself without knowing anything about him. I don't need him, or you."

Adair wrote his address and telephone number on the program for *Troubles* and handed it to her. "The world is shrinking. I can be here in twenty-four hours or less. Just call."

For a moment, he thought she was going to pitch the thing into the Thames, but Vanessa crammed the program into her coat pocket and walked away. Adair rested his arms on the parapet and stared at the wavering reflection of London's nighttime face in the river. It looked fatigued and bleary, not unlike the face that greeted him in the mirror every morning.

Like her mother, Vanessa Marlowe had a knack for reading people, and like Lydia, she wasn't afraid to load her crossbow with unflattering observations. She was right. He was too stubborn to know when to quit, too old to change.

Twenty-five years ago, Owen's instincts had told him that Phillip Abbott's co-conspirators were still active in government. Like a terrier chasing a rat, he had torn Washington apart looking for them. In the process, he uncovered a lot of secrets and made a lot of enemies.

In time his enemies had their revenge. Years later he was working the Central America desk at the Agency when the press exposed a secret CIA pipeline to the right-wing death squads in El Salvador. A Senate sub-committee laid the fault at his doorstep, and his enemies demanded his resignation.

Owen's friends, among them Billy Whistle, urged him to get out before the scandal blew him off the map, and while he could still claim his pension, but he resisted, stubbornly clinging to the organization he had served for so long, refusing to admit to himself that despite a quarter of a century of uncritical devotion, he was no longer welcome there.

A nearly fatal heart attack had finally persuaded Owen to retire, but he still believed he could trace the beginnings of the stress on his heart back to that day in 1956 when Allen Dulles had slapped a file down in front of him and told him to find out what lay behind Phillip Abbott's defection.

"Dig deep, Owen. Better to lance the boil before the gangrene spreads."

Such a long time ago, and yet the events that took place then were so vivid in his memory they might have happened yesterday.

Vanessa Marlowe was her mother's daughter, a product of wealth and privilege skilled at preserving outward appearances. She was also a professional actress trained to conceal her emotions. Nothing in the world could induce her to part with information if she didn't want to. But Owen could read faces, too, and he had seen something in her eyes that he recalled from his long-ago interviews with Lydia: worry and fear.

Owen drew his collar up around his throat and pulled his hat down over his ears. He didn't blame the Marlowe women, not one bit. Those icy blasts from the East always brought trouble.

CHAPTER 16

Moscow: May 1982

R oom 422 of the Hotel National overlooked twelve lanes of traffic on
Gorky Street. All the cars that whizzed past gleamed as if they had
just come off the assembly line. Within the Moscow city limits, the police
levied fines against mud-spattered vehicles. The drivers were subject to the
same controls. Judith heard no horns, no shouts, no screeching brakes.
Even downtown Lusaka was nosier than Moscow at rush hour.

If she stood on the left side of the alcove behind the dingy polyester
curtains and pressed her nose to the windowpane, Judith could barely
glimpse Red Square and the much-photographed *kokoshniki,* the domed
turrets of the churches inside the Kremlin walls. The room had little else
to offer in the way of entertainment. No television, no vibrating mattress.
The walls were painted hospital green, the ceiling white, except for the
brown stain in one corner where the drain under the bathtub directly
above had leaked. In addition to the double bed, the furnishings included
a lumpy armchair upholstered in brown gabardine, a battered writing desk,
the surface veneer nicked and scarred, and a table lamp that looked like
a plastic mushroom. Judith decided that the listening devices were planted
either in the ceiling fixture or in the telephone.

"The plumbing in this place is a disgrace," she informed the listening
walls. "The toilet doesn't flush properly, and the hot-water tap in the tub
is so slow it will take me a week to get enough to bathe in. Either get it
fixed while I'm gone this afternoon or move me to a better room. Otherwise you can forget about my visiting my father tomorrow. I won't be fit
to see anyone."

Judith lay down to test the bed. The hammocklike sag in the center of the mattress wouldn't kill her, as long as she was sleeping alone. She wished she could take a nap right now. She had left Zambia yesterday morning and spent the night in airports and on planes. Despite her exhaustion, she had acquiesced when Tanya, her guide from Intourist, offered to take her on a tour of the city in one hour.

"I never thought I would come here," Judith had told Tanya. "But even when I was a little girl, I couldn't help looking at pictures of your city. I wanted to see where my father had gone to live. But you really don't have to show me around, you know. I'm not here as a tourist. I've come to see my father."

Tanya was insistent. "No, it is my pleasure. I want to acquaint you with our beautiful city. Nothing too tiring, a nice tour by car."

"I hope we don't have to stand in long lines to see Lenin's tomb."

Tanya didn't blink. "That won't be necessary. You are a special visitor, which means we can bypass the lines and go straight in."

As much as she wanted to see the city, Judith wasn't looking forward to being dragged around on a fact-filled tour of Moscow by Tanya, who looked hardly old enough to be out of high school. On the drive from Sheremetyevo Airport, Tanya had been a veritable talking robot: "And here is the Dynamo Swimming Pool and over there the Sovietskaya Concert Hall." By the time Judith reached her hotel room, her eyes were glazed over and she had the beginning of a headache. She would have liked a drink, but she had neglected to purchase anything in the duty-free shop during her stopover in Paris. She wondered if she could bribe the elderly floor watcher stationed at the end of the hall to sell her something. A nice nip of vodka in a cracked teacup, perhaps, from the old lady's private store.

The telephone rang. "Mrs. Marlowe, your car has arrived."

"Already? I wasn't expecting it for another half-hour. Can't you—"

But the man at the front desk had already hung up. Resigning herself to a long afternoon of boredom and unrelieved sobriety, Judith changed from the black woolen suit in which she had traveled from Zambia into a pleated gray skirt and fuzzy white pullover sweater. She pushed her feet into comfortably soft loafers, freshened her lipstick, and slung her trench coat over her arm. Tanya had promised that it wouldn't rain, but Judith had had enough experience with Eastern bloc propaganda not to believe her.

Downstairs in the lobby, Tanya was nowhere in sight. As Judith stood looking around, a uniformed chauffeur approached her and bowed slightly.

"Mrs. Marlowe? The car is waiting."

"Where is Tanya? I didn't expect her for another hour."

"Plans have been changed. Will you come with me?"

Judith followed him out the front entrance. He opened the door to a shiny black Chaika whose rear and side windows were hung with short green curtains. Judith stepped inside and settled herself in the middle of the seat. The boxy shape and spacious interior reminded her of a car her father had owned when she was small, a chunky bottle-green Cadillac with extra seats in the rear that folded down. The driver slid behind the wheel, shouted a warning at some American tourists about to jaywalk in front of him, and took off swiftly but smoothly.

Judith experienced an initial moment of panic. "I don't understand. Why isn't Tanya here? We were supposed to go sightseeing."

The driver shrugged but did not reply. Judith questioned him further, with a similar lack of success. Suffocated by the hearselike feeling of the interior, she drew back the curtain and looked out.

They were speeding along Gorky Street away from Red Square. As they crossed the two ring roads and whipped past the Byelorussia Station, with the old Hippodrome in the background, Judith wondered if she was being summarily expelled from Russia, without even a chance to collect her luggage. Perhaps the Soviets had decided against letting her see her father.

But they passed the entrance to Sheremetyevo Airport without slowing. Building out here was less dense, with green fields and patches of forest showing between the blocks of apartments. The driver swung onto the Leningrad Highway. Was he taking her to see her father? Or perhaps the KGB wanted to debrief her in a remote place in the country, a sort of suburban Lubianka. What if they quizzed her about Dmitrov? She wondered how long she could hold out under torture.

The few road signs she saw were not helpful. She was learning to read Cyrillic and to sound out words in Russian, but after only a couple of months of study on her own with the help of books and cassette tapes, she was far from being fluent, and the signs disappeared so quickly that she doubted she could have read them even in English. They passed a corner marked with a large red *M,* indicating a metro stop, probably the last one on that particular line. If only she could escape from the car, she could make her way back to the city and take refuge in the American embassy on Tchaikovsky Street.

Eventually the boxlike apartment buildings vanished from the landscape, replaced by smoking factory chimneys and large areas fenced with barbed wire. And then they were in the country, speeding along a narrower road through a dense pine forest, heading away from the sun, which glowed weakly in an overcast sky. The driver braked, then turned into a rutted gravel lane. He guided the car over the bumps with such care that Judith barely felt them. No doubt her interrogators wanted her delivered in one piece, a clean, unbruised, unmarred canvas on which to practice their heinous arts.

The car stopped. A dozen yards ahead, Judith saw a wooden cottage with a steeply pitched roof. It was covered with cedar clapboard faded to the same whiteness as the birch trees that surrounded it. Ornate wood carvings graced the eaves, the window frames, and the ridgepole. A man was standing on the front porch.

"Sasha!" Judith threw open the door and ran toward him. He met her on the path in front of the house. She threw her arms around his neck.

"I didn't know—the driver didn't tell me. You wouldn't believe what I was thinking."

"I wanted you to be surprised."

"Surprised! I was terrified." She laughed heartily at her fantasies. "I half expected to be strapped to a gurney and injected with sodium pentothal by a man in a white coat."

"Out of date." Dmitrov gave a dismissive wave of his hand. "I have devised more sophisticated methods of extracting the truth from unwilling subjects." Judith attempted to kiss him. He allowed her a brief peck on the lips, then held her away from him. "That will have to wait until the others have left. Today is my mother's birthday, and you have arrived in Moscow just in time to help us celebrate."

"You should have told me. I'm not dressed."

"Don't be silly. We're in the country now, very casual. I hope Comrade Tanya is enjoying her free afternoon. I informed her superiors that her services would not be required again until tomorrow."

Judith took his arm and they started up the path. "Couldn't you inform them that her services will not be required again, ever? When your scientists hooked her up to a tape recorder, they neglected to provide her with pitch and volume controls. She makes even the bloodiest episodes in your history sound boring. Get me someone about thirty years older, of the opposite sex, taller, and a good dancer."

Dmitrov grinned and gave her arm a squeeze. "I can't make any promises." He opened the door and ushered her inside.

The *dacha* had been built of simple materials, but the interior made Judith gasp: deep-pile Persian rugs, two Impressionist landscapes in gilt frames, a towering malachite urn in one corner.

"My father built this house with his own hands, during a period when he was out of favor with Stalin," Dmitrov told her. "My mother furnished it. I don't know which of the two was more horrified, she at finding herself stuck out here in the woods for an entire summer, miles from her beloved Moscow, or he at finding himself surrounded by museum pieces. I wanted to clear all the stuff out—"

"But he knows I would not allow it." A slim woman came toward them from the kitchen. She wore black slacks and a black cashmere sweater. A half-dozen gold bangles rattled on her wrists, and around her neck she wore a necklace composed of hundreds of thinly hammered gold disks, which whispered and rustled as she moved. Her hair was as black as her costume, drawn into a braided coil at the back of her head. A few strands of gray at the hairline and temples attested to the fact that it wasn't dyed. Dark eyes shone in a pale but still youthful face. Judith resisted a sudden impulse to drop a curtsy. Although she knew who the woman was—indeed, she recognized her from the moment she came into the room—she waited for Dmitrov to introduce them.

"Mother, this is Judith Marlowe, Phillip Abbott's younger daughter."

The older woman studied her carefully. "You do not look much like him." She spoke English with a strong accent. "Perhaps a little, around the eyes. And your height. Your mouth and chin are strong and a bit stubborn, like Phillip's. So, you have finally come to see him? I hope you won't be expecting the man you knew as a child."

"I'm not. Everyone changes."

"But in one's heart and in one's mind, people stay the same. That is why seeing someone after a long separation can be a terrible shock. When I look at some of the men I used to sleep with . . . They have turned into monsters, with their bald heads and their fat bellies and their big red noses." She sketched these old men in the air with a few deft motions of her exquisite hands. Her fingernails were long, slightly curved, and painted crimson. Then she lifted her shoulders and let them fall. "Of course, I have changed, too."

"No, you haven't," Judith said truthfully. "You're just as beautiful as you were when I saw you dance in 1959."

Valenskaya's laughter betrayed her age, which must have been nearly eighty. It sounded like an old woman's cackle. "You have your father's gift of being able to speak the most flattering nonsense with the utmost sincerity. Sasha, you should have warned us that your friend was so lovely. Irina will hate her."

Dmitrov shrugged. "Irina hates everyone." He took out his cigarettes and offered them to the ladies first. Judith declined, but Valenskaya took one, holding it between thumb and forefinger. Dmitrov clicked his lighter. "Seventeen is a difficult age."

"With that girl, all her ages have been difficult," his mother snapped. Then she lapsed into rapid Russian.

Dmitrov shot back a sharp answer, and for a minute, Judith had a glimpse of the incendiary relationship between the spy and the ballerina. A titanic clash of wills, Wotan versus Fricka, complete with thunderclaps and jagged streaks of lightning.

Dmitrov touched her arm. "Forgive our bad manners. Let me offer you something to drink. Mother brought her own hamper to this party, because she didn't trust me to provide just the right vintage of champagne or just the right brand of vodka. She favors Dom Pérignon and Starorus-skaya."

"I grew up in an age when no sensible person ever undertook a journey of even a few miles without a plentiful supply of food," Valenskaya declared in her husky voice. "Don't be so lazy, boy. Give her something at once, before she faints."

They adjourned to a glassed-in alcove between the living room and kitchen. The triple sets of casement windows that served as protection against the fierce winter cold had been thrown open to admit the freshening breeze of late afternoon, as well as the sounds of crickets and birdsong. The U-shaped banquette table was set with four places. Valenskaya called out to someone in the kitchen, and a moment later an elderly female servant appeared bearing an enormous tray loaded with goodies: iced vodka and champagne, smoked salmon and tiny boiled potatoes, a huge pot of caviar on a bed of ice, thinly sliced black bread, herring in sour cream, mushrooms swimming in an herbed vinaigrette. Valenskaya instructed her son and his guest to sit together on the far side. She sat in the middle, beside Judith. The fourth place was still empty. After the old servant had unloaded her tray and vanished into the kitchen, Valenskaya barked another sharp phrase in Russian at her son. Dmitrov gazed at the ceiling, muttering something; then he got up from the table. He trotted up the open staircase near the front door. Judith heard him calling to someone in Russian. His tone was sharp.

"Children," Valenskaya said with an impatient movement that rattled the gold disks on her necklace. She saw Judith's interested look and touched her chest. "Do you know what these are? They are harness decorations, for the horses that used to pull the czar's troika. Gold, of course. Only gold makes such a delicate sound. Can you imagine what that must have sounded like in the dark woods, with the snow piled deep upon the ground? The thump of the horses' hooves, the crack of the driver's whip, and the sound of these little wafers, like fairies' wings beating together." She rested her clawlike hand on Judith's forearm. "I remember these things from my childhood, years ago, before everything was turned upside down. But at my age, I have experienced many upheavals."

Judith smiled at her. "I'm sure you have."

Valenskaya said, "Three years next month. That's when Misha died. My grandson. You can't see the pond from here. Sasha wanted to drain it and fill it in after the accident. I told him not to be a fool. It wasn't the fault of the water that the child drowned."

"It must have been a terrible shock for everyone," Judith said.

"It destroyed my son's family. His wife left him. They used to come here often. It was a happy place. I think Sasha hates it now. But he needs a house away from the city."

Dmitrov returned, preceded by a fair-haired girl of appalling thinness. While he wasn't actually touching her, Judith had the impression that he was urging her forward with an invisible goad. She was wearing a baggy sweatshirt with a UCLA crest on the front, a pair of faded blue jeans, and Nike running shoes. Her collarbones jutted out above the neckline of the sweatshirt, and her wrists were no thicker than the shafts of golf clubs.

"This is my daughter," Dmitrov said in English. Judith was struck by the note of weariness in his voice. He wasn't enjoying this party. "Irina, I would like you to meet Mrs. Marlowe from America."

Judith offered her hand. "How do you do, Irina?"

Irina, who had been staring sullenly at her feet, looked up and met Judith's gaze squarely. Judith was startled by the coldness in her eyes. Valenskaya was right; Irina was prepared to hate her. Irina waited until her father had taken his seat beside Judith, then she plumped herself down next to her grandmother. She grabbed a piece of dark bread, tore off a scrap, and covered it with caviar. She bit into it, made a face, and dropped the remainder onto her plate.

"I don't like that kind of caviar." She crossed her arms over her flat chest and slumped against the cushioned back of the banquette. The message was clear: she would eat no more food at that table.

Her grandmother remonstrated with her. "Don't be silly. This is the finest beluga, the best caviar money can buy. How can you waste good food like that? It is clear you never lived through a war. You don't know what it is to starve."

Judith saw the dark frown gathering on Dmitrov's forehead and broke in. "Irina, how long have you studied English?"

"Long enough," Irina answered after a long moment. "It was not my favorite subject."

"You speak it very well. What was your favorite subject?"

"Music." Irina's hair was long and straight. She lifted it and swept it behind her shoulders. "But not the kind they teach in their rotten old schools. I like jazz, and rock and roll."

"She could have been a dancer," her grandmother put in, "a fantastic dancer, with that build and that carriage. As a child, her body was perfect, straight and strong. The Bolshoi school accepted her, and she was developing brilliantly, and then what do you think she did? She left. All of fourteen years old, and she announced that she wasn't going to dance anymore."

"I did the same," Dmitrov said through a mouthful of caviar and bread.

"That was a mistake. You could have had all this"—the old lady waved a graceful hand—"and the price would have been much lower."

"I didn't want to sleep with the director," Dmitrov growled. "He was old and fat and he smelled bad."

Irina giggled, but Valenskaya wasn't ready to let the matter drop. Her next sentence was in Russian, but stated so slowly and deliberately that Judith was able to understand most of the words: "Do you mean to tell me you haven't prostituted yourself in other ways, doing what you're doing? There are worse things in life than getting poked in the behind by a foolish old man."

"Sasha, why don't we open the champagne?" Judith suggested brightly. "I would like to toast your mother's health."

Valenskaya chuckled. "You see, a diplomat's daughter knows how to save any situation."

Dmitrov poured the champagne, including a glass for Irina, who lifted it in a toast, touched her lips to it, but did not drink. Valenskaya watched her wordlessly. Her necklace rattled softly, like the warning hiss of an angry snake.

"Now my only grandchild spends her time with a lot of no-good *urli*, standing around the Nogina metro, smoking filthy cigarettes and God knows what else. This is how the last descendant of a once-proud family conducts herself, and brings shame to her parents and her grandmother. These young people today don't understand that when you waste your opportunities, they never come again. You might as well send your life down the toilet. You will never get out of the sewer."

"Mother," Dmitrov said sharply, "enough! Irina, you may be excused if you wish."

Irina got up slowly. She slouched toward the stairs, swinging her shoulders and her thin child's hips. After a minute, the three adults heard the throbbing blare of rock music over their heads.

Handing around thin brown Turkish cigarettes, Valenskaya began to upbraid her son for his daughter's rude behavior. "Her manners are abominable, but what can you expect? You don't see her for weeks and months, then you shower her with presents and expect her to love you for it."

Judith pulled smoke deep into her lungs. Dmitrov's daughter was anorexic, of course. Judith didn't know why she was so astonished to see an anorexic teenager in Russia. Somehow, anorexia nervosa seemed a more appropriate reaction to Western cultural excesses. But it was Irina's way of rebelling, of controlling her own destiny, and of punishing the people who tormented her with their demands and their expectations. It was a way of carving away excess, of paring herself down to more manageable proportions, of whittling away the only thing that stood between her spirit and the freedom she craved: her body. An effective diet, in which ultimate success was death.

Judith turned to Dmitrov. "When did Irina stop eating?"

Dmitrov grasped the vodka bottle and poured himself a stiff measure in an empty water glass. "It's just a phase she's going through. She says all her friends are doing it. They want to look like American movie actresses."

"American movie actresses don't look like that. She's in trouble, Sasha. We call it anorexia. American teenagers die of it. They starve themselves to death. Irina needs help. Psychiatric help."

"You see," Valenskaya trumpeted, "I am not the only one who thinks the girl is crazy."

"Don't be stupid," Dmitrov snapped, "you know what children are like, especially teenagers. She'll get over it. Your nagging won't help." He glared at Judith. His eyes were cold, colder than she had ever seen them. "And neither will your interference. What do you know? You've only just met her."

Judith didn't want to fuel any more arguments between Dmitrov and his mother. She prompted Valenskaya to talk about her years at the Bolshoi. Dmitrov's mother was currently teaching at the ballet school, but she insisted that none of her pupils showed as much promise as Irina had. Irina again. Dmitrov made a menacing noise deep in his throat. This time Valenskaya heeded the warning signal and changed the subject. She began to reminisce about General Nikolai Dmitrov, the handsome young soldier who had courted the budding ballerina.

What an espionage coup this was, Judith thought as she listened to Valenskaya. It was a shame the CIA would never hear about it. Here she was, visiting a high officer of the KGB in his private dacha, gaining insight into his personal life and family problems, learning the details of his father's career and death.

"Sent to the Gulag. Died of heart failure, the report said." Valenskaya sniffed. "Not such a lie. They murdered him through overwork or torture. Of course his heart stopped. He devoted every ounce of his energy to his country. In war he became a hero. Stalin saw a rival and wiped him out." She looked at Dmitrov. "I survived those horrible days because I was an artist. If my son had been wise, he would have followed my example and not his father's."

Dmitrov stood up. He had downed half a bottle of vodka, but his eyes were clear and he was still steady on his feet. "My mother is an unrepentent czarist," he said scornfully. "To her everlasting regret, she was only able to marry a general, and not a prince or a count. More vodka all around! Let us drink to those dear, dead days beyond recall."

"Show her the icon," Valenskaya urged. "I want to see it again myself. It pleases me to know that despite our wars and revolutions, beautiful things like this still exist. The icon, Sasha."

Dmitrov opened a door in the tall chest in the corner of the living room and brought out an object wrapped in blue velvet. The servant came out of the kitchen and stood respectfully just inside the doorway. Under the covering was a miniature tree stump, about ten inches high, carved of some dark wood, perhaps walnut or chestnut. A golden wreath of vines and exquisitely wrought roses encircled the base of the stump. Dmitrov set it down on the table in front of Judith so that she could admire the beauty of the carving and the metalwork, and how each petal seemed to rise out of a swirl in the grain.

"Touch this leaf," he instructed her. As she did so, the stump sprang open on concealed hinges into three unequal sections. Inside the back half was a bas relief carving of a madonna and child, their features and clothing delicately tinted, the background solidly gilded. They looked incredibly fragile, yet lifelike, almost ready to speak. The old maidservant crossed herself and murmured a prayer. The two smaller side panels were not carved, only painted, but with an extraordinary lightness of touch and great humanity.

"Saint Basil"—Valenskaya pointed to one—"and Saint Gleb. Russia's first saints. This piece is very old, a treasure of the fourteenth century, from a follower of Feodor Grek, the most famous icon painter of his time. Sasha says it belongs in a museum, but I tell him it has been in my family for centuries, and I want it to stay in my family until after I am dead. Then he can do with it what he likes. Art survives." She brushed the tiny hand of the Christ with a crimson fingertip. "Men perish. Revolutions fade. Only beauty lives on. I have devoted my life to beauty. And I have not been sorry for one minute, which is more than many people can say." She cast a dark glance at her son.

At nine o'clock the Chaika returned to collect Valenskaya, Irina, and the old maidservant. Dmitrov took Judith aside. "I'll drive you back in the morning."

"I think Tanya is supposed to come for me at ten, to take me to see my father."

"I'll get you there in time."

Dmitrov went upstairs to fetch Irina. Valenskaya and Judith stood together under the gabled overhang on the small front porch. *"Sa femme,"* Valenskaya said in French. *"Vous savez qu'il l'aime encore."*

Judith was startled. "I beg your pardon, madame?"

"They still sleep together from time to time. They think the girl doesn't know. Fools. Children always know. His wife—" She broke off as she heard Dmitrov and Irina approaching. Valenskaya kissed Judith on both cheeks. "Good-bye, my dear. Give your father my regards when you see him."

Saying nothing to anyone, Irina sashayed over to the car and climbed into the back seat. The chauffeur made an elaborate production of making sure that Valenskaya was comfortable. The servant got in last and sat in the front beside the driver. Finally the car pulled away, its headlights slashing through the birches. Judith and Dmitrov stood waving on the front steps. When the car had vanished, Dmitrov dropped his arm and went inside without a word to Judith.

Judith sat on the bottom step. From inside the house she heard the sound of glass clinking against glass. Sasha hitting the vodka again, fixing himself a nightcap, or three or four. The night air was cool, too cool to be outside without a jacket, but she didn't want to go in.

"Sa femme. Vous savez qu'il l'aime encore."

A bird began to sing. She knew without being told that it was a nightingale. He warmed up with a few glissandos and some high-range chirrups and twitters, then he launched into a wistful, heartbreaking song that made Judith long for all the things she had lost.

"Come inside." Dmitrov stood in the doorway. "It's going to rain."

"I want to go back to town." Judith rose. As she smoothed her skirt down over her hips, her hands trembled. Was it weariness or trepidation? She wasn't sure. "That is, if you don't mind driving me. It's been a long day and I'm rather tired."

"You can't go back." At last he was beginning to show the effects of all the vodka he had drunk. His words were slurred, his eyes bloodshot and bleary. "You just got here. I'll take you back tomorrow in plenty of time for your appointment."

Judith mounted the steps. "You shouldn't have brought me here. I felt like an intruder."

"You're my guest, aren't you?" He sounded surly. "If I didn't want you, I would have arranged something else."

"Irina hates me. I don't think your mother liked me, either."

"I see; the old bitch upset you. Pay no attention. That's her way. She's spoiled rotten. Because she had talent, she thought she could get away with anything and everything. By the time the rest of us got fed up with her, it was too late to change her."

"I'm not just talking about your mother and daughter. It's you. The mood you're in. I've never seen you like this."

"That's rubbish, Judith. You came ten thousand miles just to make love to me, and now you want to leave. What's the matter?" Dmitrov leered at her. "Have I suddenly sprouted green horns, or purple skin, or black teeth? Have I turned into a monster? Or maybe you've found another lover back in darkest Africa. A black man, who satisfies your taste for the exotic and the bizarre."

"I have no other lover, black or otherwise. And I don't have you, either. Maybe that's the problem." Judith moved past him toward the door. "I'll get my purse. If you won't drive me, perhaps you'll let me call a taxi."

Dmitrov grabbed her arm and swung her around. "You can't leave yet. You didn't get what you came here for."

Judith recoiled. "What's the matter with you, Sasha? For heaven's sake, stop it. Let me go."

"Where are you going to go? I haven't any neighbors, no one to hear you scream. We're nicely isolated out here, in the middle of a tract of government forest with a restriction on new construction. At least my father managed to do one thing right. He built his *dacha* far away from the KGB's spying eyes."

"You're hurting me. Stop!"

Dmitrov jerked her close. He grabbed a fistful of hair and pulled her head back. His kiss was more vicious than passionate. Hearing her furious squeal, he released her. "Is something wrong, Judith? Isn't this what you wanted? You'll have plenty to tell the CIA when they debrief you."

"I'm not planning to tell anybody anything." Judith wiped her mouth with the back of her hand. "What's gotten into you tonight? Why are you behaving like a drunken Cossack?"

"Because that's what I am." Dmitrov thumped his chest with his fist. "What did you think, that I'm like that flabby-handed sissy you married? I know what a woman wants, what she needs. She needs to be reminded from time to time that she exists solely for the pleasure and convenience of the man who chooses her. Nothing else."

He pinned her arms to her sides and kissed her again. Judith endured it for ten seconds, then she reared back and butted his nose with her forehead. Stunned by the pain, Dmitrov released her. She jumped off the porch and ran down the grassy lane toward where she thought the main road should be. A light rain had begun to fall, and the ground underfoot was slick and wet.

She was breathing so hard that she didn't hear Dmitrov pounding after her until he was almost on top of her. He tackled her around the waist and brought her down in the long grass under the birches. Judith clawed and kicked. He straddled her and pinned her wrists to the ground.

"You're crazy," she panted, "and drunk. What in hell is the matter with you?"

"This is my country, my house, my earth. I want you my way. The Russian way."

Judith blinked at him. "So now you're going to rape me," she sneered. "How original. Well, go ahead, what are you waiting for? Show me what a he-man you are. If a slobbering weasel like Byron Harcourt can do it, you shouldn't have any trouble. If I give you a hard time, you can always knock out a few teeth, break my jaw, put me in my place."

Dmitrov lowered himself on top of her. "It's not rape, to make love to a woman who wants it as badly as you do."

Above them, the young birch leaves caught the light from the house. They shimmered against the taut black fabric of the sky. Raindrops filled Judith's eyes and spilled down her cheeks. Or perhaps she was crying. She wasn't sure.

When Dmitrov ground his mouth down on hers, she tasted blood, but she didn't know if it was his blood or hers, and after a moment, she didn't care.

"I don't know why you're sulking. You can tell lies with your lips, but not with your body. Admit it, you enjoyed yourself last night."

At six in the morning, other commuters in shining Zhigulis and Zaporozhets and Finnish Ladas were speeding along the highway toward the city. A few of them cast envious glances at Dmitrov's red Mercedes, but most, like Judith, were too bleary-eyed to notice the symbol of his status, or to care.

"I didn't enjoy it. We weren't making love, we were making war." Judith rubbed her eyes. "I must have been drunk. That's what it was. We were both drunk. I know, we got drunk together once before, but this was worse. You turned into an animal, and you made me one too."

"What are you complaining about? You got what you came for."

Dmitrov rolled his window down and tossed out the butt of the cigarette he had been smoking. "A few more hours in the arms of your tame spy."

"No, I wanted to see if you really loved me. I guess I have my answer."

Dmitrov dropped her at the National. They did not arrange to meet again. She went up to the fourth floor and asked the old lady at the desk for her key. The woman barely glanced at her. Judith was grateful. Under her raincoat, her clothes were tattered and filthy. And under her clothes—even rheumy old eyes that had seen everything would widen at the sight of those bites and bruises. True, she gave as good as she got. Dmitrov had some deep scratches on his back and buttocks, and some nasty purple marks on his chest and shoulders. She hoped they would sting for a long time to come.

Judith noticed right away that her toilet flushed properly, and that the hot water came out of her tap in a steaming rush. She leaned against the bathroom sink and laughed until she choked on her sobs.

CHAPTER 17

*J*udith pressed her hand over her eyes. "I don't want to look at the passing scene, and I don't want to listen to talk. I drank too much last night, and I have a beastly headache."

Tanya, who seemed prepared to deliver a five-minute lecture on every point of interest or noninterest between Red Square and the neighborhood of Sokolniki Park, where Phillip Abbott lived, clammed up immediately with a startled expression on her childish face. Grateful for the respite, Judith leaned her head against the curtained window. She really did have one hell of a hangover. That ought to teach her to mix champagne and vodka. A crick in her back reminded her that she was probably getting too old to make love on the ground, too. But she didn't want to think about last night. That part of her brain was blessedly numb, and she preferred to keep it that way.

The Volga drew up in front of a block of apartments at Sokolnicheskaya 8. None was taller than five stories, which meant they lacked elevators. Tanya said tersely and unnecessarily, "We are here."

Judith climbed out of the car after her and followed her up a flight of cracked cement steps to the entrance of the centermost building. No trees or flowering shrubs relieved the grimness of the landscape. An ancient heap of rubble blocked the sidewalk in front of the entrance, forcing them to follow a path worn through a patch of unmown weeds. Bits of paper fluttered in the breeze like fledglings not yet able to fly.

A man in uniform occupied the glassed-in cubicle to the left of the door. He nodded to Tanya, checked the clock on the wall, and scratched an entry on a piece of paper clipped to a board.

The lobby was as stark as a prison, lit by a single flickering fluorescent tube. Beneath a layer of grime, the floor might have been linoleum, marble, or concrete; Judith couldn't tell. Streaks of green mold on the walls looked like the slime deposited on pilings by a receding tide. Judith could taste the dampness, and the apathy. She felt ill.

They climbed four flights of stairs. According to Aleksandr Dmitrov, Phillip Abbott had a bad heart. Perhaps the Soviets were tired of him and wanted to finish him off quickly. The stairs were just as filthy as the lobby floor, but because most of the bulbs in the wall sconces were either burned out or missing, the grime was hidden by the shadows. During what she called her "hopeful hippie phase," Judith had done some volunteer work in housing projects in the slums of New York and Los Angeles, but in her memory they had looked better than this. She kept her hands in her pockets and refrained from touching the walls or the banisters.

Tanya groped her way along a dingy corridor in the near darkness. She must have been counting the doors as she went, for she stopped in front of one and rapped sharply. Judith experienced a sudden spasm of nausea and nerves. Maybe it wasn't too late to beat a hasty retreat.

Then she heard a noise. Someone rattled a security chain and opened the door. "You're early," a man growled in Russian.

Judith, who had glanced at her watch when they arrived, knew for a fact that they were more than forty minutes late.

"I suppose you'd better come in." The door swung open. Tanya made a movement to enter first, then at the last moment she stood back and permitted Judith to precede her.

An elderly man sagged against the wall just inside the door. He did not look up as they entered, but stared at the bare concrete floor. As Judith walked past him, another man, much younger, emerged from the bed-room buttoning a flannel shirt over his bare chest. His jeans were skin-tight. The blue denim that covered the large bulge of his crotch had been worn nearly to whiteness. He saw Judith staring at it, and he gave her a cocky grin. A yellow pimple gleamed among the sparse bristles on his chin. Judith reared back, wrinkling her nose. Even from a distance of six feet, his animal odor turned her stomach. Garlic mixed with equal parts of stale sweat and fresh sex.

The older man lifted his head and cleared his throat. Meeting his gaze, Judith felt a tremendous rush of relief. This man wasn't her father at all, but an imposter.

Then he seemed to waver into focus, and under the sagging flesh and graying hair and swollen purplish nose, she saw her father as she remembered him, like a portrait that had been painted over with another.

The young man sauntered over to Phillip Abbott and rested a hand on his shoulder. Phillip asked in Russian for a cigarette. The younger man took the lit cigarette from his own mouth and stuck it between Phillip's lips. Their gestures had the easy familiarity that intimacy brings.

Embarrassed, Judith turned away. With gray concrete walls scored by irregular settling cracks, the room could have been the cell of a prisoner serving a life sentence. A few shabby posters from long-past Moscow art exhibitions adorned the walls. Old plastic tablecloths hung in front of the windows. The furniture was Soviet modern, mass-produced and cheaply made.

Phillip spoke first. "So you're Judy. All grown up. Yuri, meet my daughter." His English was halting, his voice thick. Judith's heart sank. The old man was drunk.

She forced herself to look around again, to face her father and his lover. For much of the flight between Lusaka and Moscow, she had debated what to call this old man. She was damned if she would call him 'Dad' or 'Daddy' or 'Papa' or 'Father.' 'Phillip' was too personal, 'Mr. Abbott' too formal.

"Didn't they tell you I was coming?"

Phillip Abbott shrugged. "I don't know. Yeah, they did. I forgot. Guess you came to satisfy your curiosity about your old dad, eh? Well, here I am. Here we are. Did you bring any vodka? We finished the last of what we had this morning."

"No. Only some books." Judith dropped her parcel onto the orange plastic-covered sofa. "Also some cigarettes. I didn't know what else you needed."

"Nothing. Only vodka." Phillip wiped his nose with the back of his hand. "Everything else in this country is lousy. God knows, the food is unspeakable. At least the vodka is passable."

Tanya piped up. "Russian vodka is the best and purest in the world."

Judith's head snapped around. "If you must be present for this interview, will you at least have the decency to keep quiet?"

Tanya leaned sulking against the doorframe. Judith fumbled in her purse for her cigarettes and lighter. The smoke had a sour taste, but at least it masked the other odors in the room.

"Your voice gets brittle when you're angry." Phillip gave a drunken laugh. "Like your mother's."

He scratched his armpit. He was wearing a baggy cardigan over a faded flannel shirt, shiny blue serge trousers, and worn-out carpet slippers.

Judith said, "I had the idea that the Russians treated defectors from the West like heroes."

Phillip lowered himself into the nearest chair. The finish on its bent plywood arms was burned and gouged. Jagged cracks in the black plastic cushions looked like suppurating wounds. "Ah, the observation and criticism phase. I think we'd better settle for Scotch. Yuri." Phillip waved his hand toward the kitchen and made his request in Russian.

As Judith smoked, she rested her right elbow in her cupped left hand. She tried to compress herself, tried to reduce the possibility that she might inadvertently touch something in the apartment.

"Why did you send for me?" she asked.

"Oh, did I send for you?" Phillip grinned at her drunkenly and patted his sweater pockets. He came up with a single bruised cigarette. Further patting produced a book of matches. "How could I have done that? Maybe I was drunk."

"You sent a message to me in Warsaw, via—" Judith glanced at the listening walls. "By way of the son of a friend of yours." Seeing Phillip's deepening frown of incomprehension, she burst out, "Aleksandr Dmitrov, Galina Valenskaya's son."

Phillip chuckled. "Ah, you've met the divine Aleksandr, have you? I invited him to pay me a visit sometime, but he never did."

Yuri came out of the kitchen with Phillip's drink.

"I can't say that I blame him," Judith said. "Maybe I will take some of that Scotch."

"Splendid. We'll drink to auld lang syne. Yuri, fetch a glass for the lady. For my long-lost baby daughter." Phillip raised his glass in an offhand toast. "And my newfound love. Isn't he sweet?" Phillip leered at Judith. "My latest catch. The underground urinals near Red Square are a veritable happy hunting ground. The Moscow that isn't in the guidebooks." He started to laugh, but the laughter turned into a hacking cough.

Yuri ducked out of the room and returned with Judith's drink. She took one look at the smudged glass he offered and shook her head. He shrugged and drank it down himself. Then he sat on the arm of Phillip's chair and draped his arm around the older man's shoulders. Phillip rested his hand on Yuri's thigh and began to stroke it unconsciously, as if he were petting a dog.

Judith was shaking. "Mother told me about you, about what you were. I didn't want to believe her. I thought, no man could be that horrible. But I was wrong. You're worse."

Phillip cackled. "Worse than Lydia? I'd have to plead no contest to that charge. Lydia was perfection itself. Do I understand that her husband has recently been elevated to statehood? Secretary of State, that is. What a joke." He drained his glass. "Ah, Lydia. My life, my love, my heart. If she could see me now!"

Yuri leaned over and murmured a sentence in rapid Russian.

Phillip smiled. "Yuri doesn't want me to talk about Lydia. He says I get too overwrought. My heart, you know. Not strong. Yuri, more whiskey." Yuri fetched the bottle from the kitchen and refilled Phillip's glass. Phillip hoisted it in Judith's direction. "Sorry you're not joining me, daughter. Bottoms up. *Nasdrovya,* as we say here. First word I learned. *Nasdrovya.*"

Judith dropped the butt of her cigarette into a cracked saucer on the coffee table. "I don't know why I came. You don't give a damn about me or Vanessa. You never did." She strode toward the door.

"You're a superior, sneering bitch!" Phillip shouted as she ran out of the apartment. "Is it any wonder I prefer boys to man-eating monsters like you and your mother?"

Judith's legs were shaking so badly that she thought she was going to collapse. Somehow Tanya got her down the four flights of stairs, out of the building, and into the car. As soon as Judith settled back against the cushion, she began to sob. Tanya and the driver waited silently for the storm to pass.

"Take—take me back to the hotel at once," Judith said when she could speak. "And, oh, God, get me on a plane out of here. I don't care where it goes—Kabul or Beirut would be fine. Any place is better than this!"

Tanya spoke to the driver, then turned to Judith. "I have only seen him once before, but he was not nearly this bad. Maybe tomorrow or next week would be better."

Judith whirled on her. "What's your father like, Tanya?" She dashed the tears from her cheeks. "Is he a nice man, hardworking, drinks a bit too much on weekends but stays sober when he needs to? Does he hit your mother around, or kick the kids? No matter how bad he is, I'd rather have had him than that drunken bastard upstairs. Can you understand what I'm saying?"

"My father is a university professor," Tanya said primly. "I am his only child."

"He didn't betray his country, did he? He didn't walk away from you when you were too little to understand. He doesn't cavort in public with boys he picks up in a public toilet and then boast about it afterwards. Whatever he is, your father isn't like the monster I just met. And if you don't want to have another American lunatic on your hands, you'll get me on a plane tonight."

Tanya said softly, "I will do my best."

Judith awakened with a start. The pillow under her cheek was damp, which made her wonder if she had continued weeping even after falling asleep. The sheer curtains shimmered behind the cheap lamp on the table. Daylight had faded, and the smudged fingers of late afternoon had gently rubbed out the cracks and stains and dirt, returning the old room to a state of newness, to an era long ago.

An era before Judith had begun to exist. Before her own tiny griefs had been added to the sum total of the world's misery. After the Revolution but before the Stalinist purges, before the War, before the Cold War and Beria and the KGB. Only the curtains fluttering gently in front of the open window had changed since that time.

Judith washed her face and reapplied her makeup. Her plane was scheduled to leave at nine o'clock, a direct flight to Budapest. From there she would catch a train to Vienna. She had ordered a taxi for six to give herself plenty of time to go through customs. Tanya had not offered her a lift. Judith had spurned Soviet hospitality, therefore she could make her own bloody way to the airport.

Judith had asked the old lady in charge of the room keys to send up a porter for her luggage. When someone knocked, she opened the door expecting to see an elderly man in a mouse-gray uniform. Instead, Aleksandr Dmitrov stood there, looking relaxed and casual in beige slacks and a lightweight tweed sports jacket over a blue polo shirt. Only his eyes betrayed his weariness.

"What are you—"

He pulled her out of the doorway and hustled her down the hall. When she started to protest, he clamped his right hand over her mouth. Judith waited for a caw of protest from the *babushka,* but that end of the hall was strangely silent.

Dmitrov opened a door and shoved Judith into a storage closet. Shelves of clean sheets and towels lined one wall. In the corner a couple of immense wheeled hampers were loaded with soiled linens. An asbestos-clad steam pipe dripped rusty water onto the floor in the middle of the room. A valve hissed. The place smelled like the Moscow subway during rush hour, of carbolic and garlic and stale sweat.

Dmitrov stood with his back to the door. Seeing Judith take a breath to scream, he said, "If you raise your voice above a whisper, I will slap you." He waited a moment for the warning to register, then he said, "I didn't come here to rape you. I want to talk to you. I heard you were leaving."

"You'd better believe I'm leaving, and if you try to stop me, I'll make the biggest stink this town has ever heard. I'll denounce you to the CIA and the KGB and *The New York Times* and—"

"If you're angry about last night—"

"If last night were all, it would be plenty." Judith pushed her hair back from her face. "I saw my father this morning."

Dmitrov grunted. "I was afraid of something like this. I suppose he misbehaved?"

"You know he did, damn you. You've had Tanya's report. Maybe you were even listening to the broadcast coming over the transmitters in his living room. I fell right into it, didn't I? You beckoned, and I followed. And what did I find? A drunken pederast who belongs in a psychiatric hospital—or a jail."

"He must have been terrified of meeting you. They might have known he'd lose control. Give him another chance. He must feel terrible."

"Don't bother to commiserate, Aleksandr. You can't make it convincing. You don't know how to sympathize. Friendship is as foreign to you as love. I know why you're here. You heard I was leaving and you hurried over to salvage the situation. Well, you can't stop me. I'm getting on that plane tonight. The entire Red Army couldn't stop me."

"I wouldn't dream of stopping you," Dmitrov said. "You are perfectly free to go if you wish."

"Free! That's another word that's not in your lexicon. It was all part of the master plan, wasn't it? Your orders were to bring me to Moscow any way you could, for a reunion with my father. Isn't that right? They didn't care what you had to do to establish a bond: make love to me, tell me lies about your kid, anything."

"They weren't lies."

"You didn't make a wrong move, not one. And like the fool that I am, I walked right into it. Love, sweet words, warm smiles—they're just the tools you use to dupe suckers like me. Good old S and T, right? I was your assignment. Just another job. Well, wasn't I?"

He shrugged. "Yes."

"You bastard." She started to laugh, and tears rolled down her cheeks. "You're good at what you do, I'll say that much. Tadeusz's apartment, that whole stupid setup, the baby's room, those pictures—"

"That part wasn't my idea. I don't like dirty tricks."

"But you played, because it was the quickest way to pull down my defenses, flimsy as they were. That whole charade of throwing that man into the river, ripping the bugs out of my apartment. The meetings and partings. 'If you want to see me again, you'll have to come to Moscow.' And I bought it all. I couldn't wait to get here, to throw myself into your arms. But last night— You slipped up there, didn't you, Sasha? You drank too much vodka and for once you let your real feelings show."

"Judith, I apologize—"

"Why didn't you tell me about your wife?" The question hung in the air for a half a minute, unanswered. Judith pressed on. "You still love her, don't you? You're still sleeping with her. You're divorced and you hate it, and your daughter hates you, and you hate me for making you unfaithful to your wife. It's a goddamn putrid emotional swamp, and you let me wade right into it. You should have told me."

Dmitrov crossed his arms. His expression was blank. "Someday my mother should learn the value of discretion."

"Your mother didn't have to tell me anything. I knew it the minute I saw you yesterday. That place is your home, your wife's home, and you didn't want me in it. Someone had a bright idea for a cozy reunion at the *dacha,* and you went along. But you hated it. And you hated me for invading your sanctuary. You drank like a pig, hoping that when you woke up from your drunk I wouldn't be there. But you couldn't pass out and I was still there, and so you played out some sick Russian-soldier rape fantasy in order to punish me."

"I don't hate you, Judith."

"But you don't love me. Do you?" she demanded. "Answer me!"

Dmitrov blinked twice. "I am fond of you, Judith."

"Listen to you! You can't even bother to make it sound convincing, because you know it's too late and you don't want to waste the energy. You're the consummate professional, aren't you? A professional liar and a professional killer, just like your father, dear old General Dmitrov. Purged the military of undesirables, did he? We all know what that means. Not only blood on his hands, but blood clear up to the tops of his hip boots. And you're no different. How much blood have you drawn, Sasha? How many deaths do you have on your conscience? You probably can't even count that high. I was warned. Oh, God, they told me what you were, and like a jerk I paid no attention. But they were right. You're scum, just like my father. You probably have fancy boys of your own. Well, don't you?"

Dmitrov chuckled. "What if I did? Would that make you jealous?"

"It makes me sick. My father wasn't interested in me. I might just as well have been a stranger. He didn't want me there. He never sent for me. That part was a lie, too. And if that was a lie, and your love was a lie, then why am I here? Why in the name of all that's holy did I fly ten thousand miles in order to shout at you in a broom closet in a Moscow hotel? Why am I here? Tell me!"

"I can't. I don't know myself."

Judith dashed away her tears with her fist. "Will you please let me out of here? I have a plane to catch."

"I'm not finished yet."

"Oh, yes you are. Let me tell you something, Colonel Dmitrov. You can keep me here, but you can't force me to speak to my father. The next time I see him, I'll spit in his eye. You can lock me in a cell with him, but I won't listen to a word he says. I should have let him stay buried. He was out of my life completely. I should have left it that way."

Dmitrov gazed at her thoughtfully for a moment, then he stepped aside. "I'll drive you to the airport."

"No, thank you. I don't want any more favors from you."

He opened the door. Judith slipped past him and ran down the hall to her room. She met the porter coming out with her suitcases. She ducked past him, grabbed her coat and purse, and followed him to the stairs. The floor lady held out her hand for the keys. Dmitrov was nowhere to be seen.

CHAPTER 18

Lusaka, Zambia: August 1982

*J*udith saw the ball coming toward her in a high, slow arc, an easy volley.

She swung too late and missed. Her partner groaned. "Lord, Judy, what is it with you? You're not hitting anything. You want to change places? I'll take the back court."

"Sorry, Mmbele, I'm not feeling very well today." In fact, Judith had been feeling nauseous since her return from Moscow three months ago. She hadn't been to a doctor to confirm her suspicions, but she had missed a couple of periods and she recognized the symptoms. After years of trying, she had finally gotten pregnant, and the baby was certainly Dmitrov's. Just another of life's wonderful ironies. It made you wonder about the hand that wrote the script. Sooner or later, she would have to tell Kenneth. Her own farewell to Africa, with nary an antelope head nor a lion pelt to show for it.

"You want to quit? We'll go sit in the shade." Mmbele's dark skin looked smooth and dry, like unvarnished ebony, and her white tennis dress was still crisp. Her husband was Zambia's Minister of Education. Lucky man, to have found one of those women with a natural talent for perfection.

"No, I'm all right. Let's finish the set." Judith pushed herself, forced herself to concentrate. At the end of the game, which she and Mmbele lost, she was staggering. The nagging pain in her groin was worse. Not a pulled muscle. Something else. She limped over to the bench under the flame tree at the side of the court and lowered her head over her knees.

"Judy, you really are sick, girl. You better go home." The two women who had won the game joined Mmbele to hover over her.

"Not home. Get me to a hospital. I think I'm having a miscarriage."

The three women joined together in a chorus of concerned cries: "Judy, why didn't you tell me?" "All this tennis, what a bad mistake!" "I'll call the ambulance!" "You stay quiet." "Don't worry, girl. Don't worry."

Kenneth turned away from the window. "I don't suppose there's the remotest chance that it was mine?"

Judith had noticed approvingly that the Africans, at least the Zambians, still believed in surgical whites. The fad for easy-on-the-eye hospital green hadn't reached Lusaka yet. The doctors who had administered the anesthesia and stopped the hemorrhaging and scraped her uterus all wore white. The only other color she remembered was red: her own and her baby's blood.

The walls of her private room were painted white, too, and so was the iron bedstead. Flowers provided the only color, red and blue and violet and gold, baskets of fragrant bouquets sent by the people at the club and the various embassies around town. Mmbele, who had stayed with her in the recovery room after the D and C, had brought something else, a black ebony carving that looked like a blunt-tipped dagger. It hung from a thong made of antelope leather, which she slipped over Judith's head.

"It's the man's—you know," she whispered. "From one of the villages. You should have told me you were pregnant and I would have gotten it for you sooner, to protect you. But this will make you heal quickly so you can start another baby. I can get some powdered root from the witch doctor for Kenneth. You mix it in his food. He'll never know. With powder like that, you get only sons." Judith had accepted the fetish but declined the powder. She didn't think Kenneth would appreciate the joke.

Now she looked away from his unblinking gaze and plucked at the sheet that lay over her lap. "I'm sorry. I guess."

"Sorry!" he exploded. "You could have told me. This came as a complete and total shock to me. I know the husband's supposed to be the last to know, but this is ridiculous. When were you going to say something, when it was time for you to deliver? At least if you'd given me some warning, I might have reacted with something more than befuddled ignorance when I got back to town and they told me you were in the hospital. I thought you'd tried to commit suicide again."

"Sorry to disappoint you. Just social suicide."

"Whose was it?" Kenneth stood over her, his face flushed and his chin quivering. August was winter in Zambia, and the breeze that came through the window was cool and banana-scented, but Kenneth was sweating inside his gray worsted suit. "I think I have a right to know."

"Aleksandr Dmitrov's," Judith said in a flat voice. "That little shopping trip I took to Paris back in the spring was a sham, as you probably guessed. I went on to Moscow instead, and while I was there, I screwed Sasha and spent twenty minutes with Phillip Abbott. Two gross mistakes in two unforgettable days. At least I had the good sense to get out before I could compound my humiliation by seeing more of them, and I spent the next week holed up in a hotel in Vienna. I drank too much and I cried a lot, but I did not pick up any men. As I recall, you waited a couple of weeks after I got back before succumbing to a moment of weakness, but by then the damage was done and I was already feeling sick. Ergo, Dmitrov. The bastard baby's bastard father."

"Jesus." Kenneth clutched the railing at the foot of the bed. "You're incredible. Unbelievable!"

Judith sighed. "As I said, I'm sorry."

He leaned forward. "What did—what happened with Abbott?"

"Nothing happened. He was a drunken pervert. Everything Mother said. We didn't hit it off. No glad reunion. No apologies or regrets. Not even a peck on the cheek."

"There must have been something."

"Nothing, Kenny. We had even less going for each other than you and I. I mean nothing." She fingered the fetish. "I suppose you're going to throw me out now?"

"I don't know." Kenneth raked his hands through his thinning hair. "I thought we were doing better. That shows how stupid I am. How many times can I let you make a fool of me?"

"I could have had an abortion, but I wanted the baby," Judith said softly. "A baby would have been nice. A tiny, fragile vessel into which you can pour your best-quality, unadulterated love. And it lasts. When you raise a child, you have a ten-year grace period where they love you back without judging you. Then, of course, the kid gets smart and starts seeing the rough places under the shining exterior, and the honeymoon is over. But that pure love, that dependence—I must need that, or I wouldn't be trying so hard to get it."

"We shouldn't have married." Kenneth paced off the dimensions of the small room. "Mother was right. She's always right. But I thought I could help you. Instead I ended up scuttling my own career. She said this would ruin me."

"You should have listened to her. Mother always knows best. It's not too late to dump me, Kenny. You're a smart boy with friends in high places. Without me, you can get your career back on track before it's too late. Funny, I married you because I thought you'd take care of me. At least I'm no worse off than I was in Las Vegas, but that's not saying much."

A nurse came into the room. She checked Judith's pulse, took her temperature and blood pressure, and asked her if she needed anything. Kenneth watched the whole ritual without speaking.

When the nurse departed, he said, "You can go or you can stay. It doesn't matter to me at this point." His voice was curiously dead. "I'll still be stuck here, doing penance, for another year."

"If it's all the same to you, I'll stay," Judith said. "I'll try to behave myself, but you know me. I'd better not make any promises. But I will try."

Kenneth said nothing. He gazed with unseeing eyes at a spot on the floor.

"They think you lost a baby, too. You ought to get some mileage out of all that sympathy."

"I don't want their sympathy!" Kenneth's head jerked up. "I want you to be my wife. Look at me, Judith. I am not fourteen anymore. I got rid of my braces and my pimples years ago, and in case you haven't noticed, my teeth are straight and my voice doesn't squeak when I yell. You can stop teasing me and poking fun at me. I'm a man now. I'm not your brother or your stepbrother. I'm your husband."

"Then why don't you act like a husband?" Judith asked not unkindly. "You push me away with one hand and pull me back with the other. I don't know if I'm coming or going, so I end up spinning until I'm dizzy, and then I fall on my face. I wish I knew why you're so tortured. You don't want to be married to me, and you don't want to let me go. Can you blame me for giving up and going my own way? What is it, Kenny? Are you trying to tell me something? Are you a secret homosexual like my father? Tell me."

"No, of course I'm not. For God's sake, Judith."

"Well, there's something. Out with it."

"I love you," Kenneth blurted. "I can't remember a time when I didn't love you. If I didn't have very much experience with women when we got married, it was because I never met one who could make me stop thinking about you. I love you. But I've got no business, no right, and . . . and you don't love me."

"I don't have to love you, Kenny. We go back a long way together. We're buddies. After Vanessa left for boarding school, you and I played together, remember? We had good times. I like you. It ain't Gable and Lombard, but it's the best we can do. We can live with it: you loving, me liking. Why not?"

"I can't give you any of the things you need."

"How do you know until you've tried?"

Kenneth sank into the visitor's chair and closed his eyes. Neither spoke for a long time. Eventually Judith drifted off to sleep. After an hour, the embassy physician came in to check on her. Judith awakened as he was leaving, and she heard him tell Kenneth that he was sorry.

"You're going to be getting a lot of that," Judith said when they were alone again. "People consoling you for the loss of another man's baby. It could make you crazy."

Kenneth's laugh was bitter. "I'm already crazy, Judith. Crazier than you are. At least you know what you want. I don't even know that. I'm teetering on the brink. I'm the one who should be in that bed, having my head examined, having a double frontal lobotomy so that I wouldn't have to think. Vanessa is right about me. I took advantage of you when you were down, but only because I wanted you so badly. I saw my chance and I took it. It was completely selfish and unfair to you, and I've treated you badly, but I just can't seem to get my head screwed on right. I love you, but I had no right to marry you. No right."

"Oh, Kenny. Come over here. Sit by me." Judith shifted over to one side of the bed and patted the space beside her. "Hold my hand. Now, listen carefully. I'll try if you will, but you can't shut me out anymore. One room, one bed, one fairly satisfied wife. That's where it's got to start. If there's any foundation to build a real marriage on, then we'll build. I'll be faithful to you as long as you'll let me. I'm afraid that's the best I can do."

He leaned over and rested his head between her breasts. "I love you, Judy." He sounded like the fourteen-year-old boy he thought he had left behind. "I don't want you to go away."

"Where would I go, Kenny?" Judith stroked his hair. "You're the only home I've got."

CHAPTER 19

London: April 1983

*E*very Saturday night before Vanessa went to bed, she took the telephone off the hook and hung a NE DERANGER PAS sign on her door to warn off her tenants. She allowed Deaf Kitty to feast on chicken livers or fish, knowing that he, too, would oversleep in the morning and not nudge her awake. And she let it be known far and wide, to friend and foe alike, that they risked life and limb by disturbing her on a Sunday while she was performing in a play. Even Judith knew better than to telephone her before six in the evening, London time. So when her doorbell sounded at ten o'clock one Sunday morning in April, she ignored it as long as she could, then she scrambled out of bed and ran to the front window, ready to do battle.

"If you don't stop ringing that damn bell, I'm going to soak you with ice water!" she yelled.

The man who looked up at her from the front steps was a stranger: mid-forties, tall, square-jawed, somewhat severe-looking, blue-eyed. "Miss Marlowe?" He had a smooth baritone voice that any actor would envy, and an accent she couldn't readily identify. "I am a friend of your sister's, from Moscow. She visited me in the spring. May I speak to you, please?"

"You! I can't believe the nerve. Get lost, comrade." Vanessa started to lower the sash. The buzzing resumed. She threw it open again and leaned out.

Dmitrov said, "I am fully prepared to stand here all day with my thumb on the button until you agree to give me ten minutes of your time."

"Like hell. I'll call the cops. They'll jail you for harassing me."

"I will claim diplomatic privilege, and as soon as they have apologized and released me, I will return. Ten minutes?"

"Five."

"I won't come up. We can walk on the Heath. I will wait for you at the end of the block."

"Shit." Vanessa slammed down the window and stamped into her bedroom. She pulled on slacks and a sweater, shoved her feet into running shoes, and grabbed her raincoat. When she caught up with Dmitrov at the corner, her eyes were snapping with anger. "All right, what do you want?"

Dmitrov began walking. Vanessa had to stride to keep up with him.

"I must see your sister at once," Dmitrov said. "It is not possible or advisable for me to go to Lusaka. I would like you to bring her here on some pretext. No one must know that I have spoken to her."

Vanessa stopped moving and gaped up at him. "You're out of your mind! You can't come barreling into London and start making demands of me."

"You gave me only five minutes," he reminded her. "I therefore skipped the preliminaries and got to the point straightaway. Perhaps you want honeyed words, an apology, a passionate declaration of my love for Judith."

"I want you to go back where you came from." Vanessa's arm shot out, her finger pointing to the east. "And stay away from my sister. She called me from Vienna right after it happened and she told me everything, how you lured her to Moscow and then kicked dirt in her face. You're an out-and-out bastard, Mr. Dmitrov, and if you think I'm going to let you exploit Judith any further, then you are gravely mistaken. Now get the hell out of my life, and so help me, if you ever ring my doorbell again, I'll scald you."

"Four minutes." Dmitrov started walking again. After a pause, Vanessa caught up with him and fell into step beside him. "You've made your point. Now let me make mine. I handled the situation with your sister badly, I know. I never meant to hurt her. But I wasn't the only one exploiting her. I thought she should get away from me, and from Moscow, and forget the whole affair."

"That's crap." They waited for the light to change at the zebra crossing, then they crossed Hampstead Avenue and entered the sprawling, scruffy meadow known as Hampstead Heath. John Keats had strolled there over a century and a half earlier, when Hampstead was a country village remote from London. Now the paths were well trodden by walkers, joggers, kite flyers, and dogs. "There are nice ways of ending an affair."

"Indeed?" Dmitrov arched one eyebrow, something Vanessa had practiced for months in her youth and never quite mastered. "I don't know of any. Someone always gets hurt. Why delude her that there was any possibility of our sharing a life together? There wasn't—then." He glanced over his shoulder. An elderly couple sharing a black umbrella had entered the park behind them. They turned off down one of the asphalt paths. Dmitrov's voice dropped. "Now things may be different."

Vanessa flopped down on a bench and peered up at him. The falling mist formed beads on her hair and eyelashes. She shook her head. "This is incredible! Are you saying that you want to defect?"

Dmitrov spoke carefully. "I am merely talking about possibilities."

Vanessa snorted. "God, we've got them coming and going in this family. Phil Abbott heads east, you move west. Why don't you just stay home where you belong? We don't want you here. Judith certainly doesn't need you."

Dmitrov played the eyebrow trick again. It looked different when he wasn't smiling. "Are you competent to judge what your sister needs?"

"Yes, I am, damn you." Vanessa crossed her legs and folded her arms in front of her. "I know her better than I know myself. I've watched her get involved with men who were totally and utterly wrong for her, and I've picked up the pieces when they've thrown her aside and walked away. She's a kid, a scared, vulnerable kid, and I'm sick of watching apes like you take advantage of her."

"She is nearly thirty-five years old," Dmitrov reminded her. "She has a right to make her own mistakes."

"No, she does not!" Vanessa's eyes filled with tears. "Every mistake she makes convinces her that people are right in the judgments they made about her long ago, that she's worthless and insignificant. Eventually, when she gets tired of screwing up, she's going to kill herself. She's tried it before, and she'll do it again, and sooner or later, she'll succeed. I know how she thinks, and I don't want to lose her. Look, I spent half my life being told I was stupid. I didn't believe it, so I told my teachers and my parents and the rest of them to go to hell. But Judy swallowed the lie. I'm not just protecting her from you, I'm protecting her from herself. And if you have just a scrap of feeling for her, you'll stay away. Leave her alone. Don't force her to make the mistake that might be her last." She searched her coat pockets for a tissue to blot the raindrops and the tears that were fogging her vision.

"You don't give Judith enough credit, Miss Marlowe." Dmitrov sat down at the end of the bench. "She is stronger than you think."

"Is she?" Vanessa's digging failed to produce a tissue, but she did find a nearly empty pack of cigarettes with a nearly empty matchbook tucked into the cellophane. She lit one and smoked furiously. "Did you know she had a miscarriage three months after she saw you? That's two babies she's lost. If I didn't have any other reason for hating you, I'd hate you for that."

"Oh. I'm sorry." Dmitrov glanced up. A male jogger approached from the south and splashed past without looking at them. "I didn't know."

"Maybe you didn't know, but you're not sorry. You're in trouble and you need her help, or you wouldn't be here."

Dmitrov shifted closer to Vanessa. "I understand your concern, Miss Marlowe. And like you, I am frustrated at the limits of love. I have a daughter. Judith has met her. Irina is seventeen. A few years ago, she was a student at the Bolshoi school, a superb dancer with a brilliant career ahead of her. Then I did something that hurt her very badly, and in order to punish me, she is trying to destroy herself. This is her picture." He pulled out his wallet. Vanessa turned away. "Look, please," Dmitrov urged. "Here she is when she was still dancing. She is lovely, I think. You'll forgive a doting father."

Vanessa glanced at the snapshot he held up. The girl was doing a pirouette on point, one leg lifted high in front of her in a skipping step, arms outstretched and raised over her head. Her smile was dazzling.

"This is how she looks now. Older than her own grandmother."

He offered a Polaroid. The girl in the picture had the eyes of a tired whore. Her cheeks were sunken, her short hair was bleached to the color of straw, then greased and pulled into spiky points. She was leaning against a brick wall in the classic posture of adolescent ennui and hostility. But the features were the same as the pert ballerina's. This, too, was Dmitrov's daughter.

"So you've screwed up your kid." Vanessa pushed his hand away. "You're not the first. But don't expect my sister to save your daughter when she can't even save herself."

"I think, if Judith knew, that she would want to help. Not for my sake, but for Irina's."

"I won't let you use her."

"Is that your decision to make, Miss Marlowe?"

"You're damn right it is." Vanessa pitched the butt of her cigarette into the grass and lit another. "It's my duty to protect her, because I love her and I don't want her to get hurt. I'd go into a tiger cage to save her. I'd lay down my life for her!"

"That's admirable, but I'm not sure Judith would appreciate the gesture." Dmitrov returned the pictures to his wallet and put it away. "Miss Marlowe, I believe you are underestimating your sister. The mistakes she has made have not weakened her, they have strengthened her. She has

survived, and she has learned. She could have shied away from an affair
with me if she wanted to avoid trouble. She welcomed it, because she
wanted to live more intensely. Very often, people who are afraid of pain
are overly cautious. They protect others, and they protect themselves, and
they work hard, but at the same time they forget to live. Your sister isn't
afraid of anything. She loves life. And she has a knack for making people
love her."

Vanessa jumped up. Her face was pale. "You bastard, you're talking
about me, aren't you? I'm the one who's scared of living, is that it? The
career-obsessed harridan, the shrew, the corpse who takes on life only
when she steps into a character that's not her own." Her voice rose. "Is
that what you're saying?"

"Am I?"

"Damn you, I've got to look after her! She's my baby sister." Tears
streamed down her cheeks. She appealed to her visitor. "I've looked after
her since we were kids, since Phillip Abbott ran away and all hell broke
loose. Mother was so busy trying to redeem us all in the eyes of the world
that she forgot to love us. I mothered Judy! I can't let anything happen
to her."

"A great deal has happened to her," Dmitrov reminded her gently.
"In spite of your love and concern. Her life is her own. Let her live it."

"How do I know you're telling the truth?" Vanessa asked, dashing
away her tears. "How do I know you're not using me the way you used
her? She's simpleminded about men. She'll believe anything they tell her,
the biggest lies, the oldest lines in the book. Look at the men she got
involved with. Only Charlie Klein was decent, and the stupid jerk went and
got himself killed. She'd have better luck picking a decent husband by
walking down Charing Cross Road blindfolded and sticking a pin into
some man at random. If I don't look after her, who will? You? Kenny?
Mother?"

"She can look after herself. She's been doing it for quite a long time."

"But I care about her," Vanessa wailed. "I love her."

"I love her, too."

Vanessa felt herself floundering. "You want an accomplice, someone
to make it easy for you. I won't be your tethered goat, Mr. Dmitrov. I
won't wriggle on the hook for you so you can snag my own sister. I won't
let you. She—she deserves better than you."

"You want to save your sister. I want to save my daughter. Perhaps
they can save each other." Dmitrov leaned toward her, imploring her.
"Please, Miss Marlowe—Vanessa—allow Judith to make her own decision.
She can refuse me if that's what she wants. If she does refuse, if she declines

to help, then I'll leave her alone forever, you have my word. But I need to speak to her. Can you bring her here without arousing her husband's suspicions? Is there a way?"

Vanessa sat on the end of the bench and drew her head down between her hunched shoulders. She was silent for a long time. Then she looked up. "Yes, there's a way. But I'm not leaving you alone with her. Whatever you tell her, you tell me, too. That's the way it has to be."

Dmitrov nodded. "Very well. I agree to your terms."

Judith poured coffee from a flowered Haviland pot. Marie Dupont from the French embassy passed the plate of little cakes and helped her hand round the cups. Judith would have preferred a Bloody Mary or a screwdriver, but the ambassador's wife frowned on any of her "ladies" setting an unsavory example by imbibing alcoholic beverages in public before cocktail hour.

The agenda at these Wednesday-morning socials never varied. Gossip first, starting with absent members and moving on to local celebrities. Then clothes. Then husbands and children, with few distinctions drawn between the two. Then domestic woes, chiefly problems with wayward and undependable servants.

International politics rarely entered the picture. Zambia was landlocked, isolated from the mainstreams of Western culture, remote even from the rest of Africa. The residents of the capital tended to look south to Johannesburg for news. They cast an occasional wary eye toward their troublesome neighbors, the Angolans. But a guerrilla war in one's back yard was a dreary subject for a tea party, and conversation rarely strayed from the home front.

Judith was finally enjoying her stay in Zambia. The slow tempo of life there had helped heal her wounds and soothe her spirit. She and Kenneth were struggling to observe the terms of their truce, and so far they were successful: at least she was faithful to him. He was still not the world's most demanding and accomplished lover, but for once, she didn't mind. At this point in her life, she needed a rest from men.

A servant brought in a small silver tray and presented it to Judith. She excused herself and opened the folded yellow telegram.

BEN. MOST URGENT. COME AT ONCE. JACKSTRAW.

"Judith, what happened? Is it bad news?" The women's voices were filled with concern. As she had on that awful day at the tennis court, Judith drew comfort from the feeling of sisterhood, something she had missed in Warsaw and back in the States. All these women knew that most cable and wire traffic was directed to the men in their families. A telegram addressed to a wife could only mean that something serious had occurred, perhaps to an elderly parent, or to a child placed in an overseas boarding school or with relatives.

"My sister." She stood up. "I—I think I'd better telephone. Please, don't worry. I'm sure it's nothing."

Mmbele ran after her. "I will help you. My brother-in-law is in charge of the telephone exchange. Otherwise it could take a very long time."

The Zambian telephone system was slow, quirky, and unreliable. Mmbele greeted the operator, a young man, and after exchanging pleasantries about the weather and inquiring about his relatives, she asked him if he would be so kind as to put her in touch with Robert Kwansa as soon as possible, thank you very much, as she needed to place an urgent call to London. Judith waited, staring at the telegram smoothed out on her knee.

This wasn't Judith's first summons from Jackstraw. Vanessa had gotten pregnant while still a student at the Royal Academy of Dramatic Arts. Alone in a strange city, she had sent for Judith, who had helped her through an abortion. From time to time, Jackstraw had received urgent messages from Ben Gunn. When that happened, Vanessa dropped everything and came running.

"The international operator is ringing London, Judith," Mmbele told her. "She is not getting any answer. Do you want me to keep trying?"

"No. No, it's all right, Mmbele. I'd better go right away. She wouldn't have sent for me otherwise."

"There is a flight to Nairobi in one hour," Mmbele said in her take-charge voice. "I will call my cousin in the Ministry of Transport and arrange everything. They will hold the plane for you. But you must hurry. I will ring for your maid. You tell her what you want to take."

In fifteen minutes Judith had her suitcase packed and her passport ready. Mmbele had booked her trip: Air Zambia to Nairobi, Alitalia to Rome, British Airways to London. An embassy car was waiting at the door.

Judith's guests had been speculating about what dreadful thing could have befallen Miss Marlowe. They all took a strong interest in Vanessa's career. The videocassette of Vanessa as Becky Sharp in a television version of *Vanity Fair* was still a hot item at parties.

Judith made her apologies and told them she would be flying to London at once. The women were dying for more information, but they knew that they would only be underfoot in this time of emergency. After asking Judith to let them know if there was anything they could do, they departed, their chatter subdued. Mmbele went with them.

Kenneth hurried in. "What's going on? Somebody told me you were leaving."

Judith explained that Vanessa was in trouble. Kenneth frowned.

"Did she say what kind of emergency it was?"

"She didn't spell it out, but I've got to go. A long time ago, we made a pact, a solemn vow. She wouldn't have used the code name if it hadn't been really serious. Please, Kenny, I've got to go. The car is waiting."

"She didn't come last year, when you were in trouble."

"I didn't want her. I was too ashamed." Judith bit her lower lip to stop its trembling.

"I see. Well, I suppose it's all right. Have a good trip. Do you know when you'll be back? We're going home on leave in four weeks. I don't have time to handle all the arrangements. That's your job."

"If I died, you'd have to handle them, wouldn't you? Look, darling, I'll call you as soon as I've found out what's going on. Meanwhile, tell your colleagues not to get out the calling cards. We may not need condolences yet."

Her driver reached downtown Lusaka in good time, but got hung up in traffic on Cairo Road in the city's busy shopping district. As usual, the streets and alleys around the Luburma Market were thronged with traders and shoppers. Judith noted the line of patients lined up outside Dr. Pasmodi's office. Even sophisticated Zambians like Mmbele swore by him, and many a Westerner had consulted the witch doctor in fun, only to find that some minor problem like headache or sinus trouble had been cleared up.

The shrill clamor of bicycle bells competed for attention with the louder claxons of the taxis. Judith perched on the edge of her seat while the embassy driver nudged his car through the press of wheels and bodies. They were stuck behind an idling bus for two minutes. When the inside of the car filled with fumes, Judith cranked down her window and asked the driver to do the same. That only made things worse.

Finally they broke free and sped out to the airport. Mmbele had said her cousin would smooth Judith's way through customs and hold the plane until she boarded, but Judith was still trembling with nerves when the car finally pulled up in front of the terminal building.

"Oh, dear God," she kept repeating to herself, "please let Vanessa be all right. Please, please, please."

* * *

Vanessa's little Triumph was still parked in front of her Hampstead house. That didn't mean anything. She had probably been taken to the hospital in an ambulance.

Judith pressed the button under Vanessa's nameplate. She could hear the muted sound of the buzzer up in her sister's flat, but no one triggered the release on the door to admit her. She punched buttons all over the board until the electric lock finally hummed and the catch on the door sprang open. Judith dumped her suitcases in the foyer and bounded up the stairs. Vanessa's neighbor, Mr. Tidyman, stepped out of his flat.

"Miss—Mrs. Marlowe. I couldn't imagine who was making all that racket. This neighborhood is usually so quiet."

"Sorry. I'm looking for Vanessa. I called from the airport and got no answer, and she doesn't seem to be home. Have you seen her?"

Tidyman drew his sparse eyebrows together. "Why, I believe I heard her leave her flat some time after noon. She went to the theater, surely. This is one of her matinee days. The curtain goes up at three o'clock, I believe."

"The theater." Judith pushed her gloved hand through her hair. "Of course, I should have thought. Look, would you mind taking care of my suitcases until we get back? I'm awfully sorry to bother you like this, but it's important. I've got to see her right away."

"Why, yes, of course." Mr. Tidyman gave her a nod. "No trouble at all. I hope everything is all right with Miss Marlowe. She's such a delight-ful person. Would you like me to call a taxi for you?"

Judith shook her head. "I'll take the tube. At this hour it might be quicker."

"Quite so, quite so. You run along, now. I'll bring your bags up. No trouble. No trouble at all."

Vanessa was appearing in a revival of Shaw's *Candida* at the Players Theatre off the Strand near Charing Cross Station. Judith arrived at the stage door just as the play was letting out. The guard told her that Vanessa had turned up for the performance as usual.

"She said you might come by, miss. You're to go on back."

Judith hurried to Vanessa's dressing room and burst in on her with-out knocking.

"Van, I was so worried!" Judith engulfed her sister in a fierce hug.

They clung together. "I know you were, and I'm sorry, but I couldn't talk about it over the phone."

"What is it? What's going on? Tell me!"

"It's complicated." Vanessa gave her a weary smile. "But I'm all right. It's nothing to do with me at all, really. But I had to get you here as quickly as possible. Look, I have to make a call, and then we can go. We're meeting someone. Just hang on a little longer, Judy." Vanessa went out and came back two minutes later. "It's set. There's a pub on Adelphi, right across the street from the Embankment Gardens. He'll wait for us there."

Judith pestered her with questions, but Vanessa refused to say anything more while she finished stowing away her makeup and brushes. Finally she was ready to leave.

"We close next week. The show has done exceptionally well, for Shaw. It seems that Zola thing I did for Thames a couple of years ago turned up on 'Masterpiece Theatre' last fall. The American tourists have been coming in droves. I have my own little fan club, all people who want to meet that slut Nana up close. Some femme fatale, huh? Even a few gray hairs showing at the temples. I never thought I would attain stardom and old age at the same time."

Judith exploded. "Vannessa Marlowe, you're driving me crazy!"

"Just a few more minutes," Vanessa promised. "Please, Judy."

They were delayed at the stage door by autograph seekers. It was just after five-thirty when they stepped into the Golden Egg on Adelphi Street. The saloon bar had only been open for a few minutes and was not yet crowded. Vanessa looked around.

"I don't see him. Let's try the lounge." They passed through a doorway into the adjoining room, furnished with padded benches and tables with checkered cloths. At first glance it appeared empty of customers. Then Judith saw Aleksandr Dmitrov as he turned away from the hatch, where he had just paid for three half-pints of bitter. Judith pulled herself up short.

"Well, well, well," she drawled. "The plot thickens. I might have known."

In the center of one of the tables sat an object wrapped in blue velvet. Judith stared at it.

"Yes, it's the Valensky icon. My mother died suddenly last month," Dmitrov said as he set the drinks on the table.

Judith blinked at him. She burst out laughing. "You! I've been scared out of my wits, worried sick, and all the time it was you!" She turned to her sister. "So help me, I'm going to throttle you, Vanessa. Why didn't you say something? If I had known—"

"If you had known, you would not have come." Dmitrov slid along the bench against the wall and motioned toward the two chairs facing him. "Please, will you sit down, Judith? I have something important to say to you."

Judith shook her head in disbelief. "You're such a bastard. You people don't know when to quit, do you?"

"Please, will you listen?"

"Judy, give him a chance," Vanessa begged. "He's right. It's important."

Judith dragged one of the chairs out and plopped herself down. "So he talked you around, eh, Van? Maybe more than talk. I was right, wasn't I? He's a *great* fuck. Too bad he's got more balls than heart."

"I did *not* sleep with him, Judy." Vanessa sat stiffly on the other chair and took a long swallow of ale. "What's wrong with you? Why don't you just hear him out?"

"Why not?" Judith shrugged. "But take this slop away and bring me a Coke. I've learned that it's best to stay sober around this character."

Dmitrov went to get her the soft drink. When he set the glass down in front of Judith, she raised it and said heartily, "To the world's most unlikely pair of co-conspirators. Up yours."

Dmitrov resumed his seat. "Judith, Vanessa told me about the baby. I'm very sorry. I had no idea."

Judith swallowed. "So you're sorry, are you, Sasha? I'm not. I decided I was glad. Whatever love and respect I felt for you died the night that baby was conceived. It would have been too ironic if the kid had survived when everything else was dead."

Dmitrov was wearing a gray suit, pearl gray shirt, and matching gray tie. In the shadowy pub, his skin looked gray as well. "Believe me," he said, "I wouldn't have brought you here if it hadn't been absolutely necessary."

"The end always justifies the means." Judith reached for her purse and got out her cigarettes. "I didn't know you were such a perfect little Leninist."

Dmitrov rested his hands on the icon. "I want you to take care of this for me until I'm free."

"Free!" The cigarette in Judith's hand stopped halfway to her lips.

Although they were the only patrons in the room, Dmitrov dropped his voice to a murmur. "Do you remember my daughter, Irina? You saw her last May, starving herself, snapping at us like a wild animal. You said then that she needed treatment. I was angry with you for speaking about it, but you were right. She is dying. Every day I see her growing smaller, uglier, nastier. I feel her slipping away from me. But I can't save her. I need help, Judith. Will you help me save my daughter?"

Judith took a long drag on her cigarette. "What do you want me to do, send her a care package from Fortnum and Mason?"

"I am planning to defect to the West, and I am going to bring Irina out with me."

Despite her seeming nonchalance, Judith looked around to see if anyone was listening. A teenager had strolled in from the bar. He was playing the fruit machine in the corner and bopping to the music coming through the earphones of his transistor radio.

"I think you've been drinking too much English beer, Sasha," Judith said. "Go home and sleep it off. You're not talking about defection. You're talking about suicide."

Dmitrov nodded. "They will certainly kill me if they find out. But I trust you not to tell anyone. Because we loved each other once. Because I love you still."

"That," said Judith, "is a load of crap."

"I am not lying to you now, Judith. I have too much to lose. My daughter is dearer to me than my own life. If I have to die while freeing her, so be it. But I have a plan. With your help, we can reach the West safely."

"There's that word again." Judith drained her Coke. " 'Help.' On your lips, it sounds like an obscenity. I helped you once before, didn't I? You wanted me to go to Moscow. And I did, I cooperated and went to Moscow. Talk about a journey to nowhere!" She shoved her empty glass toward Vanessa. "Do you mind? All this hot air is drying me out."

Vanessa took the glass away for a refill. Dmitrov said, "I have learned why the authorities were so eager to arrange a meeting between you and your father."

Judith lit another cigarette. "I see I'm in for a tale of drama and high intrigue." When Vanessa returned, Judith looked up at her. "I'm glad you're here, Van. I'll bet you've never seen acting like this. But I'm sure he put on a good show for you, too."

Vanessa sat and crossed her arms. "I believe him, Judy."

Judith laughed. "Then you're a bigger fool than I was. This man has spent his whole life serving a system that regards truth as a joke. 'Promises are as fragile as piecrust.' Isn't that what Lenin said?"

"Judith, the KGB has the idea that your father has written something. Memoirs, an exposé. Something that could be incredibly damaging to them if it fell into Western hands."

"Baloney." Judith snorted. "I don't believe he's written anything. He's too lazy and too drunk. He wouldn't have the energy. It's just another of his pranks, like that boy he produced to shock me."

"I believe it's true, and from the way my superior has been acting, he believes it, too. Phillip's apartment has been searched repeatedly, his few remaining friends harassed and dragged in for questioning. Apparently he's been working on it for years, but he's hidden the manuscript so cleverly that they can't find it, and it's driving them mad. They thought if they could arrange a reunion between you and your father, he would hand the memoirs over to you. I was assigned to bring you to Moscow. The boy Yuri was there to intercept the manuscript. But Phillip was too drunk. He drove you away."

"I made it so easy for you, didn't I?" Judith said bitterly. "I should have given you more of a challenge. No wonder you despised me."

Dmitrov met her gaze without flinching. "A man in my position falls in love at his own risk. I didn't even know I was in love with you until after I had killed your love for me."

"So now you want me to get the manuscript from Phillip and hand it over to you." Judith tapped her cigarette on the edge of the ashtray. "I'd have to be more of a fool than I am to play along with you again."

"Judith." Dmitrov reached across the table and grasped her wrist.

She jerked her hand away. "If you touch me again, if you lay so much as a finger on me, I swear, I'll brain you with this icon."

"I'm sorry." Dmitrov leaned back. "I won't touch you. I lost that privilege when I violated your trust. But I must make you understand what is at stake. Some of their operatives from the old days must still be working. It's entirely possible. Naturally the KGB has to prevent the manuscript from reaching the West. Your people and the British would like to have it for the same reason—to find out who is betraying them. And I would like to have it as insurance, to protect Irina. If something goes wrong with the escape, I can use it to bargain with them. If they are this desperate to find it, they will trade anything for it, even my life and Irina's."

Judith shot a glance at Vanessa. "I think we're getting to the crux of the argument, don't you? I can feel that four-letter *H* word hovering in the air again."

"Irina's situation is desperate," Dmitrov told her. "She drinks, she takes drugs, she sneers at the people who are trying to save her. I'm not blaming her. I know where the blame lies: with me. I was a bad father. I betrayed my wife, my son, my daughter, my whole family. She will never forgive me. But I have to do what I can for her. Can you understand that? She's the only child I have left."

"I have another question for our illustrious spy." Judith sat back in her chair. "All this talk about defection and father-daughter love. Are you sure you don't want to bring someone else out? Your wife, for instance?"

Dmitrov sighed deeply, and then he nodded. "Yes. I won't lie to you. I would like to bring Olga out as well."

"I thought so." Judith laughed bitterly. "You want me to help you bring your ex-wife and baby Irina to the West, is that it? Suppose I do. You'll set your family up in a cute little split-level or colonial condo outside the Beltway. You'll commute to D.C. to your job in some think tank, Olga will learn how to shop Western-style at Garfinckel's, and Irina will start collecting speeding tickets from the Virginia cops in that cute little red sports car you're going to buy her with your first paycheck. You say that you love me, but do you see me anywhere in that picture? I don't. I am conspicuously absent. What do you think, Vanessa? If he should succeed in this—and we all know how remote his chances are—do you think he would turn around and desert his family for the likes of me? Would you, Sasha? Tell me the truth, baby. I have no patience with liars these days. You and Olga would get together again, wouldn't you?"

Dmitrov studied his folded hands. "I couldn't leave her to cope alone in a strange country."

"Right. Strange country. Poor Olga and poor Irina need time to settle in. They need Dad. Well, sorry, Dad, but I'm not in a missionary mood today. I don't want anything to do with you or your wife or your daughter. I'll tell you, Aleksandr Nikolayevich, I wouldn't help you cross the street if you had a tin cup in one hand and a white cane in the other."

"You really do hate me," Dmitrov said softly.

"Is that so surprising? Even the good memories have turned sour, because they were based on lies. Your lies."

"Judith, if you could talk to your father—"

"Oh, no." Judith shook her head. "I'd rather roast on a slow spit over hot coals than see that son of a bitch again. Our meeting wasn't a reunion, it was an exhumation, and I've been trying to get the stink of his corpse out of my nostrils for an entire year. I think you'd better go. And take that with you." She pointed to the icon. "I'm not going to baby-sit your junk for you."

"Vanessa has promised to keep it safe for me. If anything happens to me, I want you to have it."

"No, thanks. I don't want any souvenirs of this sordid affair."

"Then give it away. Sell it. Burn it. I don't care." Dmitrov stood and draped his Burberry over his arm. "There is an old story about a *kulak* who was paid for his crop with a gold coin. He didn't believe it was real. He bit it, he tried to bend it between his fingers. He hammered at it with a horseshoe, and eventually all he had left was a little lump of metal, worth less than the face value of the coin. The point is, we Russians often destroy what we most want. Good-bye, Judith. Vanessa."

He went out. After a minute, Judith said, "Thanks for the shaft, Vanessa. I won't forget this."

"You're a fool to turn him away," Vanessa said. "He needs your help."

Judith stared at her in amazement. "I think you've lost your mind, Sis. That story was a pack of lies from start to finish. He wants the memoirs, all right, but not because he's taking Irina and Olga anywhere.

His bosses have told him to bring it back or else. Once again, I'm supposed to be the dupe. Well, let me tell you, if he thinks he can pick up the strings and jerk this little puppet around like he did—"

"I believe him." Vanessa placed a hand on her sister's arm. "He loves you, Judy. I can tell."

"Love!" Judith echoed incredulously. "You're hooked on fantasy, kid. He played the part to perfection, and you started swooning. It's all technique, the best you'll ever see, onstage or off. I've seen his show close-up, remember? And when the rotten eggs started to fly, I was the target." She stretched and yawned. "Well, that was a bore. What this girl needs is a therapeutic dose of shopping. I bet Liberty's is still open. Want to come?"

"I can't. I have to be back at the theater in an hour. I'll tell the people at the box office to save you a ticket if you like."

"No, thanks. I've heard enough talk for one day. Two and a half hours of George Bernard Shaw would send me over the edge. Give me your key. I'll see you back at the house when you're through. Maybe I'll give Kenny a call and run up your phone bill."

"You won't tell him," Vanessa said quickly.

"No, stupid, I won't tell him. I'll just say it was a false alarm, the usual female hysteria, a mild nervous breakdown." As Judith pulled the strap of her purse over her shoulder, she glanced at the blue-wrapped icon Dmitrov had left behind. "What are you going to do with his prop?"

"I'll take it with me," Vanessa said. "I have a friend who works at Sotheby's. He'll put it in their safe."

"His old lady wanted him to keep it in the family. Shows how much he thinks of her, doesn't it?"

"Maybe it shows how much he thinks of you."

After Judith had left for Harrod's the next morning, Vanessa spent half an hour searching through her apartment. She found what she was looking for in the drawer of her nightstand, the crumpled program from *Troubles* on which Owen Adair had written the telephone numbers where she could reach him. It was one of the few pieces of printed matter in the house.

She took a long time dialing. On her first try she found herself talking to a man in Baden-Baden, West Germany. She had screwed up the country code. She apologized in German, hung up, had a cigarette to calm her nerves, and dialed again. This time Owen answered.

"Hello." His voice was thick with sleep. For him, it was the middle of the night.

"Mr. Adair, this is Vanessa Marlowe, in London."

"Yes, Miss Marlowe." The sluggishness vanished. He sounded alert and wide awake. "What can I do for you?"

Vanessa took a deep breath. "Something has happened—is happening—and I don't know what to do about it. Will you come? Please?"

CHAPTER 20

Washington: May 1983

*C*ome in, Judy. Ken, good to see you." The Secretary of State stooped
to kiss his stepdaughter on the cheek and shook his son's hand.
Preston Marlowe was extremely tall, and as slender as he had been when
he crewed the Yale eight in 1933. His bright blue eyes were clear and alert,
and his vision was as keen as ever. On this day his bow tie was red, with
small navy-blue polka dots. "Can I offer you a drink? Lydia's got me on
tight rations, but that doesn't mean I can't be a good host." He grinned
at his wife, who was sitting on the sofa at the other side of her husband's
spacious office. Lydia returned a smile.

Kenneth said, "No, thanks, Dad. I'll pass. It's a little early."

"I'll take a Scotch, if you don't mind," Judith said. "Unless you think
I'll need a clear head for what's coming."

She and Kenneth crossed the room to Lydia. "Hello, darlings."
Lydia offered a soft pink cheek to each of them. "How was your flight?"

Judith glanced past her mother to the other visitors. "We got here,
so I suppose you can say it was successful."

Four chairs had been placed in a semicircle in front of the tufted
leather sofa. Three men rose as Judith and Kenneth approached. Lydia
introduced them. "You both know our chief spy."

Chester O'Brien was the head of the CIA, a slab-faced man with
heavy jowls and a rather chilling gleam in his tiny eyes. His cheeks quivered
slightly as he shook hands.

"And I don't have to introduce you to Billy Whistle," Lydia went on.
Billy Whistle kissed Judith and shook Kenneth's hand.

"And this is Owen Adair, an old friend of mine, although we haven't seen each other for quite a long time. Owen used to work at Langley. They call him back from time to time when they need brains tempered with good sense and experience."

Judith nodded to Adair, the only stranger. Everyone sat again, and Judith found herself on the sofa between Chester O'Brien and her mother. Adair and Billy Whistle occupied the two wing chairs on the ends. Kenneth seated himself on a Chippendale side chair brought in for the occasion. This left another side chair vacant. Preston insisted that he preferred to stand.

After Preston handed Judith her drink, he congratulated Kenneth on the good work he had done in Zambia. "No complaints from the ambassador. In fact, he sent back one of the most glowing reports I've ever seen. Seems that Judy made quite a hit, too."

Judith sipped her Scotch. "I didn't mess on his rug, if that's what you mean. Skip the hoopla and get to the point, Preston. You're cutting into my shopping time."

Lydia pursed her lips, but Preston chuckled. His superb manners prevented him from ever showing shocked disapproval, no matter what anyone said or did. "You're right, Judy. Well, I certainly want to welcome you and Ken home. And I've got a little surprise for you. Ken, my boy, your new assignment's come through early. You are going to Moscow. Third Secretary. Congratulations. It's a choice spot, and I know you'll do a fantastic job."

"Darlings." Lydia beamed. "I'm so proud of you both. Kenneth, what a marvelous opportunity."

"Moscow," Judith said in a flat voice. "Wow, that is a surprise."

Kenneth flushed with pleasure and stammered his thanks. "Dad—I mean, Mr. Secretary—that's terrific news. Mother, you know how long I've been waiting for a chance like this, to prove myself. Thanks for your help. I'm truly honored. I'll do my best for you both, and for my country. I promise."

Lydia leaned over, her arm outstretched, and squeezed her stepson's hand. "I know you will, sweet. No one deserves this more than you."

"Now I have an announcement." Judith took a small swallow of Scotch. "I'm staying home."

"What!" That did shake Preston's composure. O'Brien twisted around and gave her his most chilling stare. Billy Whistle and Owen Adair exchanged glances. Lydia said, "Judith, what brought this on?"

Judith crossed her legs. "This will come as a shock to some of you, but I'm not as dumb as I look. Phillip Abbott has something you want, and you want me to go to Moscow and get it for you. Well, it's a lousy idea. And I won't play. But here's a hint: send him a beautiful young man with slim hips and a sexy smile." She held up her empty glass. Preston took it and went to the bar.

"We've tried that," Billy Whistle said. "It didn't work."

No one snickered, although Lydia looked grim. Judith glanced at Kenneth. He was staring at the rug, his face a study in neutrality. If he was disappointed to learn that he had been assigned to the Soviet Union as a cover for his own wife, he didn't show it.

Lydia turned to her daughter. "Judith, we know that you met with your father one year ago and that you were terribly upset by the experience. I tried to warn you to stay away, but of course you were curious about him. That's perfectly natural, under the circumstances. Obviously you still have a great deal of anger toward him. No one understands that better than I. But there are times when we must listen to something besides our own feelings."

Preston handed Judith her drink. "Believe me, Judith, if we could think of some other way to get close to the man, we'd try it. But so far, you're the only avenue. I hate like anything to ask this of you, but I've got no choice. Will you go to Moscow with Ken? Will you visit Phillip Abbott, earn his trust, persuade him to give you what he has?"

"Preston, I won't go back there. I can't. Besides, it all happened so long ago." Judith shook her head despairingly. "Nearly thirty years. Anybody who was involved in his . . . his defection is either dead or retired by now."

"Not necessarily." Owen Adair lit a cigarette. He was the only one in the room smoking.

Judith stretched out her hand. "May I have one of those?"

"An old mole can still do a lot of damage." Owen held out his lighter for Judith. "Ask anyone who gardens. Sometimes they're the worst."

"It isn't just a question of bringing ghosts back to life," Chester O'Brien said. "Sure, if there's anyone still in place, we'd like to know about it. For one thing, the propaganda value to our country would be enormous. Relations between us and the Russians are at a pretty low ebb right now. We've been trying to get them to the conference table in Geneva, but they're balking. Since Brezhnev died and Andropov came to power, they've been in a holding pattern, pulling in their horns, coralling the horses. If we had a lever we could use, maybe we could shift them a little. They've been on the defensive since Afghanistan, and they're not eager to remind the world of past espionage activities. We think Phillip Abbott wants to get his memoirs to the West, but for some reason he won't trust any of us."

Judith grunted. "You mean you need something to blackmail them with. I bet Phil has no idea he's this popular."

"He knows." Billy Whistle folded his arms across his chest, revealing a pair of square gold cuff links. As usual, his dress was impeccable, a navy-blue pin-striped suit, white shirt, striped rep tie, and black oxford shoes with a high military shine. "We've made a few approaches, but it's tough. The KGB is everywhere. Still, we had a little luck a month ago. Phil knows what we want, but he's not prepared to give it to us."

"Why don't the Russians just get rid of him, if he's causing trouble?" Judith asked. "That's what you'd do."

Owen Adair chuckled. O'Brien and Preston seemed about to protest, but Billy Whistle preempted them. "Because they're afraid that this thing—this memoir or manuscript, whatever it is—will turn up unexpectedly. As long as Abbott has control of it, and they have control of him, they're safe."

"And they're really going to let me walk in there and try my hand again? Not a chance. I didn't do them any good the first time."

"They're like us. They don't have many other options."

Kenneth looked up, his expression grim. "We're not going. This whole business sounds iffy and dangerous and I don't want Judith getting involved. You can't guarantee her any kind of protection over there. It's their turf. I won't have her exposed to risk."

"We believe the risk is limited, Kenneth," Billy Whistle said. "The Soviets aren't in the habit of roughing up diplomats' wives; that sort of thing doesn't play well on the evening news. Obviously, the Russians think they can snatch Phil's memoirs away from Judith, but if we thought we were exposing her to any danger we wouldn't let her go. If there's a slim chance that she might get hold of what Phil Abbott has, then we've got to take it."

"How is she supposed to get this manuscript out?" Kenneth demanded. "It's crazy. They won't let her out of their sight, and if she does get her hands on it, they'll grab it before she has a chance to read the first page. Besides, from what she tells me, he's a sick man. He might die at any moment."

O'Brien shrugged. "Then we've lost. But he's not dead yet."

Judith swirled the melting ice in her glass. Moscow. Everyone wanted her to go to Moscow. Dmitrov. Vanessa. Preston. Lydia. The CIA and the FBI, and the White House, too. They would keep up the pressure until she consented.

"It's all right, Kenny," she said. "I'll go. Why not? This is a good opportunity for you. You don't want to lose it because of me."

"I don't care about this assignment, Judith. I don't think we should go. Mother," Kenneth appealed to Lydia, "you know what that man is like. You don't want to throw your own daughter to the wolves."

"Darlings." Lydia looked at her children with love and pity. "I'm so sorry. So terribly, terribly sorry. If only we had another way. But we don't." She lifted her hands in a helpless gesture.

Judith sighed. "You're sweet, Kenny, and I'm grateful. But a woman's got to do what a woman's got to do. Duty, honor, country. Right?"

"Right." Owen Adair's dry rejoinder earned him a cool glance from Lydia. Owen winked at her. She smiled back, her eyes gleaming.

The meeting broke up. Judith was the first to leave, pleading the sudden onset of a headache. Kenneth offered to accompany her back to her mother's house, but she insisted that he stay.

"You'll have plenty of work to do, getting ready for Moscow. Might as well get started."

Owen Adair caught up with Judith in the lobby. "Mrs. Marlowe, do you have a minute? I think we need to talk."

"Offer me a ride, Mr. Adair. Offer me lunch. But spare me any more talk."

"It's about Colonel Dmitrov."

The elevators disgorged flocks of civil servants. They stampeded toward the exits, determined to make every minute of their lunch hour count. Judith joined the exodus to Twenty-third Street, Adair following.

"I was wondering when someone was going to mention him."

"They didn't mention him because they don't know. But I've been talking to your sister in London."

Judith pulled up short. "That little tattletale! Remind me never to tell her another secret."

"It isn't really your secret to keep," Owen said. "For the time being, I'm keeping the information about Dmitrov under my hat."

Judith looked at him. "For a has-been, you're taking an awful lot on yourself, aren't you? Are you trying to win bonus points toward a bigger pension?"

"We were talking about risks up there." With a light touch on her elbow, Owen guided her to a bench under a flowering crab apple tree. "If Dmitrov is really serious about defecting, then he's in grave danger. More danger than you can imagine. Did you ever hear about a man named Oleg Penkovsky, Mrs. Marlowe? He worked for the GRU, Soviet military intelligence. He wanted to stop the arms race, so he fed information to a Western businessman. When the Soviets found out, they tried him, convicted him, and sentenced him to death. The rumor went around that the top GRU men stood around the furnace while Penkovsky was fed into the flames, alive. That's what Dmitrov is up against. I told your sister, and I'm telling you now, if a whisper of this reaches the wrong ears, even here in Washington, he's a goner."

"You mean there are people in the Agency who can't be trusted?" Judith laughed. "Good God, man, what is this country coming to? Leaks and spies and moles and traitors. Yesterday, today, and forever. But you're a good guy, right?"

"Yes, I am." Adair nodded solemnly. "And so's Billy. When your father pulled his vanishing act, I vetted everybody in the Agency who might have helped. Billy Whistle is absolutely clean. But I can't vouch for anyone else anymore."

"Meaning Preston? Or O'Brien?"

"Meaning anyone else. If it looks like Dmitrov is going to come out, just give me the word. I'll do what I can to help him."

"I don't think I'll be getting any word from Colonel Dmitrov," Judith said. "We are no longer on speaking terms."

"I'm not asking you to hustle him. God knows, we want what he has, but he's safer if he just stays put. But he might approach you. You don't know."

"And I don't care." Judith opened her purse, took a pair of dark glasses from a case, and put them on. She regarded Owen from behind the opaque lenses. "You ought to change your tailor, Mr. Adair. You look like hell."

"What? Oh, you mean the suit." Owen plucked at the lapels of his jacket. "I lost a lot of weight after my bypass operation a couple of years ago. Never did get around to buying anything new."

"I see. Are you a career bachelor, or did your wife dump you because she was sick of sitting up nights waiting for her spy to come home?"

"Both. She dumped me nineteen years ago, and I've been a bachelor ever since."

"Figures." Judith jumped up and ran into the middle of the street. A taxi stopped just short of running her down. She climbed in and closed the door, and the taxi pulled away.

"So now you've met both Lydia's daughters." Billy Whistle joined Adair on the bench. "What do you think?"

Owen shook his head slowly. "I think we're lucky Lydia and Phillip Abbott didn't get around to having any more."

CHAPTER 21

Moscow: October 1983

*T*he previous tenant had left a window box with a few straggly red geraniums and some parsley plants. Judith was grateful for that splash of color and life.

The apartment was a shambles, and the living room was the worst. Kenneth had reported to the embassy immediately upon their arrival, leaving her to unpack and set things to rights—one of her duties as a diplomat's wife. Their pieces of furniture stood more or less where she wanted them, but cartons of personal belongings were stacked high in the middle of the floor. A strong arm and a crowbar were needed to pull the top off the slatted crate in which their paintings had been shipped. Then there were the clothes, enough to carry them through four seasons, still locked away in trunks and suitcases.

The Marlowes' new home was in an eight-story apartment building on Moscow's Garden Ring Road, Sadovoye Koltso. This golden ghetto was restricted to foreign diplomats and journalists and off limits to all Soviet citizens, except the ones who worked there as cleaners, guards, and KGB listeners.

Before leaving Washington, Kenneth and Judith had been fully briefed on what to expect, but it was still a shock to realize that microphones were waiting to pick up even the most banal conversation. "The safest room in the house," an FBI man had told them, "is the bathroom, with the shower on full blast. So far, the bug hasn't been invented that can penetrate that noise." Judith wondered if eventually some couples got tired of retreating to the bathroom every time they craved a moment of privacy. They simply stopped caring that some dozing Russian might be eavesdropping on their lovemaking and their quarrels.

She surveyed the room with a sense of hopelessness. Ordinarily, the upheaval of moving invigorated her, but now it depressed her.

Beyond the geraniums, the October afternoon was glorious, the sky a pale wash of blue behind the yellowing trees in the Lenin Hills. Down in the street the pedestrians were wearing sweaters and light jackets. The felt boots and bulky sheepskins would come out later. Judith hoped she would be gone by then.

She decided to visit her father right away. With any luck, she could be out of Russia with his damn manuscript before the first snow fell.

Downstairs Judith hailed a cruising taxi. The green light in the front window meant that it was free. She gave the driver her father's address in slow, precise Russian. Like Kenneth, she had spent the past month in intensive language study. This was standard practice for all foreign-service spouses.

"Fine weather you're having," she said to the cabbie.

He shrugged. "It's weather. Tomorrow will be the same, or it will be different. Who cares?"

Phillip Abbott's apartment building looked even shabbier than Judith remembered. Surprisingly, the piles of trash and rubble outside had stayed the same. Judith would have expected them to grow, or to diminish. But perhaps they were a renewable resource. Like despair.

The guard's booth was empty. Judith made her way up the stairs and down the gloomy hallway to Phillip's apartment. She knocked and waited, then knocked again and pressed her ear against the door. No one stirred inside. She considered waiting, but the lobby had no chairs and she refused to sit on the filthy steps. She jotted down her new address and telephone number, and added a few lines:

> Kenneth has been assigned to the Moscow embassy. We'll be here for two years. I guess this means we have another chance to get acquainted. Hope we can get together soon. Judith.

She slid the note under her father's door and stood uncertainly in the hallway. What if he didn't even live there anymore? What if they had taken him away, clapped him in one of their hospitals or locked him up in one of their prisons? On impulse, she tapped at the door across the hall. No answer there either. Music was coming from the apartment next to Phillip's. She pounded as hard as she could. Finally a man jerked open the door.

"What do you want?" he demanded.

"My father—Mr. Abbott—he lives next door. I am his daughter from America. I've come to see him, but he's not at home. Can you tell me when he'll be back?"

"How should I know? I've never even seen the man. I don't spy on my neighbors. I leave them in peace and I expect them to do the same for me." He slammed the door in her face.

"Thank you very much!" Judith shouted. As she turned away, she bumped into a young man wearing a business suit. She let out a little scream.

"Mrs. Marlowe? I am sorry to startle you. My name is Sergei Grigorovich." He was very blond and a trifle bulky. His English was excellent. "You have come to see your father, is that right?"

"Where is he?" Judith demanded. "What have you done with him?"

"He is visiting friends in another part of the city." Grigorovich's broad, bland face reminded Judith of Elmer Fudd. She wondered if Grigorovich had ever experienced an honest emotion in his life—or shown it. "You should have let us know you were coming. We do not recommend that tourists move about the city unaccompanied. If anything should happen, we would feel responsible."

"Who's 'we'? The KGB?"

"I am with Intourist."

"Well, you needn't worry about me." Judith hitched the strap of her bag higher on her shoulder. "I am not a tourist, I live here now. My husband is a diplomat."

"That may be so. But please, in the future, we will escort you to visit your father. He is in poor health. He frequently behaves irrationally. He might even lash out at you and inflict serious bodily injury."

Judith gave him an incredulous stare. "My father doesn't have the energy to squash an insect. Are you trying to tell me that he's gone crazy?"

"Not at all." Grigorovich remained unruffled. "But he drinks too much, and one never knows what a drunk will do, is that not so? Come, I will drive you home." He stepped aside and waited for Judith to precede him down the stairs. She hung back.

"I'm not ready to go home. I'm going to wait right here for my father. I want to see for myself that he's really all right."

"I have told you," Grigorovich said patiently, "he is as well as he can be under the circumstances."

"You've told me that he's drunk and disorderly and in danger of hurting people." Judith planted her feet firmly and crossed her arms. Maybe Grigorovich would understand her body language. She obviously wasn't getting through verbally. "Which is it? I intend to see for myself."

"He is not at home." Grigorovich's voice stayed calm, his expression neutral. "He is not likely to return for some hours. You will be wasting your time if you wait."

"It's my time, isn't it?"

"Mrs. Marlowe, you had better come with me. This is no place for a woman alone."

"Oh, so now I'm in danger from ordinary Russian citizens? You make this place sound worse than Harlem."

"You will not see your father today," Grigorovich stated firmly. "I know for a fact that he will not return until tomorrow."

"Fine." Judith shrugged. "Then I'll come back tomorrow."

"You will have to telephone the Intourist office first, and arrange an escort."

"Why can't I arrange it now, with you?"

"Because I am not authorized to make such arrangements."

Judith counted to ten. If this man was typical of Soviet bureaucrats, no wonder their economy was in trouble.

"You're saying that you won't let me see him alone, without a baby-sitter?"

"It is for your own protection," Sergei Grigorovich assured her. "He might fly into a drunken rage and injure you."

"You and I both know that's nonsense."

"While you are a guest in our country, you are in our care. We would be remiss in our duty if we permitted you to endanger yourself."

They were going in circles. Judith threw up her hands. "All right, I'll go. But I'm going to call Intourist first thing in the morning to arrange a visit. Will you be there? I'll ask for you."

Grigorovich shook his head. "I may be working elsewhere tomorrow."

"Then who should I ask for?"

"Anyone will be happy to take your request."

"But that's ridiculous! An organization the size of Intourist—it could take hours to get through to someone who has the authority to dispatch an escort."

An eloquent shrug. "We do our best to be of service. We can do no more."

Judith flounced down the stairs ahead of him, too furious to pursue the discussion further. The guard had returned. He charged out of the glass booth and began to upbraid her in Russian for failing to check in with him when she arrived.

"All visitors must make themselves known to me."

"I didn't know," Judith replied in halting Russian. "Besides, you weren't here."

"That's no excuse," the guard raged. "You are supposed to wait."

Judith's temper flared. "Where was I supposed to wait? I had no place to sit."

"You must give me your name and state the purpose of your visit." He shook his clipboard under her nose. "Give me your name!"

Judith refused. "If you were doing your job properly, you wouldn't have to shout at me now."

"I insist!"

Judith turned to Sergei Grigorovich. "Tell this guy that I'm a guest in his country. He's supposed to treat me with respect."

Grigorovich soothed the guard and sent him muttering back to his booth. "Even foreign visitors are supposed to observe the rules," he said to Judith.

"Fine. I'll obey your rules. No problem. Now, when are you going to let me see my father?"

"I cannot answer that question."

Back to square one.

The next morning, Judith began her assault on Intourist. Their answers were vague, but testy. Visits to Soviet citizens were proscribed. Soviet citizens were allowed to conduct their affairs away from the curious eyes of visiting foreigners.

"Don't you understand?" Judith struggled to keep from shouting. "This man is my father. I have a right to see him."

"Perhaps," said the chilly, anonymous voice at the other end of the line, "your father does not wish to see you."

Judith hoped that Phillip might call her and initiate a meeting from his end. But she did not hear from him. She made two more attempts to visit him on her own. The first time, the guard would not let her into the building. The second time, the fifth-floor apartment was deserted.

October melted weeping into November. The bright autumn colors faded and sullen rains dragged the dying leaves from the trees. Soon those same trees would be wadded with clots of wet snow. And still the vital meeting with her father had not occurred.

Judith knew that the authorities were capable of stalling a visit for weeks, months, indefinitely. But why would they, since they had instigated their reunion in the first place? It was beyond her comprehension. She was tempted to ask Aleksandr Dmitrov for help in cutting through the red tape, but how would she reach him? And what would she say? Anyway, she wasn't about to let Dmitrov have the manuscript. Her first loyalty was to Preston and Chester O'Brien and the State Department. If she did succeed in obtaining the manuscript, she would give it to Kenneth. Dmitrov was the KGB. She couldn't let him have it.

Then one morning in late November the telephone rang. It was Sergei Grigorovich. He spoke slowly and clearly in order to make himself understood over the annoying hiss that betrayed the presence of an intrusive listener on the line.

"Your father is willing to see you this afternoon. I will call for you in ten minutes."

Judith hurriedly gathered up the gifts she had brought for Phillip: a supply of tobacco and a new pipe, some food staples like coffee and chocolate, an Irish woolen sweater, a bottle of brandy, a parcel of mystery novels. "He used to adore them," Lydia had told her. "Tastes like that don't change."

"Do you want me to send your love?"

Judith had asked the question in a wry voice, but Lydia had answered straightforwardly: "No, darling. It would be better not to mention me at all."

"Did he ask you to go with him?" Judith wanted to know.

Lydia had looked shocked. "Oh, no. Never. He knew I wouldn't have done it. I love my country too much. And can you imagine growing up over there? Horrible. I couldn't do that to my children."

The doorbell rang. Judith admitted Grigorovich. "I've brought him some presents from home. Do you want to check them over for razor blades and microdots?"

"He can buy razor blades here, and he has no way of reading microdots. Shall we go?"

Grigorovich led her to a gray Zhiguli. He drove in silence through the rainwashed streets. The dimensions of the average pedestrian were swelling, Judith noticed, as they layered coats over sweaters and added long johns under their trousers.

The blocks of apartments at Sokolniki looked worse in the rain. The same guard was on duty inside. Grigorovich waved to him and passed on. The guard gave Judith a black look, and marked the visit down on his paper. The lobby and stairways smelled like moldy rubber boots. Grigorovich carried Judith's shopping bag. Judith appreciated the gesture. Toiling up those stairs was taxing enough for a healthy person; what was it like for a man in her father's condition?

A strange man opened the door. At least this one's fully dressed, Judith remarked to herself. Dark-haired, older than Phillip's previous roommate, this man wore khaki-colored slacks, brown boots, and a black sweatshirt. He and Grigorovich conversed briefly in Russian. Grigorovich turned to Judith. "This is Piotyr. He is sharing the apartment. Your father will be out in a moment. He isn't feeling well today."

Judith lowered herself onto the cushion of the bent plywood arm-chair and waited. Eventually Phillip shuffled out of the bedroom. He was wearing a heavy sweater with a shawl collar drawn up around his throat and baggy gray slacks. Judith stood up.

"Hello. I'm sorry you're not feeling well." Seeing his face, her old rage at him softened. He looked pathetic, drawn and pinched, slightly blue around the lips. He hadn't shaved in a couple of days.

He squinted at her. "What are you doing here? Why didn't you telephone first?"

"Didn't they tell you? Kenneth is Third Secretary at the embassy now. We'll be here for two years. I've been trying to see you for a couple of months. Did you find my note?"

Phillip shook his head. "Piotyr probably threw it away. Thought it was trash." He eased himself down onto the orange plastic-covered sofa. "You look all right."

The two Russians had moved to one corner of the room, but Judith could feel them listening, taking in every word. How could she broach the subject of the memoir? Even if she got her hands on it, how would she get it past the two of them?

"Thanks." Judith looked past him to the shelf under the window. It held an old-fashioned portable record player, a few albums without jackets, a small cassette player, and a pile of tapes. "I see you have a cassette player. If I'd known, I could have brought you some tapes. What kind of music do you like?"

Phillip's hands twitched. "All kinds. I have a particular fondness for Russian folk songs."

"Really?"

After a minute, Phillip sighed. "Handy items, these *magnitofoni*. A friend gave me that one. I listen to music on it, when I can get the batteries. Sometimes I take it with me when I go walking."

The conversation floundered. Judith noticed that her father's lips were trembling.

"Are you cold? I'll fix some tea. Or coffee. I've brought some coffee."

"Did you? That would be nice."

The kitchen was horrible, a dank hole that hadn't been properly cleaned for years. Judith hunted for a coffeepot but located only a single battered saucepan, which she scrubbed as best she could with her handker-chief. She tossed out her first pan of boiling water, boiled a second batch, threw a few measures of coffee into it, and strained the brew through the corner of a towel into cups. She found lump sugar, but no milk or cream. She carried the cups out into the living room.

"Do I have to share this with them?" She jerked her head toward Grigorovich and his companion.

"Not if you don't want to. Piotyr looks after himself."

"I'm glad to hear that. He's certainly not looking after you very well. What is he, nursemaid, jailer, or boyfriend?"

Phillip shrugged. "Does it matter? He told me I had to get up and get dressed, that I was having a visitor. He didn't tell me it was you." Phillip held the cup in both hands and sipped the steaming coffee gratefully. "This is wonderful. I can't tell you how long it's been since I had decent coffee. I'm not much of a cook."

"I am," Judith said promptly. "Can you come to dinner some night? I know Kenneth would like to meet you."

Phillip shook his head. "No. I don't think he'd care to have an old defector sitting at his table. I know I wouldn't, if I were in his shoes. I haven't felt like going out much lately."

"Then I'll cook for you here, next time I come."

"You don't have to. The kitchen isn't much, just a couple of gas rings."

"I want to. It's no trouble. After all, you're my father, aren't you?"

"Yes." Phillip looked a little sad. "I guess I am. Otherwise, you wouldn't be here."

Judith returned a week later, armed with scouring powder, brushes, disinfectant, American toilet paper, and rubber gloves. She spent the whole day scrubbing the apartment, and when she was finished, she stewed a chicken with some carrots and mushrooms she had found in the market. She left Phillip's larder stocked with tinned foods that he could heat for himself. On her third visit—Intourist restricted her to one a week—the weather was mild enough to throw open the window and air the living room and bedroom. Father and daughter lunched together on good Russian bread and sausages. When they were finished eating, Phillip suggested a walk in the park across the street.

"We won't have many more fine days. Winter will be here soon."

"But those stairs; are you sure?"

"Don't worry, I'll take my time. If I collapse, we've got that Intourist fellow and Piotyr to carry me up."

He moved slowly, like an old man. But he was only sixty-seven, no longer considered old in an America whose leader was over seventy. Judith held on to his arm as they strolled. She told herself that she would do as much for any elderly or infirm person. The Russians followed, close enough to hear every word that passed between them.

"Don't they make you angry?" Judith asked her father. "I'd like to take an eraser and rub them out. I hate the way they breathe down our necks."

"It's their job. They didn't choose this assignment. I'm sure they would much rather be playing soccer out here somewhere or swilling vodka at home with their friends. There's no point in making it hard for them; they'll only make it harder for us. I learned that lesson a long time ago."

In a quiet corner of the park, amid birch groves and rose gardens and in the center of a round flower bed, stood a statue of Lenin. It was typical of thousands all over the Soviet Union, the leader enlarged to three times his normal height, hatless, wearing an unbuttoned greatcoat, striding confidently into the future, his keen-eyed but kindly gaze fixed on some point on the horizon.

"The triumph of socialism." A row of benches stood in a half-circle facing the front of the statue. Phillip led her to the one in the center. "That's what he's looking for. That's one thing about the Russians, they don't mind taking the long view. One century, two, a half-dozen—what's the difference, if you reach your goal? We in the West want everything to happen in our lifetime."

"Is that what you wanted?" Judith sat beside him. She waited for the guards to interrupt. This was the first time she had broached the subject of his defection.

Phillip Abbott sighed. "I don't remember. It was a long time ago. Certainly I was impatient to touch the future. We all were in those days. We didn't have Lenin's long view."

"So here we are. Welcome to the future, comrade." Behind them, Judith could sense Piotyr and Grigorovich tensing, listening closely. "Tell me something. Was it worth it?"

"I don't mind." Phillip smiled wistfully. "I don't really miss the old life anymore. It took a while. Years and years. But now I've accepted it."

Judith wanted to ask him how much he had missed his children. Ten-year-old Vanessa and eight-year-old Judith were women now. They had grown up fatherless, thanks to this man's hunger to touch the future. She stayed silent, gazing at the flower beds that surrounded Lenin's plinth. They were barren and bare. After the first killing frost, gardeners had ripped up the plants, tossed them into wheelbarrows, and carted them away. Like everyone else in Moscow, Lenin had to wait until spring to see some color again.

Phillip Abbott shivered. "We'd better go back. I'm starting to feel the cold."

He moved more slowly on the walk home. His color was worse and he seemed weaker. At the door to his apartment, he thanked Judith for lunch. She understood that she was not to be invited in, and she turned away with a brisk word of farewell.

"Judith." His voice brought her back. "Will you come again?"

"I guess so. If they'll let me."

He nodded and retreated into the world that he had made for himself.

As the official car pulled up in front of Judith's building, Sergei Grigorovich said, "Starting next week, two visits per week will be allowed. I will call for you on Tuesday morning and again on Friday. Good-bye."

Judith wondered what had brought about this concession, and decided that Phillip's weakened condition was the reason. If they were to learn anything at all from him, he had to be in shape to talk.

Judith was beginning to catch on to the way the KGB thought. Today, for the first time, her conversation with Phillip Abbott had touched on the past. A promising start. The strangeness between father and daughter was evaporating, and at the same time the two Americans were beginning to regard Piotyr and Grigorovich as pieces of furniture. Clever little men. Clever enough to be acting on the orders of Aleksandr Nikolayevich Dmitrov.

CHAPTER 22

Moscow: January 1984

*T*he telephone rang. Judith stood frozen, her hand poised over the receiver. She knew if she picked it up, she would hear nothing but static. If she failed to answer, they would keep ringing and ringing, one hundred, two hundred times until she did. Twice she had tried leaving the receiver off the hook. Both times, a repairman knocked on her door within minutes and told her he had received a complaint that her telephone was not working properly. He walked straight over to the instrument, replaced it in its cradle, and cautioned her to be more careful in the future.

"Stop it!" she screamed. "Stop bothering me!"

The ringing persisted. She pulled on her leather boots and grabbed her *shuba,* her heavy fur coat, along with her hat and fur-lined gloves, and ran out of the apartment. Outdoors, the accumulation of ice and hard-packed snow on the sidewalk made walking slow and hazardous, but that didn't deter the man who followed her the moment she left the building. No matter how swiftly she moved, he kept pace. Like a wolf tracking an injured deer, he was confident of his ability to overtake her if necessary.

She entered the metro at the Kutuzovsky stop and took it three stops to the Kievskaya interchange. The escalators to the street were packed in both directions with grim-faced, well-padded Russians. The citizens of Moscow took winter seriously. Life was fraught with enough hardships, but when you factored in freezing weather and long nights, the difficulties compounded themselves.

The American embassy at 19 Tchaikovsky Boulevard was guarded not only by U.S. Marines but also by Soviet policemen. The marines on duty recognized Judith and waved her through the entrance. She glanced back. Her tail had stopped outside the gates. He produced a cigarette and asked one of the Russians for a light.

"Please," Judith said to the secretary outside the administrative offices on the third floor, "I'd like to see my husband for a few minutes. I won't keep him long."

"Take a seat, Mrs. Marlowe. I'll tell him you're here."

Kenneth found her huddled on a sofa in the waiting room, still swathed in her black sable coat, her fur hat pulled down over her ears. Her face looked very small and pale under the pile of dark fur.

"Judith, are you all right? What's going on?"

She looked up at him, her eyes wild and tear-filled. "I have to leave right away—I can't do this anymore, Kenny. I've got to get out of here."

"Wait two minutes." He grabbed his coat and hat and left a few messages with his secretary, then he took her arm and hurried her out of the building. They walked north, toward the zoo. A January warming trend had pushed the temperatures into the near balmy twenties, and for the first time since Christmas, the Moscovites they passed wore their mufflers below their chins.

Judith cast a glance over her left shoulder. Two men in dark coats and fur hats were following them, staying twelve feet behind them. His-and-hers KGB men.

"Make them go away, Kenny," she begged. "I can't stand it anymore. They ring the phone constantly, and when I answer, there's no one there. If somebody real does call, I can't hear them through the hissing and the static. And Phil—when I'm with him, they're right there every minute, listening to every word we say. We tried talking French, just to get some privacy for a few minutes, the illusion of privacy. They stopped that right away. Told us it was forbidden. Forbidden to talk to your own father! What kind of country is this?"

"I'm sorry you have to be subjected to this, but they're just doing their job," Kenneth began.

"Doing their job! That's what Phil says. He doesn't even notice them anymore. Or maybe he just doesn't give a damn. But I can't ignore them. They're in our lives, right there in the room with us."

"Take it easy," he said soothingly. "It's just a form of harassment. They won't hurt you. Nobody said this was going to be easy."

Judith halted just outside the gates of the park that adjoined the Moscow Zoo. She turned to Kenneth. In the frigid air, the clouds of frosty vapor from their breath mingled in front of their faces, creating a fine gray mist that dimmed vision. Grayness was everywhere in Moscow. A sky of unrelenting grayness pressed down on the drab city, insinuating itself into every corner, every crevice. What had happened to color, to light?

"They're waiting for him to die," she cried. "It's a game of cat and mouse. As long as he's alive, they don't mind if I fish for some clue about the memoirs. But if he's dead, that's one less problem they have to worry about. They've thought of everything, haven't they?"

Kenneth stepped closer to her. They never discussed the memoirs at home, not even in the relatively safe confines of the bathroom. "He hasn't said anything? You're sure? Made some sign, maybe—"

"Nothing! I've seen him twice a week for the past two months. They started harassing us before Christmas. And it hasn't stopped. They examine everything I take him to make sure I'm not passing messages, flip through every page of every book and magazine, dig through tea leaves and pipe tobacco, soak the labels off the bottles and cans I've brought. It's humiliating, having them think that even a simple gift from me is some kind of ruse. If they want the manuscript, why don't they just torture him and find out where it is?"

"Maybe they've tried that."

Judith pressed her gloved hand over her eyes. The thought of KGB technicians putting the screws to the frail, broken man who was her father was almost more than she could bear.

"They're depending on me to do it for them, aren't they? But I can't! He's dying a slow death. Every time I leave him, I'm terrified of what I might find when I go back. I'm so scared he'll die before we have a chance to say anything important to each other. But we're tongue-tied. And so we listen to music on that cassette player of his, and we chat about the ballet and the theater, or he reads while I mend or clean house for him, like some kind of spinster daughter. For the past four months, I haven't had any life but him, and it's so—so superficial. We're still strangers to each other. I thought at least I could get to know him better, but we can't talk. We're not connecting. I think he's glad to see me, but I can't be sure. He's half asleep or half drunk most of the time. I want to shake him, to wake him up, but I can't do that, either. I'm afraid he'll just fall apart in my hands, like an old, rotten rag doll."

She was weeping. Kenneth took her elbow and guided her to a park bench. He swept a dusting of snow from the iron seat and they sat. The men who had been following them watched boldly, from a distance of twenty feet.

Kenneth put his arm around Judith and held her until her sobs had subsided. He said, "If you go home now, you might never see him again. I guess you know that."

She gulped. "He's so dependent. The way he was living before I came—like some kind of derelict in a flophouse. I don't think he saw anyone from one week to the next. That horrible apartment. Can't we get him out of there?"

"You know we can't."

"If only they'd move him to the ground floor. Those stairs will kill him. I've complained to everyone I can think of, but I'm not getting anywhere. Blank walls everywhere I turn. I hate them for what they're doing to him!"

"He brought it on himself," Kenneth reminded her. "It was his choice to come here."

"It was either that or get fried in the electric chair," she snapped. "What would you have done?" She suppressed another sob and mopped her eyes again. "I'm sorry. It's not your fault. It gets to be too much for me sometimes. And then I've got to put in appearances at embassy functions and pretend that everything's all right. I'm not fooling anybody."

"We have tickets to the ballet tonight. That will take your mind off things."

"I don't want to go. I don't feel like smiling and saying nice things to anybody for the rest of the day."

"You can't stay home alone in that apartment," Kenneth said reasonably. "You'll go crazy if you don't get out and do something for yourself as often as you can." He took off his gloves and blew on his fingers. "I know this has been hard for you, Judith. Believe me, if I could have spared you any of it, I would have. But there wasn't any way out of it. I'm glad we can still talk."

"It's hard on you, too. I haven't been much fun lately, have I, Kenny? Too tired and depressed even to screw. That must be some kind of record for me. I think I've forgotten how to laugh, too."

"You're about as much fun as I can tolerate," Kenneth said with a weak smile. "Believe me, I'm not running around with other women. My needs have shrunk pretty small these days."

"Mine, too. The winter's never going to end, is it?"

"Oh, I think we can predict with certainty that it will. But we have to be patient. Do you want to come back to the embassy with me? We'll have some lunch in the cafeteria, and you can sit in the reading room until I'm through for the day."

Judith wiped away the ice crystals that had formed on her eyelashes. "No, I'm all right. I just had to let off steam. I have a date with Phil tomorrow, and I need to buy some stuff at the *beriozhka*. I'll see you when I get home."

"Good-bye, then." Kenneth gave her a fond peck on the cheek and walked away, one of the two men trotting at his heels as if on a leash.

* * *

Two minutes before the curtain went up on Prokofiev's *Romeo and Juliet* at the Bolshoi that night, Judith glanced up from her program to see Aleksandr Dmitrov taking his seat in one of the boxes reserved for high Soviet officials. He saw her at the same moment. They continued to gaze at each other while the house lights dimmed. Judith sat rigidly unmoving through the long first act, not hearing, not seeing, sucked into a black hole of memory, conscious only of his closeness, and the unbreachable distance between them.

She and Kenneth were escorting a visiting American Senator and his wife, friends of the senior Marlowes. At intermission, Judith suggested a promenade through the marble corridor outside. As she and the Senator strolled arm in arm under the crystal chandeliers, she kept watch for Dmitrov. She finally saw him, smoking a cigarette and conversing with an overstuffed brunette. The woman was laughing, and he was smiling. He glanced up as they passed, and glanced away again quickly, as if she were a stranger, a rather unattractive stranger.

Judith's cheeks burned. She wanted to fly in his face, demand at the top of her lungs that he call off the KGB bloodhounds who were plaguing her, that he leave her in peace. Instead she concentrated on what her companion was saying. When she looked back, Dmitrov and the woman had gone.

Throughout the long winter, rumors circulated that the new Soviet Premier was in failing health. When Yuri Andropov died on February 9, 1984, the world once again witnessed the grim but stirring spectacle of a Kremlin funeral. Judith watched the ceremonies on Phillip Abbott's small television.

The new Premier, chosen within hours of Andropov's death, was Konstantin Chernenko, a close friend of Leonid Brezhnev and a stalwart member of the old guard. Phillip listened closely to Chernenko's funeral oration.

"He looks pretty bad himself," he remarked as the camera panned over the aged figure huddled in his furs in the center of the platform. "A last gasp for the old men before they pass the baton to the next generation. Andropov's candidate didn't make it this time, but if he behaves himself, he'll get another chance. From the looks of things, it won't be very long. Chernenko looks like I feel." He chuckled.

Piotyr and Sergei Grigorovich seemed interested in Phillip's remarks. "You think the next leader will be Gorbachev?" Piotyr asked.

Phillip Abbott nodded. "He's smart, he knows how to keep from antagonizing people, and he keeps his record clean. When he was Minister of Agriculture, he survived a string of bad harvests without getting blamed himself. As it is, he's made it to Second Secretary, which is pretty impressive. My money's on him after Chernenko kicks off."

Judith was surprised by her father's awareness of Soviet politics. She had never seen him show a keen interest in anything but theater, opera, or ballet. "Art is forever," he would say. "A Beethoven symphony. Michelangelo's *David*. Great art is ultimate perfection. Why talk about anything else?"

At the same time, Phillip Abbott was a Soviet citizen, and what happened in the Kremlin had a profound effect on the lives of all Soviet citizens. Try as he would, Phillip could not ignore history.

The ice on the Moskva River was just beginning to break up when Vanessa telephoned. The Royal Shakespeare Company was coming to Moscow in April for an international theater festival, performing plays by the irascible British Fabian, George Bernard Shaw, and the fatalistic Russian bourgeois, Anton Chekhov. Vanessa had snagged two plum parts, the title role in *Major Barbara* and Masha in *The Three Sisters*.

Judith's delight in the news was undiminished by the fact that Vanessa had to place the call three times before the static on the line died down sufficiently so that she could be heard.

Vanessa swept into Moscow like a breath of spring air. She arrived at Judith's apartment laden with gifts for her sister, and for Phillip Abbott.

"I got everything on your list, and threw in some stuff of my own," she said as Judith transferred Phillip's things from a heavy suitcase to a couple of shopping bags.

Judith snipped a tag off the sleeve of a tweed sports jacket. "You don't have to see him if you don't want to, Van."

"Are you kidding?" Vanessa took no part in the sorting and repacking. She felt she had done more than her share by purchasing and then transporting the stuff. She sprawled on the sofa, a mug of coffee in one hand and a cigarette in the other. "And miss the opportunity to see my old man for the first time in all these years? As an actress, I can't afford to pass this up. Who knows, I might want to use it sometime." She smoked furiously, sucking her cigarette down to the filter in less than one minute.

Judith gave a distracted nod. "We'll go over right away, if you don't mind. I told Sergei you were coming today. He's coming by to pick us up. He should be here in a few minutes."

"Who's Sergei when he's at home?" Vanessa lit another cigarette.

Judith explained that her visits were restricted to two days a week, and that she and their father were always observed by Phillip's roommate and the Intourist guide, both of whom undoubtedly worked for the KGB.

Vanessa frowned. "What would happen if you went some other time?"

"I tried it. The guard on duty wouldn't let me see him, and Intourist canceled my privileges for two weeks. They said he had been ill and they didn't want me to catch his germs, but it was just an excuse. What it meant was, if I step out of line, I can expect to get slapped."

"Stupid bastards," Vanessa grunted after a long moment. "He gave up a lot, didn't he? And for what?"

Pressing her forefinger to her lips, Judith grabbed her sister's arm and hustled her into the bathroom. She turned on the shower and directed the spray at the vinyl curtain.

"If you want privacy around here, this is what you have to do. Listen, Van, I'm at my wits' end. I've been here for six months, seeing Phil twice a week, and I can't say one word to him without the goons listening in. You've got to get them off my back, just for a couple of minutes. Can you?"

Vanessa nodded and flashed Judith an okay sign. Just as Judith was turning off the taps, the doorman rang up to announce that the car from Intourist had arrived to take them to the Sokolniki apartment.

Piotyr answered Judith's knock. As the three of them filed into the flat, Phillip Abbott struggled to get out of his armchair.

"Good morning, Phil. How are you feeling?" Judith drew her sister over to him. "This is Vanessa."

The old man levered himself up. He teetered, but he managed to stay erect. He and Vanessa stared at each other for a long moment.

Phillip broke the silence first. "It was good of you to come. I'm glad to meet you."

"You can skip the courtesies, Pop." Vanessa's voice was strained, more high-pitched than normal. "I want to get something off my chest right away, and once I've said it, that's it, I won't keep hammering away at it. The fact is, I hate your guts. The only reason I came was so I could tell you to your face. I've been waiting for this chance for twenty-eight years."

"For God's sake, Van," Judith cried, but Vanessa plunged ahead.

"Men spy because they get money for it or because they have strong beliefs. They screw other men because they can't help themselves, that's the way they're made. But they don't leave their kids without even a backward glance unless their love was a sham and a joke." Vanessa swallowed hard. "The fact that you walked out like that proves that you never loved us. Nothing you say or do now can change that."

"I'm . . . sorry," Phillip mumbled.

"Can it," Vanessa snapped. "I don't want to hear it. As far as I'm concerned, you're a fossil, a sorry piece of hair and bone that's kicked around too long. I'm madder than hell that you're still alive, and that you're sucking up so much of Judy's life. But that's her business."

An awkward silence ensued. Phillip collapsed back into his chair. The two Soviets shuffled their feet. Judith lit a cigarette and handed it to her father. He took it gratefully but didn't speak. She lit one for herself.

Finally Vanessa expelled a long, gusty sigh and looked around. "Cripes, this is awful. Judy, can't you do something? A little paint or paper maybe?" She took a quick tour of the apartment, ducking into the bedroom, the bathroom, the kitchen alcove. When she returned, she flopped down on the plastic sofa. Her expression was sour. "Well, at least it's clean."

"It's a palace compared to the first time I saw it," Judith told her.

A carpet on the floor and new drapes at the windows added warmth and color. Phillip had insisted on keeping his old furniture, but Judith had added some cushions, a couple of floor lamps, and a handsome writing desk. She also kept a vase filled with fresh flowers when she could get them, and a bowl on the end table piled with fruit. Still hoping to persuade the authorities to move him to new quarters, she had put off painting the walls, but she supposed that was inevitable. She wondered whom she had to bribe in order to get some halfway decent paint.

"Judith has made me respectable again." Phillip Abbott cast a weak smile at his younger daughter. Vanessa's open hostility seemed to have created a bond between Phillip and Judith, a conspiracy of the longer-acquainted against the newly arrived.

"That's your opinion." Vanessa took out a cigarette of her own. She struck a match so forcefully that the flaming tip broke off. The ember landed on the arm of the sofa. She brushed it away, but it left a small black hole in the plastic. "To me, you look like a bum."

Phillip appealed to her. "Vanessa, I want you to know . . . all these years, you and Judith—you were never out of my thoughts."

Vanessa threw back her head. Her theatrical guffaw bounced off the bare walls. "I've heard a lot of lies from a lot of men, and I'll bet Judy's heard a lot more, but this one takes the prize! 'Never out of your thoughts' my Aunt Fanny. What a joke. Do you know what I think, Phil? I think you're a damn coward. You should have stayed and faced the music. What if they had sent you to prison? You would have been out by now, instead of sitting in this hole waiting to die. It's disgusting. What's more, I can't believe these people have any respect for you." She sent a look filled with challenge toward the two guards. "They despise you. That's why they're making it so hard for you to live like a human being."

"Don't, Van." Judith touched her arm. "Phil's not well."

"Phil's as tough as old boots. If he weren't, he'd be dead by now. Isn't that right, Phil?"

"That's right, Vanessa." Their father sighed. "I'm quite indestructible, it seems. Or perhaps my bad habits aren't as lethal as everyone always said they were."

Vanessa eyed Sergei and Piotyr again. "Couldn't they at least have found you someone pretty to look at?"

Phillip Abbott smiled. "They tried that. It made a nice change, but it didn't last."

"Too bad. Well, to business. Judith sent me a shopping list." Vanessa dived into one of the bags they had brought. "Cassettes—Judy said you like classical music. Wolfgang and Ludwig and Johannes; all the biggies in the latest interpretations. I know the pianist on this one, and I want to tell you, his fingering is superb. And this conductor—but never mind him. Some books. A friend of mine who has made a study of your tastes helped select them. Owen Adair. He's an old-timer at the Agency, retired now. Investigated your disappearance, and he's still baffled. He sends his regards."

Phillip frowned. "Adair? I don't recall—"

"Enough of that kind of talk," Sergei Grigorovich barked. "It is not allowed."

Vanessa stared at him. "I get it. We're supposed to keep it light. Okay. Anyway, Owen hopes you like them. Caviar was out, but I've some lovely English toffee—do you still have your teeth? And some memories of New England, clam chowder and baked beans and canned oysters for stew. Oh, and Tabasco sauce, to give your boiled cabbage some zip."

Phillip's face lit up. "I haven't had any of this stuff in years. Thank you. Thank you very much."

"This book is from me." She thrust an oversized volume into his hands. "No words, just photographs by Ansel Adams. To remind you of what you left behind."

Phillip turned over the pages. "So beautiful. I'd forgotten."

Vanessa had also brought clothing, underwear and pajamas from Harrod's, plenty of warm woolen socks, a pair of soft leather slippers and a heavy flannel robe, a couple of sweaters, two pairs of slacks, a tweed sports jacket and a set of six shirts, two knitted vests, a cashmere muffler, and a Burberry with a removable fleece lining.

"When you come to see me perform, I don't want you looking like some old ragpicker. My friends are all dying to meet you." Suddenly Vanessa's eyes lit up. "I have an idea, let's go out someplace. We can't stay here all day. It's terminally dreary. I bet you two could use a change of scene. And the Hardy Boys, too. They're probably as sick of this place as you are."

Judith hid her smile. When Vanessa desperately wanted something, she campaigned so intensely that she broke down all resistance. Now she declared that they had to take "Phil and the boys" to a restaurant with decent food, good music, and dancing, someplace with life and laughter and plenty of noise. Phillip's companion Piotyr, who had been gazing at the actress from England all afternoon with a dazed expression in his eyes, caved in at once. Must be bisexual, Judith mused. Or maybe it's just a job. Sergei Grigorovich was tougher. He began by refusing permission absolutely—"It is impossible"—but Vanessa worked on him until he finally agreed to telephone someone to "make arrangements." He reported that a table was reserved for them at the Hotel Rossiya.

"They have a band there, and dancing."

Piotyr took Phillip into the bedroom to help him dress. Vanessa kept darting in and out, giving orders, adding finishing touches. Throwing herself wholeheartedly into the project, she seemed to have forgotten how bitterly she hated her father.

When Phillip emerged forty minutes later, even Judith was amazed at the transformation. Phillip Abbott looked like an English country gentleman. Judith had guessed all his sizes correctly, and Vanessa had spared no expense. Phillip's cheeks were smooth, thanks to the new electric razor Vanessa had brought. The old man's color had even improved—a discreet touch of Vanessa's blush, perhaps? And some translucent powder to tone down the glaring purple veins on his nose?

"When I was little, I thought you were the handsomest man I had ever seen," Judith told him. "You still are."

Phillip looked pleased. He stood straighter, and he seemed to have more energy. "It's pretty hard to put on a show of sartorial splendor here unless you travel out of the country. Or have friends abroad."

"Right. You look shinier than a new penny," Vanessa said briskly. "Come on, let's get out of here."

A line of patrons was waiting to get into the Hotel Rossiya's dining room, but Sergei Grigorovich marched his charges straight up to the doorman, who admitted them without an argument. They checked their coats and hats and followed a waiter to a table near the stage. A twenty-piece dance band was playing "In the Mood." The musicians all wore red jackets. The bandleader faced the audience, and the expression on his face as he rhythmically pumped his arms up and down was so grim that it made Vanessa and Judith laugh out loud.

Vanessa shouted over the din, "This guy should take lessons from Lawrence Welk!"

In that immense, garishly lit room, the music was almost swallowed up by the noise and laughter generated by nearly a thousand patrons. They secured a bottle of vodka right away, but Grigorovich warned them that they would probably have to wait for menus. He excused himself for a few minutes, after casting a warning glance at Piotyr.

"We might as well dance," Vanessa declared. "Come on, Phil." She hauled her protesting father to his feet. "Judy, you take Piotyr. He looks like he knows how to have a good time."

Despite his efforts to keep an eye on Vanessa and Phillip, Piotyr turned out to be an excellent dancer. Not in Dmitrov's league, of course, but then Piotyr hadn't had a prima ballerina for a mother and Bolshoi training as a boy. Judith swayed around the floor in his arms. When they passed Vanessa and Phillip, who were moving very slowly, Vanessa suggested that they change partners. Piotyr tried to resist, but she threw her arms around his neck, kissed him on both cheeks, and dragged him away. Judith stepped close to her father. His right arm tightened around her waist.

"We need to talk," she said into his right ear. "You've written something. Certain people would like to have it."

"Oh? What people?"

"Who do you think? Preston. The CIA. Billy Whistle. The President. Everybody."

"I'm sorry, Judy, but I can't give it to you. Not if you're going to hand it over to them."

"Why in hell can't you?"

"Let's just say they wouldn't appreciate my style. Preston Marlowe never did have a sense of humor. So, my memoirs have generated some interest abroad as well as at home, have they? Piotyr has been panting after them. Sergei Grigorovich has undoubtedly been assigned to get them, too. Anyone else?"

"Yes. Valenskaya's son, Dmitrov. But he's in the same camp as Sergei and Piotyr. He came to me in London with some ridiculous story about wanting to get his wife and daughter out of the country. He said he needed something to bargain with, like your book. He asked for my help in getting it. I told him to get lost."

"Seems you're quite a popular girl all of a sudden." Phillip's breathing was becoming labored. The unexpected exertion was taking its toll.

At that moment, Sergei Grigorovich came charging over to them and pulled them apart. He told Phillip that he mustn't tire himself with dancing. They returned to their table, Sergei walking between them. When they arrived, they found that Vanessa had rearranged the seating so that the two guards were placed on either side of her. Phillip and Judith sat together, with Sergei on Phillip's left.

Judith estimated that she had had less than two minutes to speak to her father without anyone listening in. The brief conversation had left her frustrated and annoyed. Her father had no intention of giving her his memoirs so long as she planned to hand them over to Preston or anyone else in the American government.

Phillip was watching her over the rim of his glass. "I'm sorry I'm not a better dancer," he said. "It's been a long time."

Judith smiled. "That's all right. My feet have survived worse. When you've been to as many diplomat dances as I have—"

At that moment, Vanessa dumped a glass of vodka into Sergei Grigorovich's lap. With the confusion providing some cover, Phillip carefully continued his conversation with Judith.

"I hope you won't tell any of the people who knew me how my style has deteriorated," he said. "Back in the dark ages, I cut quite a figure on the dance floor."

Judith understood his meaning. "I promise I won't say anything," she replied. He had already refused to give her the manuscript for fear it might fall into the wrong hands. But whose? Preston's? O'Brien's at the CIA? Billy Whistle's? "Still, I doubt that anyone would care at this point."

"You're wrong." Phillip gazed at her intently. "You know how some people get when their illusions are shattered. Downright hostile. You're familiar with the fate of the messenger who brings bad news?"

Blood rushed to Judith's cheeks. He was warning her off, telling her to stay out of it. "Of course. 'Off with his head!' "

On the other side of the table, the disturbance had abated only slightly. Grigorovich was sponging off his trousers with his napkin. Vanessa kept trying to drop lit matches into his lap, while Piotyr laughingly attempted to restrain her. Sergei Grigorovich's sour expression only fueled their merriment.

"The Red Queen." Phillip nodded. "*Alice* was one of my favorites when I was a boy. I remember being very concerned about the poor girl when I read it the first time. I always had the feeling that something terrible was about to happen to her."

Judith wet her throat with vodka. Her father was managing this with great skill, as if he carried on coded conversations every day of his life, but she didn't trust herself not to stammer and give the show away. So far, Vanessa's outrageous party-girl act was distracting the two Russians, but they weren't stupid. Sooner or later they would catch on.

She said, "It wasn't Alice's fault she fell down the rabbit hole. After that, she had to make the best of it."

Phillip shook his head. "She was far too curious. The bottle that said, 'Drink me,' for example. Any sensible child would have left it alone."

"But then you wouldn't have had a story," Judith pointed out. "I've eaten and drunk plenty of stuff that was bad for me. I'm still here."

"A dangerous habit." Phillip smiled. "Too often poisons come in pretty bottles. As a father, I would caution you to leave them alone."

After that, Phillip applied himself to his drinking. He picked at his dinner, which was excellent, preferring to nourish himself with vodka. The evening dragged on. Vanessa danced with each of the guards in turn, leaving the other sitting at the table with Judith and her father, who had lapsed into a smiling stupor.

"I've enjoyed this," he told them when Sergei Grigorovich announced that they must leave. "Probably the last party I'll have."

"With any luck, we've finished off your liver," Vanessa said as she helped her father on with his coat.

"Made of high-quality cowhide," Phillip wheezed. "Yankee goods. Crafted with pride in the U.S.A."

Back at the Marlowe apartment, Vanessa pulled Judith into the bathroom and turned on the shower. "What was all that crap about dancing and *Alice in Wonderland* and poison? Is the old man getting senile?"

Judith perched on the edge of the tub. "He doesn't want anyone in the State Department to have the memoirs."

"Fine. Wonderful. So give them to Sasha." Vanessa lifted her skirt, pulled down her panty hose, and sat on the toilet. "Did he tell you where to find this thing?"

Judith shook her head. "Not a clue. I don't know what to think. He seemed particularly anxious to keep it out of Preston's hands. You don't think Preston is a traitor, do you? It's not possible!"

"It's all moot until he gives you the memiors or whatever it is. Find it first, and then worry about who to give it to."

"He doesn't want me to get involved. He made that quite clear. He's worried about me. But why did he write his memoirs if he didn't want anyone to read them? I give up."

"At least you didn't have a couple of animals trying to rape you in front of a room full of people. That Sergei was a sly number. When we were dancing, he reached down between my legs and tickled my clit. I wanted to punch him."

"This means I can't even trust Kenny," Judith fretted. "If he gets it, he'll stuff it into a diplomatic pouch and send it straight to Washington, which is apparently the last thing Phil wants."

"If you ask me, even Phil doesn't know what Phil wants." Vanessa pulled up her panty hose, flushed the toilet, and went to the sink. "I don't believe there is a manuscript. He's playing one of his stupid spy games, one last fling before he croaks."

"He liked you," Judith said. "I could tell. He's proud of you, Van."

Vanessa made a face. "The old bastard can choke on his pride for all I care. I still hate his guts." She turned off the taps. "I don't know about you, but I'm drunk and exhausted and I don't know how I'm going to make a ten o'clock rehearsal tomorrow. Let's go to bed."

Grigorovich and Piotyr permitted Phillip to see one performance of each of the plays in which Vanessa appeared. They would not allow Judith to sit with her father, nor would they allow Phillip to visit with Vanessa and the other actors backstage. As soon as the curtain fell, the Russians hustled the old man out of the theater and into their Zhiguli.

On the morning of Vanessa's departure from Moscow, she went with Judith to pay her father a farewell visit. A taxi was waiting downstairs to take her to the airport. When the time came for Vanessa to leave, she stooped over and gave Phillip a perfunctory kiss on the cheek.

"I probably won't get back for your funeral. Might as well kiss the corpse while it's still warm."

As she was drawing away, Phillip grasped her hand and held it fast. "I'll never stop regretting what I've missed. Thank you for coming. Thank you."

Vanessa stared down at him coldly. "Too late, Pop. I couldn't stop hating you if I tried. It's a habit of long standing, and I'm too old to change."

After she had gone, Phillip shuffled into his bedroom and closed the door. Judith thought she heard him crying.

CHAPTER 23

Moscow: May 1984

On a mild May morning, Phillip Abbott announced that he wanted to stroll in the park across the way. Judith made sure he was well bundled up in multiple sweaters and the lined Burberry. As they left the building and crossed the street to Sokolniki Park, Phillip leaned heavily on her arm. He was definitely weaker than he had been in the autumn. His breathing was labored and shallow, and he could barely lift his feet. He shuffled along slowly, like an old, old man.

"Do you want to go back?" Judith asked before they even reached the park gates.

"No. A little change of scene will do me good."

"You've got to get a better apartment. I'll call them again. This time I'll keep insisting until they do something."

"No, don't bother."

"Honestly, it's no bother."

"You don't understand, Judy. I won't be around long enough to make it worth your while. Let's sit, shall we? Got any cigarettes?"

Judith handed him a cigarette and snapped her lighter for him. "Vanessa wouldn't approve of my giving you a cigarette in your condition. You can hardly breathe."

"Vanessa?" Phillip's laughter triggered a coughing fit, the worst Judith had yet witnessed. When it passed, Phillip gasped, "Vanessa would light the whole pack for me, stick them between my lips, and wish me good riddance."

"She called last night," Judith said. "She's starting a new film. Spy thriller. They're shooting most of it in Ireland."

"Vanessa's quite a girl." Phillip sighed. "Hell of an actress, too. I'm not surprised. She's Lydia's daughter."

"Don't tell her that. She and Mother have always grated on each other."

"Remember how Vanessa organized that dinner party at the Hotel Rossiya? That was Lydia all over: sweeping aside objections, asserting herself, gathering people in, charging them up, making the whole thing go. Poor Sergei and Piotyr. I bet their heads were spinning. I thought it would cost them their jobs, and I was right."

Sergei and Piotyr had been replaced shortly after the party by a different team. The guards were changed now every few visits, but Judith still thought of her Intourist guide as Sergei Grigorovich and Phillip's companion as Piotyr. She had asked one of the Sergeis about his predecessor. He replied with a bored shrug.

"Our old friend." Phillip Abbott looked up at the statue of Lenin, still striding confidently into the future. All around, the delicate green buds on the horse chestnut trees were beginning to swell. "There's gold on the horizon but mud underfoot. He ought to watch his step."

The heroic figure really did look as if he was about to step off his plinth into the churned-up flower beds below.

"Lenin was a good leader," Phillip said. "Ruthless, but with a firm sense of reality. Stalin made his own reality. He didn't care what it cost in terms of human lives and suffering."

"What amazes me is that so many people stayed faithful to the idea of Communism, even when they saw what Stalin was doing," Judith said.

"A lot of crimes have been committed in the name of Jesus Christ, too," Phillip reminded her. "People can't help—" He broke off. Judith looked at him. His face looked chalky and he was gasping.

"Phil, are you all right? What's the matter?"

"Nothing. Just a weak spell. I get them sometimes. Guess I'd better go back and lie down."

Escorted by the two keepers, they made their way back to the apartment building. Judith kept one arm firmly around her father's waist. He had lost weight since the winter. Under the layers of clothing, his body felt as thin as a preadolescent boy's. They stopped to rest in the lobby. The stale winter odor in the building was appalling, enough to kill a cat. Phillip's breathing was becoming more labored.

"You're in no condition to climb those stairs. I'm taking you home with me." Judith turned to Sergei Grigorovich's replacement. "Bring the car. This man is ill. He needs care."

"We will look after him."

"You'll kill him. I'm not letting him climb those stairs. It's a crime to expect it of him."

"No, no, it's all right, Judy. I'm fine. Really. Just tired."

Phillip insisted on toiling up the stairs. He took them one at a time, pausing to rest frequently, stopping for several minutes to catch his breath on the landings. Judith stayed right with him. She asked once if he was in pain. He didn't answer. The new Piotyr went ahead to unlock the door. By the time they reached the fifth floor, Phillip was staggering. Judith was certain that only a tremendous force of will kept him from collapsing before he crossed his threshold.

She urged him forward toward the bedroom. Suddenly his shoulders contracted. He cried out and slid to the floor.

"Oh, my God." Judith dropped to her knees beside him. She loosened his necktie and shirt collar and grabbed a cushion to put under his head. "Call a doctor!" she barked at the two men. "An ambulance. Can't you see he's sick? He may be dying. Hurry!"

The Russians looked at each other. Judith could see their attitude etched on their faces: it was no concern of theirs if the old American traitor died on their watch. Still, they had to go through the motions. The Sergei Grigorovich replacement picked up the phone.

"Don't do this, Phil," Judith begged. "It's not time yet. We've only just met. Please. We need more time."

His eyes were closed and he was breathing with difficulty. He needed heart monitors, a respirator, oxygen. She felt for his pulse. It was so weak she had trouble finding it, and when she did, she couldn't count the beats. They were too erratic, too slow, too feeble. The Russian was still on the phone. Judith asked the younger of their keepers to fetch her a cloth from the bathroom. At least she could wipe away the cold sweat that had gathered on Phillip's forehead. When he had gone, she leaned over and whispered into her father's ear.

"Where is it? Tell me, please. I won't give it to Preston or Kenneth either. I promise."

He didn't reply. She lifted an eyelid. His pupils were sliding upwards into his skull.

"Phil," she shouted, "come back! Can you hear me? It's not time yet. This is Judy, your daughter. Little Judy. Daddy, please come back. Please. Daddy!"

She pressed his hand to her cheek. His eyes flickered open and he managed a weak smile. She sobbed with relief.

The ambulance was an eternity in coming. Forty-five minutes after it had been summoned, two attendants trooped into the apartment carrying a folded stretcher. Their uniforms were gray in color, stained and stiff with grime. Judith wondered when they had last been washed. A young woman doctor accompanied them. She applied a stethoscope to Phillip Abbott's chest and shook her head.

"Are you his daughter?"

"That's right. My name is Judith Marlowe and my husband works for the American embassy. I want the best for him, do you understand? I don't care what it costs."

"Medical care is free to all citizens of the Soviet Union," the woman informed her. "We have the best hospitals in the world."

"Fine. Wonderful. Just get him to one, can't you? He needs help."

Judith followed the stretcher crew down the stairs. The ambulance, brown in color, looked like a scuffed-up panel truck. The two attendants rolled Phillip Abbott onto a gurney and then lifted him inside. Judith started to climb in. The doctor stopped her.

"It is not allowed."

"I don't care what's allowed." Judith pushed the doctor's arm away. "He's my father and I'm going with him. I'm going to stay with him every minute, and if you try to stop me, I'll make the biggest stink you ever saw. I know all the correspondents—*The New York Times, Newsweek, Time*, the London *Times*. I'll be on the phone quicker than you can say Joseph Stalin. Now get out of my way." The other woman yielded.

The only amenity inside the ambulance was a battered oxygen tank. One attendant drove while the other fiddled with the gauges on the tank. The doctor sat up front with the driver. Judith assumed that her two Russian guards were following in the Intourist car. She urged the attendant to hurry with the oxygen. Phillip's lips were turning blue and he was gasping for breath. At the very moment the attendant managed to place the cup over Phillip's mouth and nose, the ambulance hit a pothole and knocked the man on his rear. Judith clung to the side of the gurney. While the attendant was scrambling around on the floor, Phillip opened his eyes and smiled at her.

"Vladimir—watch his step—"

Judith called to him, but he had lapsed into unconsciousness again.

The hospital looked like a workhouse out of a Dickens novel, a sooty red-brick fortress with narrow windows and scarred doors. The concrete steps were pitted and pocked, crumbling away in spots. The attendants were gentle enough as they lifted the gurney down from the ambulance and carried Phillip Abbott into the receiving area. They parked him in the middle of the floor and departed. Judith looked around for the doctor. She, too, had vanished.

Two minutes passed. No one even glanced at the figure on the gurney. Finally Judith shouted in Russian, "Isn't anyone going to help this man?" She walked over to the desk and addressed an overweight blonde who was picking a hangnail. "Where are the doctors? I want a doctor for my father and I want him now. I am an American citizen, and this man is my father. Do something!"

"Do you have his *spravka*?" the woman asked in a bored voice. "He must have his proper polyclinic document. And his internal passport as well. How do we know he has permission to live in the city?"

Judith gaped at her. "What are you talking about? We've just come from his apartment. Of course he has permission."

"We cannot treat him if he does not live in this district. I must examine his papers."

"To hell with his papers!" Judith shouted. "He needs a doctor! He's dying!"

"He has to wait his turn along with everybody else," the woman informed her.

"Where's the telephone? I'm going to call the American embassy."

"There are no public telephones here. You will have to go outside."

"Absolutely not. I am not moving an inch until my father gets some attention."

"Within the hour." The standard reply. The Russian language had no word for "immediately." Everything was "within the hour." Judith was accustomed to being patient in shops and restaurants, but this was different.

"No, not within the hour," she insisted. "Now. I want a doctor now!"

"Others are waiting."

Judith looked at the people in the waiting room. They gazed back at her with hostile eyes. Old grandmothers in their *babushki* held their little charges on their laps. The children's eyes were dull, their cheeks flushed. They watched the scene listlessly, too feverish to care. A couple of injured workers occupied the bench nearest the door. One cradled his bandaged arm close to his chest. The other held a bloody rag over one eye. A young woman shared the same bench. She looked like a victim of domestic violence, with two blackened eyes, a cut on one cheek, and a bleeding mouth. They were sick, all right, but they weren't dying, and her father was.

"I demand to see the administrator," Judith said loudly. "Who's in charge of this hospital? I'll report all of you to the authorities. You'd better believe that the people in your government are going to hear about this, and so are newspapers all over the world. This man is a friend of your country. Do something!"

All the while, she did not relinquish her grip on her father's hand. His flesh was still warm and pliable. She thought she detected answering pressure, but when she leaned over him, he still seemed to be unconscious.

"It's all right, Daddy," she murmured. "If I make enough noise, they're bound to pay attention."

Finally a doctor-and-nurse team arrived. The doctor, another woman, checked Phillip Abbott over and ordered that he be taken to an examination room. Judith helped the nurse push the gurney. When they arrived at the entrance to the curtained cubicle, the nurse told her that she could not enter.

"It is not sanitary."

"Don't be a fool. I'm not going to spit on him. I want to be with him. If you don't like it, you'll have to throw me out bodily. But I'm warning you, it won't be easy."

"It's all right," the doctor said. She was in her forties, small and gaunt, with dark brown hair streaked with gray. She wore it drawn back into a braided knob at the nape of her neck. Her features, free of makeup, were regular and pleasing. She was still quite attractive in her way. "You can come in."

She opened Phillip's clothing to the waist and listened to his chest. She probed his vital organs, shone a light in his eyes and ears and throat, tested his reflexes.

"What do you know about his medical history?" she asked Judith in strongly accented but fluent English.

Judith was grateful not to have to struggle with Russian. "He's been an alcoholic for years. I think he's been hospitalized for it a couple of times. He jokes that he doesn't have any liver left. I don't know how true that is. He smokes a lot, and doesn't eat much. I think he's diabetic, but he doesn't do anything about it. He just drinks. I suppose you could say he's depressed. That's all I know. I wish I knew more."

"His condition is very bad. I think there is bleeding inside, but I can't be sure. He must go to surgery. If there is any hemorrhaging, they will find it. But I can't promise that he will survive."

"I know. Just do what you have to do. Please don't waste any more time."

The doctor nodded. "I will arrange for it to be done as quickly as possible."

Judith waited on a hard wooden bench outside the operating theater. She struck up a conversation with the woman beside her, whose young daughter was being operated on for some sort of rupture. Not her appendix; perhaps her spleen. The woman was grateful for someone to talk to and told Judith all about her drunken husband and her grasping in-laws. Judith brought out a pack of cigarettes and offered her one. The woman declined but accepted a roll of hard mints and a ballpoint pen. Their conversation flagged. The woman dozed. Judith smoked one cigarette after another. Her mind felt numb. She desperately wanted her father to live, but she knew from experience that wanting and hoping had no power to heal or to work miracles. Prayer only consoled the one who prayed, which was probably a good enough reason for it.

A surgeon appeared and told the girl's mother that the operation had been successful. The child had already been sent to her room. Her mother could join her there. Judith wished her luck, and the woman hurried away.

Judith lost track of how much time passed. She might have dozed; she wasn't sure if the images running through her mind were dreams or memories. Someone spoke her name. She looked up and saw the doctor who had examined Phillip.

"What's happening? Is he all right?"

The woman sat on the bench beside her. "It is too soon. I am sure you are very worried. I just wanted to tell you that the surgeon who is doing the operation is quite excellent. Our hospitals don't look very pretty, but our physicians are well trained. We practice good medicine here."

"I'm sure you do. Look, I'm sorry for the ruckus I made, but he's my father. I haven't known him very long, and I don't want to lose him."

"I understand. It is very frustrating even for Russians, but for Americans it is worse. You are used to quicker action. I . . ." She moistened her lips with her tongue. "I have heard of you, Mrs. Marlowe. My name is Olga Dmitrova. Aleksandr Nikolayvich is my husband."

Judith stared. She had trouble believing that this petite, careworn, motherly person in the stained lab coat was the wife of the elegant Dmitrov and the daughter-in-law of the imposing Valenskaya. "I remember now. He told me once that you were a doctor. I guess I'd forgotten."

"When I heard you were here, I offered to take care of Mr. Abbott. Actually, nobody else wanted to deal with the screaming American lady." Olga smiled hesitantly.

"I should have known." Judith twisted her handkerchief. "I thought it was very convenient, your speaking English. You're just another KGB plant, aren't you? I've seen them all—male prostitutes, Intourist guides, TASS reporters. Your husband even pretended to be a cultural attaché, among other things. Why not a doctor, too?"

Olga Dmitrova drew herself up. "Excuse me, Mrs. Marlowe, but I am not a *stukach* for the KGB."

"Why should I believe you? I know how they work. They can turn anybody into an agent. All they need to do is find out where you're vulnerable and exert the right kind of pressure."

"They wouldn't find it with me." The little woman lowered her voice. As she talked, her fingers plucked a button on her stained white coat. From time to time, she cast furtive glances at the other people in the corridor. "My brother Yakov was what your newspapers call a Jewish dissident. He wanted to emigrate, and when they wouldn't let him, he tried to tell the world what was happening here. The KGB hounded him and persecuted him and eventually they sent him to a psychiatric hospital, where he died. He was mistreated there. Beaten. And he was given no care when he was dying. He was a good man, a good Soviet, but they killed him. The KGB." She looked away, her teeth clamped down on her lower lip.

Judith was horrified. "I'm sorry. Sasha—your husband never told me. I had no idea."

"You have met my daughter, haven't you?" Olga Dmitrova would not meet Judith's gaze. "Irina. She told me about you, Sasha's beautiful American lady friend. Two years ago, when Irina was sixteen, she applied for her internal passport. For nationality, she could have put Russian, because of her father. Instead she wrote *Evrei:* Jew. For her Uncle Yakov. Her father was furious with her. That action ruined her life. She is on the outside now, a dissident like Yakov. She has no job, no rights, no future. I hope with all my heart that she doesn't end up like he did. The KGB tore our family apart. It took my brother. It ruined my marriage. It cast my child into a dark hole. As far as the system is concerned, Irina doesn't exist. Don't tell me how much you know about the KGB, Mrs. Marlowe. I know more."

She started to walk away. Judith ran after her and grabbed her arm. "Didn't Sasha know about Yakov? What they were doing to him?"

The pain in Olga's eyes was infinite. "Yes, he knew. He directed the operation himself. Irina learned the truth. She never forgave him."

Judith froze. "I don't believe you. He—he wouldn't do that!"

"He had no choice. They have ways. What was that you said about the point of vulnerability? Our son was dead, but he still had Irina and me. They never approved of me. They expected great things of Sasha, but the fact that his wife was a Jew held him back. From time to time, they devised ways of testing his loyalty. He had to cooperate, or lose everything."

"I had no idea." Judith dropped her hand from Olga Dmitrova's arm. Her head was spinning. "He never told me. I'm . . . sorry."

A man in soiled surgical whites approached and beckoned Olga Dmitrova aside. They spoke in hushed voices, then Olga turned to Judith. "I am sorry to tell you that your father has died. There was too much blood lost from internal hemorrhaging, and during the surgery his heart stopped beating. They tried to revive him, but it was no use."

"Thank you," Judith murmured. "I know you did everything you could to save him." The surgeon nodded and went away.

"You have had a shock." Olga Dmitrova touched her arm. "Would you like a glass of tea?"

"No, thank you. I'm all right. I'm sorry about what I said. It was terribly insulting. I never dreamed—"

"You have every right to be suspicious. I would be, in your place. You must leave your name with the person at the desk as next of kin. They will be in touch with you about the funeral. Will you be taking your father's body home to America?"

"No. He was a Soviet citizen. They gave him the Order of Lenin, did you know that? He's lived here for nearly thirty years."

"You have my very deep sympathy," Olga said. "If I can do anything for you, you may call me here."

Judith nodded. "Thank you. You've been very kind."

She walked back to the apartment on Sokolniki 8. For the first time in nearly eight months, no one was watching, no one was following. She was alone. When she arrived at the building, the doorkeeper's booth was empty. She passed through the lobby and climbed the stairs to the fifth floor.

The apartment was in ruins. Phillip Abbott's books had been ripped from their bindings and the pages scattered. The upholstery on the armchair and sofa had been slashed, the stuffing ripped out. The rug had been pulled up, crumpled, and stuffed into a corner. Letters, papers, stationery, and notebooks from the desk lay in a heap in the middle of the floor.

In the kitchen, every can, jar, box, and cannister had been opened, the contents dumped into the sink and sifted. Shards of glass and bits of pottery from broken plates crunched under Judith's feet. The single hanging cabinet had been pried off the wall.

The bedroom was the worst. Pillows hemorrhaged their feathers and the mattress oozed cotton batting and coils of spring. The seams of Phillip's clothes, including those Vanessa had brought from London, had been ripped apart, the pockets torn out. Phillip's shoes were cut open, the soles separated from the uppers, the insoles removed. His toiletries had been opened, emptied, smashed. A snapshot that Judith had given him of her and Vanessa standing on Waterloo Bridge had been pulled from the frame and shredded.

In a daze, Judith returned to the living room. Nothing had been stolen, as far as she could see, but nothing had been left whole. The pitifully few possessions that Phillip had amassed in over a quarter of a century of living in the Soviet Union had been desecrated, pulverized, vandalized. Even while his body was being probed by Soviet scalpels, Soviet knives had been destroying his belongings. Nothing was left worth saving; no keepsake remained untouched.

"What are you doing here?" The Intourist guide stood in the doorway. "This apartment is being sealed up."

"Try it." Judith dug her heels in. "Just try and throw me out of this place. He believed in your country, in your system, in your leaders. He did what he did because he wanted peace. And this is how you treat him."

"He betrayed his first country, why not his second? He was a parasite, unreliable, a danger to himself and others."

"Get out of here!" Judith flew at him, fists flailing. "This is my father's home and I'm his daughter and I'm ordering you to get the hell out of here or I'll call the police. Out! Out!"

The Russian grabbed her wrists and twisted her arms behind her back. "You must not interfere. Come. I will drive you home."

"I'm not going anywhere," Judith spat, struggling vainly. "I'm staying here. I want to mourn my father in the place where he lived out his life."

"It is not allowed. You must leave at once."

"I won't!"

A stranger appeared, a short, stocky man wearing navy-blue slacks and a navy sweater. He grabbed her right arm as the other man took her left. Together they hustled her out of the apartment and down the stairs to a waiting Zhiguli. She squirmed and kicked, not because she had any hope of escaping but because she wanted to let them know that arresting her wouldn't be easy.

The stocky man got behind the wheel. They left the Garden Ring Road and headed into a suburb in the southeastern part of the city. The driver had barely switched off the engine before a man in a uniform pulled open the rear door and helped the other man haul her out. Judith let her legs go limp, making herself a dead weight. Together, the first two men dragged on her arms while the uniformed man lifted her ankles, and the three of them bore her bodily into the building. They dumped her in a small windowless room furnished with a table and two chairs and locked her in.

Judith pounded on the door with her fists. "You can't hold me here!

I'm an American citizen! I demand to speak to my ambassador! I want my husband! I want a lawyer!"

She was just putting on a show of courage. She had sat through numerous State Department briefings detailing dangers to the foreign visitor in the Soviet Union and other Eastern bloc countries. They had the right to do anything they wanted. She could be charged with spying, expelled from the country, thrown into prison, or shipped to Siberia. The incident would create a ripple of sensation in the Western press and provoke strong protests from the ambassador and Preston and the President. But that wouldn't help. Like Phillip and Olga Dmitrova and Aleksandr, Judith was at the mercy of the system.

After an hour, her interrogator arrived. He looked like an accountant, balding, bespectacled, fussy. He wore a badly cut, ineptly sewn suit of gray serge over a hand-knit sweater vest and a limp white shirt. Behind his glasses, his eyes were gray and humorless. He carried a briefcase, from which he extracted a cassette tape recorder.

"This is a grave business, Mrs. Marlowe. You were apprehended while trespassing in the dwelling of a citizen of the Soviet Union. Attempted robbery is a serious crime."

"That Soviet citizen happened to be my father, who died this afternoon. I was looking for a memento—anything your thugs hadn't destroyed. Please congratulate them on their thoroughness."

"Did you remove any objects from the apartment?"

"Like what? A roll of film? A microdot? An envelope of incriminating photographs? A manuscript?" She watched his face for some reaction. He remained impassive, absolutely wooden. "No, Mr. I-don't-know-what-your-name-is. I didn't take anything. You can search me if you like."

"All in good time. You came to Moscow with a mission, did you not? An ulterior motive. You wanted something from the spy Abbott."

"Yes, I wanted to know my father. By a happy coincidence, my husband was assigned to the American embassy. I took advantage of the situation and started visiting Phillip."

"You must not twist the truth. We will find out everything in the end."

"Bring on the sodium pentothal, then. I have nothing to hide." She hoped he wouldn't see through her false bravado. Inside, she felt sick with fear.

"Perhaps you will be good enough to listen to this." He took a cassette tape from his briefcase, put it on the player, and pressed a button. Judith heard herself whispering, "Where is it? Tell me, please. I won't give it to Preston, or Kenny either. I swear it."

The man rewound the tape. "Would you like me to play it again?"

"No, I heard it."

"What were you talking about?"

"His wedding ring. He was wearing it when he defected. I wanted it for a keepsake."

"That is a lie, a thin, poorly told lie that betrays a singular lack of invention. Your father never had a wedding ring. And what would your stepfather, Preston Marlowe, want with the ring of his wife's first husband? You were talking about something else. What was it?"

"I don't remember. I believed he was dying and I was very upset. I wasn't thinking clearly."

"More lies. I am losing patience, Mrs. Marlowe."

He kept it up for another hour. He played the tape over and over, and asked her again and again what she wanted from her father.

"He made some sign to you, a signal, did he not? He told you where to look. If not there in the flat, then in the ambulance. After he died, you couldn't wait to get back to the flat to find the item. You found it, didn't you?"

"No."

"You're lying."

"Prove it."

"I will." To her surprise, he stood up, packed the tape recorder in his briefcase, and went out. A minute later, two women came into the room. They were both middle-aged, square and stout, one with the dark hair, dark eyes, and swarthy complexion of a Georgian, the other a classic Slav with fair hair, ruddy cheeks, and glittering, porcine eyes. The Slav said, "Remove your clothing, please."

"I'll do no such thing."

"If you do not cooperate, we will bring in two soldiers to help us. Remove your clothing and lay it on the table."

Judith scanned the ceiling for hidden cameras. She didn't see any. She removed her coat, skirt, pullover sweater, oxford cloth shirt, and shoes. The Georgian examined each item carefully, paying special attention to hems and seams.

"The rest, your undergarments. Come on, hurry up. The quicker you obey, the quicker you can get dressed again."

Judith pulled off her slip, unfastened her bra, peeled off her panty hose, and slipped off her underpants. She stood shivering under the Slav's unblinking gaze while the Georgian picked at the fine lace and silk and stuck her hand into the legs of the panty hose.

"Jewelry," the Slav said. "Rings, watch, earrings."

"Not until I get my clothes on. It's freezing in here."

"Jewelry," the woman repeated. "Rings, watch, earrings." Fighting back tears, Judith removed her jewelry.

"Now," said the Slav, "turn around, place your hands on the wall above your head, spread your feet. I will do this quickly. It won't hurt."

"I will not! If you think I stashed a can of microfilm up my vagina or my rear or anyplace else, you're crazy. Stay away from me! If you lay a finger on me, I'll scream the place down and I'll blacken both your eyes in the bargain."

The Slav shrugged. She went to the door and called out, "Ilya! Andrei!"

"All right!" Judith shouted. "Just get it over with, will you?" As she turned to the wall, she heard the squeak of stretching rubber as the Slav pulled on a glove. Tears spilled over and ran down her cheeks.

When it was over, the two women left, taking with them her coat and purse. Judith dressed hurriedly and sat in the chair facing the desk. She blotted her eyes and vowed not to cry again, no matter what they did to her.

The door opened and a new interrogator entered. He was tall, bulky, and completely hairless, lacking even eyebrows and eyelashes. Unlike his predecessor, he was a snappy dresser with expensive tastes, and he smelled like the Saint Laurent counter at a Paris department store. His hands were beautifully manicured, and a heavy ruby ring glittered on his left pinkie.

"Mrs. Marlowe." His voice was a deep Russian bass, his English only slightly accented. "My condolences. But we must not waste time." He took his place on the other side of the table. "What were you looking for in your father's apartment?"

"I—I don't know what you're talking about."

"What was the object you asked your father about? Why did you tell him you wouldn't give it to Preston?"

Judith cleared her throat. "I have nothing to say. I want to call my embassy."

He smiled slowly, raising the curtain of his upper lip to reveal two gold canine teeth. Judith shrank away from him. He was hideous beyond belief, and worse, he looked like he could make a meal of her with a single bite.

"Did your father make some sign before he died, perhaps a signal with his eyes or his hands?"

"I have nothing to say," she croaked. "I want to call the embassy."

This went on. After an hour, the ogre sighed deeply and lapsed into silence, drumming his polished fingertips on the tabletop. Judith wondered if he had finished. Then he said quite offhandedly, "Who is Vladimir?"

"Who?" Judith was startled by this new tactic.

"In the ambulance, your father spoke of Vladimir. Who is Vladimir?"

"I don't know. I never heard him mention anyone named Vladimir before." So the bumbling attendant had been listening after all. She wasn't surprised.

"Who is Vladimir?"

"I don't know. I have nothing more to say. I want to call the embassy."

The man stood and leaned over the table. "Why would a dying man use his last breath to give you a name that you don't recognize? Is it some sort of code? Who is this person? Where can we find him?"

"I don't know and I don't care."

"Tell me!" he roared and brought his fists crashing down on the tabletop. Judith whimpered and covered her ears. He slapped her hands aside. The blow was light, but the promise of violence was there, just waiting to be released. If he wanted to, he could kill her with a single blow. "I am losing patience with you, Mrs. Marlowe. Tell me the truth or you will not see your husband and sister again. Tell me!"

"I don't know!" Judith shouted. "If I knew, I'd tell you. Maybe Vladimir was one of your men. You probably know more about him than I do. Leave me alone. I want to call the embassy!"

The man subsided back into his chair and resumed the interrogation. Another hour passed. Questions followed by evasions followed by more questions followed by denials. Judith asked for a glass of water. Her questioner told her to answer him truthfully, then she could go home. Eventually, exhausted and on the verge of collapse, she stopped responding altogether and stared blankly at the wall behind his head.

"Enough." He stood up. "You will hear from us again, Mrs. Marlowe." He stalked out, leaving the door open. She was free to go.

The latest Grigorovich replacement was waiting in the corridor. He handed her her coat and purse. The Zhiguli was parked just outside, its motor running. A stranger sat at the wheel. Judith climbed into the back seat and slid over to make room for her escort, but he slammed the door and stepped back. The driver took off.

She arrived home after midnight. Kenneth was frantic.

"Where have you been? I've been calling everyone I could think of. There's no answer at your father's. My God, I've been so worried. Why didn't you let me know you'd be late?"

"I was too busy being interrogated by the KGB. Phil died this afternoon. They ripped his place apart looking for—something."

Kenneth understood. Phillip Abbott's memoirs. "My God. Are you all right? Did they hurt you?"

"They humiliated me pretty thoroughly, but I'm no stranger to the gutter. I've survived worse." She stumbled past him into the bedroom and collapsed on the bed.

Judith awoke twelve hours later to find that Kenneth had tucked a pillow under her head and covered her with a quilt. He had left a note asking her to call him at the embassy as soon as she got up. When she lifted the telephone receiver, the first thing she noticed was that the line was clear. It was over: the persecution, the harassment, the random calls and blatant telephone interference, the shadowing in the streets. All over.

CHAPTER 24

*D*espite a boycott by the American ambassador and embassy personnel, a fair number of people turned out for Phillip Abbott's funeral at the Novo-Devichy Cemetery. Before the lid of the coffin was closed, Judith pressed a white rose under her father's folded hands, and Vanessa a red one. Although she was working on a film, Vanessa had decided to come to Moscow for the funeral, and she had arranged to take a few days off.

"He doesn't look too bad," she said to Judith in a confiding murmur. "They did a nice job on him, I'll give them that much. I expect they've had a lot of practice with Lenin."

The corpse was wearing a dark blue suit purchased by Judith at the GUM department store expressly for the burial; all her father's other clothes had been destroyed in the exhaustive KGB search that followed his death. The ribbon of the Order of Lenin, the nation's highest decoration, was pinned above his breast pocket, along with the Red Banner and the Order of the Patriotic War, First Class.

Pravda had printed a short obituary that was notable for its omissions, but it had been enough to attract the attention of the professionally curious, media correspondents and newspapermen, who formed the bulk of the crowd. A few Eastern bloc diplomats were on hand, notably a representative from Hungary, the country that Phillip Abbott had helped secure for the Soviets in 1956.

A Soviet Army general eulogized the defector as a hero of the Soviet Union, a friend of the Soviet people, a champion of peace. Judith wondered what had happened to the KGB agents who had dismissed Phillip as a parasite, a traitor, and a spy. As the general spoke, she glanced around, curious to see if any of the people who had guarded her father were in attendance. They were all complete strangers to Judith. Had any of them been her father's lovers? They certainly hadn't been his friends.

"He was a stalwart Marxist, a devout Leninist, a devoted party member," the general intoned. "In death, as in life, his deeds will be remembered and celebrated. He left the country of his birth and came to live among soul mates in the country of his choice, his adopted land. He was our brother, and we will miss him. And now we must bid him farewell, and prepare to face the future without him, in the hope that many more intelligent young men of high ideals around the world will follow his example, and follow him to Moscow."

"Fat chance," Vanessa muttered as Judith translated the eulogy.

"One hero is an inspiration," the general declared. "From him, like sons of his spirit, spring a thousand heroes."

"Amen," Vanessa said aloud. The general looked daggers at her. She smiled charmingly, and he glanced away, scowling.

The pallbearers lowered the coffin into the grave. Someone nudged Judith's arm. She scooped up a handful of earth and sprinkled it on top of the coffin. Vanessa followed suit. A few more handfuls followed, but by then, the crowd was dissolving. The mourners drifted away. A camera clicked. A flashbulb flared. Then the only sound was birdsong wafting from the aspens and oaks that grew among the tombs and gravestones.

"He could be jolly fun, Phil," the correspondent from the *Manchester Guardian* said to Judith on his way out. "We hoisted a few in our time, but not lately. He hadn't been feeling good, and they were keeping a pretty close watch over him. I'm surprised they let you see him at all."

"They kept a pretty close watch on both of us," Judith said.

So far, no one else had approached them. Kenneth had offered to accompany them, but the ambassador had forbidden it. The deceased may have been Kenneth Marlowe's father-in-law, but he was also a notorious traitor. The embassy hadn't even offered Judith and Vanessa a car.

"Your government is probably relieved he's gone," the reporter said. "Fascinating people, defectors. They never lose their appeal for the reading public. One keeps wondering, what made them do it? Well, so long. I've a deadline to meet if I want to make the evening paper with this."

"Fatuous ass," Vanessa muttered at his retreating back. " 'Fascinating people, defectors.' Wonder how many he's known? They'll make journalistic hay out of this, you can bet on it. Too bad Owen couldn't be here. He'll be sorry it ended like this, before he found out the truth."

"Does he know Phil's dead?"

"I called him before I came. He said, 'I never thought that son of a bitch would die before me.' He sounded a little sad, I thought." They strolled toward the gates. "I'm impressed," Vanessa said, looking around. "For one of life's losers, Phil certainly has found himself in some sterling company. Owen Adair told me all about this place. Stalin's wife is here, and Chekhov, the dear man. Prokofiev. Gogol. All the greats. And now Phillip Abbott, hero of the Soviet people. What a joke."

"Sasha's father is buried here, too," Judith said. "General Dmitrov. Valenskaya told me."

"Want to pay a call, ask him to look after Phil in whatever part of hell they've assigned him to?"

"I don't think so."

"I thought your Colonel Dmitrov would show up today." Vanessa cast a look over her shoulder at the fine old church that lay within the walls. The place had been a convent once, where Peter the Great had imprisoned his sister. "I was wrong, obviously. Still, I thought he had an interest in Phil."

"So did a lot of people," Judith said. "All of them destined to be disappointed."

"Don't take it so hard, Sis." Vanessa patted her shoulder. "You did your best. Come on, what these girls need is strong drink."

"I don't feel up to a pub crawl, Van. This business has left me completely numb. I'm thinking of flying back to London with you when you go."

"You can't, love. I'm working in Ireland. Besides, you have unfinished business here. Phil must have given you a clue. All you have to do is follow it up. I'll help. Tell you what, let's visit all of Phil's old haunts."

"I don't know very many of his old haunts," Judith said glumly. "He wasn't haunting much when I knew him."

"Then we'll go to the ones we do know. Skip the apartment—the boys have been all over that. But there's the Rossiya dining room. We'll start there, lubricate the engines. Too bad we can't sniff around that infamous underground urinal where he picked up his boyfriends. On second thought, it's just as well. The idea makes my stomach turn. But lunch first. I'll buy."

They ate fish soup and chicken Kiev in the Rossiya's vast dining room. Vanessa polished off a couple of glasses of cherry vodka in quick succession and sighed contentedly.

"That's better. You know, if Phil was an alcoholic, chances are that I am, too. Family history's very important, I hear. I worry about it sometimes, but not enough to quit." She leaned across the table. "Now, I want you to tell me everything you can remember about the day he died. What did you talk about?"

"Van, I don't feel—"

"Judy, we don't have much time. Think. Did you fix lunch for him?"

"Yes. Potato soup. He didn't eat very much. But it was a nice day and he said he felt like taking a walk. We went to the park across the street and sat on his favorite bench under Lenin's statue, and that's when he had his weak spell."

"Did he say anything? Anything at all?"

"He made some joke about Lenin looking like he was going to walk right off his pedestal."

"That's our Phil. Talk about a wicked sense of humor. All right, so then he got sick and you took him home. Did he say anything on the way back to the apartment?"

"Not much. He was feeling pretty awful by then."

Vanessa took her through the events that followed. When Judith had finished, she shook her head. "I must admit, it doesn't look promising. Funny, Olga Dmitrova being the one to take care of him at the hospital. What was she like? Gorgeous?"

"She was probably pretty once," Judith conceded. "She's small and dark. Graying. Give her some new clothes and a month at Elizabeth Arden, and she'd be a knockout. Come to think of it, I could use a month at Elizabeth Arden myself. My looks have gone to hell."

Vanessa glanced around the Rossiya's immense dining room. The hour was late for lunch, and no one was sitting close enough to eavesdrop.

"Listen, Judith, that stuff Sasha's wife told you about Irina. That means Sasha was telling us the truth." She leaned over the table and whispered, "He really wants to defect."

"So?" Judith rested her chin in her cupped hand. She felt utterly depleted, too listless even to drink her vodka.

"Judith, so help me, I'm going to brain you with this bottle!" Vanessa's words came out in an explosive hiss. "Don't you see, that whole family is in bad trouble. Sasha Dmitrov wasn't joking when he brought you that icon and asked for your help."

Judith pressed her lips together. "The man he helped murder was his own wife's brother. He wouldn't have done—"

"What's the matter with you? You hated him when you thought he was lying to you, and now that you know he told you the truth, you still hate him. Listen, you don't know anything about what happened. From the way it sounds to me, he didn't have a choice."

Just then two solid Soviet citizens wearing ill-fitting gray suits hurried into the dining room. Out of half an acre of empty tables, they selected the one closest to the two sisters. Vanessa gave Judith a knowing look.

"Looks like my old boyfriends are back," Judith said, loud enough for the new arrivals to hear. "I hope they get indigestion, the bastards."

Outside the Hotel Rossiya, Vanessa flagged down a taxi. During the ride to Sokolniki Park, the sisters twisted around in their seats and watched the street behind them. After a moment Judith grinned and said to the taxi driver, "See that gray Zaporozhet behind us? You'd better slow down. If you lose them, they'll send you to Siberia."

Grimly, the taxi driver applied the brakes.

On that bright spring afternoon, the greening lawns in the park were dotted with bodies stretched out in the grass, soaking up the sunshine. Old men gathered on the benches to gossip and to play chess. A few pigeons pecked hopefully at grains of sand on the gravel paths. As Judith and Vanessa approached, a young mother and her two children vacated the bench that Phillip Abbott had occupied on the day he died. The women sat together and looked up at the statue. The men who had followed in the gray Zaporozhet were trying unsuccessfully to mingle with the old men and the pigeons.

"Well?" Vanessa said. "Any sudden flashes of inspiration?"

"No. I have a headache and my feet hurt. These stupid shoes—"

"Excuse please, nice American ladies." A young man plopped himself down beside Vanessa. "How you are doing? My name is Leo, like Count Tolstoy. That means lion, you know. Is fine day, no?"

"Pretty fine," Vanessa agreed. "So tell me, Leo, did you ever meet an old American gentleman who lived right over there? His name was Phillip."

"Filip, yes." Leo nodded. "We have that name in our language, too."

"Nice old guy. He would have liked you, I bet." Vanessa ignored the nudge Judith was giving her. "He used to come here a lot. Do you remember him?"

"No, lady, I do not think so. I live at other side of park. I only come here once in a while. Listen, you have any blue *dzhinsi* I can buy? I pay very good price, eighty rubles. They are not even needing to be in good condition. I will make that ninety. Ninety rubles, best price in Moscow."

"You're right, that is a good price. Too bad I left my jeans at home. If I'd known the market was so hot, I would have loaded up a suitcase."

"Yes," Leo said, nodding eagerly, "that would be smart. Next time, don't forget. I sell every Sunday at the big market near Kolomenskaya metro. I like the Levi Strauss the best, button fly, shrink to fit, crease in front. They call them *chortova kozha* here, devil's skin. Any size is okay, but bigger is probably better. Russian girls not so thin as you. I go. Very nice to meet you nice American ladies. So long from Leo." He bounced to his feet—he was wearing brand-new Nike running shoes, Vanessa noticed—and trotted away with a grin and a friendly wave.

"Just another *fartsovchik*, " Judith remarked. "Black marketeer. Near the big hotels, you can't make a move without tripping over them. They give the best rates in Moscow, triple the official exchange. And heaven help you if you're caught trading with them. See, look." The two KGB men had cornered Leo the Lion. They pointed to Judith and Vanessa, obviously questioning the boy about them.

"The nerve," Vanessa exclaimed. "Blatant, crass commercialism, right under Uncle Lenin's nose. No wonder they close his tomb at night. Gives poor old Vladimir Ilyich a chance to spin in his grave. Judy, what's the matter?"

Judith's mouth had fallen open. She made a little whimpering noise. *"Vladimir.* Lenin's name was Vladimir!"

"Sure. I had a Marxist boyfriend once. Never bathed. Used to preach to me by the hour."

" 'Vladimir needs to watch his step,' that's what Phil said." Judith clutched her sister's arm. "Van, I think Phil buried his book under the statue, right where Lenin's shoe would come down if he stepped off into space."

They stared at the flower bed at the base of the statue. Tulip and daffodil spears were well above the ground, poking up through the dark earth in cheerful green clumps.

"It's possible."

"No." Judith shook her head. "It's too crazy. Maybe it was just a joke. That's all, a joke."

Vanessa glanced at the KGB men. They were still hectoring Leo. "It's a good thing those guys are so dim. Come on, let's get out of here." Vanessa pulled Judith off the bench. "We can't go digging now, with all these people around. I'll just have to come back later."

"Van, you can't! I won't let you. It's too risky. You don't know what they're like."

"Yes, I do, and I know what I'm like, and I won't rest until I've satisfied myself that his stupid book isn't there. He wasn't strong, he can't have buried it very deep. Is Kenneth going to be around tonight?"

"I don't know—wait. I think there's a reception at the Saudi embassy. He'll probably have to go to that. But I'm not letting you come back here alone."

"If *you* come along, we certainly won't be alone, you'll have half the KGB with you. Sorry, babe, but I'm playing this act solo. Don't get nervous. The worst thing they can charge me with is desecrating a flower bed. I won't even get thirty days."

"I won't let you. It's out of the question. Absolutely not. I forbid it."

Vanessa left Judith's apartment at ten o'clock. She shuffled past the doorkeeper in his booth. He glanced at her, then returned to reading his newspaper.

She was bent over, shoulders hunched, clawed hand gripping a twig broom that she used as a cane. Having only her overnight bag and Judith's cosmetics to work with, she had effected a remarkable transformation. A maze of fine pencil lines etched her face. Over those, she had placed bits of toilet paper soaked in flower paste. When dry, they pulled her cheeks and forehead and chin into an aged pucker, which when colored with liquid foundation and face powder looked eerily like aged, crepe-paper skin. Similar heavy applications of foundation had erased her eyebrows and eyelashes. The wisps of hair that escaped from her worn *babushka* were whitened with dustings of bath powder stuck on with hair spray.

With Judith's help, Vanessa had wrapped her legs with dish towels to thicken them. Judith had given her a latex body suit into which she had stuffed two feather pillows. A stop at Moscow's vast GUM department store that afternoon had netted her a pair of the coarse cotton stockings favored by older women; a baggy dress, which Vanessa aged by soaking it in bleach and pounding it with a meat-tenderizing hammer; and a shapeless man's sweater, which when dusted with flour looked as if it had been around since the Revolution. On her feet, she wore a pair of *valenki*, felt boots with rubber soles, also purchased from GUM. Back at the apartment, Judith had dismantled a twig hearth brush that she used for decoration and refashioned the bristles around a broom handle.

"It wouldn't stand the glare of klieg lights on a movie set," Vanessa had declared when she examined herself in the bathroom mirror, "but it should pass in Moscow after midnight."

She took the metro to the Inner Circle Line, rode it to the Komsomolskaya interchange, then changed to the Red Line. Judith had plotted the route for her, mapping out exactly where she should get off, which direction she should walk, how many stops she should take between changes. She had to look like an experienced metro rider; any streetsweeper who paused to read signs might attract attention. And indeed, hardly anyone seemed to notice her. She had been counting on that, having observed herself that old women in *babushki* were such a common sight in Russia that no one ever looked at them twice.

Vanessa took the Red Line one stop to Sokolniki. Emerging from the metro station, she felt grateful for the cool night air. Under her feathers, latex, and woolens, she was sweltering.

The metro station was several blocks from Phillip's apartment building. A variety of contorted shapes towered above the ground, casting eerie shadows over the landscape: the Sokolniki Amusement Park. The rides were fenced off, the lights on the merry-go-round and ferris wheel extinguished for the night. Silent and abandoned, the place had the feeling of a deserted railroad yard or factory. Without anyone to operate them, the idle machines were just heaps of metal parts, undefined by function, a desecration of the natural contours of the earth.

A guard dozed near the amusement park's entrance. Vanessa thought he opened a sleepy eye as she passed him, but he closed it again just as quickly. At midnight, the paths and roads through the park were deserted.

Ten minutes later Vanessa found herself across the street from the block of apartments where Phillip Abbott had lived. She made her way to the statue of Lenin and sat facing it on the bench. A few benches away, a pair of lovers were tangled in an embrace, completely oblivious to everything else. Vanessa made a cawing sound to attract their attention, then made noises under her breath. Discomfited, the girl stood up, dragging her boyfriend after her, muttering. Wherever they went in Moscow, it seemed, they always fell under the disapproving eye of a *babushka*. Vanessa glared at them balefully as they tried to decide which way to go: deeper into the park toward a wooded area, or out, toward home. It was too cold for outdoor trysting, apparently. They decided to leave, trudging toward the block of apartments without giving Vanessa, the anonymous, muttering crone, another glance.

Vanessa waited for a few minutes, in case anyone else happened along. With Judith's coaching, given in the bathroom with the shower running full strength, she had prepared a few sentences in Russian: "My back is killing me." "I can't hear a word you're saying, I'm as deaf as a stone." "Dogs did this, the fiends. I'm fixing it." She repeated the words to herself now, liking the sound of the Russian syllables on her lips and in her throat.

The coast was clear. From under her sweater, she pulled a flashlight and the small trowel Judith used to tend her window box. The flashlight she would use sparingly, to locate the exact spot under the sole of Lenin's shoe. To keep it on any longer would be to court attention, which she didn't want.

She picked her way between the clumps of sprouting bulbs. Standing directly in front of the statue, she looked up and tried to gauge where

Lenin's foot would come down if he completed his stride. Two feet in front of the pillar, she estimated. She knelt and started probing with the point of the trowel.

Vanessa and Judith had decided that Phillip must have buried the memoirs after the first frost, when the gardening crews would have removed the blighted annuals that had flowered during the summer, but before the first hard freeze, and before Judith's arrival in Moscow made him the object of round-the-clock surveillance.

Nothing. Vanessa poked closer to the base of the statue, still in line with the shoe. She scolded herself for not bringing something slender that she could use as a probe, a metal skewer or a long-bladed knife. The earth was heavy clay, packed by a season of snow.

"Come on, Phil," she murmured to herself, "don't make it too hard. We're only humans, not bloodhounds."

The tip of the trowel struck something. She scooped out some of the earth and plunged her fingers into the soil. Yes, she felt an object, about ten inches below the surface, right alongside a clump of daffodils, whose shafts felt silky and smooth to the touch. She dug quickly, scattering the earth over the flower bed. It could be smoothed out later, if she had time.

Under the blade of the trowel the object defined itself to her searching fingers as flat and about the size of a book, wrapped in something slick like plastic. The earth flew in all directions as Vanessa dug. Finally, her hands closed around the parcel and she pulled it up.

"What are you doing?"

The man spoke in Russian, but Vanessa translated the sentence without difficulty, from the tone of his voice. She shoved the package under her skirt and clamped it between her knees, burying the trowel in the hole and scooping earth over it.

"Dogs, did this, the fiends!" she shouted in a deaf woman's croaking voice. "I'm fixing it." The man, a uniformed Moscow militiaman, asked her a question. Vanessa shook her head. "I can't hear a word you're saying. I'm as deaf as a stone." She struggled to her feet, pressing her knees tightly together to keep the package from slipping out. She let out a wail. "My back is killing me! My back is killing me!" The policeman offered his hand. She slapped it away and stooped over again to finish filling in the hole and to smooth it over. "Dogs—the fiends—I'm fixing it—my back."

When the flower bed looked decent again, she stepped back and gave a satisfied nod. The policeman handed her the broom and waited while she swept some of the scattered earth from the path. They walked together back to the street, Vanessa moving in a slow, arthritic shuffle that kept her thighs firmly pressed together around the package. The man turned and shouted into her ear in a bellow that made Vanessa's head ring. She croaked, "Can't hear a word you're saying. I'm as deaf as a stone."

Ignoring the policeman, Vanessa began to sweep the debris on the sidewalk into the gutter. She continued sweeping until she had rounded the corner. When she looked back, the policeman had vanished.

Vanessa shoved the package into the elastic waist of her long johns. She was sweating bullets. A touch to her forehead and cheeks assured her that a tide of perspiration hadn't ruined her makeup. One problem still remained: A *babushka* leaving Judith's apartment building at ten o'clock at night might not be noticed, but one entering at two in the morning would surely arouse comment. She had to stay away from the apartment for another four or five hours without being arrested and without being seen. The metro stopped running at one and didn't start again until six.

Still clinging to her broom, Vanessa trudged along Stromynka Street until she reached the Yauza River. She turned left along the park. At a moment when no cars were passing on Rusakovskaya Street, she scrambled up the hill into the trees. She found a clump of aspens rising out of some shrubs. Falling to her knees, she burrowed under the thicket until she felt that she was completely hidden. The undergrowth was thorny, but a few snags and tears to her costume wouldn't matter.

At eight o'clock the next morning, Vanessa trudged past the glass booth in the lobby and toiled up the stairs. Judith was waiting for her. The moment the door was closed, she pulled her sister into a fierce embrace. When Vanessa could move again, she hoisted her skirt and produced the plastic-wrapped parcel. Puzzled, Judith hefted it. It was smaller than a typescript, and lighter in weight. She placed it on the kitchen table and sliced the string that tied it. Vanessa looked over her shoulder.

Inside layers of black plastic and brown paper, they found eighteen cassette tapes, Russian-made. Frowning, Judith deciphered the Cyrillic titles: the Byelorussian Men's Chorus, the Ukrainian Balalaika Orchestra, Folk Songs of the Urals. The two women stared at their haul for a long minute, completely baffled. Then Vanessa clutched Judith's arm.

"Morning, Sis." Although her voice was thick with sleep, her body quivered with excitement. "Guess I'll wait for coffee until I've had my shower." She dragged Judith into the bathroom and started the water running. "Don't you get it? Tapes! Eighteen of them, forty-five minutes on each side. That's over thirteen hours of narration. Phil taped over the music. He talked his memoirs into a microphone, right under the noses of the KGB."

They rushed out to the living room, where their gazes fell on Kenneth's tape deck. No earphones, and maybe even a bug inside. They exchanged despairing glances. They could not listen to the tapes here. The

KGB would be on them like a shot. In the meantime, Judith had to find a place to hide them.

Vanessa returned to the bathroom to scrub off the layers of sweat, grime, and cosmetics while Judith rewrapped the parcel and looked around for someplace to conceal it. If the KGB thought she had found the memoirs, they would rip her apartment to shreds. Finally she noticed the flower box outside the kitchen window. She had taken the geraniums in for the winter and kept them blooming happily on the kitchen counter. Soon it would be time to set them out again, once the danger of killing frost had passed. She opened the window, shoved aside the earth in the box with a spoon, and buried the tapes.

Ten minutes later, Vanessa emerged from the bathroom with a huge terry towel wrapped around her like a sarong. She gave Judith an inquiring look. Judith pointed to the flower box. Vanessa grinned and gave her a thumbs-up.

"Good morning, love," Vanessa said brightly. "I feel like myself again. How about some coffee? But first a little juice." She got out a bottle of orange juice and filled a couple of glasses.

"I had a dream about Phil last night," Judith said. "He was watching you in a play—you were brilliant, never been better—and he was laughing. It made me happy, seeing him like that. To Phil." She lifted her glass. Vanessa did the same. They touched glasses and sipped the orange juice.

"To Phil," Vanessa echoed. "May he rest in peace, wherever he is."

CHAPTER 25

Moscow: June 1984

D r. Dmitrova? This is Judith Marlowe. You remember, Phillip Abbott's daughter."

"Yes." The voice that came over the wire was cautious but not un-
friendly. Judith could picture Dmitrov's wife in her stained white coat, her
hair beginning to escape from its restraints after a long day, her expression
closed and wary.

"Ever since my father died, I have been thinking about how kind you
were to him, and to me. I would like to show my gratitude and respect.
Perhaps—perhaps we could meet for a cup of tea?"

"Really, Mrs. Marlowe, no thanks are necessary. I was just doing my
job. Any other doctor in this hospital would have given him the same
attention."

"I'm sure that's true. Nevertheless, it was a difficult time for me, and
you were very comforting in what you said and did. Still, if you don't want
to see me . . ."

"No, I didn't say that." In the background, Judith could hear hospital noises: the rumble of gurney wheels, a baby crying, an intercom paging
a doctor. "I am permitted to have foreign visitors, as long as I report them.
You could come to my apartment tonight at seven. Do you know Arbat
Street?"

"Yes." The pedestrian mall was at the heart of Moscow's oldest
commercial district, the best place in the city to look for antiques and
collectibles.

"About halfway along to Smolenskaya Square you must turn left on

Kalashny, and then right on Stolovaya. It is a very small street, easy to miss. The number is forty-three–twelve. The doorbells don't work, so come right up to the top floor and knock on the first door to your left."

"Fine, tonight at seven. I'm looking forward to seeing you again, Doctor."

"Good-bye."

As Judith hung up the phone, her glance strayed to the geraniums now blooming pertly in their window box. The package of tapes was still there, waiting for her to decide what to do with them. She hadn't told Kenneth about Vanessa's escapade in Sokolniki Park. He would insist on sending the tapes to Washington at once. But if Preston, or someone on his staff, was untrustworthy, then the tapes could easily fall into the wrong hands. Judith couldn't risk that, not until she had made a firm decision about Dmitrov's request for help.

At six-thirty she set off on foot. In a wrapped parcel under her arm she carried a box of chocolates, a bottle of French cognac, and a tin of tea from Fortnum & Mason. She walked swiftly along Kalinin Prospekt. As she turned south on Vakhtangov Street, she glanced behind her. A man was following, making no great effort to stay out of sight. One week earlier, Vanessa had experienced a lengthy delay at the Sheremetyevo Airport on her way out of the country. Customs agents searched her luggage thoroughly, even opening her toiletries and probing with the tips of their pencils the contents of the small jars of caviar she was carrying. They stopped short of demanding that she remove her clothing, but a female agent nevertheless patted her down with great care. All this was enough to convince Judith that the KGB had not given up its search for Phillip Abbott's memoirs.

In the years before the Revolution, 43–12 Stolovaya Street had been an elegant private dwelling. Now the yellow stucco on the exterior was nearly gone. The rose-colored bricks underneath were pitted and porous, and the mortar that held them together looked less substantial than dust. The front door was a massive mahogany slab with an enormous blackened brass handle and a keyhole the size of a golf ball. Following Olga's instructions, Judith pushed the door open and went in without ringing. The smell of carbolic in the foyer reminded her of the hospital in which Phillip had died. At least it overpowered the musty reek of dampness and decay. A single weak bulb burned in the light fixture overhead, which at one time must have held decorative glass shades.

Judith made her way up the staircase to the top floor. A row of cards was pinned to the doorjamb on her left: O. DMITROVA was among them. Judith knocked. After a moment, Olga opened the door.

"A man followed me from home," Judith said. "If you prefer, I'll just leave these things with you and go. I don't want to make trouble for you."

Olga looked alarmed. "You think he knows you were coming here to see me?"

"I'm sure of it. I think they've taken the taps off our phone, but the bugs in the walls are still there."

Olga Dmitrova cast a furtive glance over her shoulder. Her hand fluttered in front of her mouth. "It never stops, the sneaking, the listening."

Judith turned away. "I'd better leave."

"No." Olga's voice was suddenly firm. "You have come to thank me for helping your father. There's no crime in that. Anyway, they will harass me whether you stay or not. Please, come in. Come."

Judith found herself in a small corridor, with four doors on the right and four on the left. A toilet flushed and a middle-aged man stepped into the hall. He seemed annoyed at finding the two women standing there, and he brushed rudely past them without saying a word and slammed through another door.

"This house was built by a wealthy nineteenth-century merchant, a trader in fur and leather," Olga told Judith. "His servants used to sleep up here. From two large rooms they made four apartments. Irina and I share the kitchen and the bath with three other families. And the water closets. Here we are." She opened the last door on the right. "We are lucky to be at the back of the house. We even have a tree to look at in the garden. And the Kominskys' rabbits. They live on the ground floor. Not the rabbits, the Kominskys."

The apartment was a single room, about ten feet by twelve feet. Two single beds were set at right angles to each other in one corner. They were covered with cotton spreads and an assortment of pillows and bolsters. During the day they served as sofas. A table stood in the angle between them. It was piled with books, newspapers, photo albums. A smaller table under the window held a hot plate. A pot steamed gently on one of the two burners. The shelves above held plates, bowls, glasses, and foodstuffs. An armoire against one wall was stuffed with clothing, the top piled high with boxes and parcels wrapped in cloth. The effect was of a dormitory or boardinghouse room, makeshift and impersonal. Still, the two tall windows were curtained with heavy velvet, and the carpet underfoot was a red and gold Tabriz in excellent condition. A bunch of violets in a drinking glass sat among the books on the table.

Olga accepted Judith's offerings with grave thanks and invited her to sit. "You would like some tea?" She went over to the kitchen corner and set a teakettle on top of the free burner on the hot plate.

"Yes, thank you. Is it safe to talk here?"

Olga shrugged. "I suppose so. Sasha—my husband has checked the apartment thoroughly. He says that the KGB can't spy on everyone in Russia, although they would like to. It would cost the earth, and they haven't enough people to do it."

"How long have you and Irina lived here?" Judith asked.

Olga smiled. "I have lived here most of my life. I was born here, in this room." She gestured toward the corner with the two beds.

"You mean this house belonged to your family?"

"Yes. After the Revolution, it was confiscated, of course, but they let my parents keep this room. My mother was a teacher in the Institute for Foreign Languages. I learned English and French from her, and some German. My father died in the war. Mother was still alive when Sasha— when we moved in with her, but she died soon afterwards and I inherited the apartment." The kettle began to steam. "You would like some jam in your tea?"

"Yes, please. What about Irina? Does she like it here?"

"I don't know. She never says anything one way or the other. After her Uncle Yakov died, she changed. She became . . . difficult, temperamental. She was always moody, but it was worse somehow. We decided, Sasha and I, that divorce would be the best thing, mostly because of Irina. She said she wouldn't continue to live in the same house as a . . . a . . . ." She stopped, unable to speak the word, but Judith understood.

"I'm sorry."

"Coming here was a shock for her. We had a beautiful apartment before the divorce, lots of pretty things that belonged to Sasha's mother. Even a maid. We had another child, you know. A boy, younger than Irina. He died in an accident."

"Yes, I know. Your husband told me." At least that part was real. Dmitrov had peppered his lies with truth. His sorrow over losing his son had not been counterfeit.

"Sasha didn't forget us, not for a minute. I don't know what we would have done without him. Every week, when he is in Moscow, he brings something. Gifts for Irina. Nice clothes."

Olga held her arms tightly crossed. Her fingers were busy, picking at a pulled thread on her sweater.

"It must have been difficult for you."

Olga nodded. "She was doing so well at the Bolshoi school, a wonderful little dancer, her grandmother's darling. She seemed all ready to have a big career, a beautiful life. But when Yakov died, everything changed. His wife and son blamed my husband, with good reason. They refused to have anything to do with us. Irina didn't understand. She loved her uncle, and she was a little in love with Arkadi, her cousin, but they all turned against us. Arkadi's the one who told Irina his mother's suspicions, that Irina's own father had helped to destroy Yakov. She asked Sasha if it was true. He told me later that he couldn't lie to her. He should have. We would still be together if he had lied."

"But you—surely you couldn't go on living with him after what he did to your brother!"

Olga fitted two glasses into silver holders and poured out the tea. "If he did it, it was because he had no choice. I saw what happened to him afterwards. Something in him died, too. He loved Yakov like his own brother. They were like boys whenever they were together, laughing and arguing, playing sports. Yakov was a good soccer player when he was young, not just an intellectual with one muscle between his ears. He and Sasha . . ." She put a few thick Russian cookies on a plate, arranged everything on a tray, and carried it over to the table near Judith. "The blame was not Sasha's. They made him do it."

They. The all-powerful, ever-present KGB. "You still love him, don't you?"

Olga shrugged. "They cost me everything—our marriage, our home, our life together. And my daughter. I'm losing her, too, because of them. But I am helpless."

This explained Irina's rude behavior during Valenskaya's birthday party. The tension between father and daughter was the result of Yakov's death. Irina hated her father.

Olga swallowed scalding tea. "Sasha's mother had some influence over Irina, but now that she's gone, no one can talk to the girl."

Judith set her tea glass aside and leaned forward. "The last time I spoke to your husband, he seemed very concerned about Irina. He thinks that the only chance for her to survive would be to leave the Soviet Union."

Olga shook her head. "It is not possible. They will never let her go. His job. They wouldn't let Yakov go because of that."

"It was my impression," Judith said carefully, "that he was planning on making some sort of escape. With both of you."

Olga Dmitrova's eyes flew open. "Escape! *Gospodi!* God help us, what a notion. It would never work. They would find out, and then we would be finished, all of us. No, no, it is out of the question."

"Please, Dr. Dmitrova, let me finish. Aleksandr wanted something from me that he could use as a bargaining chip. I wasn't sure I could get it, but last week, I was successful. I think he's right about its importance. He might be able to buy your freedom with it. Don't you think it's worth a try? You've admitted that Irina's only hope is to get away from here."

"No! Stop at once. I don't want to hear any more of your plans."

Olga swept the veil of straying wisps away from her forehead with shaking hands. "He took our happiness, and now he will kill us. It's crazy to think he could succeed with this. Madness."

"If anyone could manage it, he could," Judith urged. "I know people in the West who can—"

"No! I won't listen. Irina is fine, just fine. She needs some time to get used to life the way it is now. Sasha must use his influence to get her into the university. He must! She will have to work hard to make up for the time she has spent away from school, but in the end, she will make something of herself."

"She's had plenty of time to get used to her new life," Judith said. "Five years."

"It is too soon to expect—"

At that moment the door flew open and Irina came in. Or at least Judith supposed the creature she saw was Irina. She had shorn her fair hair into a crew cut and dyed it black. Her cheeks were pale and her eyes were ringed with black liner and mascara applied with a heavy hand. She was, if anything, even thinner than Judith remembered. Her jeans seemed welded to her narrow thighs. Over them she wore a black turtleneck sweater and a black leather jacket. Around her neck hung her grand-mother's necklace, the wafers of beaten gold that had decorated the har-nesses of the czar's horses.

When she saw Judith, she stopped in her tracks.

"Hello, Irina," Judith said in English, "remember me? We met at your grandmother's birthday party a couple of years ago."

"I remember. My father's American girlfriend." The corner of her lip lifted in a sneer.

"You look like you could use a friend, too," Judith told her. "How have you been?"

Irina shrugged. "All right, I suppose. Why should you care?"

"Irina!" Her mother remonstrated with her in Russian. "You must not be rude. Mrs. Marlowe is our guest. Look, she brought us lovely chocolates, and some cognac, and nice tea. Would you like some tea? I'll brew a fresh cup for you. Or have one of these nice chocolates. I'm sure they're delicious. See, all the way from Switzerland."

Irina glanced at the box. "I don't want any chocolates. They're boring."

"Then I'll fix you something for dinner." Olga jumped up and began to bustle over the hot plate. "I didn't realize it was so late. I made some soup; the butcher let me have a meaty bone, and one of my patients gave me some onions and a few turnips."

"I'm not hungry."

"But you must eat!"

"Why must I? Do you have any money? I want to see a film tonight, at the *kinotheater* at the university."

"A film?" Olga looked doubtful. "Yes, I suppose that will be all right. You won't stay out very late, will you? You know how I worry." She opened her coin purse and shook it out. "Here, two rubles and a few kopeks, all I have left until I get paid. Are you sure you don't want some soup? I know you'd like it."

"No. I've got to go. The film starts at eight-thirty."

She went out. The two women looked at each other. Judith said, "If she's going to see a film, I'll eat it frame by frame."

"What am I to do?" Olga sank wearily onto the hard chair near the table and knotted her hands. "I can't call her a liar to her face. Did you see her eyes? She's taking something, smoking something. I'm sure of it."

"Of course she is. Probably a combination of substances, all washed down with vodka. I've seen girls like her in the United States. They run away from home and live in a strange city, and they sell their bodies for drugs. This isn't just adolescent rebellion. It's a suicide course."

Tears streamed down the other woman's cheeks. "She had another abortion this winter, her third. I took her to the clinic myself, all three times, and sat with her. Her father doesn't know about any of them. If he did, he would kill her. And me, too. My God." She covered her face with her hands. After a moment, she lifted her head and wiped her eyes. "You say that you and my husband can help Irina. Will you talk to him? I will do anything you say, anything. You're right, she must get away from this country before they put her in jail or a psychiatric hospital." Olga shuddered and new tears spilled from her eyes.

"How can I get in touch with him?"

"I will telephone him tonight and tell him I need to speak to him about Irina. If I know him, he'll come over right away. Call me at the hospital tomorrow."

"No, it's too dangerous." Judith thought for a moment, then she said, "Tell him to wait for me in the car at the end of Izmailovsky Boulevard where it hits the park, between eleven o'clock and noon on Sunday morning. We'll probably need to make a quick getaway. If I don't see him, I'll know he's changed his mind. But make sure you tell him that I have what he was looking for."

"I will." Olga dashed the tears from her cheeks. "I will tell him."

Judith stood up. "Don't worry. It's not too late. She's young and she's angry and she doesn't know any other way of communicating with you. But she's an intelligent girl. She'll come around."

"I pray that you are right." Olga stood and faced her. "You love him, too," she said. "That's why you are here."

Judith drew back and picked up her coat. "What we had was over a long time ago. I'm merely trying to make the best use of a legacy. I think that you and Irina deserve a chance."

"No, I know what a woman looks like when she loves. And when she lies about it." Olga began to flutter around the room like a trapped bird. Her hands lightly brushed the surfaces of her few possessions. They beat among the curtains and groped the mirrored front of the armoire.

"He is very lucky, Sasha," she said too brightly. "I suppose if his plan succeeds, you and he will be together in America. You are lucky, too. He was a good husband to me once, a long time ago. A good father to his children. I am no longer young. But you—you are still beautiful, and young enough to give him more children. A son. He wants a son very badly. It is very natural. Of course I understand." Aware that she was losing control, Olga stopped in the middle of the floor and trapped her crazy hands under her arms. She bit her lower lip to stop it from trembling.

Judith felt the panic behind her rambling statement. If Dmitrov's plan worked, Olga faced a future in a strange country, with an alienated child and no husband to help her through the transition. The prospect terrified her. It might even be strong enough to hold her back, to keep her here, and Irina with her. The two of them floundering in a society that didn't want them, one prematurely old, the other prematurely dead.

"You're wrong," Judith said firmly. "I have no claim on your husband, Dr. Dmitrova. We were friends once, more than friends, but that's in the past. Sasha asked for my help and I'm ready to give it. For your family, all three of you. Life has been rough for you, but you're going to put yourselves back together. I won't interfere. You have my word."

Olga Dmitrova's legs couldn't support her anymore. She pulled the hard chair around and sat. "Thank you," she whispered. "I am so grateful. If you knew how awful it has been without him, how terrible. I miss him. Oh, God, I miss him so."

She was sobbing as Judith slipped out of the apartment.

CHAPTER 26

*B*oris Grishin straightened up as the Marlowe woman appeared. At nine o'clock on a bright Sunday morning, she left her apartment building and walked toward the nearest metro stop. She was wearing blue jeans, running shoes, and a red pullover sweater, and she carried a slouchy purse made out of coarse burlap fabric over her shoulder. The purse dragged at its leather straps, suggesting something weighty inside. From time to time, she switched it to her other shoulder, or else carried it down at her side.

She took the metro to the Revolution stop, where she switched to the Blue Line, eastbound toward Shcholkovskaya. The cars were already crammed with city dwellers seeking the green grass and open spaces of the parks and suburbs. Boris blended easily with the crowd of day-trippers. He had a nondescript face, and his age was hard to determine. In his baggy brown suit over a gray sweater, and with his fair hair combed into a fringe over his clear blue eyes, he could have been anything from nineteen to thirty-nine. During the ride, Mrs. Marlowe clutched the purse to her chest, as if she were terrified of becoming separated from it. Boris was getting curious about the contents of that purse.

She got off at the Izmailovo Recreation Park and started walking. Although the weather was getting warm, Mrs. Marlowe didn't slacken her pace over the three-kilometer hike through the woods. Boris, who was sweating a little, removed his jacket and slung it over his shoulder. At length they reached the riding stables. Horses were saddled, ready to ride, tethered to a horizontal rail outside the shabby office building. A mob of foreign women, English and American, were getting ready to mount up.

"Judith," a large woman brayed, "you're late. We thought you weren't coming. Hurry and check in. We're almost ready to leave."

Judith Marlowe went into the stable offices. She came out a few minutes later and spoke to the young Russian who was handling the horses. Boris had already tallied the number of horses and riders and had decided that the young man would be acting as escort and guide. It was unthinkable that a group of foreign women would be allowed to explore the woods unaccompanied. While Mrs. Marlowe inspected her mount and chatted with the other members of the party, Boris darted into the office. He charged up to the desk and demanded to use the telephone.

The woman at the desk looked affronted. "And what makes you think that you have a right to come in here—"

Boris flashed his identification. "You want to spend the rest of the day in prison? Shut up and give me that telephone. And give me some privacy." She vanished into the bathroom.

Boris called the office and informed his superior about the Marlowe woman's movements. "Shall I stop her from going with them?"

"Certainly not. She might be meeting someone. Get a horse for yourself and go along. We'll send someone out to help you keep an eye on her."

Boris described the way the woman clung to her purse. "I think she's carrying something. She might be trying to pass it to someone, or maybe it's a drop."

"Could be. Whatever you do, don't let that purse out of your sight."

Boris hung up the phone. He opened the bathroom door and told the woman that he needed a horse at once.

"That boy out there is going with them, right?"

"What do you think? If we let people take our horses without watching them, they'd make off with them and sell them for horsemeat. Ivan is going, and Anatol."

"Tell Anatol to stay here. I'll go instead."

"You? What do you know about horses?"

"What's to know? You kick them to make them go, pull the reins to make them stop. Don't waste time. Call him in here and tell him I'll be taking his place."

The riding party set off along a rutted trail through the forest. In the old days, Izmailovo had been one of the Romanovs' country estates, and it boasted breathtaking scenery, exquisite groves of birch and pine, cunning little streams that babbled through grassy meadows, and placid, shimmering lakes. As a child, Peter the Great had wandered these same paths, played with his toy boats on the lake, and dreamed of the day when Russia would be a great naval power.

Judith rode in the middle, beside the Englishwoman who had welcomed her. She had hooked her purse over the horn of her saddle, and it bounced gently against her horse's side. Ivan led the parade, and Boris brought up the rear. All the horses seemed tame and stupid, but his was the most sluggish of all. He suspected Anatol of pulling a switch to give the greenhorn cop the gentlest mount, but he didn't mind. He was concentrating all his attention on Judith's red sweater and that purse of hers. He was content just to sit astride the dirty, bad-smelling beast and let her have her head.

They rode for an hour without stopping. Boris was beginning to feel a chafing soreness along his inner thighs and on his bottom. He was a city boy who confined his recreation to indoor sports like drinking vodka and playing cards. The army had given him enough exercise to last a lifetime. Finally, at the edge of the lake, Ivan called a halt. The women dismounted and led their horses to the water. Mrs. Marlowe paused to chat with Ivan, who laughed at some sally of hers. Boris knew that she spoke fluent Russian, with an accent one of his co-workers had described as charming. No doubt the boyish Ivan was finding her very charming indeed. He simpered as the woman stroked his horse's neck, and laughed again when she told him that he had a wonderful style on a horse. Boris curled his lip. Style was not a Soviet trait. The boy would be better off applying his posterior to a seat in a trade school somewhere. Did he really expect to spend the rest of his life tending these nags?

Boris's mount greedily cropped the lush grass that grew at the edge of the lake. In the rushes, a frog croaked. Another answered. Dragonflies darted, the sunlight catching their iridescent wings. A kingfisher swooped low over the water, and a bass leapt. The women praised the beauty of the scene. Boris felt a glow of pride. His native land. Mother Russia.

It was time to return to the stable. Ivan went around, holding the horses steady while the ladies mounted up. He seemed to take an inordinately long time with Judith Marlowe's horse, who was prancing and tossing his head, eager to get back to his stall. Finally, all the women were taken care of. Ivan called to Boris, "Are you all right back there?" Boris waved his hand in a dismissive gesture.

Then all hell broke loose. When Ivan climbed up on his horse, it leapt up and bucked him off. Ivan sailed into the air and landed in the muck at the edge of the lake. The other horses, startled by this event, or perhaps startled by their riders' panicked reactions, started to mill and jostle. Judith Marlowe squealed as her horse took off into the trees, in the direction of the stable.

Boris watched the red sweater growing smaller and smaller. Frantic, he tried to mount, but his horse kept dancing away from him, wheeling and turning so that he couldn't even get a toe in the stirrup.

"Damn it, help me!" he barked to one of the women, the broad Britisher with the loud voice.

"Oh, for heaven's sake, man, grab the reins and hold his head steady."

"I can't. Get down. Help me." He looked around. Judith Marlowe had vanished.

In the woods, Judith pulled her mount up just long enough to take a navy-blue windbreaker from her purse and to slip it on over her sweater. She pulled a knitted cap over her head and stuffed her hair underneath, then donned a pair of sunglasses. While she performed these operations, she needed all her strength to keep her mount from heading back to the stable. When he accepted her as master, he allowed her to turn him onto a different path, away from the lake and away from home. She kicked him into a canter. He was unaccustomed to really vigorous exercise, but he made the most of it, stretching his legs and filling his lungs. They passed groves where families were picnicking, and fields where groups of boys played soccer. A few people waved. Judith waved back.

Judith headed north through the strip of woods that lay between the Moscow Circular Motorway and Parkovaya Street. Through the trees, she saw the apartment towers of Cherkizovo. Her landmark. She pulled the horse up and slid down to the ground. She gave him a couple of lumps of sugar, then turned his head back toward the stable and slapped his rump hard. After a moment's puzzlement, he trotted away. Judith walked west, finally breaking through the trees at the end of Izmailovsky Boulevard. A gray Volga was parked facing her. It flashed its lights two times. She slithered down a steep bank and ran toward the car. The driver threw open the passenger door and she jumped in.

Dmitrov greeted her. "You made good time. Any problems?"

"Not so far." Judith scanned the trees. "They should be combing the woods for a woman wearing a red sweater. Let's get out of here."

Dmitrov made a U-turn in the middle of the street. He headed north to the Shcholkovskoye Highway, then eastward, away from the city. He checked his rearview mirror frequently, until he was satisfied that no one was following them.

"I can't stay away too long," Judith said. "I want to be able to tell them I had a fall from my horse and that I wandered lost."

"The place I have in mind isn't far. How did you manage to shake the man who was tailing you?"

Judith described the Sunday-morning gathering of horse enthusiasts, most of them diplomats' wives or embassy employees, led by Beryl Sillery, a secretary at the British embassy.

"I went along with them once or twice last fall. This seemed a good opportunity to keep up my horsemanship. That poor man didn't know one end of a horse from the other, but I'll give him credit for trying. I slipped a burr under Ivan's saddle in order to create a diversion." She laughed at the memory. "You should have seen him flying through the air! And he was such a nice kid, too."

Dmitrov grunted. "He was probably KGB. And so was his horse." He turned to her with a smile. "I'm impressed, Judith. Are you sure you're not CIA?"

Judith stiffened. "Don't patronize me, Aleksandr Nikolayevich. Just because I was a dunce at school doesn't mean I'm not skilled in the arts of cunning and deception."

"Forgive me, I meant it as honest praise. I couldn't have devised a better plan myself, or carried it out more efficiently."

As they rode, Judith studied him out of the corner of her eye. He was wearing jeans, Topsider deck shoes, and a gray sweatshirt. His hair was shorter, grayer. He looked his age, which was forty-eight. At a time when most men are at the peak of their careers, he was ready to take the biggest career risk of all by defecting to the West. If he succeeded, he would face months of debriefing, maybe even years. After that, he would have to start his life over again, an exile, with the ever-present threat of assassination hanging over his head.

After twenty minutes, Dmitrov pulled off the highway onto a side road. The car bumped over an unpaved track through a pine forest for a few miles, then Dmitrov parked in the grass and switched off the engine. He climbed out of the car, walked around to the rear, and removed a wicker hamper and a blanket from the trunk.

"A simple picnic, nothing to arouse suspicion, even from the nosiest *plebka*."

Judith followed him along a well-trodden path through the rustling birches. A warbling thrush reminding Judith of the nightingale she had heard at Dmitrov's *dacha*. The night she had stopped loving him. Or had she? Why was her heart beating so fast?

They reached a glade, apparently a favorite place for lovers and for those who wanted to admire nature at close range. The grass was trampled, mashed flat in places. Dmitrov unfurled his blanket and opened the basket.

"Champagne or vodka?"

"No vodka." Judith knelt on a corner of the blanket. "If I intend to keep spying, I need to keep my wits about me."

"A glass of champagne. A toast to freedom. You're smart not to underestimate my cohorts in the KGB. A fatal mistake, as many people have learned to their sorrow."

Dmitrov worked the cork out of the bottle. The champagne was French, a brand available only in the shops that catered to high government officials and party members. He had packed crystal tulip glasses. He handed Judith one.

"Olga told me you have agreed to help. I'm very grateful. I have no one else I can trust."

Judith drew the fragile glass away from her lips. "Let's get one thing straight, Aleksandr. I'm here because of Olga and Irina. Not because of you, or us, or the way things used to be. Is that clear?"

"Quite clear, thank you." Dmitrov sat down on the blanket and raised his glass to her. "To your very good health, Mrs. Marlowe. Olga said you found the memoirs?"

"With Vanessa's help. How we did it is a story that will keep for another time."

Dmitrov watched her over the rim of his glass. "I can see in your eyes that you still don't trust me. You think this is just another KGB ploy, don't you?"

Judith felt herself reddening. The sun was reaching its zenith, and the sheltered glade was as warm as summertime. She removed her windbreaker and pushed up the sleeves of her sweater. "No, I don't. I'm sorry. Lately I'm suspicious of everybody. I'm turning into a raging paranoid."

"In this country, a little paranoia is a good thing." He drank. "I am a paranoid myself. I doubt I could smuggle Phillip Abbott's memoirs out of the country now, even if you gave them to me. Lately my travel has been restricted. I have been told that I have become too Western in my views, whatever that means."

Alarmed, Judith sat up straighter. "You think they suspect something?"

"I don't know. I believe I have a plan that will get us out, but I need your help. If anything goes wrong—and many, many escapes are foiled— then I may be able to barter your father's memoirs for our freedom. The KGB wants them badly. Will you save them for me, in case we need them?"

"I told Olga I would." Judith plucked a blade of grass and shredded it. "I'll do what I can to help you get out, but I can't promise to hand them over before I know what's in them. Let's hope it won't be necessary."

Dmitrov shrugged. "The restrictions on me may be simply a routine bureaucratic matter. Perhaps there's some clerk or party cadre who's jealous of the fact that I am able to leave the country now and then, while he stays home and waits for his name to come up on the list for a new car."

The champagne had a bitter taste. Judith wondered if the adrenaline rush that followed successfully outwitting the KGB fouled one's system. She drained her glass in a single swallow and dug in her bag for a cigarette.

"Olga told me what you did to her brother."

Dmitrov gazed into the depths of his glass. "Yes. I tried to tell you once or twice. But I couldn't. It is not a burden one likes to share."

"Why did you do it?"

He shrugged. "They offered me a choice. Either I could take charge of Yakov's case, or someone else would be assigned to it. I decided that if it had to be done, I should be the one to do it, and not a stranger. I was aware that the people at the top were troubled by the fact that my wife was a Jew. It stood in the way of my advancement, as a question mark on my record. Perhaps someone was even farsighted enough to know that this would end our marriage. In any case, I was transferred to the KGB's Fifth Directorate and assigned to gather incriminating evidence against my own brother-in-law, Yakov Seminov. They wanted me to stop his contacts with the Western press, to put his *samizdat* newsletter out of business, and to disband his little group of dissidents. I reported to a man named Krelnikov. He's the one who assigned me to the Abbott case. Our Pandarus. You've met him. I've heard he interrogated you after your father's death."

Judith's eyes widened. "Is he tall and bald, with two gold teeth?"

Dmitrov nodded. "They call him the Wolf, with good reason."

"Jesus." Judith shivered. "What about Yakov?"

"Yakov was harmless, a drunk and a fool. I told him what they wanted me to do. I explained the facts to him. I begged him to lie low for a while, to pull in his horns. The stupid bastard laughed at me. He kept butting, pushing, forcing the system to bend. He didn't seem to realize that he was one weak little maggot and they were powerful pistons just looking for an excuse to pound him into dust. They told me at the beginning that he would spend no more than a year or two in a labor camp. Instead they put him into a psychiatric hospital, and they tortured him, and he died."

"Just like Pontius Pilate," Judith said softly. "You turned him over to them, and they crucified him."

"I had no choice!" Dmitrov cried. At the sound, the glade fell silent. Even the breeze ceased to blow. "If I had refused to do my part, then my own head would have been in the noose. My own loyalty would have come into question. I would have gone to prison myself, leaving Olga and Irina alone, without friends, without anyone to protect them. And still Yakov would have died."

"There are worse things than prison," Judith told him. "At least your daughter wouldn't hate you now. She wouldn't be trying to destroy herself, just to punish you. I know what she's going through. I've tried it myself. Twenty-five years after my father defected, when I met you, I was still furious with him. Irina and I have a lot in common. I'd like to talk to her about it sometime. Not that it would help. She needs time. When she's made a few more mistakes herself, she'll look more kindly on yours."

"What about you and your father? Did you forgive him before he died?" Dmitrov leaned forward, his eyes pleading. He seemed to want to know if there was hope for him and his daughter.

"I never actually said I did, but I think he knew it. Part of me didn't have to forgive, because it never stopped loving him. I think it's the same with Irina. If she didn't care about you, she wouldn't be trying so hard to hurt you."

"I've tried to explain. I've forced her to sit and listen to the facts. But I can't get through to her. She always says the same thing: 'You killed Uncle Yakov.' " He ground his fists into his eye sockets.

Judith remained still and silent, staring down at her hands. His anger was searing and horrible and too familiar. Had her father ached like this? Had he shriveled at her coldness and despaired of her love? She remembered the long hours they spent together, separated by hostility and anger. But those emotions were hers, not his. Perhaps Phillip only wanted to hear two words: "I forgive." But she had never spoken them, and now it was too late. She was here today because she wanted to give Irina a chance to speak those words, and Dmitrov a chance to hear them, before it was too late for them, too.

Dmitrov rose and paced off the glade as if it were a cell in which he had to spend the rest of his life, taking its measurements, marking off time in steps and turns. He began to speak softly, but feverishly.

"I started asking myself why. Why had they done this to me? I'd always been a good Soviet, a loyal citizen. I liked my work, and I was good at it. I enjoyed pitting myself against the other side. They tried to get our military secrets, we tried to get theirs. I was moving up in the hierarchy, gaining privileges, getting a reputation as a man who got things done. Along the way, I made enemies. Krelnikov. He not only wanted to destroy Yakov, he wanted to destroy me, too. He knew that after Yakov died, I would begin to question, begin to hate. I think that's why he's watching me now. Because he knows, in his infinite, evil wisdom, that sooner or later I will want to break out. And then he can finish me off." He gave a terse, bitter laugh. "It would amuse my mother to hear me admit at this late date that she was right. I should have stayed away from them."

"It's hideous. I never imagined . . . I'm sorry, Sasha. I shouldn't have been so quick to judge."

"I could have gone over to the West at any time, but how could I leave Olga and Irina behind? I will never forgive myself for hurting them. Especially Irina. Olga understood, or she seemed to. We know each other so well. But Irina—never. Maybe I can fix things so that her life will be easier. I have to try."

"Yes, I know."

"Judith." Dmitrov knelt down and stretched out his hand toward her. She pulled away.

"Don't."

"I must. It's been so long."

"That night at the Bolshoi. You looked right through me."

"I had to. I was escorting the wife of General Zukov. She sees everything and reports directly to her husband. I wanted to speak to you. No, I wanted to sweep you up in my arms and carry you off. But I couldn't touch you."

"I wanted to murder you."

"When I heard that the Wolf had interrogated you after your father's death, I was frantic. I wanted to kill him."

Judith smiled tearfully. "I kept waiting for you to stride in and save me."

"I didn't know anything about it. I wasn't in Moscow when Phillip died. A week after it was all over, I saw the report. You fought them, didn't you? I was proud of you." He folded his arms around her and pressed his face against her neck. "I've missed you. Dear God, it's been an eternity since I've held you."

Dmitrov's kiss was hungry and insistent. His hands moved under her sweater.

Judith pushed him away. "No, don't. It's not fair. Olga still loves you. Even when she knew the truth about you and Yakov, she didn't want to leave you. But she had to, for Irina's sake. And you still have some feeling for her—don't try to deny it. You're not just doing this to make amends for past sins. The two of you have made your own kind of history. You've shared love and birth and death. She's still your wife. And when you get out of here, you'll all live together. You'll be a family again."

"I can't leave her behind." Dmitrov sat back on his heels. "They'll destroy her. She used to be strong, but lately she seems to be wearing down, as if it's all been too much for her. I owe it to her, Judith."

"She needs you, Sasha. You'll have to stay with her."

"Yes. It's unfair to you, to both of us. Judith, I—"

Judith touched his lips with her fingertips before he could say the words. "Don't. No more. We're all so pathetically human, aren't we? Russian, American, Balinese—a broken heart is the same in any language." She took a long breath. "Whatever you want me to do, I'll do. And when it's all over, if we're all still alive, I won't expect anything. I won't wait. Don't hurt them again."

Dmitrov kissed the palm of her hand before she could withdraw it. "I have no right to ask you to take any more risks for us."

"I have the right to refuse." Judith straightened her sweater, shook out her hair, and got down to business. "I know someone who can help. Vanessa's friend Owen Adair. He used to be with the Agency. I think he can be trusted."

Dmitrov nodded. "She told me about him. I never met him, but I've heard of him. He has given our KGB brothers a hard time on several occasions. Yes, I think we can trust him. But no one else. You must be very careful who you tell. When can you see him?"

"I'll arrange a shopping trip to Helsinki. We'll meet there." The Finnish capital, a shoppers' paradise only a short flight away, was a popular retreat for Westerners weary of Moscow's year-round drabness and chronic shortages. "Do you have a plan?"

Dmitrov reached into the basket and pulled out a bottle of vodka. He uncapped it and poured some into his champagne glass. "I'll need a few months to arrange the details, but I have already chosen a day, the fifth of October. I hope you have a good memory. I will give you all my requirements now. We won't see each other again until then."

"I'll do my best."

They talked for another hour. Judith made notes, studied them and committed them to memory, and then destroyed them. As they were getting ready to leave the glade, she handed Dmitrov her purse, to which she had returned the cap and windbreaker. "Would you mind getting rid of this for me? I want them to think I passed on the manuscript to someone."

Dmitrov hefted the bag. "What's inside?"

"A two-volume edition of *War and Peace*. Have you read it?"

"A long time ago. As I recall, it ends happily for Pierre and his Natasha. The philosophical hero and his bruised lady love."

"That's why it's fiction. I wish I could put myself between hard covers sometime. Good luck to you, Sasha."

"My best luck was in finding you." They stood fixed to the ground for a moment, listening to the happy rustle of the birch leaves and the muted trilling of birds. Then Dmitrov turned away. "We'd better go."

CHAPTER 27

London: October 1984

*J*udith cleared customs at Heathrow at four o'clock on the afternoon of October first. She had flown by way of Warsaw and Vienna, and she still had two hours to wait until the direct flight from Moscow arrived. She found a seat in the corner of the reception area from which she had a clear view of the concourse and the gate. She saw no familiar faces, and no one seemed to be taking more than a casual interest in her. For the moment, all seemed to be well.

At six-thirty, Beryl Sillery, the secretary who worked at the British embassy, stepped through the door from the customs area. When she saw Judith, she let out a penetrating halloo. Boris Grishin would have recognized her at once as the braying Englishwoman at Izmailovo Park. When the two women had embraced, Beryl fished out a plastic sack from her carry-on bag and handed it over to Judith.

"The customs boys in Moscow were interested in why I had so many tapes of Latvian choruses and balalaika music," she said. "I told them I was giving them to all my friends as Christmas presents. They must have believed me."

Judith stuffed the bag into the zippered side pocket of her suitcase. "You've been great, Beryl. Thanks a lot."

"As a hardened professional, I'm supposed to know when to keep my mouth shut, so I won't ask any questions, even though I'm burning with curiosity. Want to share a taxi? I'm going to Highgate."

"Hampstead for me. I'll drop you."

* * *

Vanessa had promised she would be at home to welcome her, but no one answered her ring. Frustrated, Judith did as she had done when Vanessa summoned her from Zambia: she pressed all the buttons at the entrance until one of the tenants admitted her. Now, as then, Mr. Tidyman was waiting at the top of the stairs.

"Mrs. Marlowe, your sister told me you would be coming. She's gone away for a few days. She asked me to take care of her cat. May I help you with your bags?"

"No, thank you, I can manage." Cursing Vanessa under her breath, Judith humped her suitcases up the stairs. Mr. Tidyman took one of them and led the way to Vanessa's door.

"She left me a key, you see. I noticed an envelope on the kitchen table with your name on it." He unlocked the door and pushed it open. After setting Judith's suitcase down inside, he rubbed his hands together. "There you are. I see the young master is hungry again. He misses your sister so terribly when she's gone. Well, I'll run along. If you need anything, anything at all, please don't hesitate to ask. I'm always home." He went out, closing the door.

Deaf Kitty mouthed a forlorn greeting, but when Judith scratched his ears and his belly, he rolled over and purred.

"Where in hell is that sister of mine, Deaf Kitty?"

Judith found the envelope to which Mr. Tidyman had referred. The note could only have been written by Vanessa, in a scrawl that looked like a third-grader's:

Judy, didn't think I was going to miss the fun? Tidypants taking care D.K. C U in Stambull. Luv, V.

Vanessa had enclosed an airline ticket to Istanbul dated the following day, departure scheduled at ten forty-five, with stopovers in Brussels and Vienna.

"God damn you, Van," Judith said aloud. "You promised to stay out of this."

Soon after Judith's meeting with Dmitrov, she had arranged to meet Vanessa and Owen Adair in Helsinki. Judith told them about Dmitrov's plan to defect and asked for Owen's help. Owen agreed readily. He had friends in that part of the world, useful contacts who could be trusted not to leak word of the operation back to Washington or Moscow. He and Judith both insisted, however, that Vanessa stay clear. Owen wanted her to man the telephone in London, to take and relay messages in case of a hitch. Apparently he had changed his mind, or else Vanessa had over-whelmed him. Judith wasn't surprised; she knew from experience how persuasive Vanessa could be. But this still left her with the problem of what to do with Phillip's tapes. She had been depending on Vanessa to give them to her friend at Sotheby's for safekeeping. It was too late to call anyone now, and she wouldn't have time before her flight tomorrow to rent a safe-deposit box.

In Russia, tapes of the Riga Men's Chorus and the Chernobyl Bala-laika Orchestra looked perfectly innocent. Beryl had gotten the cassettes through customs at Sheremetyevo Airport by explaining that they were souvenirs, perfect gifts for the folks back home. But here in Vanessa's flat, all those Cyrillic letters seemed to shout, *Play me first!*

Judith muttered another curse at her feckless sister. She would have to hide them here, tonight. She had no choice.

"Look, darling, isn't the sea beautiful today! So blue and clear."

Somehow Irina summoned up enough energy to produce a yawn. "It looks just the same as it did yesterday."

Olga Dmitrova sighed. So far, Irina had been sullen and uncoopera-tive, if not downright hostile.

"Can we go back to the hotel now?" Irina asked.

"Soon, Irinushka, soon. It's so lovely to breathe the clean air, to see all the beautiful flowers."

They strolled through the citrus groves in the famous botanical garden at Zelyoni Mys. Olga touched the shiny dark leaves that hung over the path. She marveled at the tiny white blossoms, the small green fruits and the ripening orange ones. Surely this was paradise, a place where the same trees blossomed and bore fruit simultaneously, throughout the year. Irina lagged behind, dragging her feet and sucking on a cheap cigarette.

Olga said, "I have a surprise for you. We are meeting your father tonight, for dinner. He is flying in from Moscow today on business."

"I don't want to eat dinner with him."

"Please, Irinushka," Olga pleaded, "don't spoil this evening for us. You know we couldn't have afforded to come here on our own, and we certainly couldn't have afforded to stay at the Intourist, in that lovely room. You've got to be one of the *nomenklatura* for that kind of luxury."

"So what? I didn't want to come here anyway. Who cares about stinking Batumi and the stinking Georgians? It's boring here. The food is boring, the wine tastes like vinegar, there are too many people on the beaches, and all of them are boring. And there's no action at night. This place is as dead as a graveyard. I want to see my friends in Moscow."

Olga felt her panic rising like a sudden fever. Tonight was the night they would be making their escape, but she hadn't told her daughter. She knew that Irina would flatly refuse to go along with the plan. She would jeer at her father for making an effort to get them out, and sneer at her mother for aiding and abetting him. She would probably create enough of a disturbance to attract the attention of the police or the KGB. Olga grasped Irina's hand.

"Sit down on this bench, darling, I want to talk to you."

Irina flopped down beside her. Birds swooped under the green canopy above their heads. Sunlight played on the rain-kissed leaves, and the gentle breeze from the sea showered them with diamonds.

"What is it?"

Olga gazed deep into her daughter's eyes. "Whatever happened in the past, your father still loves you. He is concerned about you. And so am I. You can't go on indefinitely flouting authority. It's only because he is what he is that you haven't been thrown into a psychiatric hospital or a rehabilitation camp."

"My father is a criminal and a traitor," Irina said in a hard voice. "I don't want somebody like him interfering in my life. Did you hear that, Mother? *My* life! Not his, not yours. I make my own decisions now. I choose my own friends, I go my own way. The only reason I came with you to this disgusting place is because you cried and begged and carried on. You said you wouldn't have any vacation at all if I didn't come with you. All right, you've got your vacation. But if you think you and that man are going to turn it into a second honeymoon, you can just put me on the next train out of here. I won't stand for it. I hate him."

Olga touched the tips of her fingers to her trembling lips. "I can't even talk to you anymore. We used to be such good friends. Do you remember? You would come into my room and sit on my bed and tell me all about your day at school. And I would tell you stories about my patients. And we'd laugh. Now I can't even touch you. When we walk down the street arm in arm, I feel you pulling away from me, as though you can't stand to be close to me. I know you want to be free of both of us. But I can't let you go! You're too young to know what is good for you, Irinushka. You'll disappear into the underworld with those ruffians and drug addicts, and I'll never see you again. Can you understand how that terrifies me? Everything I ever valued in my life is gone. You're all I have left."

Irina stood up. "We're not the same people we used to be, Mother. Not you, not me, not him. Besides, what difference does it make how I live? We're all going to die. No one will remember who we were. What's the difference if you die at eight or eighty? No one cares." She ran down the path toward the exit. After a moment, Olga hurried after her.

They took the bus back to Batumi. It was Olga's first visit to a Black Sea resort. Batumi was one of the busiest cities in that part of the country, a major seaport, connected by rail and pipeline to the rich oil fields at Baku. The shipyard, engineering works, and refineries provided plenty of jobs, and the people she saw in the shops and on the sidewalks looked cheerful and prosperous. Why shouldn't they, living in warmth the year round, with tons of fruits and vegetables coming to market from the nearby collectives and private farms? Washed by frequent rainfall, the rooftops and even the streets looked clean, free of dust and grime. Flowers bloomed in gardens and window boxes.

When Olga and Irina returned to the hotel, Irina locked herself in the bathroom. As always, Olga was drawn to the window, which overlooked the bustling harbor. Aleksandr Dmitrov had used his political connections to secure a suite on the top floor of the Intourist Hotel, the best accommodation in the city. To the west lay the yacht club and a row of pleasure boats lined up at a floating dock. On the jetty straight ahead, a tanker loaded its cargo of crude oil from the Baku pipeline. A few tugs plied in and out among the commercial vessels, nosing barges toward Yalta, with their cargos of machinery and lumber and gravel and fruit.

The troubled Dmitrov family would be traveling on one of those boats this very night. Wearing only the clothes on their backs, taking nothing more than what they could cram into their pockets, they would leave the Soviet Union forever. The prospect made Olga positively sick with fear. She desperately wanted a big drink of vodka to calm her nerves, but decided against it. She needed to keep her brain clear. Sasha had not told her any details, but she trusted him to come up with a good plan. After that, their fate was in God's hands.

Olga wondered if, after they reached the West, she could still satisfy Sasha in bed. He was the only man she had ever made love to. Long after their divorce, she continued to love him. But did he still feel anything for her? Or had he planned this escape in order to rid himself of guilt over Irina and to secure for himself a future with the American, Judith Marlowe? Would he take his wife and daughter to America and then abandon them among strangers?

Olga upbraided herself for allowing her fears and her doubts to get the best of her. One day at a time, one hour at a time, that was the only way to survive this agony. She caught a whiff of marijuana smoke and cast a worried glance toward the bathroom. Irina was psychologically and spiritually impaired, incapable of sound judgment. Olga reassured herself for the thousandth time that she was doing the right thing, the only thing that could save her child. But it grieved her to think that after tonight her daughter would hate her, too.

Irina pressed herself against the louvered glass window in the bathroom and sucked at the dirty screw of paper and dried *trava*. Her last joint. Her friends had told her that you could get really good hash in Batumi, smuggled over the Turkish border only a dozen miles away. But her mother had kept her on such a tight rein that she hadn't had a chance to connect with someone who could point her to a dealer. With a decent stock of hash, she could do some dealing of her own when she got back to Moscow, perhaps even earn enough money to buy herself a car. A car was real *klass*. Speed and power. Freedom from her dreadful family.

This town was boring beyond belief. Irina made up her mind. Tomorrow she would strike out on her own. No more stupid Lenin museums or public gardens or taxi rides into the country. Some sun. Some grass. A boy. A quick screw, if they could find a place.

She hid the roach and opened the door.

The Dmitrovs dined in a little restaurant on the eastern promenade overlooking the Batumi harbor. Because the place was patronized by high party officials, the food was excellent and the service almost up to Western standards. Irina ate nothing, but she drank plenty. To her amazement, her mother uttered not one word of protest, even though her father refilled her wineglass again and again and even invited her to have a cognac with them after the meal.

"Are you trying to get me drunk?" she asked teasingly.

"What if I am?"

"Drunk or sober, I still hate you."

Dmitrov sighed. "And I still love you, Irinushka, drunk or sober."

They took their time over the meal. It was nearly midnight when they pushed their chairs back. Irina stumbled, but when her father caught her arm to steady her, she twisted away from him, snarling.

"Just because I'm drunk doesn't give you permission to put your hands all over me."

They left the restaurant. Olga suggested a stroll along Batumi's waterfront to clear their heads.

"Clear your own heads," Irina growled. "I'm taking mine back to the hotel, to bed."

"I think your mother's suggestion is a good one," Dmitrov said. "She is a physician, after all. We should listen to her."

Irina noticed that the single streetlight on the corner had multiplied. Instead of one, she now saw five small moons all revolving around each other. She felt her father's arm come around her waist, but she was too dizzy to protest.

"Don't feel good," she said thickly.

"Walk, Irina." Her mother braced her up on the other side. "It's not far. Your father and I will help you."

"Where are we going?"

"We're taking a nice little stroll. That's good. Keep moving."

They walked east along the promenade. Irina's legs churned automatically. Her eyes were half-closed, vacant.

"How much farther?" Olga puffed.

"We're almost there."

They reached a patch of woods above the beach and stumbled down the trail through the pines. The sighing of the wind in the boughs seemed to echo the regular rhythmic breathing of the sea below them. The night air was heavy with fragrance, not only of sun-baked pine needles and salt spray, but also of gardenias and roses and sweet olive blossoms. When they broke through the trees, Dmitrov pulled out a small pocket torch and flashed it twice. A single answering flash came from the sea.

Irina muttered, "I don't feel well. Think I'm going to be sick."

She doubled over and vomited in the sand. When she was finished, her father lifted her in his arms and carried her toward the surf. She weighed so little, not much more than she had when she was ten years old.

Olga stifled a sob. "I will never forgive myself for this. My own daughter."

They came to a small wooden dinghy whose oarlocks had been wrapped with rags. As soon as Dmitrov and Olga were seated with Irina braced between them, the boatman shoved off and hopped aboard. He pulled with long, easy strokes. The dark mass of the shoreline, with the creamy fringe of surf lapping at the beach, gradually receded from view.

"What did you give her?" Dmitrov asked Olga.

"A sleeping powder that I dissolved in water. I know, when you first suggested it I was against it, but there wasn't any other way. I tried to talk to her this morning. She was impossible." She choked back a sob. Dmitrov reached over and squeezed her hand.

After half an hour, they drew up alongside a darkened tugboat in the Batumi harbor. At the oarsman's soft whistle, a rope ladder tumbled over the side. He grabbed it and held it steady. Dmitrov slung Irina over his shoulder and climbed up the rope. Two sailors were waiting on deck to help him. As soon as Olga's foot left the rowboat, the oarsman pulled away, back toward the shore.

"This way," a voice said. Olga groped along blindly after Dmitrov. He seemed to have no trouble seeing in the gloom, or keeping his footing on the slick, greasy deck. Irina's arms dangled limply as he carried her. Olga repeated her daughter's name in a chanting murmur. It had a calming, almost hypnotic effect on her. *Irinushka. Irinushka.*

A man wearing dark trousers and a dark high-necked sweater led them to a small cabin on the starboard side. He warned them not to come out until he called them.

"The tanker will finish loading by five in the morning. She has to leave on the high tide. She draws so much water, it's the only time she can clear the channel. We'll see her out about five miles, then we'll hook south and deliver you to your friends."

Inside the cabin were two narrow bunks, a filthy sink, and a stool. Dmitrov laid his unconscious daughter in the upper bunk and pulled a rough blanket over her legs.

"We're kidnapping her," Olga sobbed. "Our own daughter."

"We had no choice." Dmitrov's voice was heavy with regret. "She's not rational anymore."

Olga sat on the lower bunk. "All she wants is to separate herself from us. She's worked so hard at it, devoted all her time and strength to escaping. It seems cruel to take that away from her, everything she's done for the last four years."

"She may not thank us in the morning, but someday."

"Can we trust these men?"

Dmitrov shrugged. "They know if they betray us, I will tell the KGB everything I know about their smuggling operation. Gold, samovars, icons—a lot of our country's treasures leave through these Black Sea ports. I think we can trust them. The captain has done this before, many times. It's risky, but I offered him so many American dollars that he couldn't refuse."

Olga wrung her hands. "My God, I'm so frightened. What if they catch us?"

"They won't, but if they do, just tell them that I kidnapped you."

She looked up at him, her eyes wide with fatigue and despair. "What about when—when we're free? What happens then?"

"We will stay together," Dmitrov promised. "As a family. Don't worry, Olga, I won't leave you."

Olga began to weep. "That's what frightened me most of all, that we might still be apart after all this. But I didn't know how to ask. She's so pretty, the American girl. I know she loves you. She wouldn't help us if she didn't." She grasped her husband's hand and pressed it to her cheek. "I love you so much, Sasha. I never stopped loving you. I never will."

"I know, Olga." Sitting beside her on the bunk, Dmitrov put his arm around her shoulders. She pressed her face hard against his chest, as if to shut out the light and the night and the terror. "We can't go back to the old ways. It won't be the same. We've changed."

"That's what Irina said this morning. But I haven't changed. Inside, I'm just the same. I never blamed you, you know. I blamed Yakov, but what was the point in that? He was dead. In this country, you do what you have to do in order to survive. If more children found out the truth, as Irina did, there would be a revolution. Not just one poor child trying to destroy herself to spite her parents and her country, but thousands, demanding that we give them what we promised."

"That's why we're leaving," Dmitrov said soothingly. "Don't think about it anymore. It's all in the past."

Olga looked up at him. "Sasha, make love to me. Please."

He frowned. "Irina—"

"She won't waken. I gave her a big dose."

Dmitrov kissed her. She opened her dress and guided his hand to her breast. Her eagerness embarrassed and saddened him. It was easy for a man to forget an old love, even a wife of many years. All it took was a few women, a few heated encounters that burned away memory, and the heart stopped aching. But Olga had not replaced him. Her memory of him was as fresh and alive as if they had made love yesterday.

He found her body comfortingly familiar. They had known each other for nearly thirty years, since they were students, younger than Irina. In those days, Olga deflected unwanted attention with a haughty air and a sharp tongue. Dmitrov had seen through the ruse. He recognized a possible friend, a sweet girl who was plagued with self-doubt and frightened of falling in love. Marriage was good for both of them, despite his mother's interference and the disapproval of his superiors. For the most part, Dmitrov had been a faithful husband, until Misha's death drove a wedge between them and polluted their lovemaking with sorrow.

New memories blot out the old, but the old are more powerful because they are part of your fabric, assimilated into your muscle and bone. He had given his word that he would stay with her and protect her. If necessary, he supposed, he could even fall in love with her again.

*   *   *

Irina opened her eyes and recoiled from the blaze of the light bulb in its wire mesh cage. She rolled over on her side and buried her face in her arms. Her stomach felt uncertain, and the movement wasn't helping any.

Movement? She sat up too quickly and banged her head on the bulkhead over the bunk. This wasn't her bed at home, and it wasn't her room at the Intourist. She was sitting in a narrow bunk and it was tipping gently from side to side. A boat.

"Mother!"

At the sound of her daughter's voice, Olga rolled out of the lower bunk and stood up. Her clothes were rumpled and she smelled of perspiration and sex.

"Darling. Irinushka—"

"What's happening? Where are we?"

Dmitrov appeared at Olga's side. He was shirtless. "Listen carefully, Irina," he said softly, "and don't make any loud noises. We are leaving Russia this morning. This tugboat is escorting an oil tanker out of the harbor. Then it will take us into Turkish waters, just a few miles away. Friends will meet us with another boat. By tonight we'll be in the West. Free."

Irina's face was on a level with her father's. Their eyes locked. His were cool and expressionless, as usual. Hers burned with hatred.

"You can just forget it, you damn murderer. I'm not going anywhere with you, do you understand? I don't need you or your friends or your fucking boat."

"Irina!"

"You think by screwing my mother you can persuade her to let you take us away from our country, our home, our friends. I'm not going. You just tell them to put me ashore. You've got a hell of a nerve, trying to salve your conscience by pulling something like this. I've called you a murderer to your face, but from now on, I'll call you a murderer in public, for the whole world to hear. I'll tell them what you did to Uncle Yakov, and how you tried to kidnap me to keep me quiet."

"Stop it!" Olga elbowed Dmitrov aside. "You listen to me, Irinushka. I love you. Your father loves you. He cares deeply about what happens to you. If he didn't, he would have left us behind and quit the country long ago. He had plenty of chances."

"He killed Uncle Yakov," Irina said stubbornly.

"He did not! He gave Yakov plenty of opportunity to save himself, and Yakov refused. Your uncle knew that ideals were a luxury he couldn't afford. If he wanted to die for them, that was his business. Yes, your father was a tool of the KGB, an instrument of the system. The system is corrupt, and it corrupted him. It's corrupted me, too, and you. Oh, yes. For years, I've had plenty of things I wanted to shout from the housetops, too. But it was dangerous to speak out, and for your sake and my own, I've put up with things and kept my mouth shut."

"I don't want to leave," Irina cried. "You had no right to take me away without even asking me, no right to drug me and kidnap me."

"Irina." Olga grasped one of her daughter's thin hands. "Irinushka, I look at you and I want to weep. You're killing yourself, wasting your life, and I can't do a thing to help you. Only your father can save you, and he's doing it. And if you don't care now, if you don't want to thank him, if you want to sulk and carry on like a spoiled brat and keep killing yourself with sex and drugs, then do it. But do it in a place where I won't have to point to the system or to myself, because you'll be a free woman in a free country, and you'll have only yourself to blame." Olga lowered her head into her hands and wept.

Irina fell back and stared at the light. Wasn't this what she and her friends dreamed about? Going to America, indulging in an orgy of drugs and rock music and gaudy clothes and fast cars? She had prided herself on finding a way to live outside the system. But the system had drawn parameters, limited her choices, formed and shaped and molded her. A free woman? She couldn't even imagine what freedom was like.

Olga lifted her head. Her large brown eyes were swimming with tears. "I've given up asking you for favors, making requests. But I'm asking you now, because you are my life and my soul; because I don't want you to end up like Yakov, in a mental hospital or in a camp. I have seen people will themselves into madness because they can't deal with reality. I beg you, Irinushka. Just this once, listen to me. Listen to your father. Cooperate with him. Do exactly as he says. He risked his life just to bring us this far. If they catch us, they will kill him. You and I can always say he forced us, that we had no choice. In your case, that's true. But they will execute him for treason, feed him screaming into the flames while they watch. Please, Irina." Her grip on Irina's hand tightened. "Please."

"I won't forgive him," Irina said after a long silence. "You can't make me do that."

"No." Olga and Dmitrov exchanged glances. They had won, but at what cost? Olga stepped away from the bunk. Her voice was weary, drained of emotion. "You will forgive when you're ready and not before, when you learn that the cost of hating is too high, and that anger eats you up like a cancer, from the inside. But you won't believe me until you find out those things for yourself."

CHAPTER 28

The Black Sea: October 1984

*T*he captain tapped on the door and stuck his head in.

"We've left the tanker and we're getting close to the rendezvous. Get ready."

Irina swung herself out of the bunk. "Not that we have anything to get ready. Where's the crapper?"

A few minutes later, they stood in the stern of the tugboat, watching the foamy wash surge away behind them. Olga and Irina wrapped their arms around each other for warmth. The wind threatened to rip the clothes from their bodies, and the yellow oilskins a crewman had given them provided no warmth. In the half-hour before dawn, the sea and the sky were shining mirrors of each other, gray-green and softly textured, like molten lead.

Up in the wheelhouse, the first mate scanned all points of the horizon ahead with binoculars. The Turkish yacht they were meeting would have located the big tanker on its radar within minutes of its leaving the harbor. It should be heading right toward them now. Dmitrov concentrated on the sea to the north, beyond the foaming wake. From that direction danger would come.

At the same moment that he saw a dark speck on the narrow edge between sky and sea, he heard the mate cry out. He ran up to the wheelhouse. Sure enough, a white pinprick danced on the waves in front of them. They were right on target.

"There's a ship behind us," Dmitrov said.

The KGB was responsible for border and coastal security. In the

Black Sea, they maintained their own fleet of cruisers with missile launch-
ers. All the ships in the region, whether naval or commercial or tourist
craft, had KGB men among the officers and crew.

Dmitrov had chosen this particular tugboat because the family of
Georgians who ran it had assured him that they could get rid of their
current KGB *stukach* any time they wished. They were a vast tribe, as dark
as gypsies, with a host of beautiful women who were known for their
courtesy to visitors. Their parties had become legendary on the seacoast.
A KGB man might find himself sitting on a plump cushion, surrounded
by perfumed houris who fed him grapes dipped in vodka. Laughter would
eddy around him like strange music. And such food, such unbelievable
food—and in such incredible quantities! When the guest got too tired to
hold up his end of the conversation, one of the girls would lead him to
a bedroom and help him strip. In the morning, or whenever he awakened
and pulled on his trousers, he would find a hundred rubles in his pocket.

Now no one was thinking about parties. Like the other crew members, the first mate in the wheelhouse was one of the captain's relatives,
and when the captain shouted an order, the mate pushed the engines up
to maximum speed.

"Twin diesels, West German," the captain told Dmitrov. "Not bad
for an old tub, eh? We can outrun any boat they send after us."

Dmitrov didn't have much hope of that. "Transferring the passengers
will take time. Can you take us right into Turkish waters? I'll pay you
extra."

"They'll be waiting to arrest me the minute we get back to Batumi.
No, comrade. That wasn't part of our deal."

The man had been smuggling for twenty-five years. You didn't last
that long in this part of the world without being good, and careful.

"Get the women into life jackets," the captain ordered. "You might
have to swim for it."

Dmitrov buckled Olga and Irina into bulky, mildewed life jackets.
Irina was silent, too frightened to do more than stare at the surging sea.
Her father patted her shoulder. "Don't worry, Irinushka, it will be all
right." He was gone before she could flinch.

"Believe in him," Olga urged her daughter. "He's our only hope."

"I hate him." Irina's response was as automatic as breathing.

"That doesn't matter, as long as you do everything he tells you."

For a while, the tug managed to keep her distance from her pursuer
while gaining steadily on the yacht. It was low and white, flying a Turkish
flag. The captain had taken over the wheel of the tug. Dmitrov stood
beside him.

"I'm going to cut the engines now. I don't want to overshoot and have to circle around. If I do, they'll catch us for sure. I'll get as close as I can, but you'd better get ready to jump. Your people will have their lines all set to throw out. As soon as you're clear, I'm getting out of here."

Dmitrov went down and relayed the message to his wife and daughter. Olga kissed him on both cheeks. "Take care of Irina. Don't worry about me. I used to be a good swimmer, remember?"

"I'll take care of you both," Dmitrov promised.

They were close enough to the white yacht to see people on board, waving, and a weapon of some sort mounted on the prow. Dmitrov stepped between his wife and daughter and put his arms around their shoulders. Olga pressed herself against him, grateful for his strength and solidity. Irina, intent on watching the yacht, seemed unaware of his touch.

The gap between the two boats closed. Crewmen were visible on the yacht's deck, standing at the rail with coils of rope in their hands. The seas were moderately calm, with three-foot swells and a light westerly wind that licked the crests into tiny whitecaps. Dmitrov thought he saw Judith's dark blond head in the stern of the *Argos.* She hailed him with a wave of her arm and a shout. Her words were lost to him, but he felt an answering surge of affection and gratitude. She had not failed him. The boat, the timing of the rendezvous—everything was perfect, exactly as he had requested.

The engines of the tugboat rumbled and slowed to an idle. The captain pulled up within thirty feet of the yacht and swung around into the wind.

"Jump!" he called back. "Now. Good luck, friends."

Irina went first, hurling herself feet first into the water. Her head disappeared, then bobbed to the surface again, lifted by the buoyancy of the life jacket. The skirt of her summer dress billowed around her, and she slapped it down with her hands. Olga followed. She submerged, then came up shaking her head and blinking her eyes. The crew of the yacht called out in Russian, "This way! This way!" Olga oriented herself toward the sound and began to swim.

Dmitrov, without a life jacket, dived into the water and came up within a few feet of Irina, who was paddling aimlessly, a vacant expression in her eyes. As he reached her, the captain of the tug throttled up his engines and pulled away at top speed. His screws created a swell that lifted Olga and pulled her away from the yacht.

The same surge swamped Irina and Dmitrov. Irina swallowed some seawater, which hit her empty stomach like a bomb. She felt suddenly dizzy and light-headed, as if the two halves of her skull, front and back, were separating from each other. In her panic, she started to thrash. She gulped more water.

Dmitrov called to her, "Calm down, Irinushka, I'm coming."

She looked around, frantic. "Where's Mother? I don't see her."

"She's right with us. Come on, swim toward me. Over here. This way."

"No, I can't! I'm scared. I don't want to!"

"I'll help you." Dmitrov reached her in a couple of strokes. "Relax. I'll take you. Trust me, Irina. Don't fight."

But as he got behind her and passed his arm around her chest, he felt her go stiff, like a corpse. Then she began to struggle. The lower belt on her life jacket came loose, and as it floated up around her head and shoulders, she wriggled out of it and disappeared. Dmitrov called to her. She came up a few yards away, but she wasn't swimming. She went under again. Dmitrov reached her with a few strokes and dived. He brought her up, but she fought him like a maniac. He marveled at the pent-up strength in her frail body.

Olga heard Irina's desperate cries. She plunged ahead, but a strong current held her prisoner. No matter how hard she stroked, she seemed to be making no headway against the pull of the tide. Why didn't the skipper of the yacht do something? Why didn't they pull closer and haul them aboard? Why didn't they come to her rescue?"

Over the rush of the wind and the sound of the waves, she heard a more ominous sound, the drone of a powerful engine. Casting a look over her shoulder, she saw that the cruiser was gaining on them, coming close enough so that she could see its green ensign snapping in the wind. A green flag with the familiar hammer-and-sickle emblem. The KGB.

The captain of the yacht, a wealthy young Turk named Hachi Agca, maneuvered his craft closer to Irina and Dmitrov. Irina, her energy exhausted, went limp in her father's arms. He grabbed the rope Owen Adair threw him and looped it around Irina's torso, under her arms.

"Pull her up!" Dmitrov shouted. He snatched at another rope and hauled himself on board as the others helped Irina. "Olga—is she all right?"

Someone, Judith, wrapped a blanket around him. "She's in trouble, Sasha. Hachi's going to go after her."

Squinting into the rising sun, Dmitrov saw her then, a small, dark head bobbing on the orange bubble of the life jacket. And behind Olga, growing steadily larger, the KGB cruiser.

"We've got to get to her before they do!"

As Hachi swung the yacht around, they saw a burst of yellow from the cruiser, then heard a muffled thump. A rocket arced toward them and fell into the sea about thirty feet from the *Argos*'s prow. It exploded on impact, sending up a tower of water and spray and rocking the *Argos* over at a thirty-degree angle. The crew and passengers clung to the rails until the boat righted itself. The faint rattle of artillery fire coughed in the distance.

"We can't go any closer!" Owen Adair called. "They'll blow us out of the water. Hachi, let's get the hell out of here!"

The young captain executed a tight turn, then he pushed his engines up to full power and ran his yacht south toward the Turkish coast. Dmitrov grabbed Owen Adair's binoculars. He scanned the sea until he caught a glimpse of Olga, washed even closer to the cruiser by the swell from the rocket. He thought he saw her raise her arm in farewell. Then she disappeared in a trough between the waves.

Irina, shivering inside the blanket Vanessa had thrown around her, hurled herself at her father. He stood unmoving while blows from her fists rained on his face and neck and chest.

"Murderer!" she screamed. "Murderer! You let them take her. You let them kill her! I hate you! I hate you!"

Owen Adair and another crewman dragged her away from him. Vanessa put her arms around the sobbing girl and led her down the companionway ladder to the cabin belowdecks. Dmitrov's legs finally gave way and he slumped to the deck, his head in his hands. Judith knelt beside him. She wanted to hold him, but she knew she could not penetrate his agony.

"I'll get her back," Dmitrov whispered inside the cave of his arms. "Somehow. I don't care what it costs, or if I die trying. I'll get her back." He must have sensed Judith's presence, for suddenly he lifted his head and grabbed her upper arm. His fingers dug painfully into her flesh. "The memoirs," he hissed. "Phillip's memoirs! Are they safe?"

Judith nodded. "They're in London."

"We'll use them to buy her back. We must!"

Vanessa and Owen Adair watched from the other side of the yacht. "I told you this trip wouldn't be a pleasure cruise," Owen said.

Vanessa lit two cigarettes behind cupped hands and gave him one. "What a shame. That poor woman. Where did that ship come from, anyway?"

"They certainly had a bead on us," Adair agreed. "Must have had that Georgian's tub on her radar all the time. If it hadn't been for Hachi, we'd all be fish food right now."

The mood on board the *Argos* was grim. The jubilation that had accompanied the first sighting of the tugboat and her passengers had been exploded by the KGB's shells, by the loss of Olga, and by Irina's screams. The crew, consisting of Judith, Vanessa, Owen Adair, and four of Hachi's friends from the Istanbul Yacht Club, went about their tasks in gloomy silence. They were safe in Turkish waters now, with the rugged coastline creating a dark smudge on the horizon, but everyone on the yacht knew that their mission had been a failure.

Just before sunset, they pulled into a sheltered cove on Turkey's northern coast, a few miles west of the little town of Rize. Everyone except the Turks disembarked, and Hachi wished them good luck.

"Maybe I'll see you in Washington, Judith!" he shouted as the *Argos* backed out of the cove. "Your turn to buy dinner."

Judith managed a smile. She had met Hachi when he was studying international law at Johns Hopkins. Their romance had been brief but intense, and they had even been engaged for a time. When Judith broke it off, Hachi insisted that she keep the ring he had given her, a diamond worthy of an Ottoman queen. Hachi had found himself a Turkish girl of good family, and they had five children now. It was enough to make a girl feel old.

They made their way up a steep track to an olive grove where a flock of goats was grazing. A couple of the goats had climbed up on the roof of a battered Land-Rover and were nibbling olive leaves from their lofty perch. Owen and Judith shooed them away. A ten-year-old boy who was herding the goats watched shyly from behind a boulder. Judith called him over and gave him a fistful of coins and a package of chewing gum.

"Did anybody bother the truck?" she asked in English. He seemed to understand her tone and gestures, and shook his head. "Good. You did a great job." She patted his shoulder. "Thanks a lot, Kemal."

He nodded and grinned, then he rounded up his goats and moved off over the crest of the hill. The sun was pressing against the peaks of the Pontic Mountains at their backs. From the shore below them, the sea sucked at the stones that had tumbled down these slopes so many centuries ago that they were worn as smooth as bowling balls. This was harsh, rugged country, and like the sea, unforgiving of weakness.

The Land-Rover was stocked with camping gear, food, and several billy cans of water. Owen Adair told Dmitrov that they would go as far as Erzurum, a good-sized city in the interior, where they could catch a plane for Ankara, then Istanbul. They would rest there, then fly on to London. Hachi's yacht would be the red herring that would draw the KGB off the scent.

"You have passports?"

Dmitrov produced an oilskin pouch from under his shirt and handed it over. He had bought the passports from black marketeers in Moscow. They were British, stolen in Vienna and smuggled into the Soviet Union. An expert forger had adapted them to suit the Dmitrov family.

"They're good," Owen said. "At least we won't have any trouble with these. Everything is set up—tickets, hotels, cars. In one week, you'll be in Washington."

"You've done a remarkable job," Dmitrov said. "I am in your debt."

"I couldn't have done anything without Judith and Vanessa. Those two have a very interesting assortment of friends." Owen shoved his hands deep into his pockets. "Look, I'm sorry about your wife. It shouldn't have happened. That cruiser shouldn't have been there."

"But it was there, and she's gone." Dmitrov straightened his shoulders and looked over at Irina, standing slumped against the front fender of the Land-Rover. "We'd better start, I suppose."

Adair drove the first leg. They abandoned the coast road as soon as they could, and headed inland toward Erzurum. The road was little more than a dirt track the width of a single car. The Land-Rover was twelve years old, and although the man from whom Hachi had bought it had guaranteed it as absolutely dependable mechanically, its springs were shot and it took the bumps badly. The two men sat up front, with the women behind them. Irina sat between Judith and Vanessa. She refused even to look at Judith, and recoiled visibly whenever they were thrown together. Judith didn't blame her. As a friend of Irina's father and a planner of this project, she had to accept a measure of responsibility for their failure. She sympathized, but the girl's unrelenting hostility worried her. At some point it might explode and put them all in danger.

At midnight, Adair left the road. They climbed until they reached high ground, where they would have a good view of the valley and the surrounding hills.

"We'll camp here tonight and get to Erzurum by noon tomorrow," Owen told them. "Our flight is at six. We don't want to hang around any one place too long."

Judith had stocked the larder with an assortment of condensed soups, tubs of olives and feta cheese, a few sticks of dried sausage, tinned crackers that wouldn't go stale, and plenty of vodka and wine. She and Vanessa built a fire and boiled water for instant soup and tea. After nightfall, the arid mountain air turned chill. Judith had hoped when she bought the food that this first meal together would be a festive one, but they ate it without speaking, and they drank the resinous-tasting wine without any toasting. Afterward they stamped out the fire and rolled out their sleeping bags. Irina, who had not spoken a word to anyone all night, dragged hers to the far edge of their campsite.

"I guess she wants to be alone," Vanessa said to Owen.

"I feel sorry for her, but I don't trust her," Owen said. "She might be planning to run away, which would screw us up royally. I'll keep an eye on her."

Judith joined Dmitrov, who was sitting on a rock smoking a cigarette. "Sasha, I'm sorry about Olga. I wish things had happened differ-
ently."

"She put her trust in me." Dmitrov took a last drag on his cigarette
and stubbed it out. "And I promised her that I would take care of her and
Irina, that we would be a family again. She was so tired of being frightened
and suspicious. She wanted to be free. She wanted this." He lifted his chin
and glared resentfully at the spangled canopy overhead.

Judith crouched beside him. "We'll cable Washington from the con-
sulate at Istanbul. I'll ask Preston to see what they can find out about her
through their channels in Moscow."

Dmitrov's head snapped up. "No! The KGB will be holding her,
maybe even torturing her. They may be willing to make a trade, her life
for your father's memoirs. Will you give them to us, Judith? Will you use
them to save her?"

Judith sat back on her heels. "If we give them away, we'll never know
what was in them. We'll never know who ran Phil, who helped him
defect."

"A little knowledge for a life," Dmitrov said. "A few facts in exchange
for a woman who has done only good in her life. Can you really hold back
a few pages of autobiography because of simple curiosity?"

"No," Judith said firmly. "Of course not. As soon as we're safe in
London, you can call them. It should only take us another day. Don't
worry, Sasha."

"I would almost rather they killed her than put her in one of their
prisons," Dmitrov murmured.

Judith wanted to hold him, but he was still unapproachable, wrapped
in despair. "We'll do everything we can, Sasha. I promise."

He shrugged. "When you're dealing with them, everything is the
same as nothing."

CHAPTER 29

*T*hey ate a cold breakfast of leftover sausage and bread washed down with wine. Irina ate nothing, but drank more than her share of the wine. Before they clambered into the Land-Rover, she ducked behind a rock and threw it all up. She looked wrung out and corpselike, as though the sea had leached out what little life and energy she had brought with her from Moscow.

After her outburst on the *Argos,* she hadn't spoken a word to anyone. She refused to look at her father. Judith wished the girl would find a way to vent her grief, by screaming or weeping or tearing at the clothes they had provided for her: jeans and a sweater and a denim jacket. Anything was better than the kind of frozen silence that didn't let anything in or out.

They left behind them the green fringe of the northern Turkish coast, with its cornfields and tea plantations, and entered a scrubby forest of pine and larch, the trunks stunted and gnarled by the fierce winds that blew down from Russia.

As they approached the Soganli Gecidi pass through the mountains, the trail grew steeper. Owen Adair shifted down into first gear. Both Irina and Vanessa were smoking sickly sweet Turkish cigarettes. Combined with the jarring bumps and jolts, the smoke gave Judith the worst case of motion sickness she had ever had. She closed her eyes and wished for the torment to end.

Suddenly there was a loud crack. The windshield shattered. Dmitrov shouted, "Rifle! Get down!" Another shot glanced off the hood. From under the front seat, Adair grabbed two automatic rifles and a pistol. Dmitrov took a rifle.

"Everybody out of the truck! Take cover!"

Judith latched on to Irina's arm and dragged her across the seat and out the door on the left side of the Land-Rover. As another shot ricocheted off the rocks over their heads, they dived for the shelter of a large boulder. Dmitrov crouched beside the truck and scanned the rocks at the top of the pass. Sharpshooters, most likely. He saw no movement, no splash of color on the barren slopes. The snipers were well hidden, or well camouflaged.

Adair appeared beside him. "Cover me. I'll see if I can find them."

"No, I'll go. I know how they think."

Dmitrov studied the mountain on their right, from where the shots had come. A tower of rock commanded a view of the road through the pass. The shots must have come from there. Straight ahead of them, the mountainside was scored by a gully, a cleft created by an avalanche in the distant past and worn deeper by wind and rain and melting snow. Dmitrov darted across the road and began to climb. A bullet whizzed past his ear and buried itself in the trunk of a tree. Adair tried to distract the snipers by returning their fire.

Dmitrov made his way up the gully, picking his way carefully over loose stones and the trunks of fallen trees. He had a pistol in his hand and the rifle slung across his back. He had hoped for a longer grace period before the KGB gave chase, but they had found him, and he must deal with them. The paralyzing inertia of the previous night had vanished. This was one situation he could control, one battle he had a chance of winning.

A sheer cliff face rose abruptly in front of him. He skirted it to the right, keeping the mass of stone between him and the sharpshooter stationed at the peak up ahead. From down in the pass came another exchange of gunfire—Adair keeping the sniper busy. The climb was a rough one, but Dmitrov noticed he was breathing without difficulty. In his core, he was calm and quiet. Failure was behind him. From now on, he had to concentrate on saving Irina, and saving himself so that he could get Olga out of the Soviet Union.

Hearing a noise to his left, he ducked behind a wedge of rock and held his pistol ready. A man wearing green fatigues crept through the trees below him.

"Tovarich!" Dmitrov called out. The man threw himself flat out on the ground, but not before a bullet from Dmitrov's pistol had buried itself in his heart.

He would have to kill them all, every one of the death squad of four or six men that had been sent to ambush them, to retrieve or destroy the defectors and their rescuers. This was no time to negotiate. They were all in danger, Irina, Judith, Vanessa.

Dmitrov kept climbing. He was above the tree line, but the thrusting rocks still gave some protection. Then a shot chipped a boulder right in front of him, sending a splinter of stone into his face. He took cover and touched his hand to his left eye. It was filled with blood, but the cut seemed to be just above the socket. He wiped away the blood with his shirt sleeve and peered across the gap to the other side of the pass. A movement, a flash of something caught his eye, dark against the light-colored sandstone. He steadied the rifle, took aim, and fired. The shot flushed the other shooter, who scrambled across the face of the hill. Dmitrov fired again, and his quarry fell head over heels to land face down in the road.

The sniper in the rocky tower above him was still exchanging fire with Adair. Dmitrov made his way around the back of the mountain until he reached the foot of the tower. Then slowly he worked his way upward. From time to time he paused to look back, but he saw no one. The slope was more gradual here, and he found a path of sorts, worn by goats or deer.

He stationed himself just below the cleft in the rock where the sniper was lodged and readied his pistol.

"Comrade!" he called. "The traitor Dmitrov is coming after you. Look out!"

A face appeared. Dmitrov fired once, and missed. The sniper returned fire, and struck him in the right shoulder. Dmitrov rolled down the slope while bullets churned up the dust around him. He scrambled behind a boulder. He had lost his pistol, but he still had the rifle. He lay still and waited. Two long minutes passed. Finally he heard a noise and peeked out. The sniper, thinking him dead, was coming to make certain. Dmitrov braced the rifle on a ledge of rock and fired with his left hand. The sniper pitched forward, tumbled toward him, and lay still.

The pass was silent. Holding the stock of the rifle under his wounded right arm, Dmitrov made his way down the mountain. He approached the Land-Rover from the rear. A second dead gunman lay in the road. Judith was standing over him, a pistol in her hand.

"I heard him sneaking up on us. I shot him." She gazed at Dmitrov with dazed eyes. After a moment, she shook her head vigorously and focused on him. "You're hurt!"

"It's not too bad. Is everyone else all right?"

"Yes, we're fine. There's a first-aid kit—"

"Later. Give me the pistol and let's get out of here."

They rolled the bodies out of the way and scrambled into the Land-

Rover. Adair muttered a prayer of thanks that no shots had pierced the engine block. The truck started readily and he stamped on the accelerator.

They had gone about ten miles when Dmitrov pointed Judith's pistol at Owen's head.

"Pull over. Now. We have to talk." He twisted around and pressed himself against the dashboard. He had them all covered.

"Sasha, what's this all about?" Judith asked.

"One of you three has betrayed us."

The words cut through the fug of terror and dust inside the cab. "That's ridiculous!" Judith cried. "You can't really believe—"

Dmitrov silenced her with a look. "That KGB cruiser must have been following us from the moment we left port. They knew exactly what we were doing and where we were going. The same with the snipers. They were waiting for us. They failed, but there will be more. They'll keep at it until they find us, and they will either destroy us or take us back."

"Sasha, we didn't, I swear it."

"I'll vouch for Judy, and she'll vouch for me, and we'll both vouch for Owen," Vanessa said. "We're not KGB. Not that you'll believe us."

"I don't believe you. It was too easy for them. They know where we're going to be every step of the way."

"Then we'll change our plans," Adair said. "Somehow they got wind of this—I'm damned if I know how." He turned to Judith. "Hachi?"

She shook her head. "His cousin was killed in a demonstration at Istanbul University in 1973. The Soviets organized it. Everybody in Hachi's family hates the Russians." She leaned over the back of the seat and touched Dmitrov's arm. "Sasha, you have to trust us. You're hurt, you're weak, and you'll never get anywhere on your own. They'll catch you for sure."

"Let them catch us." Irina broke her long silence. "I don't care. They'll get us eventually. Why prolong the misery?"

"Because we're not going back," her father said. "I'll never let them take you back."

"You said the same thing to Mother." Irina sneered. "You lied to her, too. Why should I believe you now?"

"She wanted this for you," Dmitrov barked. "You have a chance to make a new life for yourself."

"What makes you think the new life will be any better than the old?" she demanded.

"It can be if you want it to be," Vanessa told her. "We'll help."

"Yes, like you helped them catch my mother. You're disgusting, all of you." Irina crossed her arms in front of her and slid down onto the base of her spine.

"Well, Colonel Dmitrov," said Owen Adair, "what'll it be? Are you going to shove us out and try to go it alone, just you and Irina? You won't get very far."

"We didn't betray you," Judith said passionately. "Why would we? Sasha, look at me. I love you!"

Dmitrov set his jaw. "Love is the other side of betrayal."

"Only to a twisted Russian mind." They glared at each other for a moment, then Judith sighed. "We're at a stalemate, aren't we? You have to trust us as far as England. You need us."

"You're right." Dmitrov lowered the pistol, conceding the point. "We'll stay together, but no more trusting. One of you is a traitor, or else very careless." He looked at Vanessa. "Everyone knows women have loose tongues in bed."

Vanessa snorted. "Men don't do so badly in that department either, sweetheart. Maybe your own pillow talk got out of hand back in Moscow."

"All right, cut it out." Judith reached under the seat and pulled out a metal box. "I'll patch you up, and then we'll get out of here. We have enough enemies. We don't need to fight among ourselves."

Judith did what she could to disinfect Dmitrov's wounds and to bandage his upper arm. The bullet had passed through, shattering the humerus. The bone needed setting, which was more than she dared attempt.

They bypassed Erzurum and drove another two hundred miles to Malatya. There Dmitrov vetoed the suggestion that they catch a plane from Malatya to Istanbul. Having failed to ambush them in the pass, the KGB would be watching all the airports and the main roads. Instead they would travel overland to Ankara, the capital, where they could telephone Hachi to ask for help. Judith insisted that they stop in Malatya long enough to seek out a doctor who could set Dmitrov's arm and give him an injection of antibiotics to ward off infection. He resisted that idea, too, but Judith overrode him.

"You're no good to anybody if you're half out of your mind with fever. Or dead."

"You should have brought antibiotics with you."

"I should never have gone to bed with you in the first place," she retorted. "That was my first mistake."

The atmosphere in the Land-Rover was heavy with anger and suspicion. Dmitrov kept his left hand on the pistol in his lap. Irina sulked. Vanessa chattered nervously, but when no one responded, eventually she, too, fell silent.

In Malatya they took two adjoining rooms on the second floor of the

Ugur Palas, a small hotel on a dusty side street overlooking the open-air marketplace. Vanessa, testing the beds in the women's room, declared that the owners should be sued for misrepresentation. "This dump is no palace, Ugur or any other kind."

Judith examined Dmitrov's arm. The area of the wound was red and inflamed. "You've got to see a doctor right away. I'll go with you."

"I'll take him." Owen tucked the pistol into the front of his trousers and covered it with his shirt. "You're too conspicuous. We'd have half the men in this town following us."

After the men left, Vanessa went down the hall to look for a shower—"Owen should have left me the pistol to fight off the cockroaches." Irina lounged on the cot under the window, her back pressed to the wall. Judith sat beside her.

"Cigarette?"

The girl took one. Judith snapped her disposable lighter. "It wasn't your father's fault, you know."

"Whose was it? My mother's?"

"Nobody's. Things happen. Even the best-laid plans sometimes go wrong."

Irina belched smoke. "One of you betrayed us. You're as much to blame as he is, for bringing the KGB down on us."

"We didn't. We—" Judith stopped herself, realizing the futility of arguing. "I can't prove that. You'll just have to take my word for it."

"Your word!" Irina's pretty face puckered into a sneer. "You're a typical example of perverted capitalistic thinking. You American women are all prostitutes. You look like prostitutes, you think like prostitutes. You dress up and paint your faces and keep yourselves beautiful, and for what? To capture an old man like my father! It's pathetic. I say you're welcome to him. I don't need him. I never needed him. My mother doesn't need him. We were doing perfectly well without his help."

Judith tapped her ash over a cracked saucer. "Were you? Starving your body, destroying your mind. Sorry we foiled your success. In another six months, you might have been dead."

"What business is that of yours?" Irina demanded.

"It's my business because I understand what you're doing, and why. I did it myself, for longer than I care to admit. Drugs, sex, alcohol—a blind girl groping for a quick route to eternity. I thought I could punish my father for betraying us. Sound familiar? I've got bad news for you, kid. There's a rebound effect at work that says that your chief victim is yourself. Your father is going to go on living no matter what you do. Mine did."

Irina drew her feet up under her and turned her face to the wall.

"Leave me alone. I won't listen to you anymore. You're an old woman. What do you know about anything?"

Judith stood up. "I've learned a few things in my day. Just thought I'd share them. Your father's a good man, Irina. He loves you very much. He wouldn't be putting himself through this if he didn't."

"Go fuck yourself," Irina said flatly.

Vanessa returned. She took in the situation at a glance. "How's the captive princess?" she asked. "Bratty and sullen as ever?"

"Too bad I have scruples about hitting someone who's smaller and weaker than I am." Judith dug in her knapsack for a change of clothes. "This kid needs a good spanking."

"Go fuck yourselves," Irina said from her bed.

"Nice command of the plural imperative," Vanessa remarked as Judith passed her on the way to the toilet. "Hey, kid, want to learn some really juicy Anglo-Saxonisms? They'll come in handy next time you want to tell us off."

The men returned at dusk. They had located an elderly physician on the outskirts of the town. He had dug out a few bone chips from Dmitrov's arm, packed the entry and exit wounds with sulfa drugs, and stitched them closed. Afterward he gave Dmitrov an injection from a vial of antibiotic that was three years out of date.

Dmitrov insisted on mounting a guard in the hall that night. He took the first shift, from ten to two. Owen would take the second. They would be on the road before dawn.

"For all we know, that doctor could be talking to the KGB right now."

"Fine," Judith said, "but that doesn't mean you have to spend four hours sitting out here with a rifle across your lap. You need rest more than we do. I can handle a pistol. If I need help, I'll call."

"I am responsible for my daughter's safety," Dmitrov said stubbornly.

"Which means you don't trust us to look after her, is that right? You still think one of us betrayed you."

Dmitrov refused to meet her gaze. "I am certain one of you did."

Furious, Judith stormed into the room she shared with Vanessa and Irina and slammed the door. She lay on the narrow, lumpy cot, too exhausted to sleep. The walls were thin; she could hear Owen Adair's rhythmic snoring in the room next door. She dozed off, then awoke again when the men switched places. She got up, threw a sweater on over her nightgown, and went out into the hall.

"If you hear any cries for help," she told Adair, who was just settling down in the hard chair, the pistol bulging under his shirtfront, "ignore them." He gave her a knowing grin.

She entered Dmitrov's room without knocking. He whirled around from the dresser, his rifle aimed at her chest.

"Put that thing away. I'm not the enemy. Neither is Vanessa, and Owen's worked too hard and risked too much for you. He's not going to turn you over to the KGB."

Dmitrov lowered the rifle. He propped it against the wall near the head of the bed, where he could reach it easily if needed. "Then someone was careless. You should fly home, the three of you. Irina and I will move more quickly without you."

Judith made a scornful noise. "Oh, that's a brilliant idea. If you don't die of blood poisoning, the two of you will end up shooting each other." She folded her arms. "We're staying together. Don't bother to argue. You'll just be wasting your breath."

Dmitrov stood in the center of the floor, his arms at his sides. "I love you, Judith," he said. "I want you to know, whatever happens, that not everything I said to you in the past was a lie."

The blood rushed to Judith's cheeks. "Why are you doing this to me? You're going back to your wife, remember? Why don't you just slug me, or kick me, or tell me that I'm ugly and that you don't want me around? Why—"

He captured her with his good arm. Her hands contracted into claws and reached for his face and eyes. He didn't try to deflect them. But his kiss dissolved the tension of her anger before she even touched him.

"Bastard," she whispered tearfully, "bastard," but even while she was saying the word, her right hand was snaking slowly down the length of his torso, dipping between his legs. He caught his breath. Desire came over them like madness. He took her standing up against the outside wall, in order to avoid putting weight on his wounded arm. She unsheathed her talons again, only this time she raked his back and buttocks ever so lightly, inflicting just the right amount of pain. It was all over very quickly.

As they leaned against each other and listened to the thunder of their breathing subside into sighs, he cradled her face in his hands and kissed away the tears from her eyes.

"Judith, I love—"

She stopped his mouth with her fingertips. "I'm going to forget I ever heard that word from you. Otherwise, I really will go crazy." She moved away from him. Her nightgown fell like a sheer silken curtain. "Good night, Sasha."

* * *

The journey to Ankara, a hundred and fifty miles to the west, took two days. They stuck to back roads whenever possible, and avoided narrow mountain passes. Rather than risk a hotel again, they camped out, taking turns keeping watch. Judith and Vanessa each insisted on taking a shift. Irina didn't offer, and no one asked her.

Judith noticed that Dmitrov was growing weaker, although he insisted that he was as strong as ever. He refused to allow her to examine his wounds.

They planned to telephone Hachi from Ankara. They needed a place to rest in Istanbul, and his villa on one of the Prince's islands would be perfect. Owen stopped the Land-Rover outside the main post office, and he and Judith went inside to place the call.

They waited twenty minutes for the operator to make the connection, but finally the phone rang at the villa. Judith asked for Hachi. After a moment, he came on.

"Go away. I don't want to speak to you again."

"Why? What happened?"

"A bomb. Yesterday, in my car. My nephew was taking it to the garage for repairs. There isn't even enough of him left to bury. This morning a man telephoned. He said that if I saw any of you again, the rest of my family would die, too, one by one." He hung up.

Judith looked at Owen. "Looks like we're on our own." She explained what had happened.

"They'll be watching the airports."

"We could keep driving into Greece," Judith suggested.

Owen shook his head. "Dmitrov will never make it. He needs a doctor right away. Besides, they're probably watching the borders, too."

"We could go to the embassy. Dump it on them."

"No good. Some of our Turkish embassy employees are certainly KGB co-opts. They'll alert their bosses. Dmitrov won't live to see morning."

"Well, this is a fine mess." Judith leaned against the wall. "Any ideas?"

"We could push ahead, shoot it out again if we have to."

She shook her head. "No good. I don't want anyone shooting at Vanessa. Or me, for that matter."

"Neither do I." Owen hesitated for a moment. "I know of one person who could conceivably put us in touch with someone who might help."

"Who's that?"

"Your mother. She knows everybody worth knowing in most of the embassies around the world. And if you girls are in trouble, she'll move heaven and earth to save you, and she'll keep quiet about it. Do you have any better suggestions?"

"I'm fresh out. Let's do it."

Judith told the clerk at the desk that she wanted to make an overseas call to the United States. The clerk directed her to a booth and told her to wait while he got the international operator and placed the call. Eventually the phone in the booth rang. Judith lifted the receiver.

"Hi, Mom," she said brightly. "Guess where I am?"

Lydia Marlowe switched off the speaker phone. "Who do we know in Ankara or Istanbul?"

"Robbins, at the embassy. He'll fix it."

"Find him, wherever he is. And then arrange for two seats on the Concorde from here to London."

At six-thirty the following evening, someone knocked on the door of their room in the Celik Palas Hotel in Ankara. Dmitrov steadied his rifle on his knee. He was trembling with fever, almost too weak to hold the grip. Adair moved to the corner behind the door, his pistol ready. Vanessa and Irina waited tensely while Judith turned the key in the lock and admitted the visitor.

"Evening, folks." A tall beige man stepped into the room. His hair, eyes, complexion, and rumpled suit were all the same sandy color. He spoke with a sharp Texas twang. "I'm Robbins from the embassy. Miz Marlowe says you need a hand. Sorry it took so long, but I had to make a few arrangements."

In less than an hour they were airborne, on their way to Athens in a Lear jet belonging to a rug merchant who had once been the Turkish ambassador to France. Robbins accompanied them. He was armed, with a pistol in a holster under his left arm and another smaller one in his sock. He stood guard while they transferred to a commercial jet bound for London. Dmitrov and Adair had given him their weapons in Ankara. He bade them farewell at the gate and wished them luck.

"Someone will meet you in London. It's all taken care of."

A man met them at Heathrow and escorted them through customs. He led them to a waiting Bentley outside the terminal. Judith could tell that both he and the driver of the car, a young man wearing jeans and a brown leather jacket, wore guns. Both had a way of standing on the balls of their feet, arms slightly away from their sides. The greeter saw the Bentley off, and followed in his own Austin.

To Judith's amazement, the car pulled up in front of Vanessa's house in Hampstead. Another man stepped out of the shadows and approached them. The driver rolled down his window.

"All clear. Get them inside."

By now Dmitrov was shivering, so weak he could barely stand. Judith and Owen helped him up the stairs while Vanessa went ahead to open the door. Irina hung back and asked the guard for a cigarette.

"There will be cigarettes upstairs, miss. Please get off the street."

The door was unlocked. Vanessa walked into her flat to find her mother sitting on the sofa, sipping a glass of mineral water. Kenneth was dozing in the armchair. The London *Times* in his lap was folded around the crossword. Deaf Kitty crouched under the credenza, glaring at the strangers who had invaded his sanctuary.

Lydia set down her glass. "Here you are at last, darlings! You don't know how relieved I am to see you all."

Vanessa picked up Deaf Kitty and hugged him. "Will wonders never cease? How did you get in here?"

"The gentleman from across the hall," Lydia told her. "Mr. Tidyman, I believe he said his name was. He was just coming by to feed your cat. If we hadn't seen him, I'm sure we would have found another way in."

Vanessa headed toward the kitchen, still holding the cat in her arms. "Well, I see you've made yourselves at home. I'd say the rest of us have earned ourselves a drink, too. How about brandy all around, and a Coke for the kid?"

"I will have brandy, too," Irina called after her. "Unless you have vodka."

"Me? Never touch the stuff."

Judith helped Dmitrov over to the sofa. Lydia frowned. "I had no idea his condition was so serious. You should have told me, Judith. He should be in a hospital."

"No," Dmitrov gasped. "No hospitals. No doctors."

"You heard him. He's one stubborn Russian." Judith settled Dmitrov on the sofa and wedged a cushion behind his back. As she straightened up, she brushed his cheek with the back of her hand: he was on fire. "You'll have to think up something better, Mother." She glanced over at Kenneth, who was watching the scene with studied impassivity. "Hello, Kenny. Sorry I ran out on you in Moscow the way I did."

"You said our marriage was over, that you had no reason to stay after your father died." Kenneth couldn't conceal his bitterness. "You should have told me what you were up to. I could have helped. Don't you trust me, Judith?"

"Of course I do, Kenny. But considering your position at the embassy, it was better not to involve you. If too many people knew, it might have been dangerous."

"Sounds like someone found out anyway," Kenneth said. "You should have let me handle it."

"Instead you turned Colonel Dmitrov's defection into an international circus. No, thank you, darling." Lydia waved away the brandy snifter Vanessa offered. "At least you had the sense to call when you'd exhausted your other options. I would have hated to read about a shootout in tomorrow's newspapers. I was shocked, to say the least, to find my girls involved in something so dangerous." She turned to Adair. "If anything had happened to either one of them, Owen, I would have held you personally responsible. You of all people should have known better. Why couldn't you let the professionals handle it?"

"A matter of caution, Lydia." Owen took the glass of brandy Vanessa handed him. "I couldn't find any I could trust with Mr. Dmitrov's life."

"Owen? Lydia?" Vanessa grunted. "I didn't know you two were so cozy."

"Oh, Owen and I are old friends," Lydia said with a smile. "Still riding the same old hobbyhorse, Owen? The Agency has been penetrated. The State Department is alive with traitors. There are moles burrowing away in the highest echelons of government. You're not waving that flag anymore, my dear. It's waving you. And it's a tiresome sight."

Owen raised his snifter to her. "Like the stars and stripes, Lydia. Some flags will be worth waving as long as there are enemies who want to shoot at them."

Irina pulled open the glass doors of the stereo cabinet and selected a tape, which she shoved into the cassette slot. Judith tensed.

"Irina, I don't think—"

The screech of an electric guitar ripped the air. Everyone jumped except Lydia, who had turned her attention to Dmitrov. Irina lowered the volume, helped herself to one of Vanessa's cigarettes, and crouched on the floor between the speakers, jerking and rolling to the music.

"Well, Mr. Dmitrov," Lydia said, raising her voice to make herself heard over the noise, "now that we've got you here, what are we going to do with you?"

"FBI." Dmitrov gulped down the brandy Vanessa had given him and waited for it to dull the pain in his arm. "I won't talk to anyone but the FBI."

"You won't talk to anyone period if you don't get some help at once. My suggestion is this: The State Department maintains a sort of guest-house in Brighton, a haven for weary diplomats or traveling politicians who want to get out of the limelight for a while. We'll go there at once. We have a doctor we can call, completely reliable. If necessary, I'm told, he can even perform surgery there. Then as soon as you're back on your feet, we'll fly you to the States in an Air Force plane. What do you say?"

Dmitrov's good hand tightened around the bowl of the brandy snifter. He glanced at his daughter. "Irina—"

"I'll look after her," Judith promised. "I'll stay right with you every minute, I promise."

"With Irina," Dmitrov said. "I don't care what happens to me. You look after Irina. Don't let her out of your sight."

"Nothing's going to happen to either one of you," Lydia said reassuringly as she stood. "Well, there's no sense wasting time. The car is downstairs. Kenneth, dear, would you call ahead and arrange for that surgeon? I want him waiting for us when we get there."

Kenneth went to the phone. He dialed a number, spoke two sentences, and hung up the receiver. "It's all set."

Dmitrov closed his eyes. He had no choice. He had to trust these people. "All right," he said. "We'll go with you."

Vanessa picked up her shoulder bag. "I hope you have plenty of bedrooms. Owen and I are coming, too."

Lydia shook her head. "Sorry, darling, but it's not wise. The Russians almost certainly know you're back. We can't all fit in the Bentley, and two cars make a caravan, which is a trifle conspicuous. You sit tight until we call you."

"Where is this place?" Adair asked. "I never heard about any State Department house in Brighton, official or otherwise."

"You've been away from Washington for a long time, Owen. A lot has changed in your absence. Kenneth?" Kenneth fetched Lydia's purse and helped her into her raincoat. "I know we'd all like to rest and chat, but we'd better push on." She kissed Vanessa on both cheeks. "Don't worry, your charges are well in hand. You've been awfully brilliant, dar-lings. But now it's time to turn this whole business over to people who know what they're doing."

After they had gone, Vanessa took a cigarette from the box on the coffee table, stared at it, and threw it down again.

"Damn her. I hate it when she does this. She sweeps in, pushes everybody aside, and takes over without even a 'May I?' I've put twenty years and five thousand miles of distance between us, and here she is, right in my own house, giving me orders, taking over. I feel like a goddamn ten-year-old again."

"We did call on her for help," Owen reminded her. "So far, her men have handled everything pretty well."

"So why did she have to butt in? Did she fly over on her broomstick just so she could put her imprimatur on things? Is she trying to give Kenny a boost by letting him have first crack at debriefing Dmitrov? Is the whole point of this to keep the Brits away from her defector? And why couldn't we go along with them? That Bentley is as big as a house. I don't know about you, but I don't like the way this is ending. I hate seeing Judy vanish into the night with that crowd."

"I'm sure your sister is perfectly safe." Owen walked to the window, pushed the curtain aside, and looked down. The street was empty. The watchdogs had been pulled off the job. "In any case, it's out of our hands now. I admit I'm disappointed, too, but I forfeited my right to oversee this case when the KGB started shooting at us and I ran out of options. Dmitrov was right, we were compromised. But was it from his end, or our end? I'd really like to know." He turned back to the room. "It'll keep, I guess. I'll call you in the morning."

Vanessa frowned. "You're not going?"

He returned a weary smile. "Do I hear an offer?"

She flopped onto the sofa and stretched out her long legs. "Suit yourself," she said frostily. "You and Lydia were pretty friendly, I noticed."

Owen lit a cigarette. "We've known each other a long time, Vanessa. While we may not always have seen eye to eye, we still respect each other, maybe even like each other."

"Don't give me that." Vanessa jerked her chin up and glared at him. "You were in love with her, weren't you? Maybe you still are, a little. Way back in the dark ages when you were debriefing her about Phil, trying to find out what she knew. Poor Lydia, poor little bruised blossom. Who could resist? What a scenario: Mother, all blond and fluffy and deeply distressed; you, dark and skinny and intense. You must have noticed the contrast, appreciated it, wondered what her body looked like under those ever so proper clothes she always wore. You can't kid me. She was a knockout in those days, as people insist on telling me. I haven't been a knockout since I was in diapers, and then maybe for six months. You'd better get out of here. I don't sleep with any man that my mother saw first. I've got some standards."

Owen sat on the arm of the sofa. "I'm surprised, Vanessa. As old as you are, as much as you've accomplished, you're still comparing yourself to her."

"It's the family curse." Vanessa threw her arm over her face. "Judy and me. You don't know the agony we put that poor little woman through. Her face was a perpetual study in disappointment. I couldn't read. Judith couldn't sit still. Later it was boys. They were never good enough, and we were subnormal because we wanted to go out with them. She was so bloody perfect, every hair in place, the beautifully modulated voice, the erect carriage, the always appropriate clothes, the impeccable manners, the unshakable poise. It was like growing up in a goddamn charm school. And when we rebelled, she was the one everyone felt sorry for. 'Poor Lydia, she's tried so hard with those girls.' You always got the idea that it was Phil's fault for abandoning us. Never hers. Poor bastard. No wonder he turned to men. I'll bet you anything that he couldn't measure up, either. In any department." Vanessa expelled a weary sigh. "Oh, God, I'm tired."

Owen reached down and smoothed her hair. " 'Fair consort,' " he quoted, " 'th'hour of night, and all things now retired to rest mind us of like repose.' "

She looked up at him. "I won't be Lydia for you. I'm not perfect. I'm not even polite."

Laughing softly, Owen leaned over and kissed her. Then, taking her by the hand, he drew her up from the sofa and led her toward the bedroom, quoting softly:

"So hand in hand they passed, the loveliest pair
That ever since in love's embraces met,
Adam the goodliest man of men since born
His sons, the fairest of her daughters Eve."

CHAPTER 30

Batumi, U.S.S.R.

Olga Dmitrova sat shivering on the hard stool in the interrogation room. The sailors from the cruiser *Yalta* had draped a rough blanket around her shoulders and had given her some hot tea to drink. But once the KGB men on land had taken charge of her, even minimal courtesies vanished. They ordered her to strip and searched her and then made her put on her wet clothes again. Then they left her in the small room, bare except for a single stool and a table.

As the day warmed up, her clothes finally began to dry, but as the chill in her bones eased, terror tightened its grip. They were counting on that, of course. They knew that the longer they let her simmer, the more frightened she would become. Her own imagination would do half their work for them. She knew their methods. In the early days of his persecution, Yakov had ranted about his various periods of detention. Yakov had been foolhardy but brave. Olga knew she was not brave. She couldn't stop shaking.

She was almost grateful when the questioning started. Two men, taking turns. One of them kept sneaking peeks at his wristwatch. He was doing his job, but his heart wasn't in it. He wanted to go home. To his wife, his family. His girlfriend. In his late thirties, he was no longer young, but his fair hair and cool blue eyes reminded her of Sasha.

She recognized the second man, even though she had never seen him before: This was Krelnikov, Sasha's boss, the man they called the Wolf. He was elegantly attired in a light gray suit. He smoked small brown cigars that he took from a pack with a Cuban label. The two canine teeth in his upper jaw were gold, and he used them to good advantage, concealing them with a broad smile one moment, baring them in a fierce snarl the next. She was grateful she had been given nothing to drink; she would have wet herself long ago.

Back and forth they went. Olga concentrated on the story Sasha had drilled into her: Her husband had forced her to agree to this plan; she went along against her will because she was afraid of him. Look at what he had done to her brother. She was too frightened to tell anyone else in the KGB because Dmitrov might find out. All the while Aleksandr Dmitrov had been abducting them, Olga had been terrified for herself, for her daughter. But she was innocent. Completely innocent.

"Come, now," said the Wolf, "do you really expect us to believe this pack of lies? You gave the girl drugs so that she wouldn't put up a fight. A waiter in the restaurant saw you put something in her wineglass while she was in the bathroom. Why else would you have done it unless you were cooperating fully with that traitor your husband?"

The Wolf kept referring to Sasha as "that-traitor-your-husband." Another one of their techniques. Soon she would be thinking of him that way herself. No, she told herself. He is Sasha. He loves me. He promised he wouldn't leave me. Where is he now, when I need him so desperately? Where is that-traitor-my-husband? No, I'm sorry, Sasha. I didn't mean it. You're not a traitor. I love you. I love you.

"You went along with this plan even though you knew it was wrong!" the Wolf cried. "You knew he was a traitor, didn't you? Didn't you!"

"Yes, yes," she wept, her teeth chattering. "He is a traitor."

"And you're a traitor, too. Do you know what we do to traitors, Dr. Dmitrova? Either we shoot them, one bullet through the base of the skull, or else we bury them alive in the Gulag. You are just like your brother Seminov, another Jew-traitor. Traitors run in your family, don't they? You are born of traitors, you marry traitors, your children are traitors."

"No, not my Irina! She is innocent!"

"We know how innocent she is, with her promiscuous behavior and her drugs and that bunch of parasites she calls her friends. We know about her abortions, about the boys she screws when she wants a pill or a little bag of *trava*. They say she's easy, an easy lay, a free fuck. They cheat her. They screw her and they don't give her anything. She was starting to cut in on the prostitutes' trade, did you know that? A few of them ganged up on her a month ago and beat her up. She had been sidling up to the tourists. Why not? She speaks English and a little French, and she's cheap. But she's too skinny. I know. I had her myself once."

"No, no, no," Olga moaned. "She wouldn't. She never did that! You're lying!"

In fact, Irina had come home bruised and bloody a few weeks ago. She said she had been walking through the woods behind the university, looking for mushrooms and collecting autumn leaves, and she had fallen into a patch of briars. Olga had wanted to believe her. Fool. Fool.

"No, Olga Feodorovna, I am not lying. You are lying. You are lying to yourself if you think you have done anything less than befoul our country with traitors. You are vermin."

On and on they went. After countless hours, Krelnikov and the other man went out and a new team started. But they were only filling in for the Wolf while he ate his dinner. When he returned, he dismissed them and started on her by himself. His breath reeked of garlic and wine.

Olga could tell that the Wolf enjoyed this work. He was in his element. But he was still playing with her, warming up. He didn't touch her, but the threat of physical danger was there, clinging to him like body odor. One blow from his meaty hand and she would find herself on the floor. Two blows would kill her.

Sobbing, she wailed, "If you're going to kill me, why don't you do it now? Get it over with!"

The Wolf laughed. "All in good time, Olga Feodorovna. But first I'm going to squeeze you dry. What's the point in slaughtering the cow while she can still give milk, eh?"

She wished he wouldn't use her patronymic. It was too friendly-familiar, and it reminded her of her own father, so long dead that she wondered if he had ever existed as more than a legend in her life. Her mother said that he had played with her, adored her, lavished affection on her. But she couldn't remember any of that.

The Wolf asked questions about her husband's friends in the West, but he wasn't really interested in her answers. He listened to her denials and her lies for an hour or so, then he thrust his ugly face close to hers and hissed, "Traitors sleep with traitors. Your husband was sleeping with Phillip Abbott's daughter. You knew that. She visited you in your apartment, didn't she? She took you gifts. She poisoned your mind against your own country!"

Olga waggled her head. She was too weak to answer. She had eaten nothing all day. She wanted to sleep, but she knew there would be no sleep for her. If necessary, they would give her an injection of a stimulant to keep her awake. She would not be allowed to lie down, to close her eyes. After a few days, she would die of the stresses caused by sleep deprivation. But what a sweet sleep death would be, deep and endless and peaceful, in the soft womb of the earth—

"Wake up!" The Wolf's bellow was more effective than a slap in shaking her out of her stupor. He curled his lip at her, exposing his horrible teeth to their roots. "You disgust me. Such a weak, pitiful creature, mewing your lies like a two-day-old kitten. Do you really think that your husband and daughter can get away from us? We know about them. We were watching every move you made, every move they're making now. We're waiting for them. Just waiting for them to walk into our open arms."

Traitor. Olga's brain clicked over. They had been betrayed. Not by the tugboat captain. What did he know about their movements after this morning? Someone on the outside, someone who had participated in the planning. Judith Marlowe. The beautiful temptress. She had lured Sasha and Irina to their deaths. That explained the Wolf's confident swagger. The temptress had poured her secrets into his ear, made his saliva run.

"We will have a trial," the Wolf promised. "And what a trial! Two Jewish bitches and an officer in the KGB. If I am in charge, you will hang publicly. Your husband will watch. Your daughter first, her skinny neck snapped by the rope like a string bean on a stem. Then you, wailing and weeping and crying to God for deliverance. By that time, his pants will be full of shit and his knees will be knocking. I'll open the trap under the bastard myself, with pleasure."

At that moment, a young officer opened the door and poked his head in. "Comrade Krelnikov, a telephone call for you from Moscow."

"Keep an eye on her," the Wolf barked on his way out.

The room went dark. With a groan, Olga slipped off the stool. The young officer revived her with a few stinging slaps and a glass of water. She drank, grateful to be able to wash the foul taste of fear out of her mouth.

Krelnikov was the officer who had forced Sasha to run the "investigation" of Yakov's activities. The Wolf's specialty was counterterrorism. Sasha had talked about him. Krelnikov had been trained and nurtured by Beria himself, Stalin's henchman and chief executioner. The Wolf was so feared among other agents of the KGB that they tiptoed around him and never said a bad word about him where it could possibly be overheard. Sasha said that Krelnikov's personal files were filled with damning information about the most important people in the government. Premier Konstantin Chernenko was his willing slave. Chernenko would happily lick the mud off Krelnikov's boots. Although former KGB head Yuri Andropov had found Krelnikov useful, he had loathed him and kept him away from KGB headquarters in Dzerzhinsky Square. But Andropov was dead, and once again the Wolf's black star was in the ascendant.

The officer helped Olga back onto her stool. He whisked her water glass away before Krelnikov could see it. An unauthorized kindness might cost him dearly: a new posting to one of the camps in the Gulag. Olga folded her arms on the table and put her head down.

Krelnikov hated her husband. The hatred was of long standing, born

of a long-ago grudge that Olga knew little about, and fed by class differ-
ences and mutual antipathy. Krelnikov, the fifth son of a farmer and the
only child to survive past the age of three, and Aleksandr Dmitrov, pam-
pered son of the sterling General Dmitrov and the beautiful Galina Valenskaya, had done battle in the past. Some said that Krelnikov had gathered
the information that had sent Sasha's father to his death. As chief of the
KGB's counterterrorism division, Krelnikov had personally been charged
with controlling or eliminating dissidents like Yakov. In a brilliant stroke
he had demanded the cooperation of Colonel Dmitrov. Sasha's career had
survived that encounter, but the cost to his family had been terrible. Olga
had no doubt that this last confrontation would be decisive, and that
Krelnikov would win. Why not? He had the American spy up his sleeve.

Olga hardly noticed that Krelnikov had returned. He stood over her
and laughed. "So at last Olga Dmitrova has met the Wolf. You have good
reason to be pissing in your shoes, woman. As for your husband, let us
hope he has sweet dreams tonight." The Wolf let out another raucous
laugh, like the clatter of a machine gun. "They will be his last."

CHAPTER 31

London

Owen and Vanessa slept soundly until eight in the morning, when Deaf Kitty trampled all over them demanding to be fed. Vanessa dragged herself muttering to the kitchen. After a few minutes she returned, carrying two mugs of steaming coffee.

"All I have left is instant, and no milk or cream. I'm afraid my larder is bare, unless you want cat food." Carefully balancing her brimming cup, Vanessa slipped back into bed and snuggled against Owen's warm flesh. "I don't feed men after sex. It gives them ideas about matrimony."

Owen sipped his coffee. It tasted terrible, acrid and rancid, as though the jar had sat on the shelf for too long. "What's wrong with matrimony?"

After one sip, Vanessa grimaced and set her cup aside. "I decided long ago that I wasn't smart enough to do a whole lot of things well, so I'd better concentrate on just one. I wanted to be an actress. The wife-and-mother routine isn't for me. I like being alone."

"I'll keep that in mind, although I think my heart could use the regular exercise."

Vanessa dragged her fingernail down the long vertical scar that ran through the grizzled hair on his chest. "I'm amazed we didn't pop this in all the excitement."

"Maybe we should try again." Owen's blue eyes gleamed.

"I was just waiting for you to ask." Vanessa wriggled down beside him and drew the sheet over both their heads.

* * *

"The tapes!"

The shriek wakened Owen from his doze. Vanessa ran dripping from the bathroom. "The tapes with Phil's memoirs! They're right here in the apartment. If you hadn't gotten me so stupid on sex, I would have remembered."

Vanessa threw on a pair of jeans and a ragged sweatshirt with the faded logo from the musical *Hair* on the front. Owen dressed hastily and followed her out to the living room. She was kneeling in front of the stereo cabinet.

Vanessa looked up, her eyes blazing with excitement. "He put them all on cassettes, remember, and Judy got a friend to help her smuggle them out of Russia. She told me she hid them here before coming out to meet us in Istanbul. I forgot all about them. They're probably the drunken ravings of a dying man, but maybe they'll tell us the names of the people you've been looking for."

Adair eyed the collection with amazement. "I've never seen so many records and cassettes. When do you find time to listen to them?"

"I have a horror of silence." Cassettes tumbled from the shelves. "Wanna hear the Talking Heads? Or how about me and Mick Jagger whooping it up at a party in 1978?"

"No, thank you."

As Vanessa searched through her cassettes, she explained her filing system. "Red is for theater, blue is for music, and then I have a system of subdots. If it's theater, then green is drama, pink is comedy, purple Shakespeare, brown contemporary, and so on. Music's the same. Green for classical, pink for jazz, purple is Beethoven, whom I worship above all other gods, brown—well, you get the idea."

Each cassette was stored in a small rectangular box with either a commercial label or a homemade one, and its distinguishing marks had been drawn or pasted onto a strip of white tape stuck to one side.

"Judy said she switched boxes and threw the Russian ones away, but she didn't say where she put Phil's. We'll start with the plays. See if she made any notes on the labels."

Owen picked up a cassette. "What's this?" he asked. "Looks like, 'Show M. B.'"

"Shaw. *Major Barbara*. Reading and writing don't come easily to me, so I've developed all sorts of little codes and shortcuts to help me along."

"You're dyslexic?"

"Am I ever. For years, everybody thought I was stupid, or that I lacked motivation in school. But in fact, my brain confuses the shapes of the letters, especially when they're lower-case: *b* and *d, r* and *n, a* and *u, m* and *n, j* and *y*—they all look alike to me. I didn't generally have any trouble with *s*'s—except mixing them up with *z*'s once in a while. *H* and *k* and *p* and *q* were bad—sometimes they all looked like *b* or *n*."

"But you're better now?"

Vanessa shrugged. "I have a little trouble with numbers, and it takes me twice as long to read through a script as most people. Cold readings are still rough. I usually memorize all my lines before the first read-through, even if I have to stay up all night learning them. I record everything. All these red dots are scripts I've put on tape."

"That's a pretty big hurdle," Owen said. "I had no idea."

"I figure everybody has some sort of disability they need to over-come. Just so happens I had three: dyslexia and my parents." Vanessa stood up and began sorting through tapes from another shelf, where she kept plays. "Wait a minute, look at this. See what it says?"

Owen peered over her shoulder. " 'H-M-L-T?' "

"It's *Hamlet,* but somebody's stuck a pink dot on it, which means comedy. That must be Judy. She helped me work out the system. Well, there's only one way to make sure."

She shoved the cassette into the tape deck, pushed some buttons on the amplifier, and hit the Play switch. They heard a soft, hissing sound, then a couple of clicks. Suddenly the flat was filled with the happy din of traditional Russian folk music.

"Balalaikas?" Vanessa stared at Owen. "Are you telling me we risked our lives for one thousand and one balalaikas?" Vanessa started to remove the tape from the machine, but Owen stopped her.

"Hold on a minute." Owen fast-forwarded the tape for a few seconds until he reached the middle, then he hit Play again. A Slavic chorus with string background was chanting and clapping a dance tune. With a glance at Vanessa, he pulled the tape out of the player, turned it over, and put it back.

—must have felt the sting of his stick. I was mortified by being beaten in public, but all of us began to respect him as an excellent schoolmaster. Mr. Hillary was passionately interested in almost ev-erything, and he inspired—

"That's him," Vanessa whispered. "It's Phil! What's he talking about?"

"Sounds like the early years." Owen hit the Rewind button and ran the tape back to the beginning of the B side.

When I was eight years old, my mother died, and Father's sister, Aunt Esther, moved in with us. I hated Aunt Esther. She spied on me constantly, and she told Father lies about me. He always took her side, and if it hadn't been for Mrs. Tippett in the kitchen, my life would . . .

"It's memoirs, all right," Owen said, "but I don't think this is the chapter we're looking for." He ran the tape ahead and hit the Play button again.

—a sense of victory mingled with guilt. I learned that one can never gain anything of value without losing something else. Father—

Owen hit the Fast Forward button and let the tape run until it stopped. Vanessa was already searching the bookcase for another tape. "See, he always left the tapes with the A side wound and ready to start," Owen said, "so that if anyone accidentally played one, all they would get was music."

"Here's another one!" Vanessa cried. "Ibsen's *A Doll's House* shouldn't have a pink dot. With any luck, Judy put them all in boxes from the drama shelves and labeled them as comedies. Try it."

Owen inserted the B side of the tape and ran it back to the beginning. Phillip Abbott's voice came out of the speakers.

In the spring of 1932, Martin Crossett's father wrote to my father asking if I could join their family in Europe that summer. Father thought it was a splendid opportunity, and he readily agreed. He came to regret the decision, after Aunt Esther and Aunt Lizzie began to raise objections, but he stood by his promise, and on June third I joined the Crossetts on the *Evangeline* for my first crossing—

Owen hit Fast Forward. *"I've met Martin Crossett. He teaches at Harvard Law."* Owen hit Play again.

—same bed. I was almost asleep when I felt Martin touch me, and I awakened with a start. Martin's hand was inside my pajamas. He asked if he could kiss me. I was terrified. It was the first time—

Vanessa reached over and gave the Stop button an angry jab. "What is this garbage, his version of *Remembrance of Things Past?*"

"It's his life story," Owen said with a shrug. "Have you found any more?"

"*All My Sons,* the laugh riot of my 'seventy-eight, 'seventy-nine season. Come on, Phil, I don't want to listen to seven hours of your sordid little life."

Vanessa pushed the cassette into the slot and ran it back halfway, then she hit Play.

—arrived in Pskov in the pouring rain. Ivan was my escort once again. Of all the KGB men who had handled me since my defection, he was the only one who ever showed me any compassion and kindness, and the only one who shared my interests. The next day was clear, and we drove out to the monastery at Izborsk. I will never forget the sight of those blue onion domes against a paler blue sky, and the blinding glitter of all that Russian gold. For the first time, I felt something more than rage at the bitter debacle of my life. Perhaps—

"This time we've overshot." Vanessa punched the Rewind button, then Stop, then Play. She was so intent on her task that she didn't realize they had a visitor.

"Will you back away from that cabinet, please?" Ernest Tidyman, her elderly neighbor, stood inside the door holding a .38 pistol. "And keep your hands away from your body," he said sharply. "Leave those tapes right where they are, Mr. Adair, and go sit on the sofa with Miss Marlowe. Keep your hands on your knees."

Vanessa retreated until she felt the sofa nudge the back of her legs, then she sat, stunned. "What in hell is going on, Mr. Tidyman?"

"Well, Miss Marlowe, it just so happens that I've been looking for these memoirs since you left for Istanbul."

Phillip's soft voice continued in the background:

—the advanced age of the monks, relics from the last century who had somehow survived revolution, terror, and famine—

Vanessa frowned. "I didn't tell you I was going to—the ticket! You read my note to Judy and saw the plane ticket. And the tapes? How could you? You—you've been listening to us, haven't you? You dirty old pig, you bugged my apartment! Jesus Bloody Christ! Sasha was right, somebody did betray us. It was you! No wonder the KGB knew every move we made before we made it."

We visited the cemetery, tombs carved into the walls of underground caves. The elderly monk who showed us around told us—

"Very boring it was most of the time," Ernest Tidyman said. "I will be greatly relieved never to have to listen to your dreadful music again, or your stupid friends, or your torrid and unappetizing love affairs." He backed over to the cassette deck, hit the Eject button, and dropped the tape into the pocket of his suit jacket. "And all this time, I was looking for a manuscript or a microfilm. My mistake. But easy enough to rectify. You've done half my work for me."

"You're going to kill us, aren't you?" Owen stated quietly.

Mr. Tidyman nodded. "With no regret whatsoever. You, Mr. Adair, will shoot Miss Marlowe while your mind is unhinged. Perhaps you were experiencing the jealousy an older lover might naturally feel toward his younger rivals. Or maybe the spy phobia that has gripped you for so many years finally erupted into full-blown madness. You will then shoot yourself. A nice little murder-suicide, just the sort of sordid end an immoral tramp like Vanessa would be likely to meet."

"You stink, Tidypants," Vanessa hissed. "All this time I thought you were just a harmless, nosy old fart, and you turn out to be a filthy spy."

Deaf Kitty awakened from his nap on the armchair. Noticing that his mistress had finally settled down on the sofa, he rose, stretched, and kneaded the cushion with his clawless paws for a moment. Then he sprang into her lap.

Owen Adair grabbed the cat and hurled him at Tidyman's face. Deaf Kitty yowled, and Tidyman reeled backward. The gun went off, sending down a shower of plaster over the sofa. The cat darted into the bedroom and dived under the bureau while Owen tackled Tidyman and brought him crashing down among the litter of cassettes on the floor. Vanessa stepped on the old man's outflung wrist and wrenched the pistol from his grasp.

"Good move," she gasped, "but I wish you hadn't manhandled Deaf Kitty like that. He'll never trust you again."

"He'll live. And so will we. Give me the gun." Vanessa handed him the pistol. "Bring that chair over here." Owen indicated a straight-backed Windsor near the door to the bedroom. "All right, Tidyman, take a seat. I'm afraid you're going to have to listen to a few more tapes before we turn you over to MI6."

"You're a skunk and a rat, Tidypants." Vanessa fetched a pair of panty hose from the bedroom and used them to tie their prisoner's hands behind his back. "I suppose you and your cronies were all set to snatch Sasha and Irina last night, only Mother and her soldiers got in your way, didn't they? Well, they're safe now. What have you got, Owen?"

"Eugene O'Neill, *Mourning Becomes Electra,* with a pink dot. Here goes."

—little atoll would be the scene of such horror and bloodshed. I saw my sergeant fall, and when I crawled over to him, I realized that his face had vanished in a smear of blood. The Japanese guns crackled over my head—

"Junk it," Vanessa said impatiently. "We can listen to his war stories some other time. Any more?"

"Here's a pink dot, but I can't read the title."

"*You Can't Take It With You*. Forget it. What about *The Duchess of Malfi*?"

Owen punched buttons. The cassette deck whirred and clicked. Then Phillip's voice began again.

—confessed to her that I had had some amorous adventures with classmates, as well as that servant girl Aunt Esther hired, but she didn't care. I fell madly in love with her, and she made me forget everyone else. I had never known anyone like Lydia. Brilliant, exquisitely beautiful, as fragile as—

"Yeecch." Vanessa made a face. "Do we really have to listen to this tripe?"

Tidyman spoke up. "You're wasting your time, you know. Phillip Abbott no longer knew anything important. He would never have endangered his daughters by entrusting them with vital secrets."

"Then why are you so damn eager to get your hands on these?" Vanessa demanded.

Owen shushed her. "Listen to this."

—that her father had looked like an overstuffed walrus and that her mother had literally died on her knees, scrubbing the floor of their mansion on M Street because she had a pathological fear of germs. Lydia despised them both, particularly her father, the Senator. But to look at them together, you would think that no man ever had a more loving daughter. That was her genius, the ability to live a lie so completely that she actually became the person she had invented.

Owen frowned. "That's weird. Lydia worshipped that old man. And he was crazy about her."

—first year together was heaven. In 1945, we Americans had just won the war, and we thought we could do anything. I was out of the service, back at the State Department and enjoying the work immensely, and I was madly in love with my beautiful wife. She was everything to me, and when Vanessa was born in March 1946, I thought we couldn't be happier. After Judith came along two years later, Lydia announced that our family was complete. I made no objection. I would have liked more children, but my two daughters were so delightful, so dear, that I—

Grimly, Vanessa ran the tape ahead and hit Play again.

—naturally brought a lot of work home with me. Lydia took a keen interest in what was happening in Europe, especially with the Soviets. We talked at length about Soviet hegemony and aggression. Lydia shared my passion for international diplomacy. Once I awakened early and found her poring over a report she had taken from my briefcase. I didn't think anything of it, despite the fact that the paper was stamped Top Secret. Maybe I was blinded by love. Maybe I was just stupid. I never thought—

"No." Vanessa stabbed the Stop button, then Fast Forward, then Play. "He's making this up, all of it."

—ordered us not to allow top-secret documents to leave the office. I told—

Stop. Fast Forward. Play.

—Christmas party. I gave my coat to the maid, and when I turned around, I saw Martin Crossett. He told me he was working at Justice, as a special assistant to the Attorney General. When we met for drinks the next day, Martin poured out his heart to me. He spoke of the yawning emptiness, the hollowness he had lived with since we parted, and I realized he was describing my own feelings. Needless to say, we were lovers before the day was out. We met frequently after that, two or three times a week. I was determined to keep the two loves of my life completely separate. I still cared deeply for Lydia and the girls, but my relationship with Martin was a thing apart. Special. Through Martin, I met other members of Washington's homosexual community: Congressmen, a Senator, lawyers, a cabinet member. All living secret, shame-filled lives, all terrified of being exposed.

"Get out the violins and handkerchiefs." Vanessa ran the tape forward for thirty seconds.

—how she got those photographs of Martin and myself at the party. Lydia said quite calmly that she needed my help, and that if I refused her, she would expose not only the two of us but every other man present that night. She promised me that the scandal would rock the nation and destroy a dozen careers and even more lives. You have to understand, the homophobia in America in 1956 was nearly as acute as the fear of Communism. I was horrified. I knew those men. They were loyal Americans every one, good men who—

"He's raving." Vanessa punched buttons. The tape whirred. "He's a traitor and a drunk who's been working on these lies for thirty years in his head, and now he's trying to vindicate himself." She hit another button.

Lydia was very matter-of-fact. "Because you can be useful to us." I didn't know where to turn. I had inadvertently betrayed my country, and now my own wife was ordering me to keep on doing it. I had no choice. If I gave myself up to the FBI, I would lose everything. Not only my job and my reputation, but my little girls. And I would bring Martin and the others down, too. And so I went along with her, and as I compounded betrayal with betrayal, I started drinking more and more. I felt myself sliding deeper into disgrace and despair. I wanted to end my life. Only the thought of my children kept me from doing it.

"No." Vanessa pushed buttons frantically. "No!"

—to talk about it. Things were going wrong. The Agency and the FBI were getting close, and I was to be the scapegoat for Lydia.

The voice on the tape quavered.

She gave me no choice: either I went through with the charade of defecting, played it up right and stuck to it, or I would die. The first time I made a misstep, the Russians would kill me. She insisted they were doing me a great favor by letting me live, although having me defect was certainly a brilliant propaganda coup for the Soviets. I told Lydia she'd never get away with it. But she said, "Oh, yes, I will. In twenty years I'll be the First Lady, if not President myself.

Vanessa groped for Owen's hand and held it in a grip so fierce he felt his fingers going numb.

I wish I hadn't waited so long to reveal all this. The damage Lydia has wrought within the U.S. government is impossible to calculate. And now there's talk of Preston Marlowe becoming Secretary of State. I could have stopped her years ago, but I was too much of a coward. Perhaps it's not too late.

Owen switched off the tape. "I can't believe it," he murmured. "All that time—"

Vanessa was rigid. "If he's telling the truth, then—" She whirled and grabbed Tidyman's lapels. "It's true, isn't it? He's right about her. She was the traitor, not him. It's Lydia, isn't it?"

Tidyman's eyes flashed, but he said nothing.

"She's got Judy!" Vanessa screamed. "She's got my sister and you know where they are, you old bugger. Tell me! Tell me or I'll kill you!"

Tidyman narrowed his eyes and shook his head.

Vanessa shook him. "You bastard!" she cried. "Bastard! You knew—you were in this with her."

"Won't tell," Tidyman croaked. "Kill me if you like. I'm an old man. No good to anyone now."

Vanessa slapped him. He gasped and made a small, whimpering sound, but he kept his lips pressed shut even when she slapped him again.

Owen caught her arm. "That won't do any good," he said. "He's turning himself into a martyr for the cause."

"Oh, he is?" Vanessa ripped off Tidyman's glasses, then plucked off his toupee and tossed both items into the corner. "Not so cocky now, are we?" She pinched his nose. Tidyman squirmed, but eventually his jaw dropped. Vanessa stuck her hand into his mouth and pulled out his dentures, a full set, upper and lower. She clacked them in front of his face.

"You know what you look like now, Tidypants? Your own corpse. A bald-headed, sunken-cheeked corpse." Vanessa dropped the dentures on the floor and crushed them under her shoe. "And if you think I have any qualms about killing you, you lousy old fart, you can think again. You are going to talk. Where is my sister?"

"Don't know." Without his teeth, the old man mumbled through his gums. "No idea."

"You're a damn liar! When my mother and Kenneth were hatching their plans yesterday, you were right in here with them, weren't you?" She slapped his face. "Weren't you! You know where they are. Tell me!"

A tear trickled down Ernest Tidyman's cheek, but he said nothing.

"Where's Judy?" Vanessa screamed.

"Russian is a traitor—can't be allowed to live."

Vanessa slapped him again, so forcefully that the chair nearly tipped over. "The only traitor I'm interested in now is Lydia. Either you start talking, or I'm getting a knife from the kitchen. And I will cut off your very old and very shriveled balls and stuff them into your very shriveled mouth. Do you think I won't? Well, just watch me."

While he squirmed helplessly in the chair, Vanessa opened his fly.

"Killing you would be too easy," she seethed. "I'm going to take my time. Think I'm playing a part now? I'm not. I'm going to rip you apart with my bare hands. Tell me!" She reached into his underwear and grabbed his testicles. Tidyman howled with pain and terror. "Where is Judith? Where did that lousy bitch traitor mother of mine take them last night? Tell me!"

Tidyman groaned and muttered something incomprehensible.

"What's that?" Vanessa shouted. "I can't hear you, you disgusting piece of crap." She clamped down hard on his scrotum. "Where?"

"In Victoria Crescent," Tidyman blurted, sobbing. "Brighton. Number four-oh-three." He began to retch. A small trickle of vomit ran down his chin. "Please, please," he cried between spasms, "get her away from me!"

Vanessa straightened up and stepped back. "We've got to get Judy out of there."

Owen picked up the phone. "I'll alert MI6. Tidyman will hold until someone gets here."

"Tell them to meet us there. This one's coming with us." Vanessa untied Tidyman's hands and dragged him to his feet. "He's a slippery old snake and I don't trust him an inch. Let's go."

CHAPTER 32

*T*he brass plaque under the doorbell read OAK HOUSE, although no oak tree
grew either in front of the house or in the walled garden at the rear,
and the interior doors and moldings were all milled of chestnut. The house
stood near the end of the crescent, tall and narrow, identical to the other
houses on the street in every detail, even to its Regency portico and its
heavy brass door knocker.

Inside, the furnishings were outdated but not antique, and the carpets were only slightly worn. The kitchen dated from the Fifties, but it was
spotlessly clean. The cupboards were stocked with tinned and packaged
foods, and the refrigerator held fresh milk, eggs, a pound of bacon, and
a jug of orange juice. The sheets on the beds had been freshly laundered.
The hot-water tank in the basement looked big enough to provide baths
for twenty people rather than six. In all, the place reminded Judith of an
inn whose thoughtful hostess had provided for her guests' every comfort
and then vanished.

A medical team had been waiting for them when they arrived—
surgeon, nurse, and anesthesiologist. They took Dmitrov up to the third
floor and installed him in a bedroom at the rear of the house. Judith stayed
with him while they treated him. Irina went to bed.

Dmitrov refused a general anesthetic. He remained fully conscious
throughout the procedure. After the anesthesiologist dulled the area with
novocaine, the surgeon probed the shoulder wound, removed the shattered bits of bone, stitched up the lacerated muscles, and closed the wound

again. He then splinted the upper arm, wrapped it with tape and gauze, and administered a powerful shot of antibiotic laced with painkiller. Judith sat by Dmitrov's bed all night. By morning, his fever was gone and he was sound asleep. She took a shower and lay down in the adjacent room for a couple of hours.

Judith awakened at ten, threw on her clothes, and checked on the patient. He was dozing peacefully, clearly exhausted by the rigors of the past few days. Downstairs, she found Kenneth and Irina in the living room watching a BBC documentary on Australia.

Irina snorted. "I can see stupid programs like this in Moscow," she said. "I don't need to look at them here. I want to go out for a walk. This is the free world, isn't it? I want to be free."

"It's not safe," Kenneth said. "The Soviets may have followed us. We can't allow you to leave the house."

Irina lifted her eyebrows. "Are you going to stop me?"

"I won't have to. Douglas will."

Douglas was the strapping twenty-year-old who had driven the Bentley. As he had helped Dmitrov out of the car his jacket gaped open, and Judith had seen a holstered pistol under his arm. At the moment, he was sitting in the front hall, reading a tabloid newspaper.

"Where's Mother?" Judith asked Kenneth.

"I took her breakfast up half an hour ago. She should be down soon. There's coffee in the kitchen."

"It tastes terrible," Irina said. "Like melted rubber."

Judith went back to the kitchen. The electric percolator yielded only a half-inch of dregs. Judith dumped the sludge into the sink and put on the electric kettle for tea.

While she waited for the water to boil, she decided to use the telephone on the wall beside the refrigerator to call Vanessa. She put the receiver to her ear.

" . . . ready to leave at any time," Judith heard her mother say.

"Good," a man answered. He had an upper-class British accent. "The ambulance will pick them up at noon and take them to Worthing to meet the helicopter. Is he strong enough to travel?"

"Too strong. I made sure they gave him plenty of dope with the antibiotic last night. I can give him more if he needs it."

"As long as he's in shape to stand trial when he gets back to Moscow. But in case things go sour, you know what to do."

The whistle on the kettle started to scream. Judith hastily replaced the receiver and busied herself making tea. Her hands moved mechanically, even though her pulse was crashing in her ears.

* * *

Truth is a fearsome thing, a terrible thing. Nothing matches the devastating impact of being confronted with the way things really are: You have cancer. Your husband is having an affair. Your mother is a spy.

As long as he's in shape to stand trial when he gets back to Moscow.

Back to Moscow. Trial. The KGB was eager to capture Dmitrov, to return him to Moscow, to stage a show trial and convict him, to execute him.

I made sure they gave him plenty of dope.

Mother doped Sasha. Mother is working for them, for the Soviets, the KGB. Oh, God, no! Not my mother. And not just Mother. Kenneth, too. My husband. And the boy Douglas. They brought Sasha and Irina here. Not to protect them. To trap them.

In case things go sour, you know what to do.

Mother is a spy. Mother is going to kill Sasha, or have him killed. Mother knows what to do. Mother is in charge.

Judith reached for the telephone. Who could she call? She knew a few people in London, most of them friends of her mother's. She couldn't trust them. The local police? What would she tell them? My mother is a KGB spy and she's trying to kidnap this man; he's a Russian defector and he's here illegally. Would anyone believe her?

Vanessa and Owen. She would call them first. She waited for a minute, then she lifted the receiver again. The line was dead.

"Who are you telephoning, darling?"

Lydia stood in the doorway, holding her breakfast tray. She was wearing a gray silk suit and a black blouse, low-heeled shoes, some discreetly glimmering jewelry. Her hair was perfect, not a strand out of place. Ageless and beautiful. A traitor and a spy. Had she and Phillip Abbott worked hand in hand? Had he defected to protect her, to keep her working for them all these years, to make her the wife of the Secretary of State and the duenna of the State Department? In her forty years as a master Soviet infiltrator, how many scores of young men had she recruited? How many Kenneths? How many Douglases? Robbins from the embassy in Istanbul? The man who had met their plane in London?

Judith jiggled the receiver hook. "I wanted to call Vanessa, but this phone doesn't work. Funny, I picked it up a minute ago and heard you talking. Wonder what happened?"

Lydia set the tray down on the table. "Yes, I've been making plans. As you no doubt heard."

Judith got huffy. "Mother, I have plenty of faults, but I don't eavesdrop. You cured me of that habit years ago."

"Of course. I think I'll join you in a cup of tea." Lydia put some more water in the electric teakettle and switched it on. "We're flying home today. It's of the utmost importance that we get your handsome Russian out of here immediately. An ambulance will fetch Mr. Dmitrov and Irina at noon and take them to Heathrow. It's all arranged. A special plane is being fueled up right now. They'll be in Washington tonight."

"What do you mean, 'they'? Aren't we going with them?"

"Surely you can see that we need to distance ourselves from this whole business? We can't embarrass Preston or the State Department."

Preston Marlowe, Secretary of State. Judith shivered. Was it possible that her country's chief diplomat was a KGB spy, too? Or was he just another one of Lydia's dupes? Judith took a swallow of tea.

Lydia went on. "It must appear that the Agency is handling these defectors. I can't allow you to be linked with this man in any way. Sorry, darling, but we Marlowes will travel under separate cover. Douglas will drive us up to London and we'll take a commercial flight tonight."

"Sorry, darling, yourself." Judith set down her cup. "It won't do. You're not talking about some ordinary spy. It just so happens that I used to be in love with this man, and I'm going to stick to him like stale chewing gum until I know he's safe. Besides, I promised him I'd look after Irina. I'm going with them. But it'll be all right. We don't need to advertise the fact."

"People talk. Pilots, crew members. No, it's too dangerous, Judith. I can't risk it."

"We could all get some good publicity out of this: 'Secretary's Stepdaughter Snags Spy.'" The kettle began to rumble and hiss. Judith gave it a quick, anxious glance.

Lydia pursed her lips. "This is no time for levity. I can't allow you to—"

"You have no choice, Mother. I'm going with him, and that's that." Judith yawned and stretched. "Can't we stay here a little longer? We're all exhausted. Call the CIA station chief at the embassy. He'll send some men over to look after us."

"We want to keep this as quiet as possible," Lydia told her. "You don't know what I went through to organize his departure."

I have some idea, Judith thought. She smiled. "I'm not going to leave him, or his daughter, not for a minute. And that's that."

Lydia reached over and touched Judith's shoulder. "Darling, I know you're tired. You've put yourself through a lot for that man."

Judith drained her teacup and stood up. "That man is probably wondering what happened to me. I'd better go up and tell him we're leaving. And I am going with him, Mother. I have to."

Lydia shrugged. The teakettle produced a shrill whistle, the same sound Lydia had heard over the wire when she was speaking to her Soviet contact on the telephone. The two women looked at each other for a long moment, then Judith switched the kettle off. The noise ceased abruptly.

"Your water's boiling," Judith said unnecessarily. "Shall I make your tea before I go up?"

"No, thank you, darling. That's one kitchen chore I can manage alone. If you see Kenny, tell him I'd like to speak to him, please."

"Of course." Judith went to the living room at the front of the house and delivered Lydia's message. Kenneth heaved himself out of his chair and hurried out of the room. Judith turned up the volume on the television, then she went over to Irina and sat beside her.

"I need to talk to you."

"So?" Irina puffed idly on a cigarette. "Talk. I don't know how I'm supposed to listen with that noise going on."

Judith leaned close to the girl and whispered, "We have to get out of here. It's dangerous. If you don't help, you'll be on your way to Moscow in a couple of hours, and your father too. Is that what you want?"

Irina looked at her in amazement. "I don't care one way or the other. Besides, if you're in trouble, why don't you let your mother and step-brother help you?"

"Because—because they're working for the Soviets."

Irina blinked, then she started to laugh. "Ah, that's a good joke, a really good joke. So they're all KGB, like my father? Why don't we all go back to Moscow, have a big party?"

Judith gripped Irina's arm. "They'll kill him. The KGB will kill him. And I—I don't want to lose him. You're too young. You don't understand about love—when it happens, how rare it is." Tears spilled down her cheeks.

"I understand." Irina jerked her arm away. "People who believe in love are fools. Your tears won't help, you know. I have cried so many tears that the blood in my veins should be all dried up by now. Tears of blood. Now you know how I feel."

Judith stood up. "Years ago, I did just what you're doing now. I retreated behind a barrier of bitterness and cynicism. I drowned myself in liquor, I took any pill or powder that came my way, and I had sex with every man who looked at me and licked his lips. It was easier than facing the truth and accepting responsibility."

Irina stared woodenly at the television set. Judith leaned over and spoke directly into the girl's ear.

"I pulled out of it, but you never will, and do you know why? Because we're different. Americans fight for what they believe in, whether it's love or democracy or the right to make as much money as we can. We're not sheep and we're not brooding fatalists, like you Russians. As long as we have energy and strength, we'll go after what we want. Give up. I don't care. But when you're sitting in the Lubianka next week, remember that you had a chance to do something to help yourself, and you didn't take it."

Judith ran out of the room and up the stairs. She was aware that Douglas was watching her from the hall, but she ignored him.

Dmitrov was still sleeping soundly. Judith leaned over the bed and shook him. "Sasha. Sasha, wake up! We've got to get out of here. There's danger. Please, Sasha."

He groaned. His eyelids flickered, but they didn't open. Judith slapped his cheeks and spoke Russian to him. He worked his mouth and muttered a curse: "Devil take you—leave me alone."

The door opened and Irina came in. "What's the matter with him?"

"He's been drugged. They gave him something along with the pain-killers. I can't get him up."

Irina shook him. "Papa. Papa! He is like a dead man. Can we lift him?"

Pulling on his good arm and bracing his back, they dragged him into a sitting position. Judith shoved his legs over the side of the bed. "Sasha, please!" she whispered. "Oh, God, what have they done to you? You've got to wake up!"

"Wha—Judith?" He snorted and shook his head. "Can't keep my eyes . . . Irina, you okay?"

"Yes, Papa, fine. But we're in trouble. We have to get away. These people are KGB." She tugged at his hand. "Come on, let's go."

Dmitrov's eyes filled with tears. "Irina, Irinushka, my little doll, my precious jewel," he mumbled in Russian. "Do you know how long it's been since you called me 'Papa'?"

"Don't worry about that now. Stand up! Stand up and I'll call you 'Papa' five thousand times, all right? Please, Papa, try to walk."

They got him on his feet. His knees started to buckle, but together Judith and Irina managed to support him. Irina exhorted him to walk. He shuffled a few feet, then stopped.

"So tired. Can't I do it later?"

"No, they're taking us back to Moscow later. You must do it now. Here." Irina lit a cigarette and stuck it into his mouth. "Take a big draw, all the way down into your lungs."

Dmitrov obeyed. He started to cough. Judith slammed him on the back, and he snarled at her to stop. "This shoulder hurts, damn it."

"Good," Judith said, giving him another thump, "at least you're starting to feel something. Take another puff on that cigarette and start walking. We don't have time to waste."

They walked him around for two minutes, until he shook them off. "I'm all right now. Let me go. I have to use the toilet."

Dmitrov went into the adjoining bathroom and closed the door. "Do you think he'll wake up?" Irina asked.

"He'd better." Judith glanced at the nightstand beside the bed. Among the bottles of painkilling pills the doctor had left was a flat box. Inside was a syringe loaded with a clear liquid. "This must be the dope Mother was going to give him before they took him away, to knock him out." She lifted the syringe out of the box and tapped the plunger with her thumb. "I'm going to jab Douglas with this and get his gun. While I'm gone, you take your father down the back stairs and wait outside the kitchen door. I'll create a disturbance. When you hear it, get him outside. Go down through the garden and run. Grab the first person you see and tell him to call the police. Then keep running until you find someplace to hide."

Irina took the syringe from her. "That is a good plan, Mrs. Marlowe, but I will do your part. Mr. Douglas wants to go to bed with me; I know because he licked his lips at me last night. Maybe I will give him a chance."

"Irina, you can't!"

"Why not? Sex is no big deal if it gets you something you want. Besides, he won't go all the way. There is a big closet by the front door, near where he is sitting. I will take him inside for a quick one, and when he pulls his pants down, I will stick him with the needle." She brandished the syringe.

A hundred objections rushed into Judith's mind. "The stuff might not take effect that quickly. He might hurt you."

"I can take care of him," Irina promised. "You get my father away from this house and bring the police back here. The KGB won't take me to Russia without him. They want him more than they want me."

Judith thought for a moment, then nodded. "You're pretty good at this."

Irina tossed her head. "You will see, we Russians aren't all sheep. We are trained all our lives to resist authority without getting caught. I must go. My lover is waiting for me."

She went out. Judith opened the bathroom door. Dmitrov was standing under the shower. "You're not supposed to get those bandages wet," she protested.

"I'm sure the KGB will take pains to keep them dry." He rubbed his face. "I feel lousy. Like I've been poisoned." He turned off the water. Judith helped him out of the tub and started rubbing him dry.

"You have. They shot you full of dope last night."

"Where is Irina?"

"She's already gone. We've got to get out. The ambulance is coming at noon. They're going to take you to Worthing and fly you out of here."

Back in the bedroom, Judith had to keep slapping him awake while she helped him dress in the jeans, running shoes, and sweater he had been wearing since Turkey. When she pulled the sweater over his shoulder, he winced. Then his eyes closed.

"Stay awake, damn you!" Judith hissed. "If I have to pull that arm out of its socket, I will."

"Mmmuh . . . trying," Dmitrov groaned.

"The back stairs to the kitchen are over here," Judith whispered. "Lean on me." They stepped into the hall, pausing for a moment to listen. Except for the canned chatter on the television, the house was quiet. They started down the steps. Dmitrov was weak and dizzy, and he had to stop frequently to rest and catch his breath. Judith kept her arm clamped tightly around his waist. "Only a little way now."

The house creaked as it settled deeper into history. In the street outside, a car horn blared. A dog barked. Where was Irina and the commotion she had promised?

Then Irina started to scream. "Help! Help, he attacked me! Somebody, come quickly!"

Judith and Dmitrov blundered down the staircase. As they neared the bottom, the door to the kitchen swung open.

"Going someplace, you two?" Lydia stood silhouetted against the light, a small pistol in her hand. "Come ahead, then. We might as well make ourselves comfortable while we're waiting for reinforcements."

"Where is Irina?" Dmitrov demanded in a cracked voice. "What have you done with my daughter?"

"She got a taste of her own medicine. She'll sleep like a baby until your plane lands in Moscow."

Twisting free of Judith, Dmitrov hurled himself at Lydia. As she leapt backward out of his way, her gun went off inside the stairwell. Dmitrov tumbled down the steps and landed in a heap on the kitchen floor. Judith rushed after him and threw herself to her knees beside him. He was writhing in pain, clutching his bad shoulder. Blood seeped through his fingers.

"Sasha! Oh, God, Mother—why?"

"I didn't shoot him. But I will. I'm warning you, Judith, don't try any more heroics or I'll kill him."

"Then kill me, too!" Judith cried. "Could you do that, Mother? Who do you love more, the KGB or your own child? Kill me, then. Go on, kill me!"

"Stand up," Lydia ordered in a hard voice. "You're behaving like a fool. I warned you to stay away from him. I told you he was dangerous, but you didn't listen." In the distance, they heard the pulsing shriek of a siren. Lydia permitted herself a small sigh of relief. "Right on time. The question is, what am I going to do with you? This whole operation has been a fiasco from start to finish. I should have put an end to it the minute you got involved with him. But it's too late now."

"We have Phillip's memoirs on tape," Judith told her. "Vanessa will find them. Once Owen Adair hears them, you're finished."

"We'll see about that. Kenneth!"

Kenneth pushed open the swinging door from the hall and staggered into the room. His left cheek was scored with scratches. "The little bitch fought like a tiger before that damn stuff knocked her out. Douglas is meeting the ambulance. What happened?"

"Tell them that Mr. Dmitrov will need a strong sedative. Judith, too. When we get to London, you will call Dr. O'Neill and have Judith committed to his care. A severe nervous breakdown compounded by manifestations of latent schizophrenia. She is becoming paranoid and delusional."

"I'm your daughter!" Judith shouted. "You can't do that to me! What about Vanessa? She knows I'm not crazy!"

"Vanessa will keep her mouth shut, or she'll find herself sharing your room at the sanitarium. I'm sorry, darling, but you must understand. The Party comes first. It always has."

Judith appealed to Kenneth. "Kenny, you've got to stop her. You're the only one who can. You said you loved me, remember? Kenny, I'm your wife. Help me, please."

Judith saw a flicker of something in his eyes. He turned toward Lydia.

Just then they heard a deafening crash in the street in front of the house. Kenneth pulled himself up and rushed through the door to see what had happened. Despite the commotion, Lydia's attention never wavered. She kept her pistol trained on Dmitrov.

"Mother!" Judith screamed. This time Lydia's head jerked around. Dmitrov grabbed a chair by the leg and hurled it at her. It struck her squarely in the center of her chest and she fell backward, losing her hold on the gun, which skittered across the floor and came to rest in front of the refrigerator. Judith snatched it up and pointed it at her mother.

"Get away, Sasha," she pleaded. "Go now, out the back door."

"Not without Irina."

"I've got Mother. They'll make a trade."

"They won't, you know." Lydia pulled herself to her knees and nursed her bruised elbow. "You'll have to shoot me. Do you think you can do it, darling, now that our situations are reversed? Can you put a bullet into your own mother's skull?"

The pistol felt as heavy as lead. Slowly, Judith sat down on one of the kitchen chairs and steadied her trembling wrist in her lap. "I will if I have to." Tears rushed to her eyes. "You would have done it to me."

"No." Lydia shook her blond head. "I couldn't. You're part of me. You are me. That was always the trouble with me and my two girls. We were too much alike. You, me, Vanessa—"

"Give me the gun, Judith." Dmitrov's words were still slurred but his hand was steady. "I need it."

Judith hesitated a moment, then let him take the pistol from her. "Be careful, Sasha. I love you."

Trying desperately to overcome the effects of the sedatives, Dmitrov stumbled through the inner door to the hallway. Judith and her mother stared at each other. After a moment, Lydia pulled herself up stiffly and stepped over to the back door that led to the walled garden.

"I think it's time for me to leave. I trust you won't try to stop me."

"You're not quitting now? Your side might be winning."

"I don't think so." Lydia shook her head. "Too much has gone wrong. When the shooting starts, the police and the neighbors get curious. However, I have an escape route ready. Safe houses, people to call. My friends will make the arrangements."

"You'll hate Moscow," Judith told her. "Phil did."

"Your father was a fool. I should never have had children by him. But you did help my cover. I thank you for that. And I thank your sister."

As Lydia opened the back door, Owen appeared, gun in hand. "Hold it, Lydia."

Lydia backed away from him, circling behind Judith's chair. "Owen, my dear. What exquisite timing." She shoved her hands into the pockets of her jacket. The casual gesture was so totally unlike her that it should have told them something.

Suddenly, Lydia flung her left arm around Judith's throat, choking her, and from her right pocket produced a small pressurized perfume atomizer. "Lay the gun on the table, Owen, the grip toward me. This is prussic acid. One shot in the face and Judith will die. Forgive me, but I don't intend to spend the rest of my life in a cell."

"Why don't you use that stuff on yourself?" Owen suggested.

"Not my style. Put the gun down."

Owen did as Lydia requested.

"Judith, my darling, you and I are going to walk down through the garden. Mr. Adair will step aside and let us pass, because if he doesn't, I will kill you. Stay still, please." She released Judith from the stranglehold, transferred the atomizer from her right hand to her left, and picked up the gun. "Now rise slowly, that's right, and go to the door."

Judith turned to her. Her eyes were wet as she searched her mother's face for some spark of affection. "You never . . . loved us. At all. Did you." It was a statement, not a question.

"This is business," Lydia said coldly. "You should have kept out of it, darling. Let's go. Move!"

They started across the kitchen, Judith in the lead, Lydia following at a distance of two yards. She kept the pistol trained on the back of Judith's head. Owen watched helplessly. Where in hell was everybody?

"Judith!"

Kenneth came bursting through the door at the bottom of the back stairs. Startled, Lydia turned. "Kenneth. Thank God you—"

He shot Lydia once through the heart. The force of the bullet hurled her against the refrigerator. She stayed there for a moment, her arms thrown out to the sides, her eyes staring, then she crumpled to the floor. Kenneth stumbled forward and stood over her, his shoulders heaving.

"She wouldn't let me go," he sobbed. "I loved her, but she never loved me. I thought when I married you that she would have to leave us alone, but she wouldn't. She needed me too much, she said. All those years, she forced me to be her lover, but she never loved me—and—and— she wouldn't let me love you." Kenneth turned his tear-streaked face to Judith.

"Her lover?" When he fired, Judith had thrown herself out of the way. Now, clinging to the doorjamb, she pulled herself to her feet.

"Yes, from—from the time I was sixteen. I tried to get away. I told her I loved you. She wouldn't let me go."

"You should have told me, Kenny."

He shook his head. "No. She would have killed you. She never loved anybody, you know. Me. You. Vanessa. She liked to pretend, but she didn't. She couldn't love anyone."

Kenneth knelt down and very gently lifted Lydia's blood-soaked upper body, cradling her in his arms. "I loved her once. Mother. I really did. She told me I had made a terrible mistake by marrying you. She was right. Remember the Kami—the Kamikaze Rabbits? We should have called it quits right then." With great tenderness, Kenneth lowered his burden, reached over her body, and began feeling around on the floor for something.

"Marlowe, no!" Owen shouted.

Kenneth gave himself a blast in the face with the atomizer. He convulsed, clutching his chest, and toppled forward, falling across Lydia's body. Judith started to move toward them. Owen intercepted her and dragged her away.

"Stay back. That stuff is lethal. Leave him. This is what he wanted."

Vanessa rushed in from the hall. "Judy! Are you all right?" The sisters clung together for a moment, then Vanessa became aware of the carnage at their feet. "Oh, my God! Mother? Kenny . . ."

"She was the one. She used people. Daddy. And Kenny. Us. She never loved us, Van. Any of us. All—lies."

"I know." Vanessa looked grim. "I heard the tapes. Poor Daddy. She used him and then destroyed him. I hope she burns in hell for the next three centuries."

"Sasha?" Judith asked in a dazed voice. "Is he . . . ?"

"He's okay. God, you should have seen it, Judy. We drove up and saw that ambulance and I knew, I mean I just *knew,* and so I crashed the Triumph right into it, and Owen came out firing and Douglas fired at him, and then Sasha came blasting out of the house like a superhero, and all of a sudden there were cops everywhere. It's like Beirut out there." Vanessa stared down at her mother's body for a moment, then she turned away, her face ashen. "Come on, Sis. Let's get the hell out of here."

As they passed the living room, Judith saw Dmitrov sitting on the floor beside the sofa, holding Irina's hand. Her face was flushed but she seemed to be sleeping peacefully.

"Is she going to be all right?" Judith asked.

Dmitrov nodded. "A doctor just looked at her. He says her heart is strong, that she's in no danger. She was trying to save me, Judith." He looked up at her, his eyes alight with new hope. "She didn't want them to take me back."

"It's all over now. You're both safe."

Judith stood watching them for a long time, the father and the daughter. Then Vanessa spoke softly to her, and together they walked out of the house.

Uniformed policemen and detectives were milling around in front. Police barriers of sawhorses and orange ribbons had been set up at both ends of the crescent to block it from traffic, and already the curious were beginning to gather in clusters at the edges of the disaster like bacteria multiplying on a petri dish. The crew from a police wrecker was trying to disentangle the front of Vanessa's Triumph from the radiator of a red ambulance. A second ambulance was parked nearby, and two attendants were loading Douglas inside. His brown leather jacket was soaked with blood. Two men in civilian clothes were questioning Vanessa's neighbor,

Mr. Tidyman, who was sitting on the curb, his bloodied head in his manacled hands.

The plane trees that lined the crescent were yellowing, their leaves beginning to fall. Overhead the sky was limpid and clear. The sound of the sea was hushed, barely audible, and its bracing tang barely penetrated these civilized precincts. Instead, the ripeness of the earth was in the air, with its promise of harvests and deepening cold and long terrible nights.

The season of endless heartbreak.

CHAPTER 33

Moscow

*O*lga had been bounced around in trucks and planes all night before
being deposited in another cell. No one told her she was in Moscow.
She knew it instinctively.

Olga's new cell was darker, colder, and dirtier than the one in
Batumi, but certain sounds and smells penetrated the walls and raised her
spirits. At least she wasn't among strangers anymore. She had probably
queued for meat and vegetables with the wives of the same men who kept
watch over her now, her jailers. They were a link to the world she had
known, the world she would never see again.

Krelnikov had made the move with her. He interrogated her soon
after her arrival, but it was largely ceremonial, to show off his technique
to subordinates and to demonstrate his own close interest in the case.
Although his manner was as brusque and the way he berated her just as
poisonous, Olga sensed that he was preoccupied. He kept leaving the
interrogation room, allowing his second-in-command to take over her
questioning. And when he returned, his eyes glittered dangerously. The
Wolf was hungry, and he was on the prowl.

Time outside the prison was like an accordion. It required the regular
squeezing of routine and events to give it shape and meaning. Here Olga
had no notion of how many hours or days or weeks were passing. The light
in her cell never went out. The rest of Moscow's municipal buildings were
illuminated by dirty twenty-watt bulbs. Bulbs of greater wattage were
reserved for state reception rooms and prison cells. Olga Dmitrova would

never again lift her face to the sun without remembering the relentless blaze of the ceiling fixture over her cot.

Olga had no window from which to observe the stately march of that sun from horizon to horizon, no cellmates with whom she could exchange conjectures about season and weather. Her warders were forbidden to speak to her except to issue orders. Between interrogations, she was sent back to her cell. Sometimes they brought food. Most times they didn't. She could no longer tell if the gnawing in her belly was hunger or worry. She wondered if she would see Sasha and Irina again after they were captured and returned to Russia. One day she found herself wishing that Irina would die before Krelnikov could get his hands on her, and the thought made her weep.

She tried to pray, but her prayers sounded trite and childish to her ears. Her parents had not been particularly devout Jews, and even before Yakov's death, Olga had been wary of associating herself too closely with rites and rituals that might cause the government to lump her with the dissidents.

Could she ever empty herself of tears? She thought not. She cried and cried, but the reservoir never ran dry.

Then one day a current of excitement ran through the prison. Olga heard scurrying in the halls, a shout, whispers among the warders. Something had happened. Perhaps Sasha and Irina had finally arrived.

Her tin meal tray slid through the slot on the door. Of all things, they had given her a piece of beef and a whole potato. She had just picked up her spoon when her door swung open and they dragged her out for questioning. Instead of her usual dread, Olga experienced a surge of anger. Damn them, she was hungry. Couldn't they at least permit her to finish her dinner?

Arriving in the interrogation room, she understood why her warders had not dallied. Krelnikov was in a rage and they were trembling.

"Everywhere I go, I'm surrounded by idiots!" he bellowed, teeth flashing. "Damn you, get out of my sight!"

His fury gave Olga secret pleasure. He was on top, in control, the big boss, and something had gone seriously wrong.

He began his questioning, his voice ringing against the bare walls. Olga wanted to plug her ears with her fingers, but she didn't dare.

"Did that-traitor-your-husband ever mention tapes, tape recordings? Don't lie to me. He kept them at your house, didn't he? You hid them for him. You grew up in that house, you know all the little places there are to hide things. How did he smuggle them out of the country? Did you help him? Someone must have helped him. Who was it?"

He was sweating. Olga had never seen him sweat before. He hopped around the room like a bead of water in a hot skillet. His eyes were bulging and his color was high. Olga had a professional urge to caution him about the dangers of high blood pressure and stroke, but she kept silent. What did she care if he dropped dead right in front of her?

"Did you ever meet the American Phillip Abbott?" Krelnikov wanted to know. "Did you meet Mrs. Marlowe's sister when she was here? Did Phillip Abbott say anything to you before he died?"

He was grasping at straws. He knew very well that she didn't know either of the people he mentioned, and that Phillip Abbott had been in no condition to speak when she examined him. Krelnikov was on the spot, then. In trouble.

Infuriated by her denials, he lashed out at her, striking her across the face with the back of his hand. The blow knocked her off her chair and sent her sprawling. Olga knew that the punishment had not been premeditated. Krelnikov was losing control.

His own fear reduced him in her eyes. He reminded her of a spoiled little boy having a first-class tantrum because he couldn't get what he wanted. And what had Krelnikov wanted? To see the Dmitrovs hang together.

He had lost them. Somehow, by some miracle, Sasha and Irina had slipped out of his grasp. Krelnikov's spy had not undone them. They were safe. They were free.

Olga felt like laughing. It was over. No matter what they did to her, it didn't matter, because only her life was at risk now, and not Sasha's and Irina's.

Krelnikov struck her again, and when she tried to stand, he aimed a kick at her middle that doubled her up with pain. She diagnosed a couple of broken ribs, maybe a ruptured spleen. Her head was ringing: probable concussion. Still, if he kept this up, she wouldn't survive, and then he wouldn't have any of the Dmitrovs left to pick on.

I'm winning, she thought. I'm stronger than you are and you know it. You can't take anything else away from me, only my life, and if you don't take that, you'll have to start giving things back. I'm not afraid. I'm not afraid of you anymore.

Krelnikov looked down at her, his lips curled back from those ludicrous teeth. She thought he was going to kick her again, and she closed her eyes and waited. After a moment, she heard the door open.

After that, more voices spoke to her. Hands moved over her body, but they were there to help, not to hurt. Someone, not Krelnikov, gave an order to remove her to the infirmary at once. She felt herself being borne on a stretcher. In the hospital, she absorbed the familiar sounds and odors with something approaching joy. Krelnikov couldn't touch her anymore.

That evening a doctor came by to fill in her chart. Olga's hands lay quietly on her chest. Under her hospital gown, her ribs had been bandaged so tightly she could hardly breathe. Still, the prognosis looked good. No blood in the stool, no pain except from the bruising. A dislocated jaw and a couple of swollen eyes. And her brain was clear.

"Name?" the doctor asked.

"My name is Olga Dmitrova." Olga thought of Yakov. And Irina. "Where it says nationality, you can write 'Jew.' "

CHAPTER 34

Tel Aviv: Spring 1986

J udith had occupied her room at the Tel Aviv Hilton for only ten
minutes when she heard a knock at her door. Aleksandr Dmitrov
thrust a bouquet of yellow roses into her arms. He was grinning.

"Welcome to Israel, Judith. I was afraid you wouldn't come."

"Sasha! How lovely." Judith gave him a quick kiss and slipped out
of reach before he could embrace her. "How did you know I was here?
A spy at the airport?"

Dmitrov laughed. "I don't need a spy. I am a spy, remember? First
I called around to all the hotels to find out where you had reserved a room
and when you expected to arrive, then I started telephoning every fifteen
minutes to see if you had come in yet. How was your flight?"

"Uneventful. Thank God. That's the best you can say for air travel
these days."

Judith found an empty water carafe in the bathroom and arranged
the flowers in it. She was grateful for something to do. Anything was
better than awkward, idle silence. Dmitrov sat in an armchair near the
sliding door to the balcony, from which he had a fine view of the sea and
the city.

He watched as Judith unpacked. She had brought only one small
suitcase.

"I had no idea you were in Paris until Vanessa told me. I had a hard
time finding you. Don't you ever answer your telephone?"

"Yes, when I'm there, which is practically never. I'm working long hours. I had to beg for this job on my bended knees, and I want to do well."

Judith was covering the European fashion scene for a New York magazine. She interviewed designers, reviewed their collections, and analyzed trends.

"Oh, yes, you people in the West place such great importance on what your wealthiest women will be wearing next season."

Judith refused to let Dmitrov bait her. "A lot of people find it interesting. Besides, I wanted a job. I heard that a friend was starting a magazine, and I swallowed my pride and threw myself on his mercy. Old lovers have their uses."

"Besides, you couldn't wait to get away from me."

"Yes, I wanted to get away. Too much of my life has revolved around . . . involvements. I needed a break from you. We needed a break from each other."

"Before we got 'involved' again."

"That's right." Judith tossed her lingerie into a drawer and slammed it shut. "Sasha, I only came because I didn't want to disappoint you or Irina or Olga. I didn't want you to think I was angry with you for any reason, or that I didn't care anymore. I do."

"So today you will join us at the airport to greet Olga. As soon as you have reassured yourself that all is well with her, with the entire Dmitrov family, you will leave. I suppose you already have your plane reservation?"

"How did you know?"

"More spying. You only brought enough clothing for two days."

Judith turned away from the closet, a hanger in one hand and a linen jacket in the other. "Stop it, Sasha. You're tormenting me, and I don't like it. I didn't want to come at all, but I—I had to."

"To witness the reunion, and to persuade yourself that you did the right thing by running away from me."

"We both know what I was running away from. Olga and I talked about it. You and I talked about it. After what this woman has been through, she's going to need some strong arms to hold her. You promised her she could rely on you, and I told her I'd stay out of the way. If you turn your back on her now, you might as well say good-bye to Irina forever. Whatever tentative steps the two of you have taken toward reconciliation won't be worth anything. She'll despise you again, and she'll hate me, and I'll hate myself. It's a rotten situation, but we both know that real life isn't all sunshine and roses. We're not kids anymore. We can live without each other."

"Vanessa says you're depressed."

"Vanessa has a big mouth."

"You spent a year of your life fighting for Irina and me. You stayed with me through those long hours of CIA interrogation and State Department debriefing. You argued with the bureaucrats at Immigration and Naturalization on our behalf. You paid our bills and found me a job and persuaded me it would be a good thing for Irina to come to Israel and live on a kibbutz for a while. And when she wanted to stay, you told me to respect her choice, to leave her alone. At the same time you were telephoning people, writing letters, collaring Soviet citizens at Washington cocktail parties, threatening your own government with scandal, sending telegrams to Gorbachev. Owen Adair said to me that your mother couldn't have done it better, and I believe it. You broke every rule, and you won. They finally agreed to let Olga go. You couldn't have done all that if you didn't love me."

"Of course I love you!" Judith cried. "There, are you satisfied? Now, if you have any feeling for me at all, you'll go away."

Dmitrov sighed and pulled himself to his feet. "Olga's plane gets in at two this afternoon. Irina and I will stop here on our way and you can ride out to the airport with us. That's if you don't mind. We may not get another chance to talk."

"We don't need to talk. You don't owe me anything, Sasha. Olga needs you more than I do."

"We'll stop by at one. Good-bye, Judith." He kissed her on the cheek and went out.

Judith called down to room service and ordered a bottle of vodka and a liter of fresh orange juice. Little rich bitch, can't stand losing, poorest sport in the tennis club. It served her right. She was thirty-eight years old, twice widowed, and nothing to show for it but a scuffed and shopworn heart. Why had she worked so hard for Olga Dmitrova's release? Because she wanted to be able to live with her conscience. But rich bitches aren't supposed to be noble and self-sacrificing. They don't push the men they love into the arms of their rivals with warm wishes of love and happiness. She wasn't noble—she was stupid.

The fallout from the Abbott affair had been devastating and far-reaching. Within days of the shoot-out in Brighton, the KGB had started to reshuffle operators in all parts of the world. Projects that Dmitrov had been involved with were scrapped or altered. Agents went to ground or disappeared.

In Washington, the State Department summoned home a long list of foreign-service employees. A spokesman told the press that the department was revitalizing its operations abroad, and that the flurry of appointments and resignations was merely coincidental. The President, persuaded that Preston Marlowe knew nothing of his wife and son's activities on behalf of the Soviets, asked Preston to remain in the Cabinet after Lydia unexpectedly died from heart failure while visiting her daughters in England. After two months Preston resigned and faded into retirement. Judith had heard he was working on his memoirs.

Meanwhile, Judith and Dmitrov pursued negotiations with the Soviet Union. But once again, the leadership in the Kremlin changed. Konstantin Chernenko died in March 1985, and, fulfilling the expectations of Phillip Abbott and others, Mikhail Gorbachev became the head of the Communist Party. The new regime seemed ready to pursue international peace more aggressively; otherwise, nothing had changed. Aleksandr Dmitrov and his daughter were traitors. Olga Dmitrova was a traitor. No negotiations were possible.

In return for quashing formal publication of Phillip Abbott's memoirs, Judith and Dmitrov implored Mikhail Gorbachev to release Olga Dmitrova. As Judith remarked, they might have been asking for a ban on medium-range nuclear missiles instead of the freedom of a lone woman who had no knowledge at all of Soviet government activities. Foremost in their discussions was the demand that the KGB leave Dmitrov and the members of his family in peace. When the subject was broached directly, the Soviet Foreign Minister bristled.

"These people have turned their backs on their country. We have nothing to do with traitors. To us, they have ceased to exist."

Judith didn't believe this disavowal. For the rest of his life, Aleksandr Dmitrov would have to exercise unusual caution. His home would have to be secured. He would arm himself with an alarm as well as a small-caliber weapon. This was the price he had to pay for his freedom. He had to live every day as though the KGB were going to take its revenge.

As Gorbachev settled in, a new period of *glasnost,* openness, began. Jews in greater numbers were leaving the Soviet Union. But Olga Dmitrova was still denied an exit visa. Then, a year and a half after the escape from Batumi, the Soviet bureaucracy relented. Tomorrow, Olga would be a free woman.

Irina's face was as sunny and bright as the load of flowers in her arms. Six months on a kibbutz had erased the sullen rebel who had dropped out of Soviet society. Her hair was curled in a tight perm, and her face was tanned and free of makeup. She had enrolled at Tel Aviv

University, where she was following a curriculum heavy in biosciences and chemistry. She had decided that she was too old to become a dancer, but she could still become a doctor, like her mother.

She kissed Judith on both cheeks. "Papa has told me everything you've done. We are so grateful. You are a good friend."

"I'm glad you're happy."

"Who wouldn't be happy? My mother is coming home today!"

Traffic on the road to the airport was slowed by security checks. Further checks were necessary before they could enter the lounge outside the customs area.

"So this is what it's like to live in a war zone," Judith remarked.

"We Jews aren't sheep," Irina said tartly. "If we want to be free, we have to fight for it, every one of us, every day of our lives."

Judith felt queasy from the heat and from nerves, and from the spicy falafel she had eaten for lunch. The sight of Irina, hopping up and down with excitement, only made it worse.

"I hope they haven't hurt her. I kept asking in my letters. She never answered me. They told her what she could and couldn't write. Nazis." Irina had developed a passionate interest in the persecution of the Jews under Hitler. She visited Holocaust monuments and talked to survivors. Everyone else in Israel had been born a Jew, she said. She had had to learn for herself what it meant to be Jewish.

The flight from Vienna was late. Finally a few passengers started to come through the double doors.

"There she is!" Irina shouted. "Mama! Mama!"

Dmitrov reached for Judith's hand and grasped it tightly. "Her hair," he said in a grieving voice. "It's turned white."

Mother and daughter embraced and kissed, and kissed again. Irina wept unashamedly, and kissed her mother's hands, and pressed the flowers into her arms. Judith saw her touch Olga's hair. Her weeping renewed itself, and she cried out in Russian, "What did they do to you? What did they do?"

Finally Dmitrov and Judith came forward. "Welcome to the West," they said. Dmitrov kissed his former wife on both cheeks. She opened her arms to accept the bouquet he gave her.

"Sasha, Sasha, I can hardly believe it. It's like a dream, a beautiful dream."

"Your hair."

Olga laughed. "It's nothing to worry about. My mother's hair was snow white when she was my age. That's the way it is with the women in my family. Irina, too, someday. That's life, no?"

"Did they hurt you?"

She shrugged. "It's past. They didn't do anything that I couldn't tolerate. Mostly they talked. I learned to stop listening. Then one day, it ended. They left me alone, and let me go back to work. And a few days ago, I got my visa. Like a miracle. You did that, didn't you?"

"You can thank Judith." Dmitrov drew her forward. "She talked to everybody she could think of. And she wrote letters, hundreds of them. She sent them to Gorbachev and all the members of the Politburo, United States Senators and Congressmen, the newspapers."

Olga took Judith's hands. "I thank you. You have been a good friend to our family. Think of it! I'll have to go to school to learn how to be a physician all over again, in the modern world." She pushed a strand of hair away from her face. "I'm like a new baby. Don't be surprised if I cry a lot at first, Irina. The shock of being born. Everything so bright, so many colors after so much darkness, so much loud noise. I'm not used to it. It will take a while."

"Not so long as you think." Irina slipped her arm around her mother's waist. "I got used to it right away. You'll like it here."

"I have to learn a new language."

"Not in one day. There are plenty of Russians in Tel Aviv and lots of people speak English. Don't worry. You have suitcases?"

Olga's eyes clouded over. "They took everything away for inspection at the airport. I had gifts, keepsakes. They were taking so long and the plane was leaving. I had to come away without them. I felt terrible."

"We'll buy everything new," Irina declared. "Who needs that old Russian stuff anyway?"

They walked toward the front of the terminal building. Olga seemed to shrink from the babble of languages around them: Hebrew, Yiddish, Russian, Arabic, English. And the people looked so strange. Sephardic Jews in long black coats mingled with Hasidim with their earlocks and black felt hats. Most of the men wore yarmulkes. Half the younger men were in uniform.

"I have been exempted from military service," Irina said. "I'm too small to carry their weapons. I told them I would treat the soldiers' wounds instead."

"You have a boyfriend? Someone special?" her mother asked.

Irina shrugged. "Maybe. Every week it's someone different. I like the boys here. They grow up early. But they don't take life too seriously. Wait until you see my apartment, Mama. Color television and a videotape recorder!"

They emerged from the air-conditioned cavern of the terminal into the blazing sun of the parking lot. Irina turned to Judith. "I am having a little party to welcome Mama to Israel. I would like you to come, too."

Judith demurred. "No, it's a family affair. I don't want to interfere."

Olga protested. "No, no, you are the best friend we have. Of course you must come."

Dmitrov asked the cabdriver to stop at his hotel for a moment. He went inside, and returned with a small brown-paper carton.

Irina lived in a new high-rise on Dizengoff Street, in the bustling heart of the city. The small apartment overflowed with guests. Irina's friends and classmates greeted Mrs. Dmitrov warmly and presented her with gifts of candy, flowers, wine, and fruit. Several were recent Russian immigrants themselves, eager for the latest news of their Jewish friends back in Moscow. Irina kept a close eye on her mother, and when she saw Olga's state of dazed joy turning to exhaustion, she began urging her guests toward the door. Judith came over to bid Olga farewell.

Olga grasped her hand. "She is so different, my little girl. I hardly know her. So free! Thank you. Thank you for all you have done for us."

"Really, Olga, it's not necessary to keep thanking me. I was happy to help."

"You and Sasha . . . ?" The sentence drifted into a question mark.

"I've honored the pledge I made to you," Judith said evenly. "We're just friends. And after today, not even that."

"You still love him." It was a statement, not a question.

Judith shook her head. "His place is here, with you. Good-bye." She embraced Olga, kissed her on both cheeks, and started toward the door. Dmitrov intercepted her.

"So, you're really leaving tomorrow. I won't see you again."

Judith didn't trust herself to speak. She shook her head and went out. Dmitrov turned back to the room, a cheerful shambles of food and flowers and empty wine bottles. Irina had thrown open the door to the balcony to air out the fug of cigarette smoke. A muffled cacophony of street sounds drifted up to them: honking horns, the blare of a loudspeaker promoting a political candidate, a police siren, the squawk of a hundred radios, echoes of chatter and laughter. Olga sat on the sofa, her hands limp in her lap. She looked infinitely weary, but she was smiling.

"Irina has nice friends. We are very lucky to be here, all of us. It's a miracle, and it all happened after I had given up believing in miracles. Irina, will you take me to the synagogue tomorrow night? I've never been to a real sabbath service."

"We'll go early to get a seat," Irina said. "It's always crowded."

"Imagine," Olga murmured, "so many Jews that they won't all fit inside the synagogue."

"Dozens of synagogues, Mama. In this country, you could throw a hundred pebbles and hit a hundred Jews. We'll get our shopping done in the morning. Everything closes at one o'clock in the afternoon and doesn't open again until Saturday night. Different from what we're used to. But in many ways the same. The people here don't trust the government, and they cheat and bribe, just like home. The thing is, they're not afraid to put themselves forward, to speak out. And they do it—we do it—without being afraid."

Olga was watching Dmitrov, who had poured himself a stiff vodka. "And what about you, Sasha? Will you come to services with us tomorrow?"

"If you want me to. It will be a new experience."

"So, you live in Philadelphia now, and teach at a university there. Do you like it?"

"Pretty well." He shrugged. "I teach global history and economics. They seemed to think I was properly qualified, and my students like me. Actually, Judith found me the job. She knows a lot of important people. I also travel to Washington now and then as a special consultant to the State Department. I assist in interpreting top-level messages from Moscow, so I can tell them what the Russians are really thinking."

He spoke wryly, but Olga could tell that he was satisfied with his work. Nevertheless, he was unhappy. He only drank like that, glass after glass of vodka, when he was disturbed about something.

Dmitrov finished his drink and brought out the package he had fetched from his hotel. He set it in the middle of the table and cut the strings, then opened the carton and lifted out a bundle wrapped in blue velvet. Olga knew what it was. So did Irina. The Valensky icon.

They gazed at it in reverential silence. Dmitrov turned the gold leaf that unlocked the triptych and the two side panels sprang open, revealing the Madonna and Child within and the two saints who guarded them. The object looked out of place in this modernistic room, among Irina's newly acquired possessions.

"This is for you, Irina," he said. "I promised your grandmother that it would stay in our family. But you are under no such obligation. You may do what you like with it."

Irina touched the glowing wooden shell. "I don't know what to say, Papa. It's very beautiful, and valuable, I know. But it—it isn't—" She appealed to her mother for help. "Mama?"

Olga said, "We are Jews, living in Israel. What do Jews need with a Christian icon? We came from Russia with nothing, Irina and I. No reminders of the old days. That's the way it should be for immigrants. A new life, a future and no past." She smiled at Dmitrov. "Sasha, you have your own life in America, different from ours. I want to stay here with Irina. This is our country now. But it is not your country."

Dmitrov seemed stunned. "But you will need help, money."

Olga shook her head. "The refugee organizations will look after us until I find work. And I have Irina. I'm not afraid of what lies ahead. I'll never be afraid of anything anymore. I've been in prison. I've seen hell. Once I knew the two of you were safe, they couldn't touch me. I laughed at them, and they lost their power to terrify me. I was wrong to make you promise to keep us together as a family after we got out. It wouldn't have worked, I can see that, and all of us would be unhappy, just as we were in Russia. Go now, Sasha. Go to her."

Dmitrov took her hands and drew her to her feet. "I forgot that before you were anything else to me, my wife or the mother of my children, you were my friend."

They held each other for a long time. Then Olga gave him a gentle push. Her eyes were swimming with tears, but she was laughing.

"Look at him, bolted to the floor. He still can't believe he's a free man. Make him go, Irina."

Irina had replaced the icon in its velvet sack, and she handed it to her father. "My gift to you and Judith, for all you have done for us." Then she threw her arms around his neck and gave him a fierce hug. He heard her whisper, "Papa, I forgive you."

Judith's gold silk caftan was crumpled. Her hair was tousled and her makeup smeared. She had been crying.

Dmitrov handed her the icon. "This is yours to keep, if you want it."

"Yes." Her eyes widened. "Oh, yes. Yes!"

New tears welled up and spilled over. Seeing them, Dmitrov smiled. He took the icon from her and set it aside, then he brushed the teardrops away with his fingertips and framed her face gently with his big hands.

"No more weeping," he said with mock sternness. "The time for tears is over."

"I don't know—" Judith's lips were trembling. "I've forgotten how to be happy."

"Have you?" Dmitrov kissed her soundly, again and again, making loud smacking noises, until she began to laugh with him, then he scooped her up in his arms. "Come. We will learn it again, together."

Later they stood on the balcony and Dmitrov told her about Olga's gentle dismissal of him, and Irina's farewell. Judith leaned against him and lifted her face to the sky. A few faint stars were flickering behind the glare of the city lights. The breeze from the sea was soft, scented with orange blossoms.

Papa, I forgive.